TROUBLE RIDES TALL
CROSS THE RED CREEK
DESERT STAKE-OUT

This Large Print Book carries the
Seal of Approval of N.A.V.H.

TROUBLE RIDES TALL
CROSS THE RED CREEK
DESERT STAKE-OUT

HARRY WHITTINGTON

WHEELER PUBLISHING
A part of Gale, Cengage Learning

GALE
CENGAGE Learning®

Farmington Hills, Mich • San Francisco • New York • Waterville, Maine
Meriden, Conn • Mason, Ohio • Chicago

GALE
CENGAGE Learning®

LIBRARY OF CONGRESS CATALOGING-IN-PUBLICATION DATA

Names: Whittington, Harry, 1915-1989, author. | Whittington, Harry, 1915-1989. Trouble rides tall. | Whittington, Harry, 1915-1989. Cross the red creek. | Whittington, Harry, 1915-1989. Desert stake-out.
Title: Trouble rides tall ; Cross the red creek ; Desert stake-out / by Harry Whittington.
Description: Large print edition. | Waterville, Maine : Wheeler Publishing, 2017. | Series: Wheeler Publishing large print western
Identifiers: LCCN 2017009059| ISBN 9781432838409 (softcover) | ISBN 1432838407 (softcover)
Subjects: LCSH: Western stories. | Large type books.
Classification: LCC PS3545.H896 A6 2017 | DDC 813/.54—dc23
LC record available at https://lccn.loc.gov/2017009059

Published in 2017 by arrangement with JET Literary Associates, Inc.

Printed in Mexico
1 2 3 4 5 6 7 21 20 19 18 17

TROUBLE RIDES TALL
CROSS THE RED CREEK
DESERT STAKE-OUT

■ ■ ■ ■

TROUBLE RIDES
TALL

BY HARRY WHITTINGTON

■ ■ ■ ■

ONE

Until his dog scented something and tried to bark it out of a greasewood thicket, it had been a shiny new-penny kind of afternoon. A world full of sun, the earth reflecting it from sand-washed flats and from foothills where rabbit brush and sunflowers glistened like dry gold. The best day young Will could remember of all his eight years, with the sky cloudless, the wind cutting into you so you felt good just to be alive.

He raced his willow-pole pony across the dry-crusted ground with Sanky Konki at his heels.

Sometimes he forgot that like most important things in his life, Sanky Konki didn't exist except in his imagination. There were no other children near for him to play with; anyhow he spent most of the day helping his father around their shack outside Pony Wells. It was hard work following his father who took long steps and drove himself;

sometimes the chores seemed endless. But when he was finally free, he had a yard full of imaginary friends, or he played alone with his dog and Sanky Konki.

He was never lonely. To him the Sage River Valley was the most wonderful place in the world. You could hunt arrowheads, track a band of Indians in the arroyos, fight savages in the brush. Such a secure world, with gray hills to bound it in and keep it warm. In Spring, willows reddish brown with the sap in them, and in Summer the whole valley went dry with calves bawling and cows nosing the air for just the scent of water. In Autumn you gathered flowers in secret places and made Ma smile when you thrust them out to her, so she smiled even when you were late to supper. Autumn was finest in his valley, hidden canyons red and gold with wild currant and wild roses, and golden aspen like a woven mat hung to dry on the sheer walls.

His pa had told him the floor of this valley had been gouged out by a glacier more than a million years ago. Through its middle wound a stream ice-blue in winter, but mud dry in summer. What a wonderful land that glacier had created for him. He drew a deep breath, owning it all from shadowed crags to sun-blasted hills, from rich soil where farmers plowed to the cattle grazing ranges of thin-crusted sand that danced away like thistles on the first night wind.

From the stream you could take crappie and perch and blue gills, if you had the patience to fish. You could chase a picket-pin gopher with no hope of catching him but with the fine feeling of forcing him to run. You could lie on your belly and watch sage hens, chukar partridge or maybe a cock-ring pheasant. Twice a year migratory birds settled: plover, tatler, godwit and coots. Then like some miracle the sky turned black and the world echoed the scream of wild geese, so the hair stood on the nape of your neck at the wonder of it.

"Hurry, Sanky!" he yelled. "Hurry!"

Young Will had played alone so long he'd have been uncomfortable with playmates. Since earliest childhood he'd made his own games, invented and named his own friends.

He called over his shoulder. "Come on, Sanky Konki. Let's see what that fool dog is barkin' at."

Young Will never permitted the thought to reach the top of his mind, but there was a reason he loved this imaginary friend.

He loved to lead. In his mind, he was a leader of his people — on wilderness treks, out of Indian attacks, into order from

11

lawlessness, the way the marshal at Pony Wells had done, so people talked about it in awe.

Young Will felt born to lead; Sanky Konki was born to follow, loved to follow, never wanted anything else. Usually Young Will spoke to him over his shoulder. "Wonder what ole Charley has got treed?" Sanky Konki called. Here was another reason to love him. Sanky Konki never *knew* anything, he was always asking questions. Young Will's father sometimes lost his patience at Young Will's eternal questions, but Young Will's patience was of sterner quality.

"Must be that dern fool ornery ole hell that 'scaped from jail," Young Will called over his shoulder. He loved to swear when he was out alone, away from his mother's disapproval, the back of his father's hand. Sometimes he got off enough cussing to last him a month of Sundays. Tension never got bottled up in Young Will. Sanky Konki didn't mind how much he cussed. Sometimes he'd even join him a little.

Today they were Marshal and Deputy hunting an escaped prisoner in the arroyos and along the rim of the sweetgrass country that marked the cattle ranges. Lately, being Marshal was young Will's favourite game.

The marshal at Pony Wells was the most

talked about man in the valley. Even people who disapproved of him, like Young Will's father, had to admire him.

Sometimes he felt disloyal, unable to decide if he wanted to grow up a giant among men like the marshal, or a good man as Ma said Pa was. A good man meant you couldn't fight, or sling a gun, or even wear one; you seldom cussed, you always went to church, never had much fun.

There was something frantic about Charley's barking. Young Will slowed. That barking had a quality of wrong in it, a harried sound that persisted, taking the glitter off the sun and putting clouds where there hadn't been any clouds.

"I know one thing," Sanky Konki said. "I don't care much about going over there where Charley is."

"Oh, don't be a derned scared baby." But knowing how Sanky felt reassured him. He could whistle old Charley to heel and they could turn back, they'd strayed too far and Ma was going to raise the dickens now, they agreed on that.

He felt a nagging worry. Would Sanky admire him if they turned back? Pa said the marshal at Pony Wells was a stubborn man who never turned back, even when he was wrong. Wouldn't Sanky admire him more if he were like the marshal? If he retreated now, would Sanky want to go on following him, or would there be an unspoken barrier between them?

"Why damn-smoke it," Young Will said, "how are we going to capture the Bad Kid if we don't go where Charley's trailed him?" His laugh was shaky. "Don't you worry, Sanky. I got my gun. I'm faster on the draw even than Marshal Shafter."

He slapped his hip, drew and fired once just to prove it. But the sound of his gun was frail against the anxious yapping of old Charley.

"Here, Charley!"

Young Will stopped at the crest of an arroyo to blow his pony. He himself wasn't winded, but a man knew he had to treat his horses gently.

In a rock-strewn thicket he saw Charley poised, hairs like a brush along his spine, barking without ceasing. Maybe it was a rattler. Pa had told him what to do about rattlers. You threw something at a rattler, making him coil if you could and then you ran like old billy-hell.

"Charley! Come here."

It was as if Charley were deaf. Young Will moved forward slowly. Maybe Charley had found a dead gopher. Pa had told him the

Shoshone Indians dreaded a dead gopher. He didn't blame them. To come upon a dead gopher suddenly made his stomach churn, short hairs bristle on his neck, and disgust-wrinkles rib his nose.

He stepped up beside Charley, stopped and stared. First there was the mound of new turned earth, thrown up by a dog or a hungry coyote. And then there was the body, the human body, and the woman's shoes.

Young Will backed away, sickness gorging up in him. He looked around wildly.

He spoke to Charley and when Charley didn't respond, grabbed the scruff of his neck and pulled him away. Somebody was dead. The horror numbed him and he could not think. He stood holding Charley tightly. Charley whined.

In the blue-hazed distance he saw the roofs of houses in Pony Wells, the ash gray line of the road, and cattle grazing, and beyond the cattle the stand of scrubby pines in the foothills. A faraway train whistled. A cow bawled. A whisky jack screeched and then the silence pressed in. "Charley, we got to tell Pa."

He turned and walked through the sweet-grass, moving stiff-legged, half-dragging the dog. Pa. He wished he could see him working about the place, but he was still too far away, and suddenly he was too tired to run. He could only plod forward, seeing that body, the woman's black shoes, and the way the earth had been turned up from the shallow grave.

What was Pa going to say? What was he doing over here across the creek? What did he mean finding a body?

What if Pa blamed him? Pa wouldn't. Sure, Pa would know better. But what about the marshal at Pony Wells? Even grown people talked about him in fearful whispers. Mothers said, "Be good — or the marshal will get you." When Pa got mad, he said: "Step lively, boy. You'll never outrun the marshal like that."

His stomach churned and his mind wheeled like a bird sick with fright. It was his first sight of death. His mind cringed from it and longed not to think about it, not to have to tell anybody about it.

Maybe he hadn't seen it. Maybe he'd wake up and be in bed, and he'd call Ma and she'd light a lamp, and it would be a bad dream and he wouldn't have to tell anybody.

But he had to tell Pa. There was a body out there.

"Whose body?" Pa'd say. "Where? Who

found it?" And the marshal would look down at him, and know in his mind who was guilty. How many times had he heard grown men talking about the relentless way the marshal was when he believed a man guilty of crime. He'd hound him and ride him down, and all hell couldn't change him when he'd made up his mind.

Young Will took two running steps toward home and then slowed again. I can't tell, he thought. What if the marshal looks at me and sees me guilty and nothing I can say, and all hell can't change him?

He released Charley suddenly and ran. The breath burned in his throat. He stumbled once, reaching out for support and taking five long steps before he caught his balance.

He saw his father, but his back was turned. Young Will slipped through a fence and ran behind the lean-to. He pushed the cow out of the way and crawled into the hay. He lay there panting and shivering. The world was no longer good or secure or warm. He was frightened and lonely and sick with horror. The world had turned as black as dirty water.

He stayed there until he fell asleep from fatigue and weariness. He didn't even answer when his mother called him in to supper.

Two

Bry Shafter came awake slowly. He lay sprawled on his back, a lank-bodied man with gray-splotched temples but youthful muscles, wiredrawn shoulders and a hungry, rugged face. His size thirteen feet hung over the end of the bed.

He lay for the moment listening to the noise from the front of the house, people's voices urgent against Maudie's quiet tone that he knew she always used when she refused to let them disturb him.

The urgency of the voices did not rouse him. He smiled grimly, knowing he was an old fire horse; he responded to the clang of bell-clapper, but it was just another fire by now. Voices were always urgent at the marshal's front door. Life and death. It was one or the other, or people seldom came.

He wriggled his little toe, first one foot, then the other just to be sure he still could do it. He pawed around for the sheet without opening his eyes again, turned on his side and curled up his legs.

He wore only underpants and these were made of sacking. These allowed him freedom of movement he discovered vital many years ago. He pulled his legs up, still pawing for the sheet and not finding it. He couldn't say why he needed a sheet, the mid-afternoon sun blazed against the side of the house and heated the drawn window shade. There wasn't a breath of air in the whole town, yet he was chilled.

With legs curled up dog fashion, he should have been able to sink into sleep again even with the chill tracing through him.

He could not, and finally admitted he didn't want to go back to sleep. He was afraid of sleep because unless he was bone tired, his sleep was forever beset with dreams, some of them more real than any waking moment, and he hated them.

It was a satanic thing to hope the people at the front door had trouble so vile that even Maudie couldn't turn them away. She would if there were any chance. She would quietly and firmly remind them that Deputy Marshal Zach Adams was on duty. She would turn them away, would that sixteen-year-old little lady.

He smiled, thinking about Maudie. She's all I have left of you, Hannah, but she's the good of both of us, what little good there is in me, and all the good that was in you.

It wasn't right to make a grown woman of

Maudie, with house to keep, anyway not a barn of a house like this. Old Judge Warren Blair's place. Eight rooms. Too much house for the judge when his wife died and his kids married away. Too much house for anybody.

He sighed. He'd bought it for Hannah. He'd wanted to impress her. Ten thousand a year. He couldn't offer her security, he couldn't even promise he'd come home alive from his work. But he could buy her the biggest house in town. And that's what he'd done. Only, after all their troubles and privations, Hannah never lived to enjoy the good.

I'm getting old, he thought. Lying here looking backward with all my mind and all my heart. Dreading sleep, dreading the night hours ahead, unable to turn back, unwilling to go forward. What surer sign a man was getting old?

He sat up on the side of the bed, placing his feet squarely on the floor. A studied gesture. He had to be always ready, always balanced and watchful. Sure, this was his own house, a second-floor window opened only to the sun, but he'd learned this was where trouble came from, where you never expected it.

He scrubbed his hand through his thinning hair and squinted his eyes against the intrusion of painful light. He was in his late thirties, but years didn't count, it was the way a man had lived. He stood up and the room seemed to shrink. It wasn't large and even a large room seemed small when he was in it.

He tugged the shade, releasing and sending upward on its roller so the sun speared inward, and he looked out upon his bare yard and the backs of Main Street buildings. Quiet out there in the mid-afternoon, no more sound than the gnats made, or the deerflies.

There were the voices again, a man's voice, insistent. He barely heard Maudie's voice rising against it, but he nodded, knowing Maudie's will was made of steel.

He drew a deep breath, drinking in the faint-touched alkali air of the valley. It was a good smell and the only way he could express its effect upon him was that it was the kind of air a man breathed in the place he called home.

He scowled, shaking this thought from his mind. Two years he'd been here; he had sunk no roots into the ground of this valley. He had no roots anywhere. He knew what he was, and knew there was no place he called home. . . .

He scratched his ribs, running his hands roughly across the flatness of his stomach. He could feel these muscles relaxing, too. He drew his hands away.

The door opened behind him and he spun around.

It was Maudie. At sixteen, she tossed a light of her own back toward the sun. He tried to find Hannah in her fair hair, blue eyes, baby-softness of her cheeks and chin. Dark, slender Hannah wasn't outwardly there. She'd bequeathed Maudie her goodness and gentleness, and tempered steel. Heaven had taken his rough-crag features, toned and styled and softened them so Maudie resembled her father and yet was beautiful. He smiled behind his eyes, paying tribute to Hannah: I just don't see how you did it.

"Papa," Maudie's voice was shocked. "Standing there in those awful underpants. Suppose somebody saw you like that?"

"If they'd ever seen anything like me before, they'd know what I was. If they hadn't — it wouldn't matter much, would it?"

"Come away from that window." Maudie smiled at him without in any way condoning his actions. "I think you're vain of yourself, Papa. I really do. You think you're all trim in the hips, and with those big muscles in your chest. You'd like people to see you like that, wouldn't you, Papa?"

He felt confusion on his face and in his eyes. He tried to laugh it off. "Well, you must admit, Angel, we don't know how much longer an old man like me will be pretty like this."

"Wouldn't you just love to have me tell the men down at the Blue Dollar that you called yourself pretty?"

"If you don't care anything about sitting down for the next few days, you go ahead and do it."

"You get dressed and we won't say any more about it."

She picked up his whipcord trousers from the chair where he'd dropped them last night. She looked at them a moment and then tossed them to him. "There are people downstairs to see you," she said.

"Couldn't get rid of them, eh?" His voice teased her and loved her.

"I tried," she said from the door. "They've no right, coming here, waking you up. What's Zach Adams for?"

He was stepping into his pants. He glanced up. "I got no answer for that," he said.

"Hurry." She closed the door behind her.

He stood a moment listening to her go away down the hall toward the stairs.

He buckled his belt about his trousers without buttoning his fly. He poured water in a white basin from matching pitcher. He lathered his hands with the brown bar of lye-and-fat soap. He scrubbed at his face, washing it a long time, washing away the remnants of sleep and the need for rest. He was awake now. It would be sixteen hours before he'd get back in bed. Another night ahead. One more night.

He washed his arms and his ribs with soap and water. He rubbed himself with the clean-smelling towel Maudie had laid out for him.

He found a fresh shirt in the top drawer of the squatted bureau with its ornate scrolls. The shirt was full in the shoulders. He wore them that way so they never impeded his movements.

He winced at the thought that such a trivial thing should be a life-and-death matter. The sleeves should never bind or arrest the free movement of his arms. On such trifles his very existence depended.

It was like this with the homemade short underpants. Once he'd worn the knee-length union suits in summer and ankle-hugging woolens in winter. That was Han-

24

nah's idea of guarding his health. But he'd learned more important secrets of health and longevity. You stayed alive in his profession only if you could move faster than the man facing you. If woolens suddenly bound instead of stretching, that split-second loss of movement could cost your life. Long ago he'd drawn some sketches of the underpants he needed. At first, Hannah had cut them from his union suits, but then it was easier to sew them from sack lining. She'd made them for him until she died, and then Maudie had learned to cut and sew them.

He felt taut in his chest: such a bad thing for a child — to make clothing that might help keep her father alive one more night. It was the sort of knowledge from which you wanted to shield your child.

He buttoned his shirt, stuffed it into his trousers, fixed his clothes and strapped on his gunbelt. He broke the chamber out of his revolver, checked the five cartridge faces, shook the chamber back into place, thrust the gun into its holster.

The leather vest had his badge pinned to it. He shrugged his arms into it, trying not to see the sun glinting on the tin star.

He spent another moment rubbing oil into his lifeless hair and pushed a brush through it.

It took another moment to work his feet into hand-tooled boots. He studied a crack in one, slapped at it with some of the oil he'd massaged into his scalp. Dressed, he looked about the room and then walked out of it.

They were waiting in the downstairs living-room. Maudie had raised the shade so the room was lighted, overstuffed couch, bow-legged center table, wide stone hearth, the faded place where the judge's picture had once dominated the wall.

Shafter paused in the doorway. He was surprised to see the man and the little boy with Maudie.

The man was coyote-lean, deeply tanned, and his hair overgrew his collar in a way that said if he had money for a hair-cut, there were too many other uses for it. His worn denim shirt and levis were faded, much washed, and his cheap boots were run over. Wilbur Brown was a proud and stubborn man barely eking out an existence on the subsistence farm he'd homesteaded outside town limits.

The boy squirmed with excitement. His sandy hair was tousled and he shoved it back from his face in a continual nervous gesture. There was more than excitement in young Will's face, it was white with fear and he bit at his lower lip.

In the father's face, Shafter saw something more: the ill-concealed disapproval the good people felt toward him and the gun at his side. The nice folks, the church element, he knew what they thought of him. And with Wilbur Brown it went even deeper. Wilbur Brown knew the marshal was paid ten thousand a year. Wilbur wasn't fated to see that much money at once in all his life. When you worked your guts out and you had nothing and your kids went hungry, you didn't take kindly to a man who collected ten thousand for packing a gun.

Shafter knew how Brown felt and wasn't moved one way or the other. It never occurred to him to wonder how he felt toward Wilbur Brown; he simply never gave him a thought.

He listened as Brown told what young Will had found in a greasewood thicket. Wilbur's voice shook and it was as if he apologized for his son's having found this terrible thing, this corpse.

"We came to you, quick as we could," Brown said. "We figured you'd know what to do." He stood up and the boy jumped up from the couch and stood hard against his father's side, eyes distended and fixed on the marshal.

27

Brown tried to put aside the disapproval. He tried to smile. He touched his son on top of his head in a gesture that told Shafter better than words his deep affection for his son. Brown smiled, "Young Will here, he wants you to know — for sure — that he didn't do it."

Shafter moved his gaze down to the boy's worried face. He did not laugh, he met the boy's eyes levelly. His voice was low. "I'm sure you didn't," he said. He nodded, giving the boy an equal's trust. "No matter what I hear, Young Will, it won't change my mind about that."

THREE

A crowd gathered before they reached the greasewood thicket. Not a word was spoken, and the people who followed did not talk among themselves. Bry thought wryly, they knew where the marshal went was trouble. They trailed him, but hung back, to see it without becoming involved.

The sun dipped behind the humpbacked ranges that formed the west wall of the valley. There was still light and it would be light for another hour, a fantastically sharp glow that illumined people and trees and rocks in brazen etching-like clarity.

Sage River was little more than a trickle this time of the year. Bry Shafter walked across, unmindful of his boots. Wilbur Brown beside him hesitated at the water, then lifted young Will, swinging him across by both hands. The boy exhaled in pleasure, forgetting the terror ahead.

"Up there," Brown said.

Shafter glanced back. He nodded and strode forward. Young Will noticed that not even his father's long strides could keep him apace the marshal.

The crowd was crossing the creek when Marshal Shafter stopped before the new mound of earth. Revulsion spread through him, and in the deep recesses of his mind he shuddered, thinking, "Oh God, no." But his face remained impassive.

For a long time there was this silence with everything etched clearly against the gray-silvered sky.

The crowd moved close enough to see the body on the knoll at the marshal's feet. The sight of the body congealed them into a mass and they receded slightly along the incline. None moved nearer.

Shafter stared at the girl's body, knowing at once who it was, yet unable to believe it, not being able to see how such a thing could be.

He looked back across the heads of the townspeople, across the creek and the grassy fields, pocked with rocks and stubby piñon. This was such an open place, in sight of town and the shacks of the dirt farmers.

Still, in another way, its very openness gave it a kind of isolation. A sand-washed boulder stood like a huge grave marker atop the knoll, greasewood and mesquite tangled into a thicket. The rocks and thin crusted sand rendered the place worthless and shunned, a barren spot nobody wanted. His deputy pushed through the crowd and started up the knoll.

"What you got, Bry?"

Zach Adams was what Bry remembered he once had been, or perhaps what he liked to think he'd been, recklessly good looking, insolent, hard-muscled, lean — and most of all, devilishly young, with contempt for anything or anyone older than himself.

Bry inclined his head toward the body and did not speak. He watched young Adams' face pale, and his soul withdraw from the shock of what he saw, and watched him swallow back the bile.

"Good lord," Zach whispered. "What a mess."

"She's been dead a few days. Somebody buried her here. Coyotes must have dug up the grave last night."

"Yeah."

Zach had stopped a few feet down the incline, his nostrils distended with revulsion.

Shafter swallowed hard, reminded himself he'd seen a lot more deaths than Zach had. He was pushing forty and Adams was twenty-five. Yet he knew as soon as Zach had adjusted himself to the sight of this violent death, Zach would feel the wrong less than he did.

Death is my business, he told himself, and I'm concerned with it in every way. I see them dead, I try to keep them from killing each other. I try to patch them up and delay their death a while. Sometimes I even bring death. It doesn't look as though it will ever change: I'll always withdraw from it, retreat inside.

His fists clenched, taut against his hips. Sweat peppered across his forehead beneath the band of his dust-smeared Stetson.

When he spoke, he kept his voice more casual than ever: "Is the doctor here yet?"

There was no reason for his being upset like this, yet he felt as though a fist had closed on his guts and shook him, twisting his insides into knots. He looked about at the unmoving people in a mass at the foot

31

of the knoll, at the way the dust spread in slow puffs from beneath their feet.

He recognized the faces down there. Amos Cowley, in town from his ranch and missing no excitement. Bry did not probe into the unreasoning depths of dislike he felt toward Amos Cowley. What was there about him to despise? He had a country-man's open and guileless face, direct eyes, a strong mouth, flesh seared by range suns and winter winds. There was nothing about such a man to dislike, but there it was. Maybe it was the foppish watch chain he wore across his tight vest.

Trumbo Gilley was there, too. Bullnecked, thick chested, a dangerous unthinking man with death in his past, a gun thonged at his thigh, a man who spent his days and nights doing nothing unless ordered to take action by his boss. Him, Shafter didn't like or dislike. He tolerated him, knew what he was. He expected to find Trumbo in a place like this.

Sam Pickens had run out from behind his meat counter and now was wiping his hands on his blood-spattered apron. Young Tolliver shifted from one leg to the other, dissolving back into the crowd so he would not be near enough to see the corpse again, but not wanting to miss the only excitement in months. Young Tolliver was a good boy and would grow into a good man, the church-element kind who'd disapprove of Shafter's kind of marshal.

Shafter sighed, supposing that was the way he would order it anyhow, and moved his gaze to Albert Tishkin. He watched Tishkin bob along at the rear of the crowd. Albert seemed to dance from one foot to the other, taking awkward bounds into the air, trying to see over other people's heads. Albert was the butt of town jokes. He lived alone in a one-room shack, collected bottles and rags and pictures from eastern magazines. Talk was that for the first two or three years of his life, Albert had been normal, but his progress in the last twenty or thirty years had been slow. Nobody knew exactly how old he was. The Tishkins had moved to California more than eighteen years ago, but Albert had run away from them and found his way back to the valley alone. He'd been half-dead when he arrived, but he'd never left the valley again, or wanted to. Albert was anywhere there was noise or excitement, always on Main Street until the last dog was hung.

There were others there, sod farmers and ranchers, a few merchants, all watching, storing up this moment to chew over in the months ahead. Nothing much happened in Pony Wells any more, and when something did happen, the eye witness was the center of attention in Wu Sing's Barber Shop for months afterwards.

Shafter wondered if these people had recognized this girl at once as he had? It they did, how could they stand there, unmoving, unmoved?

Shafter said again, "Is the doctor here yet?"

Zach had his emotions under control. His mouth twisted into a grin, faintly touched with contempt. "What can a doctor tell you, Bry?"

Bry flushed. His voice was cold. "I don't know. How she died. How long she's been out here."

"What difference that make? She's dead. You think you'll find who did it after this much time?"

Shafter's voice remained cold. "I think I'll try."

Zach shook his head. "You take your job real serious, old fellow."

"She's been murdered. Investigating is our job."

"Yeah." But Zach remained where he was, not more than half way up the incline.

Shafter glanced at Zach, then turned his

34

back on him. Zach said, "Here comes Dr. Gaines."

Shafter nodded but did not move.

Zach swore at him. "What you staring at, Bry? You like to look at things like that?"

Wilbur Brown muttered under his breath, unwillingly: "He's a man got no feelings."

Shafter's shoulders hunched, his fists tightened, nails digging into his palms. He did not speak.

"Tell me what you see, Bry?" Zach said. "What's there to see?"

What was there to see? The body that remained here, the torn clothing, the clotted hair? Or was it the way she had looked the last time he saw her?

He jerked his head around.

"Nothing. Just this girl, that's all. Lying here dead. Somebody killed her and left her here."

"All right. So she's dead. I guess I'm not crazy enough about death to stand right there in it."

"Then get to hell back to town."

He heard Zach catch his breath all the way from down the knoll. Zach said, "I'll stay."

Dr. Gaines moved past Zach and walked up the knoll, narrow-shouldered, slender, walking primly. The light was fading, the clearly etched people and trees and boulders now wore fuzzy shading, and the orange streaks across the sky faded to dirty yellow. The wind had quieted right at sundown, and for the moment there was silence across the whole valley.

The doctor stood across the body from Shafter. His voice was mild, carrying its chronic self-abnegation. "Don't glare at me like that, Shafter. I didn't do it."

Shafter shook his head, unaware so much anger showed in his face.

"Sorry, Doc. It's the Hogarty girl, isn't it? The kid from the Blue Dollar?"

Dr. Gaines knelt beside the body. He was a compact man with thick brown hair, rimless glasses pinched on fine straight nose. His dark suits were expensive, his white shirts showed the ruffle of lace beneath his vest. The thing that most impressed Shafter was the doctor's hands. They were pinkly clean and white, the nails showing no trace of dirt. There was an antiseptic smell of cleanliness about Dr. Gaines, yet Shafter knew he was certainly Pony Wells' "other doctor," the man people visited when for some reason they could not see Doc Swilner, who looked like a butcher and had hands like a butcher.

"I don't suppose you're very impressed by death any more," Gaines said. He glanced at Shafter. Their gazes met across the body, Shafter's the gray of slate and the doctor's bitter green.

Shafter breathed shallowly. In Gaines' patrician face he saw repugnance, a distaste for this violent death, this violated shallow grave on a knoll, the ugliness of uprooting a corpse days old.

"What does it matter what I think about death?" Shafter stared at him. "How long has she been here? Do you know?"

"No better than you do. Obviously, a few days. Her skull was crushed, across here. Can you see the cranial fracture, Bryant? Her flesh shows markings but —" His slender body was wracked by an abrupt involuntary shudder — "but they might not have contributed to her death."

"They might have happened after she was dead?"

"Yes."

"Somebody murdered her though?"

"Yes."

"And buried her here."

Gaines stood up. "I believe Pillans Metz is there in the crowd. Turn her body over to him and his funeral parlor, Bryant. That's the last we can do for her here on this earth."

Shafter went on kneeling there.

"What do you expect to find?"

Shafter's voice was an abrasive. "I don't know. What is there to find? Do you agree it's the Hogarty girl?"

"It looks like her. I never knew her too well. She came to me once about an abortion — about a year ago. I had to refuse her. She never came back to me."

"Somebody killed her," Shafter's voice remained low. "Somebody killed her at night and buried her here."

"You know it was at night?"

"He was scared," Shafter said. "He dug only a shallow grave. He did it at night all right. He couldn't even have dug a grave this deep without being seen by day."

Gaines gave him a twisted, bitter smile. "Already you know this much, Bryant. And soon you'll know more. You won't let it alone, will you? Why, Shafter? Is it because you care about her, a girl the town never wanted? Or is it that you want the violence, Shafter? Is that what you want? To find the man and shoot him with that gun at your side? Is that what you want?"

Shafter stood up slowly. He looked down at the doctor, at the girl beside the open grave, at his knotted fists.

"What difference does it make?" he said. "What does it matter what I want?"

FOUR

The darkness crept in across the valley and the wind stirred, moving a tumbleweed slowly down the knoll. The brush bumped Zach's boot unnoticed, hung there a moment and then toppled around it, falling along.

For a long moment it was a tableau in black and grey against the darkling sky. Below the boulder, the doctor stood and Bry knelt over the body. Halfway down the knoll, Zach waited, neither willing to go forward nor return to the crowd. The faces of the townspeople were blurred now, hazy and featureless beneath their hats.

Zach Adams moved first, and it was an involuntary movement of his shoulders, either he shivered or shrugged his shirt collar up against his neck. He scowled toward where Bry and the doctor were beside the body, feeling there was some official action he should take, unable to think of any. Perhaps if someone in the crowd tried to get too near, he could restrain him. He winced, hoping Bry would not ask him to touch the body. . . .

"You going to spend the night here?" Gaines said, keeping his voice low.

Bry glanced up but did not speak or rise

from his knee. He felt chilled and unmoving, but his mind was alive and tormented. He could not push Maudie from his mind, and kept telling himself he could not imagine why he thought of her and dead Gloria Hogarty at the same time. Still, Maudie kept thrusting into the forepart of his mind, the way she talked, the way she laughed, the way she was so young and so much like Hannah. That's fine, old man, he taunted himself, but why think of her now? And why not, came the bitter answer, why not think of the young living when you looked at the young dead?

Through his mind pushed thoughts of Gloria Hogarty, and the things he'd known about her. It wasn't much. She was busy fouling her life, and he'd been going to hell his way. Their paths crossed infrequently. Once, there'd been something about a cat and the Hogarty girl. It escaped him at the moment, nagging at him, and he wished he could remember what it was; it angered him that he couldn't, and angered him that he considered it might be at all important.

She'd been a pretty little thing, this he remembered, and he'd always been a man with an eye for pretty girls. Even under enough make-up to preserve an Egyptian mummy, her young beauty had shone through: teasing blue eyes, up-turned nose, full lips and rich blonde hair. A skinny little thing with girl breasts, but the way she dressed screamed at you she was a woman, with a woman's knowledge; a common woman, approachable and easy.

He scowled, pushing himself upward. His gaze moved to her arms, and the marks on them, and to her hands. He looked again, feeling the sure warning of wrong. He glanced at the doctor, thinking maybe Gaines would be more perceptive than he. The doc was the smartest man he knew. He cursed himself, wishing he were smart enough to *know* what it was he should see, looking at Gloria. He stood up, shaking his head.

"What's the matter?" Gaines said.

"Nothing."

He did not meet the doctor's gaze now. He was studying himself inwardly, trying to ferret out whatever it was he should know about Gloria, and missing it. He felt it buzz close, like a bee at a thistle, and then dart away. It did not help to stand, staring down at Gloria's body.

Zach took one step up the incline. His voice was cold and low. "It's plain to me, Bry."

"Yes?" Shafter spoke over his shoulder,

41

glancing at his deputy.

"It ought to be to you."

"I'm listening."

"She was robbed, most likely, maybe raped. You know how she was swishing her skirts around, and rolling her eyes. She promised every man she met, everything she had."

"It was just her manner. She didn't mean it."

"Didn't she? There ain't enough women in these parts for the ones that are here to make fake promises. They got to know their place. Or they're plumb asking for bad trouble."

Gaines' voice was as twisted as his smile. "Your young deputy is entirely correct, Marshal."

Zach nodded, feeling bolder. He took another forward step. "I am right. Somebody robbed her and raped her and left her buried up here. She's been gone from town almost a week. Some passing man might have done it. He could be in Nevady by now."

When Zach spoke, the crowd surged nearer to hear what was said. They moved as one man, and stopped, seeming not to have moved.

Sam Pickens stepped forward from the

crowd. He wiped his hands on his apron. "She was leaving town, Marshal, almost a week ago. I remember that. She was in the store, shopping for a dress fitting to wear on the coach."

"Is this the dress?" Bry nodded toward the corpse.

Sam licked his lips, shook his head. He did not come nearer. "I don't remember, Marshal. I don't recall. I sell a woman a dress, I can't say five minutes after what it was like."

"How did she seem?"

Sam cupped his hand behind his ear. "What, Marshal?"

"When you talked to her, was she worried?"

Sam scratched at the side of his pudgy jowls, his nails making a scratching sound against his whiskers. "Well, now I think about it — seeing her dead there like this, she acted kind of scairt, Marshal. Probably, though, if I never saw her dead like that, I'd never of thought about it."

"Maybe she was finally frightened by what the women of Pony Wells threatened unless she got out of town," Gaines said under his breath.

Shafter glanced at the doctor, didn't answer him. "Did she say why she was

43

scared, Sam?"

"Oh, no. No. She didn't even mention being upset. It was just the way she acted."

Trumbo Gilley spoke. "I seen her just before she got on the coach. Seemed just like herself to me. Why, she slapped me across the face when I tried to kiss her goodbye."

A short tense laugh wavered through the crowd. In their minds they could see the arrogant little Glory, lashing out to strike big Trumbo across his whiskered face. Hard to believe such a lively one was dead like this, forever dead, forever gone.

Bry said, "Thanks, Trumbo."

Trumbo rubbed the side of his face, remembering. "Sure. Just want you to know she seemed okay to me."

Shafter said, "Pillans Metz, you take her body back to your funeral parlor. Try to fix her up. We'll give her a decent burial."

Pillans Metz came out of the crowd and walked reluctantly up the knoll.

"What's the matter, Metz?" Bry said. "Since when did you shy away from a funeral?"

Metz looked at the body. "I'll have to get my wagon. I'll come up and get her."

Bry's voice stopped him. "You still don't sound really happy about this. Tell me why."

44

Metz turned, staring at the marshal. "Who's to tell me what price funeral, Marshal?"

"Oh," Bry said. He sighed. "You worried about getting your money."

"Caskets don't come free to me, Marshal. And she's got no family that I know."

No, Shafter thought, she's got no family. Her mother died, then her father was killed, and there was nobody to want Glory, or take her, and it was plumb easy for her to drift into the Blue Dollar — and end up here.

"I'll pay for the casket, and whatever it costs you to get her decently buried."

Young Will glanced up at his father. He could not see how his father could despise a man as kindly and as strong as the marshal. Yet there was a twisted smile about his father's face, and young Will knew him well enough to see that his father had given some hidden meaning to the marshal's gesture, a meaning that left it stripped of goodness, young Will knew, even though he could not understand his father's precise thoughts. It looked as though when grown people hated, no matter what happened, they went on hating.

Dr. Gaines hefted his black medical kit, spoke briefly to Shafter and went, walking erect and prim down the incline, crossing the creek and going toward Pony Wells, a lonely bitter little man.

"That's all," Shafter said, his voice rising. "You people can saddle up. You can get back home now."

Some of the crowd moved back towards the creek, but only Pillans Metz and the doctor actually moved toward town. Pillans Metz was hurrying, his shoulders hunched up in his black coat, well ahead of the doctor.

Young Will shivered. He was sure he'd forever remember the way the undertaker looked, striding across that flat land. In his black hat and black suit, he looked like death itself, hurrying to get you, walking faster than the doctor who was helpless and frustrated against him.

Shafter came down the incline to where Zach stood. Young Will and his father followed.

Zach glanced at the sky. "Not full dark yet," he said. "We could get in a couple rounds of target shooting on the flats, Old Man."

"No."

"We could set up a lantern. See if your eyes are still any good in the dark."

Shafter's voice rasped. "Forget it . . . I

46

said, forget it."

Zach's voice made a joke of Bry's anger. "Afraid I'll outshoot you?"

Shafter lifted his head, staring at Zach. He did not speak.

"You need it, Old Man. You're getting elderly. You need that practice worse than I do."

Shafter's face was pulled in an inscrutable frown. He moved his gaze across Zach's face as if puzzled by something.

He turned then and took long steps, moving through the crowd, bumping any of the people who didn't move fast enough to get out of his way.

FIVE

Bry set up the target. It was a straw man and resembled a scarecrow, with wisps of straw jutting from beneath the preacher's black hat, a chest stuffed full enough to bulge the cast-off vest and dust-smeared coat. The levis were ripped and more straw burst out.

He hung the target on a peg in a four-by-four post they'd driven into the hard crust of a dry lake half a mile from Pony Wells' town limits.

Darkness hovered like encroaching clouds

above the sheer cliffs that walled the valley far and away to the west. It was not yet full dark, a grey haze settled over the valley, making shadows of trees and rocks and blackening the crevices and ravines in the hills. The dry lake glistened alkali-white and by moonlight would shine white and flat and bare.

Shafter lighted a lantern and hung it on the second four-by-four. The lantern lay a sheen across their faces, and seemed reflected from the dry flats. It tossed a wide clearly-defined circle and Shafter walked slowly with Zach Adams to the rim of light. This was their target range and empty cartridges were strewn about their feet.

"All right," Shafter said. "Let's get it over with."

Zach straightened, facing the target, tall, handsome and scowling.

"What's eating you, Pop? You're gettin' paid, ain't you? You been growling ever since I talked you into this deal. What more can you do that you don't do? Pony Wells is so respectable it's downright dull. So a tramp got herself killed, and it's eating at you. Not even you can make everybody be good, Pop. Tell you what. You act nice," he looked around broadly, making certain he was not overheard, taunting Shafter. "Tell you, I

48

might let you outshoot me tonight."

"All right. Like I said. Let's go. Let's get it over." Shafter was staring across Zach's shoulder at the town lights of Pony Wells; they appeared slowly, weak and mild against the growing darkness. A shiver ran through him.

What am I doing out here? he thought, acting stooge for young Adams so he can build his ego by outshooting me on a range that never mattered, at a target without meaning.

He knew better: he'd come out here because after dark he was seldom alone in Pony Wells. Zach's presence did not disturb him. When Zach talked, all that mattered was that Zach listened. He could stand here on the windy flats, watching the night bugs fly against the lantern, throwing lean shadows across the white crust of the dry lake. Out here, he could think with only the sound of Zach's gun and the sound of Zach's voice to beat against his conscious mind.

They checked their guns, placed feet apart and addressed the target. The lantern glittered on a vest button. "Whisky or box of shells?" Zach said across his shoulder.

"Make it easy on yourself."

Zach glanced at him, that faint impersonal

contempt playing about his mouth. Zach viewed deprecatingly anyone older than himself. As far as Zach was concerned, Marshal Shafter was an old man, a tired old horse ready to be turned to pasture.

Zach raised his gun, taking his time. He fired rapidly, one, two, three. The gun bucked in his hand but he held his wrist as Shafter had taught him. Smoke erupted white in the yellow lantern glow, and the sound barked across the valley and echoed wanly from some far canyon.

The target bucked three times in almost exactly the same manner. Shafter did not have to go near it to know how closely the three bullets had traced each other into that straw padding.

But Zach was not content with anything less than certain knowledge. He strode into the lantern glow, tall, wide-shouldered in black boots, black whipcord trousers and black vest.

He turned when he reached the target. The wind riffled a lock of hair on his forehead. He grinned.

"See that shooting, Old Man?"

"What?"

Zach snarled at him. "I drilled this scarecrow three times in the heart, and you don't listen. What's the matter, Old Fellow, don't

50

you want to know how good I am?"

"As long as I got ears in the sound of your voice, I'll know how good you are."

Zach jammed his forefinger into the single tear made in the scarecrow's chest by the three bullets. "That's right. I'm good because I think about what I'm doing. What are you thinking about, Bry?"

"That kid out there on that mound tonight. When you're as old as I am, Zach, and got kids, you'll know what it can do to you, seeing a girl left out there like that."

"A saloon girl got the wrong guy excited, got herself killed. It happens all the time, Bry."

"Yeah. But not like that." He shuddered, thinking how it had been: ugly and brutal, a savage killing, a careless burial.

Zach started toward him in the light, his long shadow lunging toward Bry and the rim of dark. "She didn't mean anything to you. You hardly knew her."

"That's right. She danced at the Blue Dollar. Gave the come-on to the suckers. That don't make me like what happened to her."

Zach was checking his gun. "And I don't either. But women that live like her take their chances. You could spend your time better than chasing some guy a week gone from here."

"Don't it make you want to find that killer?"

"No."

Shafter shrugged. Zach clicked the chamber back into place, thrust his gun into his holster.

"You ought to have something to go on, Pop. You haven't, have you?"

"No. I got nothing. Just hate."

"Maybe I could string along with you if you'd give me something to go on."

"I'm not asking you."

Zach shrugged. "Sure you're not. Maybe I feel big hearted. But you told me a law-man had to have something to go on."

Shafter sighed. "When he don't have something to go on, he can look at it another way, Zach. That's the way I do. I take the known facts. Even if it's just one. If I got one bit of truth, and something fits it, fine, that adds to it. If it don't fit — then I don't go on with that clue, no matter how interesting it looks."

"You're a nice old gentleman, Bry. But you let things upset you." Zach turned and faced the target. "We'll draw and fire. I'll beat you to the draw."

Shafter nodded. He counted. One. Two. Three. His hand slapped his holster, but in the split second before he pressed the trigger of his gun, he heard the roar of Zach's, and the harsh ring of Zach's laughter. Shafter fired and the sounds reverberated from the pines.

They heard the creak of wagon wheels, clop of a trotting horse, the crackling of the dry crust of the lake.

Zach turned. Shafter returned his gun to his holster, feeling a chill that was not in the rising wind.

The carriage was a richly upholstered two-seat runabout, with painted sides, canvas covered top and curtains to snap on the uprights against rain. The carriage was open tonight and they saw Troy Vance was driving it.

She pulled the horse slightly past them into the light. "I knew just where to find you two boys," she said.

"What are you doing in town?" Zach's voice was insolent. "Your old man send you in to foreclose another mortgage?"

"He came with me," she said. "He figured there were enough widows and orphans for both of us." She turned her head, the lantern tracing her sharp fine features and glowing in her dark hair. "Hello, Marshal Shafter, aren't you getting kind of careless the company you keep?"

Zach's voice cut across hers. "I just gave

53

the old man a lesson in shooting."

"That's just fine," she said, voice overly sweet. "And what happens to crime in this town while you two are out here learning to shoot?"

"She rides out here to us," Zach said. He leaned against the wagon. "Anybody ever tell you that you're the pertest little heifer ever nibbled a blade of grass?"

She smiled. "Not in just that well-worded way."

He reached up for her. "Oh, say, when you grow up, you'll drive the boys wild."

She drew away from him. "But I suppose I don't interest you at all?"

He spread his hands. "Well, that's the way it goes. You're just not my type."

"Oh, you'll regret that," she said. "Oh, how you'll regret that."

"Come on," he motioned with his hands. "I want to show you my kind of shooting. I want you to see it. Then you can tell those no-goods that hang around your father's rancho what I'll do to them if they don't stay away from my girl."

She tied the reins, and leaned forward. He slipped his hands slowly under her arms, pressing her, and staring up at her, mouth twisted and eyes insolent. He waited for her to protest. She said nothing. When he set her on her feet, she stayed for a moment close against him.

Zach's gaze met Shafter's over the top of her dark head. Zach pulled down the corner of his mouth and winked. The rich girl, said his eyes, the richest girl in this whole valley, in this whole territory, and look at her, nibbling right out of Zach Adams' hand.

Zach put his arm about her and the three of them crossed the lighted ring to the scarecrow. Zach said, "Mister Scarecrow, I want you to meet Troy Vance. Miss Vance, here's the man I just shot in the heart. He made a mighty insulting remark about you. He said the bustle there wasn't a bustle at all, that it was you — all you."

She reached up and put her hand over his mouth.

"You're not supposed to notice such things."

"Then why do you wear them, except for me to notice?"

She laughed. "All right, notice then. But don't talk about it."

Zach shrugged, and Shafter looked at him, thinking Zach belonged in the saloons and the sheriff's office. Troy's old man wanted a gentleman for her. And Troy wanted this roughneck.

Zach pulled her close against his side with

one arm and reached out, jabbing his finger into the bullet hole in the scarecrow's vest. "I did that," he told her. "One. Two. Three. Ask the old man here. Then you know what I did? I outdrew him." He laughed and threw back his head. "Bry Shafter — the trouble marshal. The man they hire because he's fast with a gun."

Troy didn't look up at Shafter. Her voice was low. "I'm proud of you, Zach."

"You ought to be." His voice rang with generosity. He slapped Shafter on the shoulder. "The old man has treated me like a son, Troy. I got to give him that. In his time, he had it. He can't help getting old, can you, Pop?"

"Guess not, Zach."

Zach laughed. "How does it feel, Dad, knowing I've learned, and now I'm better? He's been teaching me his tricks, Troy." He faced Shafter again. "Well, I've learned them all now, huh, old fellow?"

Bry smiled. His hand touched the scarred butt of his gun. "Almost," he said.

Troy touched Shafter's arm. "Is he good, Marshal? I mean is he even nearly as good as he says he is?"

Shafter smiled down at her. "Nobody's that good," he said. "But he's fair with a gun."

"That's fine," she said. She looked Zach over. "He's the kind of man I want in my family."

Zach pulled her after him towards the carriage. "I'll see you in town, girl," he told her. "A couple more rounds, and I'll call it a night. We'll take a ride in this parlor on wheels."

"You promise?" She turned up her mouth and Zach kissed her, his lips rough, and his hands moving on her. She shivered, sagged against him.

He nodded and swung her up into the carriage. "Can't I stay and watch?" Troy said.

His voice went cold. "I keep my mind on what I'm doing — just one thing at a time, Troy. I mean that."

She bit her lip, her shoulders quivered as if with a sudden chill. She took up the reins, turned the horse and pulled out of the light, returning toward Pony Wells.

The moment she was gone, she was out of Zach's mind. He checked his gun. "Time for another round, Dad?"

"No. I've had enough."

He wanted to get into town. He'd had enough of Zach Adams and dry firing at inanimate targets. He sighed, thinking no man knew what he was or what he could do, until he faced a living man with a deadly gun in his hand.

He could not get Gloria Hogarty from his mind. He could not stop thinking that if Gloria's father had lived Gloria would never have ended this way. Hogarty never meant it to be this way. Why, she could be any man's daughter . . . it could be his own daughter. He closed his fists tightly.

Zach laughed. "About time for you to retire, ain't it, Marshal? When you know there's one faster man, there might be two. And just one — that's too many. No . . . think you ought to retire."

Shafter turned on his heel, facing Zach suddenly. His face was as white as the crust of the dry lake. His voice lashed out savagely, but low, through his taut throat.

"There's been a lot of men faster than me, Zach. A lot of them. But they're gone . . ." He exhaled heavily. "And I'm still here."

SIX

Shafter saw lights brightly lit in his office even before he got there. He walked across the flat fields, coming into Main Street from the darkness, walking fast and alone.

He stepped up on the narrow plank stoop of the frame building that housed his office and the two cells of the jail. It was set apart from the other frame buildings of Main Street, and Shafter reached it from the dry lake without going into town at all.

He paused a moment, reading the small sign tacked to the door: Marshal, Pony Wells. Through the lighted window he saw swirls of cigar smoke. Whoever his company was, they'd been waiting for some time.

He pushed open the door and the three men sitting before his desk stood up, and turned toward him. "Marshal Shafter?"

"I'm Marshal Shafter."

The man who'd asked the question studied him and some of the tension in his face relaxed. Shafter felt his jaw tighten. They liked what they saw, these three. It was almost as if he were horseflesh on display. The buyer looked him over and decided if he wanted to buy. He supposed he should be pleased that men such as these still liked what they saw when they inspected him. He recognized the whole deal, he'd been through it often.

Standing in the doorway of his office, he had the odd sensation of walking into a situation that had happened before in exactly the same way . . . many times.

Once there had been some exhilaration, an uplift to walk into a room like this and find three worried men awaiting him. He had known he was wanted and needed, desperately. There could not help being that sense of pride at knowing they talked your name around campfires and across bars, so the stories of you traveled, and when there was a town in trouble, the man they thought of was Bryant Shafter.

But now there was no pleasure, no excitement, there was only the sense of having ridden this trail before.

He had to stare at his office to be sure this was the place he'd worked from for the past two years, and not some other office, in some other town, in the years that were past. He felt a slight sickness at the thought that all the offices were the same, and the worried men were the same, and their malignant trouble was always the same.

He saw the framed drawing of Maudie on his desk, the way the gun closet was kept closed so he no longer had to look at the shotguns and the Winchesters arranged on its pegs. He had allowed Maudie to put curtains at his windows; he had no tintypes of other peace officers. He realized suddenly how completely different he had tried to make this office. It had angered him that his office was like every other marshal's office or sheriff's office in the territory. He had tried to make it unlike any other. And now these three harried men, with their cigars, and their looks of satisfaction at the size and build of him, they destroyed everything he had worked for. This office was the same, nothing had changed.

He looked at them, knowing them, knowing what they wanted.

He closed the door behind him and moved around his desk, thinking he didn't know their names or their town, but these were details, he'd seen these men before, or men precisely like them until he knew which was the banker, which the rancher, and which of them owned more of the town and of its troubles than he would ever admit.

The biggest of the three men stepped forward. "Marshal Shafter, I'm Sim Linnot. I know you haven't heard of me. But I've heard of you, sir." He laughed heartily. "I don't think there are many men in this territory who haven't heard of you."

The small man in the expensive suit winked suddenly. "I swear, I thought you'd be bigger. I heard a lot about how big you were, Marshal."

Shafter studied the winking man. This one he knew best of the three, this was the man a new marshal dealt with most closely, because this one had more secrets. This one owned the brothel, the land it was on, the house that encased it, and the women in it. The wink meant nothing, certainly not that the little man had a bright and sunny nature. The wink was a tic in his left eye, and was so much a part of him by now that he'd forgotten it happened, the way he forgot that he breathed.

"Oh, they have bouncers in whorehouses bigger than I am," Shafter said, watching the winking man.

The three men laughed. They would have laughed if he'd given them a weather report. They wanted to ingratiate themselves with him.

Linnot's voice boomed in the close, smoke veiled room. "When a man is talked about, he grows, just like the stories about him grow. That's the way it is. That's the way it's always been."

The third man had not spoken. Now he pressed close on the edge of his chair. "We ought to get right down to business, Sim." He stared up at Shafter. "We can tell you frankly, Marshal, we've come almost a thousand miles to call on you."

Shafter said, "I'm right flattered."

Linnot said, "We won't waste no more of your time than we have to, Marshal. Like I said, I'm Sim Linnot. Now, the three of us, we're from Gravehead — in the Utah Territory. You heard of it?"

Shafter nodded, feeling that old familiar emptiness in the pit of his stomach.

"Well, sir, I'm Linnot, owner of the Lazy L ranch, that's about the biggest in that territory." Shafter heard the voice, thinking two years ago it was Old Man Vance and he owned the biggest ranch within six hundred miles of Pony Wells. Now it was Gravehead in the Utah Territory. Now it was a hearty man named Sim Linnot. Linnot was well-fed, with large balding head and jowls that shook when he smiled or frowned.

Shafter studied the rancher, thinking, here is the man who grows fat in the lean years.

Linnot was saying, "The little fellow here is Abel Queen." Shafter moved his gaze to Queen just at the second the little man's eye closed in a leering wink. Shafter studied him as they shook hands. Gray, wispy hair. The expensive suit that had been shipped west from a New York tailor, and the soup stains on Queen's white shirt front. "Abel owns the mercantile store in Gravehead."

Abel Queen was nodding. He owned the mercantile store. Then he winked. It was the tic at work, but it was as if the wink were saying, obviously Queen owns more of Gravehead than the general store. A man who owns the general store in any town gets many opportunities to buy into all manner of ancillary businesses.

Queen said, "I crossed this country and most of Utah in a wagon-train, Marshal Shafter. That was a good many years ago. I fell in love with that spot, sir. Looked like the kind of place a man like me had been looking for." He sighed and his shoulders sagged, as if he were a man without hope. But at that instant, he winked again.

Linnot laughed. "Sure. Abel's got his troubles. I swear I went to see Doc Seavy out home with Abel one time. Abel had every pain the doc had any remedy for." Linnot stopped talking so that he could laugh, remembering. And Shafter recognized this routine, too. Linnot was telling him Gravehead was a place where good men lived, men of good will who wanted him to come out there and be among them. God, he thought, how old I'm getting. How often this has happened.

Linnot dropped a heavy arm about the narrow shoulders of the skimpily made man in the cheap black suit. Here's the real money, Shafter thought, looking at the tight-fisted, screw-mouthed man. "This here is my good friend Lius McHercher, Marshal Shafter."

Shafter shook McHercher's soft warm

hand. McHercher tried to smile, but pulled his hand away, knotted it into a fist and pressed it against his diaphragm.

McHercher belched. "Pardon me, Marshal. I got me a pain here in my middle that's like fire. Like that all the time. Pains me when I eat, even when I drink water. Thought it was my heart, but Doc Seavy says it's not. Says he don't know what it is, but I tell you sometimes, Marshal, I feel like that pain will burn my insides out. Doc Seavy says I'm not to worry so much, or I'm headed for my grave. Now I ask you — how can I help worrying?"

Linnot made a sympathetic clucking sound. "McHercher is president of our bank, Marshal Shafter. . . . Now I tell you, sir . . . we're all plain men, and mighty proud that a man as well-known, as talked about as you, will take the time to hear out our troubles. But then maybe I don't even have to tell you. Gravehead has earned a name that stinks both ways to the border, Marshal."

McHercher nodded, digging his fist against his vest. "It shouldn't be that way. It's a lovely town. On the Rio Grande and Western railway, on a lovely river, got grazing lands and farm lands — why, there's sheep country so there's never even dissension between men like Linnot and the herders."

"I try to get along with folks," Linnot said. "They don't force me, they find me right friendly."

"Just the same, the situation there is bad," Queen said. "There's no law any more. The marshal that's there was put in office because he would not enforce the law. That was the only reason he was wanted, to stand between the decent element and the bad, and to work for the bad." Queen sat forward, cracked his knuckles, winked.

"Men with bad gun reps are turning up there," Linnot said. "Men on the prod, and other men with a price on their heads. When gunmen call a place like Gravehead home, Marshal, you know as well as I do that town is dying a quick death — it's a stench hole that honest people avoid."

"Why, Marshal, known prostitutes walk the street and solicit trade right in front of our wives and our children, and laugh in our faces." McHercher's voice shook. One incident was new in his mind, and still rankled.

"And cowpunchers — why, even the men who work for Sim Linnot — when they get into Gravehead at the end of the week, they shoot up the streets, or knife each other.

There's never a Saturday night that two young men don't lay each other open with their knives," Queen said.

Linnot said, "Marshal, I'm a man that knows his evil times. When I 'steaded my land out there, there was nothing out there but the mountain men, the Indians and some hidehunters. It wasn't easy, Shafter." Linnot was staring into the past, his voice ringing in the small room, filled with the memories and the hurts and the triumphs. "I buried my wife, and I lost my oldest son. There was grief, Shafter, the kind of hurt that I thought I could not stand. But I was big enough to face it all, and live through it. But now this evil in Gravehead is something else, and organized terror, so a decent man cannot make a living."

"That's what we're all up against, Marshal," McHercher said, "and Doc Seavy tells me to stop worrying. Now, I haven't been out there as long as either Sim Linnot or Abel. I came with the railroad. Gravehead was the land of opportunity then, and I saw the possibilities. I invested all the money I could borrow. For years there, I had more debts than I could face or meet, but I fought through it. I will say that I brought a lot of fine people to Gravehead. Both Linnot and Queen will tell you that. But I stand to be ruined if those good people leave Grave-head, and that's what they'll do if this lawlessness continues."

"And that's why we've come almost a thousand miles to see you, Marshal. Something has got to be done, or we stand to lose our homes — maybe our lives — and see our town turned into a pesthole."

McHercher said, "That's it, Mr. Shafter. We've got trouble, and we heard you were the man — they call you the trouble marshal. God knows, that's what we need."

Shafter looked from McHercher to Linnot. He had heard the story of Gravehead before. The name of the town was different. But the story was the same, and the trouble was.

His stomach felt empty, and there was a sense of loss in him. He thought about Pony Wells, and the longing need to call this place home, the wish to stay here, and enjoy the quiet and the peace that he had made — and he alone, walking the streets in the dark, standing up to men who had never backed down, seeing them back down or, draw. He thought about Main Street, the way it had been two years ago, the way it was now. Sure the bad was here, but it was controlled, under the surface, leashed. It was what they wanted, and Pony Wells was what he wanted. He looked at his hands, wondering if he wanted a home, or was it that he was getting old and tired? Whatever it was, he was sick of danger and death and trouble.

He exhaled heavily, standing there behind the desk they'd given him two years ago along with the tin star.

"You gentlemen have my sympathy. I'm sorry. I've heard about Gravehead, and I know your problem. But it don't look like there's anything I can do. I'm marshal here at Pony Wells — and that's about a full time job."

His gaze touched Abel Queen's, and at that moment, the little man winked.

SEVEN

Linnot laughed. The bluff hearty sound banged against the walls. Linnot was accustomed to the open places, the ranges where wind smashed a thin voice to atoms. "Now, just a minute, Marshal. We've heard all about Bry Shafter."

"Have you?" Bry touched his chin.

"Shafter never wastes his talents in a town that's dead and dull," Queen said.

McHercher cleared his throat. "We have investigated you pretty thoroughly, Marshal

69

Shafter, because we were very interested in you — and, ah, your record."

Linnot laughed. "We heard about Abilene. We know about you in Abilene, Shafter."

Shafter felt as though he were not breathing, but standing breathless, waiting for them to say it all.

"Before Abilene, it was Dodge City." Queen wriggled in his chair. "The report is that Shafter is a quiet man, but hell with a gun. That's what they said about you in Dodge City."

"I believe your record was best in Cheyenne," McHercher said. "And we spent the day talking to the folks here at Pony Wells. Your two years here has made a new and peaceful town of Pony Wells — and the whole valley."

"But that's it." Linnot leaned forward. "This town is too quiet for you, too quiet for a man like you."

He held up his hand. The others stared at him, frowned, but were silent. They heard crickets at the windows, the neighing of a horse. Two men laughed, talking together, boots clumping on the board walk. From far along the street came the tinny sounds of a piano. Somebody drove past in a wagon, goods clattering in its bed. Above all of it threaded the singing of choir practice

70

at the First Baptist Church.

McHercher swallowed. "Hard to believe that Pony Wells was ever a pesthole, Marshal. This is a good place for a man to live."

"Yes," Shafter said.

"But not for a man of action," Linnot said. "You're a man whose whole life has been spent in the middle of violence of one kind or another. Why, what will happen to you, living in a place like this?"

"I don't know," Shafter said.

McHercher got up, went to the door, opened it and looked out upon the quiet street, laced with yellow shafts of light from quiet windows. "This is what I want," he said. "This is the way I want my town."

"Like I said," Shafter told them. "I'm not free to go."

Queen winked. "If the price were right, you could get free."

Shafter shook his head. The price right? After sixteen years of it, he wondered if there were a right price to place upon a man's walking into hell. He was a professional marshal, the kind they called a trouble marshal. But as a man grew older, he grew wiser, had a better knowledge of the hazards and the odds. Once, there'd been excitement. There was nothing exciting about it any more.

Perhaps, the truth was that since Maudie had grown up, he'd felt a greater sense of responsibility toward her, a need to see her secure and happy. Perhaps, seeing Hannah die, hating his profession and the tin star he wore, had made him see himself and his job differently. Whatever it was, he could envision the killers holed up in Gravehead, and he knew the price for facing those men was not right. There was no price for that sort of gut-wracking labor. There wasn't that much money . . . not any more.

"I'm almost forty," Shafter said half to himself. "Have you thought about hiring a younger man?"

"We talked about it," McHercher said.

Linnot's face flushed. "We don't want a younger man, Marshal. Why, I reckon you remember your own younger years. It was harder for you to catch on in a new town. Right?"

Shafter exhaled, did not answer.

Linnot's flushed face worked into a confident smile. He leaned forward, putting much implied meaning into his words. "We mistrust a younger man, Marshal."

Queen nodded at Linnot, winked. "Experience, Marshal. That's what you've got. That's what we told McHercher we wanted to buy."

McHercher nodded. "And I agreed. I believe in experience, especially in matters of law enforcement."

They were talking around it, Shafter told himself, and a new feeling worked itself through the emptiness in his diaphragm. This was something he'd never felt before in any office in his past, when confronted by any town fathers in his past. This was something that came as his inner contempt grew for men who said one thing, and meant something else.

The other two hinted at it, but Queen really said it: "We know you, Mr. Shafter. We've talked to people who know you. You understand our problem. That's most important." The eye closed in a sudden wink. "You know what we want, Mr. Shafter."

Shafter let his gaze move through the clouds of cigar smoke to the window, to the dark street, and the town. He knew what was out there; it was more than choir practice at the First Baptist Church, and women walking safely along the avenues at night, an end to knife fights. He saw that Pony Wells was just what he'd promised those other town fathers two years ago he'd make of it. He'd understood then what they wanted, really wanted.

His sweated hands closed. They had paid

their money, and they had got what they wanted.

Everything that had been in Pony Wells when he arrived two years ago was here now. A man could gamble at the Blue Dollar, get a woman at Mrs. Sefner's boarding house, drink as much as he liked in any of the bars along Main Street. Only the wild element was gone. The violence was all right out there, but it was a controlled violence, pushed beneath a hypocritical surface of respectability and smelling of flowers in a Sunday morning church.

He'd arrived two years ago on the stage with Hannah and Maudie. He'd stepped off the stage and seen the evil in Pony Wells.

Gunmen swaggered on the streets, carrying dodgers sent after them, boasting of the reward some town further east would pay on them. Drunken cowboys knifed each other in the alleys. Women worked the dark places. It was no place to bring a wife and a fourteen-year-old daughter. But he'd brought them here.

The fugitives were profitable to nobody, and they were driven out. A knifing made nothing but blood on Doc Swilner's kitchen floor; the deadly weapons were outlawed. Women who worked for themselves weren't even profitable to themselves, because most of them were fools or drunks, and unless they would fall in line, they were given enough money to get them out of town.

It had not been easy. If it had been easy anybody could have done it, and they would never have brought Bryant Shafter to Pony Wells. But easy or not, he had accomplished it. Tonight the loudest sound was choir practice in the First Baptist Church. The evil was tamed, the violence controlled, all of it arranged so there was profit in it for the men who ran this town.

Shafter's jaw tightened. And that's what these men wanted at Gravehead in the Utah Territory. A cap on lawlessness, the fugitives exterminated, and a profit from evil that was pressed under the surface.

That's my experience they find so valuable, that's what I understand that a younger man might misunderstand.

His hands pressed against his desk top. And maybe that's why I don't sleep well, maybe that's why I've come to hate myself, and despise these men who whine and lie about what they really want.

Linnot glanced toward McHercher, cleared his throat and leaned toward Shafter. "What are you paid a year in this town, Marshal?" Linnot laughed and knocked ash from his cigar, an expansive

75

man, implying that whatever he made here, a higher salary awaited him in God's country, the pesthole named Gravehead.

Shafter regarded them, moving his gaze slowly. Queen, winking and satisfied, certain they had found a capable man and a worldly one who understood the facts about a clean town. Queen winked, knowing human beings were going to gamble, wench, drink, but feeling somebody ought to profit from it. As things were in Gravehead, men sinned, but nobody profited.

Linnot wanted the town clean so it was safe as a railhead for his business. Lawlessness cut into his profits, and there was no redress for wrongs committed against him. He wanted lawlessness controlled, and he wanted to feel he controlled the man who enforced the law.

McHercher was closest in approaching honesty. He had realized his town was doomed if it continued wild and evil, a nesting place for gun vultures who couldn't exist where there was law and order.

But McHercher would have rebelled at the suggestion that the painted women who insulted his wife be dispersed from Gravehead. All he wanted was that they stayed behind drawn shades and closed doors where they belonged. His bank would lose money if the saloons closed, and he didn't want them closed, and gambling put money on deposit that could be used to build other businesses as long as it gained interest for the depositor.

"I'm paid ten thousand a year," Shafter said.

At first they thought he was joking, but when they met his gray eyes, they knew better.

He smiled mirthlessly, holding their gazes. "Oh, they squealed, like stuck pigs, and swore they'd get along without me. But I told them I wouldn't come here for less." He shrugged. "I've been here two years."

McHercher shook his head, pressing his fist against the burning ulceration in his middle. "Ten thousand dollars. For one man . . . That's a good deal more than I make, Mr. Shafter. A good deal more." He tried to laugh but could not unscrew his mouth.

"Why, ten thousand dollars," Linnot said. "Why, that's a fortune, Shafter."

Shafter shrugged. "You asked me. I told you."

McHercher belched. "No wonder the men we talked to were so reluctant to discuss your salary. Obviously they didn't like to boast what fools they'd been."

Shafter just stared at him. McHercher's face turned red. "Don't misunderstand. I'm sure you've been worth many times more than you've been paid. But ten thousand a year is a big salary in these times."

Queen winked, and winked again. He wiped his hands across his trousers. "Well. We just have not considered anything like this, Mr. Shafter."

Shafter was tired of them. He walked around his desk, moving deliberately. He stood facing them. His voice was mild, but thick with contempt. "Gentlemen, they don't pay me by the year. They pay me by the gunhand." He held them out, first the right, then the left, staring at them. "Five thousand each."

They tried to smile, could not. They looked at each other. "You want to hire a gun," Shafter said relentlessly, "That's the way you've got to consider it. The price is cheap. That's what I'm paid here. But — I wouldn't come to Gravehead for that." He looked directly at McHercher. "Perhaps twice that, Mr. McHercher. That pain in your stomach is pretty bad. I might contract something like it — even worse. My health is pretty valuable to me."

They did not look at him. They felt his contempt, but knew they needed him. The higher he set his price, the more valuable they felt him to be. But the first year at Gravehead, the money he demanded would come from their own pockets. It would be the first year that was so painful. They had not thought that a gun would hire so dear. The evil that infested Gravehead was a thousand miles west of them, but the threat to their pocketbooks was here and immediate.

"We'll have to talk it over," Queen said.

"We need you in Gravehead, Mr. Shafter." Linnot no longer laughed.

"Your price is stiff," McHercher said. He pressed his fist hard against his middle and belched again.

EIGHT

He sat at his desk for twenty minutes after they were gone, thinking about them, their visit, and what it meant.

He looked around the office that he'd worked so hard to make just a little different. There was an alien feeling in the room, as if something had ended and he no longer belonged here.

He clenched his fists on the desk before him.

The door opened and he straightened,

alert. He dropped his hand to his side. Always be ready, he thought, you've always got to be ready, everytime that door opens.

Maudie came in. She wore a new print frock and a bonnet with a single flower. She carried a tray covered by one of Hannah's linen handkerchiefs.

Maudie wrinkled her nose. She set the tray on his desk and blinked at the solid streamers of smoke. "What have you been doing in here?" she said. "Burning old love letters?"

She opened the door and pushed up a window. A breeze stirred the smoke and it swirled lazily and slid in wraiths around the door.

"I know you won't be able to stand the fresh air," she said.

He pulled the tray across the desk, peeked under the napkin. "And I know you came down here alone, too. In a new dress and a new hat."

She turned on her toes so he could look her over. "How do you like it?" she said. She nodded her head toward the door. "Lon is outside."

"Not Lon Tolliver?" He pretended to be astounded. "I think he followed you down here last night, too."

She smiled and blushed. "Eat your supper."

He mocked her, scowling. "Is young Tolliver annoying you? I'll have a word with him."

She stood against the desk, staring at him. "Lon told me — about the poor girl. The one the little boy found. Do you know who did it, Papa?"

He shook his head, let the napkin fall back over the tray. The pleasure went out of seeing Maudie, the good went out of having her with him for a few minutes in the evening. He looked forward to her coming, and always felt better when he knew that Lon was out there to walk her home and sit with her in the swing. That was Maudie's world, and that was the way he wanted it, apart from what he was, what he had become.

His mouth pulled. "Maudie, will you be a good girl?"

"What are you talking about?"

"I mean it, Maudie. No matter what happens to me."

"What's the matter with you?"

"Never mind what's the matter. You answer me."

She laughed, the flower bobbling on her hat. "Papa, how can I answer that?"

He stared at her. "I mean it, girl."

She formed her lips in a teasing kiss. "Why, Papa, I'm so good all the time that I'm bored stiff with myself."

He exhaled, pleased with her answer. He looked at her new dress, the new curves developing under it. His voice was low. "You just remember. Your mama was a church woman. No matter what I am."

She stopped smiling, came around the desk. She stood close against him, touching his forehead the way Hannah had done, fretting about him in the silent office.

"Papa. What's the matter?"

"Nothing." Her palm felt cool against his face.

"You're worried."

"No."

She moved away, looking at the office and the cells behind it, hating it all. "You've got to quit, Papa. You've got to quit all this."

He managed to smile. "Sure. And what would I do? Dig ditches, string fences?"

"There are a lot of things you could do."

He shook his head. "No. When you're my age, Maudie, and know nothing, you realize what a bad spot you're in. You know one job. The job you're in. You might be too old for it, but it's all you know."

"You're not too old. You're young. You're

82

much younger than any other man your age in this town. It's just because you've got me, and worry about me. If you didn't have me, you could be as young and wild as Zach Adams."

He caught his breath. "What do you know about Zach Adams?"

"Why nothing. Just that he thinks every woman is crazy about him."

"I guess they've got him convinced, honey."

"Oh, if you just knew. He's nothing beside you. Nothing." She came back to him, laid her hand on his shoulder. "But there are so many things you don't know, Papa. Things like thinking you've got to go on being a marshal."

He looked around him. "It's all I know."

"What will you do?" Her voice was soft up through her taut throat. "What will you do? Just go on until some stupid killer shoots you?"

He tried to smile. "Why would they want to do that?"

"Don't think I don't know. Lon told me."

"Damn that Lon."

"He told me. Men who think they're gunfighters. They hear about you. They want to build their nasty reputations."

"Lon's been dreaming."

83

"No. It's true. You know it. They seek you out. Don't they? They come here because you're here."

"I don't worry about them."

"Don't you? You think I don't know. Out there tonight, in those dark alleys, getting drunk in some saloon may be some man who — who's going to try . . . . to kill you — tonight."

"It's not that bad, baby."

"It's worse. I just never knew before. When I heard Mama crying, I didn't understand. Now I know."

"I can take care of myself, Maudie. You've got to get this business off your mind. You tell young Tolliver if he talks any more of this to you, I'll slap him sillier than he is."

"No, Papa. Lon tells me the truth . . . .You don't. You try to lie to me."

He stood up. His throat felt taut. "I don't lie to you, honey. This work — it's all I know. Ten thousand a year. Maybe — next year — twenty thousand."

She turned her head away, pressing her hand against her mouth. "Yes. Sure . . . . Unless you're killed — tonight."

"No, Maudie. Don't talk this way."

"It's the way I must talk. You've got to stop, Papa. It's peaceful here now in Pony Wells. You made it that way. You alone. They must be grateful. Somebody will be. Somebody will hire you for some good job —"

"No. I know better." His voice sounded tired. "I wouldn't lie to you about that. I'm a trouble marshal, Maudie."

She turned and looked up, smiling.

"You mean a peace marshal," she said.

He shook his head. He looked down at her, the tears glistening in her dark lashes, the soft waves under her new bonnet, the fresh young loveliness of her.

Yesterday, she was a baby. Sixteen years ago? Impossible. It was last night. There was trouble, and he sat all night in the darkness of an open corral waiting for a killer to come for his horse, and in her agony Hannah cried for him, and he never heard her. And from her agony, Maudie had come, and when he walked in in the morning, the neighbors were with Hannah, and the baby was born. And Hannah looked up at him from her pillow. And Hannah had tried to forgive him. Hannah always tried to forgive him.

"No, baby. I'm a trouble marshal. All I've ever been. They want me only when there's trouble." He shook his head. "And only as long as there's trouble. A trouble marshal. He's a different breed, baby."

NINE

Shafter finished off the quarter of apple pie Maudie had put on the tray to top off his supper.

He got up then, feeling better, spread the napkin over the tray. He turned down the lamp, set his hat on his head, and closed the office.

He walked across the street to Wu Sing's Barber Shop. Two ladies leaving the Baptist Church waited on the walk until he passed. They did not look at him.

He opened the door at Wu Sing's. Half a dozen men sat in the chairs along the wall. There was no one in the barber chair. The little Chinaman gave Shafter a bob and smile, shaking out the cloth.

"Need a shave, Wu Sing." The men had stopped talking and sat watching as Wu Sing took a heavy mug marked "Shafter" from the shelf.

"Found the devil that killed the Hogarty girl, Marshal?"

Shafter shook his head. Wu Sing let down the chair and wrapped his face in a steaming towel. Bry was thankful.

"Never will catch him, either," a man said. "I figure it was some devil passing. You all know there ain't no man lives around here would do a thing like that."

"I'd hate to think so, anyhow," said another. "No woman would be safe around a man that would do a fiend's trick like that."

"Must have been some foreigner," said another. "No civilized Christian would do what that fiend done." They began to talk about the things that rumor had had happen to Glory Hogarty. Hacked off one breast. Chopped off her fingers. The cruelest things a man could think, those were the horrors they said had happened to Gloria.

Lord, Shafter thought. It was bad enough as it was. These men professed shocked horror at what had happened to Glory, but they urged each other for more details, gasping or cursing their shock when they heard.

Wu Sing finished shaving Shafter, working silently. The marshal paid him, and the Chinaman brushed his hat and clothing with a long brush.

One of the men leaned forward in his chair.

"Marshal?"

Shafter turned, setting his hat on his head, his face feeling fresh and clean. "Yeah, Wally?"

The little man licked his lips, watching the marshal's face. "Heard something, Marshal, might interest you."

"Yeah?"

"Heard down at a bar today that a fellow named Rio is drifting this way. You ever hear a gun toter called Rio Kid, Marshal?"

Shafter sighed. "I think so. Saw a reward dodger. Can't be much. A hundred dollars. That's all they offer for him."

Everybody laughed.

Wally looked around, unsmiling. "Way this fellow told it, Rio is building a gun rep."

Shafter's mouth tightened. "Somebody always is," he said.

"This fellow said Rio is like lightning with a gun."

Shafter took a step toward the door. Wally's high tenor voice clutched at him. "What will you do, Marshal, if Rio does show up here?"

Shafter put his hand on the doorknob. He looked back at Wally, wondering what it was the little man wanted to see? Fear?

He shrugged. "I don't know, Wally."

He saw the Vances' fancy runabout parked in front of the shadows near the Main Hotel. The leather and polish caught faint glitters of light, gleaming. He was surprised to see Troy Vance sitting on the front seat, alone.

She was huddled, arms across her breasts, as if she were chilled, as if she had been waiting for something for a long time.

He nodded, touched the brim of his hat and started past her.

Troy said, "Marshal."

He walked to the side of the carriage, put his hand on the seat guard. "Yes, Troy?"

She drew a deep breath. "He's not with you?"

He smiled. "I'm getting more particular of my company."

"When did you see him last?"

"Who are we talking about?"

She smiled. "I am being silly, aren't I?" Her shoulders moved. "I don't know. I don't get in from the ranch every day. I guess I was looking forward to tonight. I — thought he'd be as anxious as I am."

"Who are we talking about?"

She laughed now. "You're very nice, Marshal."

"That's a terrible thing to say to a man — even an old buck like me."

"You're not old. And you know you're not. But it pleases you to pretend you are, doesn't it? That way you don't have to notice the way you excite all the women."

"That sounds interesting."

She sighed. She stared at him. "You're doing it now," she accused him. "The first time I saw you — I got all mixed up, and didn't know what to say. You treated me like an infant. I kept expecting you to pat me on the back for colic."

He laughed. "Believe me, Troy. I never felt that way."

"Yes you have. I'm not the only woman you've treated that way. You like to hold them away from you. A brave man like you — I think you're afraid."

He nodded. "I tremble. Every time I look in your eyes."

"Stop it, Marshal. You'll make me forget I'm waiting for Zach. You'll — make me wish I weren't."

"Oh. That's who we were talking about."

She laughed. "You are nice, Marshal . . . I don't see how they can say such things about —" She stopped, biting her lip.

"About me? What things?"

"Nothing, Bryant. I'm sorry." She looked about the dark street. "When did you see Zach last?"

"Left him out on the target range. He wanted to admire his shooting a while. He was to bring in the lantern."

"It must have been a heavy lantern. I'm not going on sitting here, waiting all night. I'm beginning to be mad to the soles of my feet."

He touched his hat again. "I can't imagine

90

you waiting for anybody, Troy. I can't even imagine you having to."

The words burst from her. "Oh, I don't have to. And I wouldn't. Any other time I'd be halfway back to the ranch by now, and the next time Zach Adams showed up, I'd sic the dogs on him. But I've got to wait anyhow."

"Your father in town?"

She nodded, and in the faint light from the hotel window he saw her face flush faintly. Troy looked embarrassed.

"Yes. He had some business."

He glanced at her, trying to read in her face what it was she left unsaid. Her father's being in town often happened, and in itself was nothing to cause Troy to be confused, unless it had something to do with the marshal himself. Shafter waited a moment, shrugged, deciding to let it go at that.

"Marshal."

He'd already turned. He stopped, glancing over his shoulder.

"Whatever bad things anybody says about you, Bryant. Please . . . . believe me, I know better — for whatever that's worth to you."

He nodded, thanking her. Sam Pickens was locking the front door of his store, and Shafter watched him test the padlock. A wagon rolled tiredly around the corner of

Main Street. From within the hotel a man laughed suddenly once, loudly, and stopped laughing.

"If you see Zach," she called after him. "Tell him where I said he could go. Even if I'm still waiting here, I'll be waiting for father, and not for him."

Shad Withers' Blue Dollar was the talk of every cowhand within a hundred miles of Pony Wells. It was the place they looked forward to, saved money for, dreamed about. A man could let himself go inside the Blue Dollar. No matter how drunk he got, there was a sense of being protected from the law in there. They had rooms where they dragged you and let you sleep it off if you put away too many. They never kept a woman when she began to show her age. New women and uncut liquor, gambling rooms in the back, free lunch.

The Blue Dollar wasn't the largest saloon in Pony Wells, but it was the one with the finest bar, gleaming and reflecting the lights. It was always freshly painted and newly decorated. Shad Withers took in a lot of money, and he put a lot of it back into his business.

Shafter pushed open the batwings and stepped inside the Blue Dollar. Piano music, gushing talk and the smell of beer struck him.

He looked about noting how many people were in the garishly lighted room, how many he knew, how many were strangers, and what the strangers looked like.

It was early for the Blue Dollar. A few men lined the bar. There was a table of poker. Six girls sat together at a table in the rear, talking and waiting.

He went across to the bar, standing around the curve of it so his back was to a wall and he could see the whole room. The bartender shoved a bottle and shot glass toward him.

He saw Shad Withers come from a door beyond the other end of the bar. Shad came directly toward Shafter without even glancing at the other customers. Somebody had told Shad when Shafter walked in. Shad had been looking for him this evening.

Withers flicked imaginary lint from his expensive wool suit as he walked toward Shafter, a self-conscious gesture because people stared at him. A slender man in his middle thirties, Withers had blond hair neatly trimmed and carefully brushed. His lapel was set off with an artificial white flower, his clothes were sharply creased and lovingly pressed.

He came around the bar and smiled. "Shafter. Good to see you." He spoke to the bartender. "There's no charge on this bottle, Tom."

The bartender nodded, smiling. "Right, Mr. Withers."

Shafter inclined his head, thanking Shad. He pulled a shot glass near and filled it, pushing it in front of Withers.

Withers lifted the brimming glass, touched it to his lips, drinking less than a third of it. He set the glass on the bar.

"Hear you had visitors tonight, Bry."

Shafter nodded. "Word gets around fast."

Withers pulled a small knife on the end of a chain from his vest pocket. He opened it and cleaned at his nails. "Not necessarily, Bry. I'm a man makes it my business to know what's going on in Pony Wells."

"Yes. I know. That's why I thought maybe you could tell me something about Gloria Hogarty."

Withers scowled. "What about her?"

"You know she's dead?"

"Of course. Trumbo told me before six o'clock."

"Yes. Trumbo was out there."

Withers frowned, regarding his nails. "What is that supposed to mean?"

"Nothing. Except that Trumbo has noth-

94

ing else to do. He always turns up where something happens."

"You don't like Trumbo, do you?"

"He doesn't matter to me, Shad. He's the kind of man I'd lock up as a vagrant."

"How can you? He works. For me."

Shafter smiled. "I know. That's why I don't lock him up."

"Trumbo is a good man. He's worth a lot to me."

"The little Hogarty kid. She was worth a lot to you, too, wasn't she?"

"She was until she wanted to quit."

"Quit? Why would she want to quit?"

"Am I on trial, Bry?"

"No. My God. A girl has been killed."

"A tramp has been killed. She quit here, was leaving town. That's all I know. She quit my place, I know nothing more about her. I don't want to know."

"Couldn't you even tell me where she was going?"

"No. I didn't ask her."

"Was she going to meet somebody?"

"Have another drink, Bry. It looks to me as if a man like you — a man with a full-time job could tend to business and forget a girl that's as well off dead."

"Who says she's as well off dead?"

"Don't get sore at me. I knew her. When

she worked here, I knew her. Sure, she was a peppy kid. She made men spend more — and like it — than any six other dames. But she was a lush, and when she drank, she cried."

"What about?"

"Holy God, man. How do I know what about? Did I ever hold her head? I'm a busy man. And so are you. Forget Hogarty."

Bry's voice was low, coldly angry. "It's a killing, Shad. A murder. In my territory."

"There have been other killings."

"She was a lonely, homeless kid — not more than nineteen."

"I grant you all that."

"She was buried up there, in a grave not even knee deep. Somebody crushed her skull, dragged her up there."

"I'm as sorry as you are about all that . . . Now tell me, about this company of yours tonight?"

Shafter breathed deeply, closing his fist around the empty shot glass. The man at the piano started a ballad, one of the girls leaned against the piano, singing. A man glanced up from the poker table, moved his gaze back to his cards. The girls stopped chattering at the rear table.

"Fellows from out Utah way, I hear?" Shad prompted.

"That's right. I suppose they came here to see you this afternoon?"

Shad smiled, taking another sip of whisky. "That's right. They did stop in for a drink."

"All right. Why ask me about why they visited me?"

Shad frowned. "I thought you were my friend, Bry. Don't take your hate out on me. Those aren't the first men who've offered to hire you in two years."

"No." Shafter's voice remained low, he stared at Withers. "No. It's just they're the first ones that you people hoped *would* hire me."

"Now, Bry. Don't talk like that. They seemed desperate. That town out there. Really needs a man like you. I figured they'd pay you enough — make it worth while. We'd hate to lose you here — but after all, Pony Wells is pretty quiet — and we can't expect to stand in your way when you've a chance to make more money than we can offer you."

The sense of emptiness spread inside Bry. He poured another shot glass of whisky, stared at it.

"You think I ought to take it, eh?"

"Why, Bry. I didn't say that. Why, a thing like that. A man has to make up his own mind. Like I say, we'd hate to lose you."

Shafter stared at the poker table.

Withers said, "You've been here two years, Bry. You've done a fine job. Nobody can deny what you've done for this town."

"Sure."

"You came here when we were sick with our troubles, Bry. Two years. A lot of changes. Things are different now. We don't have much trouble here."

"That's right."

Withers took another quick drink. "Your fame sure has spread, Bry. A thousand miles away in Utah Territory, they hear about you. One bad thing about having a rep like yours."

"Yes?" Their gazes locked.

"Well, Lord knows, I don't like to say this, Bry. But you must know it's true. There's just one thing lures the gun toters to Pony Wells any more."

The men at the poker table were arguing. The girl at the piano had stopped singing.

Shafter stared straight ahead. "Yes?"

"Well, Lord Almighty, Bry. It's you. Those gun slingers don't come because Pony Wells is a tough town. It's not tough. Not any more. They come — because you're here. They want to test their gun skill, build their own reps. They come looking for Bry Shafter."

One of the men jumped up at the card table. He lunged across it, grabbing at the man there. This man shoved back in his chair. He stood up, fighting a knife from his pocket, springing it open. He stood there, waiting, knife blade gleaming.

Shafter moved away from the bar, started around Shad.

Withers caught his arm. "Forget it, Bry. A little trouble like that. We can handle it. A lot better than you can, Bry. You arrest them — they'll be sore. I'll lose customers. Let us handle it — it's all friendly. Just a little mix-up. Why, that's not your kind of trouble, Bry."

TEN

Shafter walked down the steps from the stoop before the Blue Dollar, feeling the chilled malice following him from inside. He shrugged his collar up against his neck, aware his face was moist with faint perspiration.

"Hmph."

The sound didn't really stop him. The expression of womanly scorn had long since lost its sting. It happened to any man leaving or entering a saloon, it happened to any man wearing a gun on public streets. It could happen to any man.

But he slowed, feeling he was the unfair target of outraged citizenry suddenly. And when he saw who the woman was who'd expressed herself so scornfully, he did stop, standing outside the saloon, a shaft of light across his shoulders.

He forced his voice to remain level, friendly. "Hello, Wilton." He bowed slightly. "Hello, Ada."

Ada Jenkins was on the inside of the walk, holding her husband's arm. She was a tall, vinegary woman and when you looked at her, it was hard to believe she'd ever been warm and sweet and fragrant. She must have been but it must have been a long time ago, too. Her hair was brushed severely from her face, pinned in a taut bun at the back of her head. Upon this sat a black hat trimmed with blue velvet. She was flat chested, wasp-waisted and full-bustled, which was the style then in Pony Wells.

He knew Ada had seen him, knew she recognized him. She was the only woman near. That scornful "hmph" had been hers and he'd been its target. Through his mind raced the quick memory of the party Ada Jenkins had given for him and Hannah when they first arrived in Pony Wells. The way the soured woman had forced her smile at the man who was going to save their town, fawning upon him.

Now she turned, looking into the darkened window of the store beside the saloon, pulling on Wilton Jenkins' arm so the banker paused like a dog on a leash.

Whatever it was Ada saw in the darkened window, it held her attention so completely that she neglected to speak to him.

The man on her leash was a different matter. The time hadn't yet come when Wilton Jenkins could cut the marshal dead on a public street. Not yet, Shafter thought, not yet.

Jenkins looked flustered. Through his mind must have darted a dozen thoughts. Bryant Shafter was one of his largest depositors. Shafter had invested his money well, and was on his way to being a rich man by Pony Wells standards. If for no other reason, the banker was forced to be courteous. And he looked ill at the way his wife was behaving.

Like all men who make money their lives, Wilton Jenkins became ill easily. His thin face got pale and his eyes got haggard and he looked around at everything so he did not have to look directly at anyone.

Jenkins was not as tall as his wife, and was even thinner. His nose was a hawk's nose and his jutting chin resembled the dulled blade of a hatchet.

He said, "Evening, Marshal." His voice was curt, but his face jerked into a perfunctory smile.

Shafter smiled, wondering if Jenkins were afraid he was going to hit him up for a loan right there on Main Street.

He passed them, nodding again. He was thinking, it's about over, Shafter, your welcome is about gone. They don't need you any more. They don't want you any more.

Now they looked at him — seeing him not as the man who had risked his life night after night. Evidently they didn't even remember that. Now they saw a man who didn't work, raised no cattle, put in no winter wheat. They saw a man almost forty years old who lived by his gun.

He lived by his gun. He could look at himself with Ada Jenkins' eyes and see why she would cut him on the street. For two years he'd been their marshal in time of trouble. Now there wasn't any trouble and he was a professional gun man who somehow had managed to masquerade on the side of the law.

Wearing a gun made him different. It set him apart. It made women like Ada Jenkins afraid of him. Once there had been a good reason for his being in Pony Wells. Now that reason was gone. Yet he was still here, still packing his gun. Still collecting ten thousand a year.

He walked slower, remembering the way Shad Withers had stopped him in the Blue Dollar. "This isn't your kind of trouble, Marshal." That said it. Pony Wells had no trouble any more that they couldn't handle. And ten thousand a year. It hurt them in the pocketbook. They felt robbed.

They saw him as a professional gunman and the ten thousand a year was tribute money.

Vividly before his eyes, he saw Maudie, remembering what Lon Tolliver had told her. The gunmen come to Pony Wells now seeking Bry Shafter. And Shad Withers, telling him the only trouble they had in Pony Wells now was the trouble that came looking for Bry Shafter.

He went up the steps, pushed open the batwings of the Main Street Bar. This was less than half a block from the Blue Dollar, but belonged in a different world. The bar was homemade, square, rough topped. The tables were kitchen tables, stained with whisky and beer and slashed with knife carvings.

The owner was bartender. He shoved a bottle across the bar toward Bry. Bry shook his head. He glanced about the room. The working men came in here, the laborers who could not afford the elegance of the Blue Dollar, or felt out of place in their sweated, body-smelling clothes.

A Mexican laborer was shooting dice with two cowhands at the end of the bar. The Mexican was drinking and winning. His head went back and his teeth flashed.

Turning, he saw Shafter watching him. He held the top of his sombrero with one hand, gulped down the drink in his other. Then he slapped his palm over his winnings.

He heeled around at the bar, keeping his hand over the crumpled bills he'd won. His greasy hair was toppled over his forehead in tight-sprung crow-black ringlets. His chin was weak, and there was about him an appearance of weakness. His eyes shone and his face began to work.

He screamed, yelling something in Spanish. Until then Shafter had not realized how drunk the laborer was.

"My *dinero*." The Mexican yelled it. "You don't touch it. You don't take it."

He wailed this at Shafter, his mouth pulling taut across his stained teeth. "My money."

He shook his head back and forth, working at the knife in his belt. He jerked it free, springing the catch. The blade gleamed.

The bartender ran down the inside of the bar. "Angelo," he said to the Mexican. "What's wrong with you?"

"My money." That was all Angelo would say. That was all he could think.

He clawed at the bills, picking them up from the bar, spilling the loose change, never taking his crazy-lighted eyes from Shafter's face.

With the bills in the pockets of his levis, he pushed his hand around on the bar, mopping up the change he'd spilled.

When he had most of it, he moved away from the bar, making a circle around Shafter. His shoulders were hunched, his hands spread wide at his side so he resembled a fighting cock in some Sonora cockpit.

He did not look at the bar to see if he had all his money. He didn't take his eyes from Shafter's face.

"What's wrong with you, Angelo?" the bartender said again.

Angelo shook his head, not looking at him. "I drink. I gamble with some my friends. He not arrest me. Por Dio. He not arrest me. Take my money. I keel him first."

105

"Put away that knife, Angelo," Shafter said.

Angelo stopped, frozen, arms extended at the sound of Shafter's voice.

"Don't try to touch me." He screeched it. "You don't want to get keel. You let me alone."

"I told you. Put away that knife."

Angelo's face twisted, and screaming, he lunged at Shafter, chopping at him with the long-bladed knife. Shafter pressed against the bar, watching him.

Angelo swiped at his face with the knife, missed. The knife blade hissed through the air, barely scraping Shafter's shoulder.

Shafter caught the wrist as it passed on the downward thrust. Angelo screeched, baring his teeth. He swung all the way round, trying to writhe free.

He leaped backwards, pulled himself free, knife still gleaming in his fist. He crouched low and sprang forward, jabbing with the knife.

Again Shafter snagged his wrist. This time he twisted so hard the Mexican wailed in agony and every man watching in the room could feel his own tendons giving. The knife clattered to the floor.

Shafter caught Angelo's shoulder in his fist, brought Angelo's body down hard and his bent knee upward to meet it. The sound of Angelo's chin against his knee cracked in the silent room.

Angelo's head snapped back. Shafter released him and he crumpled to the floor like empty sacking and lay still. Greenbacks showed from his levi pockets.

Shafter glanced around the room. The faces of the watching men were cold, dangerous. Some of them were the same men who'd been here two years ago when he arrived in Pony Wells, many were doing the same things, too.

He studied the faces of the dangerous ones, the toughs who'd been hoping Angelo's knife would find its mark.

Looking at them, Shafter knew he was seeing the bottled violence, seeing something he'd turned his back on for two years. Men who stayed in line because they were afraid. He'd never feared these men, didn't fear them now. They didn't have guts enough between them to strike against strength; they were the petty ones who gambled, drank, fought, ducked for cover, and paid off.

All the old violence was still here in Pony Wells. But now it was the controlled, profitable violence those men had wanted two years ago when they'd paid him to clean up their town. This kind of violence profited men like Withers, Jenkins and old Pike Vance.

The bartender said, "Little rough, weren't you, Marshal?"

Shafter turned on his heel, face white. "That was my head he was chopping at. Sober him up. When he sobers up, tell him to get back on his job and stay there. If I see him inside town limits for the next two weeks, I'll lock him up. You tell him, you understand?"

"All right, Marshal. Poor guy was just drunk."

"Just crazy drunk. Wait until it's you he's jabbing at with that pigsticker."

He turned and walked toward the door, thinking, this town's cleaned up, just the way they hired me to clean it. Wonder if they can see that?

In his mind he saw the way it had been in his marshal's office at River Bend. It was a sudden, bitter memory, vivid against the darkness and his sharp cold anger.

The talks had been going on for a long time. He had heard their story of Pony Wells a dozen times, and he had named his price, and they had haggled, and they had walked out, and they had come back, and made him another offer, and he had told them his original terms stood, that he did not want to come to Pony Wells, and if they did not want to meet his terms, they could forget it.

Wilton Jenkins had half-knelt from his chair. He was wringing his hands and tears brimmed his eyes. "My God, sir," Wilton Jenkins had said. "It's not money. We're in hell at Pony Wells. We're in hell. We've got to have you there. Come to Pony Wells, Mr. Shafter. God have mercy on us if you don't. I speak for all of us. We've agreed to meet your terms. Men in hell have no choice. Let's not talk about money any more, Mr. Shafter. I'm begging you in the name of all that's humane. Come to Pony Wells, Mr. Shafter, come at any price."

ELEVEN

Shafter walked out of the Main Street Bar and crossed Third Avenue, going toward the railroad station. He heard the muffled sound of men's voices from the darkness out of Third, and paused at the corner.

Third was unlighted and he stood, letting his eyes become accustomed to the darkness. First he was aware of the shapes of horses and then of men pressed against the wall of the hay-and-grain store.

He felt himself go tense; the fight down

there was violent and brutal; the kind that had no time for words and loses its voice because it fears interference.

He drew his gun, strode along the dark street. Two men had another pressed with his back to the wall. As Shafter approached, he saw the big man with his back to the wall had a knife and only his knife was keeping the other two at bay.

These two were trying to catch the big man off guard. One had a short bull whip. It flicked suddenly at the big man, lashing and snapping in the dark. The big man took the whip across the shoulders. He grunted, but that was the only sound. He did not take his gaze from the other man who was armed with a short club.

"Here," Shafter said. "What's going on here?"

The bull whip was raised. The man kept his arm up, letting the whip go lax over his shoulder. The man with the club took a backward step.

Only the big man against the wall did not move. He held his knife low, ready, watching the two and did not glance toward Shafter. With a flare of anger, Shafter recognized the big man. It was Shad Withers' hired gun. Shafter's voice rasped. "What's going on here, Gilley?"

Gilley did not relax. His voice whined, full of self-righteousness. "Why don't you ask these two, Marshal? They jumped me."

"Drop that whip," Shafter ordered. The man was poorly garbed in faded levis and a sheep-lined coat with a rent at the elbow. He stared at Shafter a moment, at the knife in Gilley's hand. He released the whip, letting it slip to the ground at his feet.

"And the club," Shafter said to the other man. This one was young, small of frame and as poorly dressed. Shafter recognized neither of them.

"Wait." The young one tightened his grip on his club. His voice shook. "You his partner?" He jerked his head toward where Trumbo stood with his knife poised.

"I'm the marshal here," Shafter said. "You don't want to end in jail, you'll drop that club."

"End in jail?" the youngster's voice trembled. "Sure. We'll end in jail. First this man robs us, and when we try to get our money back, you come along with a gun to put us in jail."

"Shut up, Jamie," the older man said. "It don't matter. He's got the gun. That's what matters."

"Not to me," Jamie said. He hefted the club again. "You going to help him rob us?

111

Is that what you're going to do? If you are, go on, shoot. Go on." His whole body shook. "Go on, shoot me. I ain't giving up no other way."

"You better come to jail," Shafter said. "Maybe by morning you'll have some sense in your head."

"That's right, Marshal," Trumbo Gilley said. "Lock 'em up. They can't come in here jumping people."

"Put up that knife," Shafter said. "You're under arrest, too. Just the same as they are."

"Me?" Gilley sounded mortally wounded. "What you arresting me for?"

"For carrying a concealed weapon, Gilley. Let's go. I'm tired talking about it."

The youngster was staring at Shafter. When Trumbo closed his knife, thrusting it into his pocket, the youngster dropped his club.

The older man said, "We didn't want this trouble, Marshal. We bought horses from this man."

"They were no good," the younger man broke in. "When we saw that, we turned around, came back here, tried to get Mr. Gilley to give us our money back. He just laughed at us."

"A sale is a sale," Trumbo said. "You fellows got sense enough to know that. The buyer has to look out for what he's buying."

"I know that," the older man said. "But you tricked us. Them horses had been doped. And the man at the livery stable said you must have been putting arsenic in their water to make them coats shine like that. I'm a man that takes his chances, but you just plain swindled us, Gilley. No man does that. Not to me."

Shafter's voice was hard. "Another horse deal, Trumbo?"

Trumbo looked ill with his outraged innocence. "Why, them was good horses, Marshal —"

"How much did they pay you?"

Trumbo didn't answer. He stared hard at Shafter.

The older man said, "We give him sixty dollars."

Jamie said, "It was all we had."

"That's why we came back. We need horses, Marshal. We're doing some prospecting. We can get some money in a few days — but not if we got no horses."

Shafter said, "All right, Trumbo. Sixty dollars." He held out his hand.

Trumbo's face paled and his eyes glittered small and enraged. He stared at Shafter without speaking. His expression said clearly they were both working for the same man,

113

and the boss was going to hear about this.

"I don't want to have to ask you again, Trumbo." Shafter kept his voice low. "You'll go to jail unless you turn over that money."

Trumbo's voice mocked him. "Now, why put me in jail, Marshal? That would just make you a lot of trouble for nothing."

Shafter did not speak. Trumbo stared at him a moment longer. Trumbo shrugged his jacket up on his shoulders.

Trumbo tried to laugh. "All right. All right. I'll give 'em the money. You're going a long way past your job, Shafter."

Still Shafter didn't speak. Trumbo reached into his pocket, pulled out a Mexican leather wallet. He counted out the paper bills. He laid them in Shafter's hand.

"Sixty dollars?" Shafter said to the older man. He nodded, and Shafter saw Jamie brush relieved tears from his eyes. Shafter counted out the money into the older man's trembling hand. Shafter said, "You can buy horses at the livery stable."

"Yes, sir."

"Next time you buy 'em from the livery stable. If you hadn't been trying to force a bargain, you'd never have run into Trumbo. This wouldn't have happened."

"Please, sir," Jamie said. "We done learned. Can we go, Marshal?"

The older man picked up his whip, coiled it, stood waiting.

Shafter said, "You two men leaving town?"

"Soon as we buy new mounts, Marshal. Yes, sir."

"All right. I'm not locking you up. If you went to court for disturbing the peace and assault, you'd lose most of that sixty. You see that, don't you?"

"Yes, sir, Mr. Marshal."

"Next time you have trouble in my town, you come to me with it. You ever do this again, you'll pay."

"We just lost our heads, Marshal. We was just sick."

"All right. Get down to the livery. Get your new mounts. Get out of town."

He stood in the shadows, watching the two men hurrying toward Main Street. Trumbo's voice was heavy with mock servility. "You still holding me, Marshal?"

Shafter drew a deep breath, turned, looking at Gilley. "You've already said it," he said. "What good would it do?"

Trumbo let his gaze move over the marshal and he laughed. He hitched his trousers up, stepped past Shafter, moving too close to him. He walked out into the street and went across it, going toward the Blue Dollar.

Shafter looked both ways along Third, the lights at Main, the darkness of the valley the other way. He heard a movement behind the hay-and-grain store. He walked toward the end of the frame building, gun at his side.

As he entered the alley behind the store, he saw a shadow flicker against the darkness of a window at the rear of the building. Something slithered out of the window, letting it fall closed, and toppled to the ground. Must be a kid, Shafter thought, to rob in spite of all the noise we made outside.

Before the person could move from the darkness where he'd landed, Shafter holstered his gun and sprang into the shadows, clutching at the body.

His hands closed on flesh taut-drawn over frame. A wild cry came from its mouth and the body shook uncontrollably. He pulled him out into the alley. It was Albert Tishkin. He was shaking so badly that he dropped the sack of beet sugar he'd stolen.

"Marshal!" Albert wailed. "Oh, Gawd, Marshal, don't kill me."

"I'm not going to kill you, Albert. I'm just going to beat you till you wish you were dead. What you doing in that store?"

Albert's teeth chattered. "S-stealing."

"Sure. I know you were stealing. But what

116

for? Why do you have to steal?"

"I don't know . . . I know . . . It was sugar, I like sugar, Marshal."

"Why don't you ask Mr. Ballinger for some sugar? He'd give it to you."

Albert shivered all over again. "I — was in his store. I ask him. He said he too busy. I saw that window. I knew he forgot to lock it."

"All right, Albert. You take that sugar back."

"Now?"

"Right now."

"It's terrible dark in there, Marshal."

"Albert, you want to go to jail?"

"I sure wouldn't like that, Marshal."

"All right. You take that sugar back. You can bar that window."

"How will I get out?"

"I ought to let you stay in there."

"Please, Marshal, not in the dark."

"Stealing in my town. I ought to lock you up."

"I wasn't thinking about you, Marshal . . . My Gawd, I don't think very good, Marshal. I — can't think about many things at one time. I wasn't thinking about you . . . if I'd been thinking about you, Marshal . . . I'd of been too scared, even for sugar. You know that."

117

"What were you thinking about? About Zach? Don't you think he'd lock you up as quick?"

Albert's face changed, getting white and defiant. He did not answer. He writhed free and Shafter released him. Albert climbed back up, let the sugar drop inside the window. He fell to the ground again. Shafter grinned despite himself, decided to be satisfied with this.

"I'm telling Ballinger about his open window," Shafter said. "He'll come down and lock it. I'm warning you, Albert, don't ever steal again — in my town."

Albert nodded. He stood up, shoulders round, head hung. He stared up at Shafter.

"I never heard of you stealing before," Shafter said. "What's the matter, Albert? What got into you?"

Albert shook his head. He drew a ragged breath. "Told you. Wasn't thinking about you. But I don't have to steal. I could be rich if I wanted to." He stared at Shafter and his pale eyes were crafty.

Shafter said, "All right, Albert. You could be rich. But you could be in jail, too. You get out of this alley. Don't ever let me catch you here again."

Albert nodded, cringing. He slipped past Shafter and darted out into Third. Puzzled,

Shafter stood there a moment and then walked slowly through the alley toward Fourth.

Ahead he saw the lines of light edging all the drawn blinds at Angie Sefner's boarding house. This two-storied building faced Fourth across an alley from Main Street.

He walked slowly past the house, aware of scabbed paint even in the dark, and the odor emanating from the shadowed yard. He looked at the drawn blinds at all the windows, and all the windows with lights in them.

He used the brass knocker at the front door and waited in the darkness. There was noise and laughter within this house, a subdued and perfumed tension. He glanced about at the unpaved street, the sagging fence, and the lights of Main Street almost a block away.

The door was opened without hesitation or caution. The woman who stood in the doorway was painted, bustled and curled. Her face appeared abnormally white with powder, abnormally bright with rouge and her eyes were deeply lined with blue pencil. "Marshal." Angie Sefner's voice was whisky-hoarse. "Why, we're real honored, Marshal . . ." she paused and looked up at him. "That is — unless there's some kind of trouble. There ain't any, is there, Marshal?"

He stepped into the perfumed foyer and she closed the door behind him. She took his hat and hung it on a hat-tree that blossomed hats of all kinds, Stetson, derby, fedora, slouch hat.

"No trouble that I know of," he said.

She sighed and taking his arm, led him into her private office. He glanced toward the public parlor that was empty at the moment.

"Business seems to be good," he said as Angie closed the door behind them.

"I can't complain," Angie said. She patted his arm, sank into her rocking chair. It fitted her generous form. She sighed again and he glanced around the room, brought his gaze back to the stack of poultry magazines on the table at her elbow. "See you admiring my poultry gazettes." She laughed and touched them with her jeweled fingers. "I don't know what I'd do without my chicken books, Marshal. I truly dream of the day when I can settle down on a chicken farm all my own."

He leaned against her desk and laughed at her. "I think your chicken farm is the kind of dream all the rest of us have, Angie. It's not something you really want. You like to think about it. If somebody told you you had to go live on a chicken farm, you'd screech your head off."

"No," Angie said. "That's where you're wrong. I've had it tough, Marshal. I don't expect you to take out and start weeping over my troubles. But I've seen me some tough towns in my time. A woman is young — she thinks she can take all kind of men, all the time and nothing can do her any harm. But when she gets my age, she knows better. Only it's too late then . . . No, Marshal, when I've enough money saved, I'm going to buy me one of them chicken ranches and raise barred rocks." She laughed. "And no men around. Why, I ain't going to have any more roosters than necessary."

She patted her gaudy hair, watching him. He saw she was still wondering at the reason for his visit. He had told her there was to be no trouble, but as she said, she'd had a rugged life, and at her age, she no longer believed everything she heard.

He looked about the crowded office, letting his gaze pause at the nude paintings, the calendars, the witty sayings Angie had had framed for her own pleasure.

From outside this small room, he heard the sudden shrill yelps of laughter, the steady hum of subdued talk. But it was very quiet out there. The only time there was noise at Angie Sefner's was when all the girls were down in the public parlor at the same time.

He frowned slightly, wondering why Angie had suspected his visit might mean trouble. He knew that Wilton Jenkins owned this house, this property and that he took the profits from it. He recognized bitterly that until he had come here, there had been no profit in places like this, because it had not been controlled. Still, Wilton Jenkins did protect this house, and everything that went on inside it. It had never occurred to Shafter to close it up, and now it seemed odd that Angie might even imagine he would.

"What's the matter, Angie?" he said. "What's up? Why are you jittery?"

"Jittery?" She patted her hair, tried to laugh again. "Why should I be jittery?"

"I don't know." He moved his gaze about the room. "Didn't Glory Hogarty room here, Angie?"

Angie's face paled slightly under the powder. "Yes. She roomed here. But that was all. She didn't work for me."

"Oh?"

"No. She didn't. I didn't know nothing about her. She had a room up at the Main

122

Hotel, but the church women in town got pretty snotty about her. Shad Withers asked me if I didn't have a room that Gloria could rent. I said yes. You know me. Glad to do any friend a favor."

He nodded. "Did you know Glory planned to leave town?"

She chewed at the underside of her lip. She nodded. "Yes. Glory was in the dumps there at the last. Something was on her mind. She was upset, talked about leaving. Then one night she came in and said she was going."

"She ever say what she was upset about?"

Angie had been staring longingly at her chicken gazettes. Her head jerked up. "You mean you didn't know, Marshal?"

He scowled. "No. I didn't know. Should I? If I should, tell me about it."

She swallowed hard, shook her head. "No. I got nothing to say." Her voice went lame. "I only meant — a small town like this, I thought everybody knew everything."

"If there's anything you can tell me about Glory that might help me, Angie, you better do it."

She tried to smile, "I told you. I got nothing to say." She leaned forward, putting a leer on her mouth. "Don't you want a girl, Marshal? We got a new girl — from Laredo.

I tell you, Bry, what them Texas girls don't learn —"

"Did she take everything with her?"

"What? Who?"

"Glory. Did she take everything she owned with her?"

"Marshal, you're a man got a one track mind, all right. Fine looking fellow like you." She laughed, shook her head. "I reckon with all the church women in this town, a nice looker like you'd never have to visit my place."

"I asked you a question."

She laughed again. "Marshal, I'd sure hate to have you hating me. Now, as far as I know, Glory took everything she owned. It wasn't much. A few clothes, a picture of her folks. Carried everything she had in a straw suitcase. And then of course, there was her rings."

Shafter, straightened from the desk, feeling the excitement flooding through him. Rings. That was what had been wrong up there on that knoll this afternoon. Her rings. Glory's rings had been ripped from her fingers.

"She put all her money in rings," he whispered.

"That's right." Angie nodded. "Glory said she knew Mr. Wilton Jenkins and that made her mistrust all banks. She figured rings would always be worth what she paid for them."

"Wore them on every finger."

"Poor kid. In a lot of ways, Glory was a good kid. But she led men on till it was a crime sometimes. Looks like one of them just wouldn't stop."

Shafter was deep in thought. He turned, scowling at Angie. "Maybe you're wrong," he said. "Maybe there's a chance to find who killed her. All of a sudden, I don't think rape had anything to do with it." He smiled, nodding. "Whoever killed her will have to get rid of that suitcase — and somehow he's got to try to get rid of those rings."

TWELVE

Angie was watching him — the painted and accented planes of her face intense and faintly sad. He knew her sadness had little to do with Gloria's death, or with him, except as its consequences hovered like a cloud over her, and this profitable business of hers.

He stood tall and still as she'd seen him stand often before in the past two years, at moments when faced by a gunman who might yet back down; in a courtroom when he heard testimony he knew to be lies and paused, waiting for the witness to correct himself. She'd talked about what a big man Bry Shafter was, had heard others talking about it, the fact of his bigness and the way you were never more aware of it than when he paused, giving you one final chance to be better than you were.

"You're sure she left nothing behind in her room?" Shafter prompted. "No letters, nothing I might use?"

"No," she said. "if there had been anything, the maid would have thrown it out . . . we're using her room now."

He nodded and turned to leave the room. She got up from her chair, followed him to her door. "You're not leaving, Bry?"

He glanced at her, and her bold eyes admired the height of him, and the width of his shoulders, the depth of his chest. This pleased and flattered him. He remembered what Maudie had told him this afternoon, he was vain of himself. He liked to be admired. All right, he thought sharply, show me any guy that doesn't.

Angie laughed, "I swear, Bry Shafter, you're the first man ever came to my place — to talk."

He set his hat on the side of his head, still pleased with the way she'd looked at him,

126

vaguely stirred by it. "Maybe I'll come back," he said.

She shook her head, earrings bobbling. "No," she said. "You'd be surprised at how many times you've promised that, Marshal. But you've never come back."

There was a burst of laughter from a room across the dark corridor and two doors down. He recognized the laugh and jerked his head around at Angie. She smothered a smile and shrugged.

He walked along the corridor, feeling Angie's gaze following him from her doorway.

He knocked on the door, and for the barest instant there was breathless silence within. Then a girl's voice, faintly accented, said: "Go away."

Zach Adams laughed again, and in his laughter there was hard unconscious cruelty. "Come on in. I was just leaving, anyway."

The door was unlocked, all of them in the whole house were, Bry knew by now. There were too many things could happen behind barred doors that would cause Angie Sefner trouble, the kind that not even Wilton Jenkins could buy her out of.

Shafter stepped into the room and closed the door. Blind drawn at window, a dresser with pocked mirror, a chair and washstand were the furnishings. The girl and the bed

127

were one, and she was reclined on it now, sheer kimono caught over her navel in her fist.

Shafter glanced at the girl, not recognizing her. She was dark, with black eyes, small high breasts and a faint line of hair like a drawn pencil line down the inside of her leg to her red garter. Her face was taut with her anger, and Shafter knew Zach had made a new conquest.

"What you want?" she said with an accent from south of the Rio. "Can't you wait — in the parlor?"

Zach was knotting his tie at the wavy mirror. He glanced over his shoulder and laughed. "That's no way to act, Mamie. This here is a friend of mine. Marshal Shafter meet Mamie from Laredo."

"Hello," the girl said. She did not meet Shafter's gaze.

Shafter said to Zach, "I could be wrong, but I thought you were working until ten o'clock tonight?"

Zach turned around, leaned against the dresser. He snugged his tie into place and regarded Shafter. He shrugged. "All right, so I'm working."

"When I was a kid we had another name for it."

Zach laughed. "When you were a kid it

probably wasn't even invented yet."

"This your new office?" Shafter's gaze raked the room, moving across Mamie's rigid face.

"Now don't get excited, Marshal. I'm just patterning myself after the old master. I learned all your tricks with a gun . . . now I'm learning all about women."

"None of my business," Shafter said, "but there was somebody waiting in a rig for you in front of the Main Hotel. She said you could go to hell and I was to tell you if I saw you."

Zach shrugged. "She'll wait. She's hooked, and you know she's hooked. All that money, all that land, all them cattle." He laughed. "She'll wait."

"All right."

"You sound angered, Marshal. You sound jealous. Now, let me tell you how it is. I got to play it cagey with the Vances. Right? If I went to see the Vances feeling the way I felt when I walked into Mamie's room, I might queer the whole deal. Now I can be real stand-offish. Drive 'em crazy trying to figure how cagey Zach Adams can be in the face of all that beauty and all that money."

"It's your life."

"Why don't you stay here and visit with Mamie, Shafter? Mamie is from Laredo.

Brand new in town. I tell you what them gals learn down in Texas is a caution."

"Some other time," Shafter said.

Zach grinned at Mamie. "He's just an old man, honey. You got to forgive him." He set his slouch hat on the side of his head. He winked at Mamie. "See you, baby." He glanced at Shafter. "By the way, Marshal, Mamie has some news for you. Ain't that right, sugar?"

"I guess so."

"Sure she has. She says there was some young guy in here from down in Texas. Name of Rio. Said he was gunning for you."

Shafter laughed at him. "Is that why you holed up in here, until the shooting was over?"

Zach laughed, too. "Why, I was on my way to protect you, Old Man. Really. I just wanted to give Rio one decent chance at you first."

Shafter sighed, following Zach into the hallway. It was quiet out here again. Angie's door was closed and he supposed she was whiling away her time with her poultry books until some new customer used the brass knocker. He glanced around, the dark corridor, the narrow stairs leading upward into darkness, all doors closed, all rooms lighted and all blinds drawn. And in one of

130

these rooms, a gun-wild kid calling himself Rio had paused for relief on his way to keep a date of another kind of passion.

They walked out into the street, walking shoulder to shoulder. Zach pulled in lungsful of night air. Shafter was glad to get the cloying perfume from his nostrils. Strange that an overly sweet scent like that could carry with it the smell of evil.

When they reached Main Street, the first thing Shafter saw was the Vance buggy before the Main Hotel. Troy was sitting alone in the front seat. When she saw them turn the corner, she sprang down from the carriage and hurried toward the hotel entrance.

"Troy!"

Zach's voice was sharp in the still night. Horses pricked their ears at the hitching rails. A man down the street paused, looking over his shoulder. Troy stopped in the lighted doorway and Zach hurried toward her.

Shafter paused on the board walk, watching. Zach came into the light with her, standing tall, looking down, their shadows ragged down the hotel steps. Her head was high, but he saw the rigidity seep out of her shoulders under Zach's laughter. And then Zach put his hands on her arms, drew her

131

close against him in the lighted doorway, and after a moment, she smiled up at him. He pulled her close and they walked down the steps together.

At the carriage, Zach slipped his hands under her arms to lift her into the seat. But for the moment he did not move, only held her, hands caressing her. Into Shafter's mind flashed the picture of Mamie from Laredo lying on that rumpled bed at Angie Sefner's, kimono loosely caught over her navel. He shook his head, turned away thinking that Zach hadn't even washed his hands.

THIRTEEN

Shafter walked the other way alone down Main Street. His boot heels cracked against the board walk, his shadow flickered now in front, now beside him.

He remembered Rio. He'd heard about the gunman first tonight in Wu Sing's Barber Shop, and then in Mamie's room. This was an old pattern, and he recognized it. The gunslinger did a lot of talking first, keeping out of sight until the intended victim did a lot of thinking, a lot of worrying. Gun battles were won that way, many times.

Lord, Shafter thought, how old I'm getting. How old all this is to me. In his mind he saw young Rio, feeling he had a new deal working for him, passing the word around Pony Wells that a tough man with a price on his head was throwing down on the marshal at sight. It's all so old, Rio, Shafter thought. It's all happened so often.

A horse wickered in an alley and Shafter paused, tense, arm out over holster, waiting. The sound was not repeated. Saddle metal clanged as pony shifted at the rail and Shafter walked again in the light.

He could have asked Mamie for a description of the Rio kid. He liked to know these people in advance. But he couldn't let them think he was interested in Rio, or worried about him at all. Whatever he felt, he had learned to keep within himself. A troubled marshal was a breed apart, a lonely man.

It didn't really matter what Rio looked like. He'd know him on sight. There was the chance that Rio would ambush him from a dark alley, but that was a risk he ran every night along this street. In that case, it would not matter about Rio's description.

He paused before the darkened grocery store and looked both ways along Main Street, from the depot to the marshal's office; his whole life was bounded by this narrow plot of land. From the dark could come Rio's bullet, or Angelo's knife, and his life would end.

There was more light than usual in the bank and Shafter walked toward it, hurrying. He slowed when he recognized Jenkins' rig out front and Shad Withers' bay snubbed at the hitching rail.

Before the bank he paused, hearing the riffling of a breeze in the cottonwood that grew in the parkway. He glanced into the window and saw the men sitting around Wilton Jenkins' desk, the same three men who had brought him to Pony Wells two years ago. Something was up and that was certain. Pike Vance in from his ranch, Jenkins worried in his swivel chair, watching the faces of the others to know what to do. Only Shad Withers was relaxed, and by now Shafter recognized the saloonkeeper's pose.

He drew a deep breath, wondering why he had not even been briefed about this meeting. Then he remembered the odd way Troy Vance had looked when she'd explained she was in Pony Wells on business with her father.

He shrugged. The hell with them. He stepped off the board walk, moving past Withers' big bay horse, smoothing the sleek neck as he passed.

A wagon rolled by and he paused in the middle of the street. The sod farmer and his sleepy family nodded at Shafter as they passed. When they were gone, he moved forward watching a lone man walk out of the Home Style Cafe.

He felt a quickening of his pulses when he saw Ellen come around the counter at the rear of the small room and walk between the white-clothed tables to the door.

The Home Style Cafe was not large, a small counter and five tables. The building had once been a cottage, but Ellen's imagination and energy had converted it into a square frame store flush on the walk.

Ellen Thomson was not large herself, a couple inches over five feet tall, maybe a hundred and ten pounds. But she was made of energy and drive and ambition. She was the golden tan of a fair Indian, with straight black hair in braids across the crown of her head, well-set ears, and purple-brown eyes. Her profile always made Shafter think of a woman on a cameo, or a new minted coin, and when her squared jaws were set, she was beautiful but immovable.

They reached her front door at almost the exact same time. Her head jerked up and she recognized him. For the fleetest instant, pain flickered in those grape-brown eyes.

She said, "I'm sorry. I'm closing."

He caught the heavy door, held it. "Just coffee."

"It always starts like that."

He stepped inside, closed the door.

"Please, Bry," she said. " 'We've been through this. It gets us nowhere."

"Maybe I'm not interested in getting anywhere. Maybe I just want to be near you."

She'd already reached the counter on her way to the kitchen. She half-turned, spoke over her shoulder. "It's too dangerous near you. A person could be shot, just standing near you."

She went behind the counter, poured him a cup of coffee, set it before him. She leaned against the counter, watching him hold the steaming cup in his fist.

"Why are you so bitter?" he said.

She frowned. "I don't want to talk about it, Bry."

"Why not?"

"Because we've talked about it before. It gets nowhere. I'm not going to waste my time talking about things that don't get anywhere. I'm too busy. You never knew anybody as busy as I am, Bry. Why don't you let me alone?"

He set the cup down. "Do you want me

to say it?"

Her chin tilted, her gaze struck against his. "No."

"Because I love you. Because I still think you and I could be happy."

"Happy? Doing what? Am I to go on here waiting tables, cooking meals for men who don't even know what good food is supposed to taste like?"

"I never asked you to do that, Ellen."

"No, and Sam Thomson never asked me to do it, either. But I'm doing it. I'd been doing it for two years before he was killed. No, Bry, I buried one husband. I'm not going through that again."

"You've had it tough, Ellen. I admit that. You won't have to do any of this if you marry me. We'll sell this place first thing."

Her expression did not alter. "Sure. So I can have all the fun and drudgery of starting a new place later on when they bring me the news that somebody has killed you." She took the cup from him and dropped it into a pan of hot suds. "I'm sorry, Bry. I'm closing up."

He sat on a stool at the counter and surveyed the cafe. She was right. Sure, he'd put Hannah through hell without intending to. He admitted he worried about living through one more night so that for a while longer Maudie would be protected.

He exhaled sharply, speaking as though Ellen had been following the complicated line of his thinking. "Still, a man has got to have something. A man finds a woman that he loves — and that he knows loves him."

"You know nothing of the kind." She placed hands on hips, glaring. "Sure, you've made me say I love you. You've made me weak enough to say a lot of fool things. But I've been married. To a man like you. He was so unlike you that you were identical. He was a weakling, a drunk, a braggart gambler who went out every night to own the world. And I waited tables and cooked to support us, and waited until they came and told me he was dead. And they came. Oh, they came. They came and said that he had started a fight, and a man had killed him. Well, Sam Thomson excited me, too. I want you to know that, Bry Shafter. He was exciting — maybe not as exciting as you — or maybe he's been dead and I've forgotten, so you seem more exciting. But this I remember. I had excitement with him. That's all I had. But had enough of it to last the rest of my life."

She pushed open the door and walked into the kitchen. He got up slowly and followed. When he entered the large, scoured room, she was putting things away, moving swiftly.

"I don't know anything else, Ellen, except my job."

She turned, eyes flashing. "I know you don't. You couldn't change."

He stepped close to her, put his arms about her, pressing his hands against the small of her back, lifting her so she pressed against him. Her mouth parted, and her breath quickened, for a moment her eyes went sleepy, but she tried to writhe free.

"I'm not asking you to change, Bry. You're what you are. A hired gunman. A man who has to use his gun against other men. A man whose life depends on his being faster on the draw than another man. I want security. And peace. I want life to be smooth and —"

His mouth covered hers, and the taste of her excited him and he held her closer and after a moment her arms went around him, fiercely, and her mouth crushed under his.

At last he released her and she stepped back against the serving table. She stared up at him, eyes moist and starry.

He reached for her, but she batted his hands down. Her voice was breathless. "You've nothing to offer a woman, Bry Shafter. A moment with you before you're dead. Why don't you get out of here? Why don't you leave me alone?"

His voice was husky. "Because you don't want me to."

Her voice went chilled. "Oh, you can make me weak and hot and trembly. Why should I try to deny that? That's what you want, isn't it? That's all you really want. All right, you've had that. I'm through. Get out. Let me alone."

"I want to marry you. I've told you that, too."

She cried out as though hurt. "Why do you want to marry me? So there'll be somebody to take your daughter in when you're killed?"

His voice was as cold as hers. "All right. Maybe it would be fine to know that Maudie was with you — if anything did happen to me. But that has nothing to do with it. I'd want Maudie with you because you're good people. I want you with me — because you love me, and because I love you."

She laughed at him, sharply and coldly. "I don't love you. Oh, yes, you excite me. You overcome me when we're alone, because I — have no defenses against you. But I don't change. I only love what you could be."

"I could be whatever you want me to be."

"Would you give up that gun? That tin

140

star?" Her mouth curled. Under her armor was the forlorn sound of hurt.

"I would. If there was anything else I could do."

"Then give it up." Her voice raked at him. "I'll wait tables here, I'll go on cooking, and washing dishes. We'll live right here."

"You know I can't do that."

"Of course I know it. You've too much pride, haven't you? Too much stupid ugly pride to live and let me support us. Then get out. That's all I ask you. Get out."

He looked about the gleaming kitchen. The big pots and the boilers, the knives and the cutlery, everything in place because Ellen was an ambitious, orderly woman. It didn't matter when you looked into the kitchen, at five in the morning she was here, baking, cooking, getting ready for the next day. She worked every minute and by now she only paused, he knew, when he took her in his arms and made her put these other things from her mind.

Tears glistened in her deep eyes. "You're a hired gun, Bry Shafter, with a tin star. And I'll always hate that."

He tried to laugh at her, but tonight there was no laughter. It was as if those words were her knife, probing deeper every time until suddenly they twisted into the vulnerable unprotected places within him. He winced, hurt and instead of moving close to take her in his arms, he stepped back.

Tonight, he felt the terrible finality in the way she spoke. She'd cried before but her tears never looked so cold. It was as if at last she was through with crying, she was through with him.

And it was not only this finality that hurt him. It was the accumulation of hurts so that now he admitted she was lost to him.

It was Hannah's dying, and the three men from Gravehead making his office like all those other offices. It was that girl buried on the lonely knoll. It was a kid named Rio out to make a gun rep. It was a laborer named Angelo fearing and despising him. It was the lighted office in the Pony Wells bank and the three men who had brought him here, talking about him over that desk. It was Ada Jenkins looking into a shop window so she wouldn't have to speak to him. It was Lon Tolliver telling Maudie what her father was, a lure for gunmen. It was knowing that Pony Wells was a good town now, as good as any town its size, and it was good because he'd made it that way, and because he had, they didn't need him here any more, they didn't want him any more. He didn't belong here, he belonged nowhere: a trouble marshal where there was peace and quiet.

He shivered, chilled in the warm kitchen, knowing there were no words that would change Ellen. Whatever she had been to him, it was over, and he didn't even belong here any more. He turned, walking woodenly toward the front door. When he reached the kitchen exit, her voice stopped him, and for a second his heart lurched with hope she was calling him back.

Her voice was forlorn. "Don't come back, Bry. Don't ever come back."

FOURTEEN

Shafter closed the door of the Home Style Cafe behind him. He stood with a hand on the knob, looking both ways along the wind-teased street. He had the feeling of being alone and alien in this place.

"Marshal."

He turned and saw the small tow-headed boy step from the shadows at the side of the cafe.

"Yes, boy."

Shafter recognized young Will. The boy said, "I seen you go in the cafe, Marshal. I waited out here because I wanted to talk to you."

The marshal glanced along the street

143

again, seeing horses at hitch rails, men talking outside lighted windows, no shadow that might be a kid named Rio.

He said, "It's late, boy. After nine. What you doing out by yourself this time of night?"

"Wanted to talk to you, sir."

"Your father will tan your pants."

Young Will smiled. "He's fast asleep. I waited until I was sure. I heard him snoring. I sneaked out of my window."

"All right, what is it?"

"I couldn't sleep, Marshal. I couldn't sleep at all. I wasn't scared. Why, I don't want you to think I was scared."

"Oh, I don't think that." Shafter turned toward the jail, moving slowly so Young Will could walk beside him. Young Will skipped once, then took long strides to match the marshal's.

Shafter covered the top of Young Will's head with his hand and moved him across the walk in front of him so Young Will was walking on the inside. Young Will smiled, not questioning him.

"I used to be scared of you," Young Will confided, grinning.

"Did you? When you were little?"

"No. Until today. Until I got to know you. See, all I ever knew about you until this

afternoon was just what I heard people talking, saying about you."

"I reckon they say some pretty strong
things."

Young Will grinned. "I reckon."

Shafter sighed. "I reckon folks use me to
frighten children, eh?" He watched the boy
skip along at his side. Young Will had a sudden fit of inner laughter that he attempted
to conceal behind his hand. "Isn't that right,
boy?" Shafter prodded.

Young Will's eyes were bright. He nodded. "I reckon so, Marshal . . . I don't
know."

"Oh, not you," Shafter said. "I don't mean
you. But the younger kids — mothers and
fathers threaten them with the marshal to
make them be good. Eh?"

"Yes — I reckon they do."

They were silent a moment, walking
through the night. Bry smiled, glad the boy
had stolen away from his house, feeling
some of his loneliness dissolving. He felt
warm toward Young Will. Here was the kind
of boy he would like to have, like to have
had if Hannah had lived. He felt a twist in
his solar plexus, it wouldn't be too late, with
Ellen, if only he could have her.

His mouth tightened. Have Ellen, and a
son like this? For what? Out here, away from

the strong pull of Ellen's beauty and his need for her, he had to admit she was right. It was just that longing for her, he refused to admit the truth. How wonderful, he thought bitterly, to have a son like this, have him grow up to know his father was a hired gun with a tin star.

"I want to be just like you," Young Will said.

That knife twisted again inside Shafter. He tried not to growl at the boy. "You forget it," he said. "You grow up like your pa. Your pa is a fine man. He works hard. He's got his own land. He's — sunk his roots in that land. You don't know now, boy, how important that is."

"Yes, sir . . . I do, too. Oh, Pa talks to me about it. How hard he works, and how it's for me, so I'll have that place when he's old — and gone."

"He's right."

"Yes, sir. But maybe that's because that's what he wants. Is that — is that what you want, Marshal Shafter?"

The wind curled around the rim of the buildings and loose sand whirled along the hard-packed street. The choir practice had ended at the Baptist church and people came out the front doors, laughing and calling to each other. Shafter breathed deeply.

"It's what I would want," he said. His voice was sharp. "If I had been as smart as your pa, it's what I would have done when I was younger. It's too late now."

Young Will strode silently a few moments. "I don't understand," he said at last.

"It doesn't matter. You get on home and get to bed."

"Yes, sir." Young Will's steps did not pause. "But it seems to me that making a whole town safe like this for all these people, that seems a lot more important to me."

"Not important. You're a kid. It sounds like excitement. There's nothing exciting about it."

"Not many people could do it. Oh, I've heard them talking. It ain't just knowing how to use a gun, or how to fight. I've heard men talk. They say you — they say you know when to use a gun, when to give a man a chance. I've heard them. A tough man can't make a good town. I've heard 'em say that. So it seems to me — it would have to take a good man to make a good town . . . wouldn't that be true, Marshal?"

"I don't know, boy."

"Gosh. That's what I want. To be somebody. To be a man people know is good — even when they don't admit it out loud."

"Don't get mixed up, boy," Shafter said.

But his voice had softened, and the warmth in him had spread. He looked down at the tousled little head, the manful strides. Lord, he thought, make me that, just almost as good as this boy thinks I am.

His hand brushed the butt of his gun, and he recoiled, feeling with almost primitive superstition that brushing this gun had been some god's answer, a negative answer.

They had reached the doorway of the Marshal's office. Shafter paused outside. He looked down at Young Will.

"Would you like to come in, Will?" He tried to smile. "Maybe you'd like to see the jail and my office."

"Gosh," Young Will said. His eyes were round. He touched Shafter's hand. "You got — anybody in the jail?"

"Not tonight, Will. It's early. We'll have some before morning."

Young Will trailed him into the office. He wandered around, touching the desk, the chairs, seeing everything, memorizing it.

"We keep the guns here," Shafter said. He opened the closet. Young Will stopped as if in a trance, eyes round. Shafter forced himself to add, "We never use them — unless there's a jail break, or a bank robbery."

Young Will scarcely heard him. He asked the name of each rifle, what kind of shells it used, what was its range; had the marshal ever used these rifles?

Young Will stared into the cells, tested the bars in his fists. He returned to Shafter's office. Shafter was rooting around in his top drawer. He came up with a bent deputy badge. He repaired the pin on it while young Will watched, awed.

"It's what I'm going to be," Young Will whispered.

"Then you get home, get some sleep."

"I couldn't sleep, Marshal."

"What was on your mind?"

"That lady — out there on that mound. That dead lady I found. I keep thinking about her. It's something terrible, Marshal. I'm afraid to go to sleep."

"You got nothing to be afraid of. Poor woman is dead. She can't hurt you."

"Somebody killed her, didn't they?"

Shafter nodded.

"They live around here?"

"I don't know."

"You're going to catch him, aren't you, Marshal? When you catch him, you'll shoot him, won't you? For what he's done?"

Shafter exhaled. He knelt before young Will, pinned the deputy badge on his shirt.

"I'm giving you this for a reason, Will. Because of what you did today, the way you found that poor woman's body, and came right with your father to tell me —"

"Not — right — straight, Marshal."

"But you came. That's what matters. You knew what was right. And the other reason is, a deputy or a marshal or a sheriff never shoots anybody — not even the kind of man that did that terrible thing today — not unless he has to. He brings him in, Will. He brings him to trial . . . It's hard work — and sometimes it's dangerous. But it's not fun or exciting like you think. I want you to wear this badge and I want you to think about that."

"But you will catch him, won't you, Marshal?"

Shafter nodded. He had to promise. Young Will was keyed up taut and needed reassurance. They walked together out of the office. Young Will waited until Shafter closed the door.

Shafter said, "You get for home, Young Will."

Young Will touched the badge, stroking it. He grinned up at Shafter. "Good night, Marshal."

"Good night, Deputy."

He stood on the walk, watching Young Will run along the shadowed street, one arm swinging at his side, the other clutching the star pinned to his chest. A boy full of the goodness of his mother, the tenacity of his father, and the strength right out of the iron-worked earth of the valley. And watching, he went tense. Young Will streaked past the lighted windows of the Blue Dollar, turned to look over his shoulder as he started across Third. A horseman raced around the corner into Main. Young Will turned back too late, threw up his arm. Shafter stood motionless, hearing himself yell the child's name. The boy's scream, the horse's wild neighing, the rider's curses all mingled together into one sound.

Shafter stood paralyzed, weak in the small of his back. He was unable to move. All he could think was, oh, no, God damn it, no.

He tried to move and could not. He tried to run and his legs would not support him. He was afraid he would fall. The horse reared, its forepaws coming down like lethal blades against the fallen child's head. Shafter stared and didn't see it. He didn't see it happen there before his eyes, but knew that all the rest of his life he'd be afraid to close his eyes because he would see it.

FIFTEEN

At last Shafter could move.

He stepped off the walk, astonished the earth supported him, surprised the world didn't reel about his head. In the whole stricken world, everything that moved slid along in some insane kind of slow motion. All that happened occurred swiftly and yet watching it was like trying to find movement in some gigantic avalanche that stirred only inches a day.

The people from the Baptist Church ran out into the street, yet they seemed not to move at all, restrained by some kind of horror. The batwings of the saloon parted and men erupted from the light into the vague gloom of the street. People came from everywhere, yet it seemed to Shafter it was an eternity before anyone reached the fallen child.

There were no sounds, at least none that reached Shafter. He moved along, taking giant strides, trying to run, unable to.

Dust stirred under the boots of the men, forming puffs and smoking along the street, so that abruptly there was nothing but silent eternal motion on Main Street and only Young Will did not move from the place where the horse had knocked him sprawling at the curb.

Shafter thrust through the ring of people, shoving them aside when they did not move quickly enough. They whispered, staring at him and falling back, waiting for him to take over. "Get a doctor," Shafter said. He did not recognize his own voice.

A man was hunkered over the boy, his hand pressed against young Will's chest. The bent Deputy badge glittered on his shirt.

Shafter stared at the man holding the reins of the horse. For a moment he was unable to recognize him. He saw only that he was drunk, weaving on his legs and leaning against the horse for support. Finally Shafter recognized him, knew it had to be this man. It was Trumbo Gilley.

He swallowed back the bile, turned away from Gilley, knowing if he went on looking he might lunge forward and kill him.

"Anybody go for Doc Gaines?" he said.

"Perkins went," a woman said. "He went the minute you told him, Marshal."

"There ain't no heartbeat," the man hunkered over young Will said. "Leastwise none I can feel."

Shafter felt his nails digging into his palms. "Go after Perkins," he said, voice cold and dead. "Tell him to have Gaines go out to the Browns' house. Now."

153

Somebody said, "Yes, sir, Marshal." They moved away from the crowd, running along Main Street.

He heard Zach leap from the Vance buggy, felt him push through the crowd. "What's the matter?" Zach said, and then he said, "Oh, my God." He stood at Shafter's left and did not speak again.

Trumbo Gilley pulled hard on the reins. "I didn't mean to run the kid down," he muttered. "I wouldn't do nothing like that." Nobody spoke. Gilley's voice got louder. "Kid should have seen me. I came around the corner. Kid should have seen me."

He jerked the horse around savagely. His voice got defiant. "I don't want to hurt anybody. Sure don't want to hurt no kid. I came around the corner. I didn't see him. My God, I wouldn't do anything like this. You people know I wouldn't do anything like this. It just ain't my fault, that's all. Kid should have seen me. What's a kid doing out this time of night by hisself, anyhow? Yeah. What's that kid doing out this time of night?"

Gilley stepped forward, words spilling across his mouth. "I didn't see the kid. I sure wouldn't want to hurt him. But you people can't blame me. I mean it's the kid's fault."

Shafter brought the back of his hand around with all his strength, starting it from his left thigh. His knuckles, his wrist, the bones and tendons of his hand cracked against Gilley's head. A gasp went through the crowd. The impact of his hand against Gilley's face sounded like a stressed planking released to slap against a wall.

Trumbo's hands fell loose from the reins and he went sprawling backwards half across the street. His boot heels struck the boardwalk plankings and he toppled to his back.

The breath gushed across his mouth, and he tried to catch his breath. By the time he could breathe he was trying to get to his feet.

He raised himself as far as his elbow. Then his gaze struck across Shafter's face and what he saw there turned his will to whey. People standing around saw his face pale and his gaze drop under Shafter's. Afterwards they said it was as though Gilley knew if he made a wrong move, or drew a wrong breath, he was about to die.

Gilley stayed there on the ground.

Shafter stood a moment not looking at Gilley, but watching him without looking directly at him.

Shafter said, "Zach. I want you to take

155

this man to jail. I want you to lock him up. There's no bail. Do you understand?"

Shafter turned his back on Gilley. He knelt beside the boy. He put his arms under him, slowly, cradling the tousled head in the palm of his hand. Slowly, infinitely slowly, he stood up, holding the boy close, resting his head at the base of his throat.

The crowd parted and Shafter walked slowly down the middle of the street with the boy in his arms.

They watched him from the walks, and from the windows and none of them spoke. The people who had been crowded around did not move away, but stood, silently watching him.

Ellen Thomson stood before The Home Style Cafe. She had just come out of the darkened front door and she stood talking with Amos Cowley. Shafter did not look toward them. He did not take his gaze from the dark shack far down Main Street.

Ellen nodded briefly toward Amos Cowley. She stepped off the boardwalk and came into the street, angling out to where Shafter was passing.

She fell into step beside him. She did not speak. He did not turn to look at her, but felt the touch of her skirt against him in the rising wind, was aware of a damp curl touched by the breeze on her forehead.

They walked silently. Shafter was thinking nothing. Once he prayed young Will might speak or move in his arms. But the child was still.

They walked across the yard. Ellen hurried ahead and beat on the Browns' front door.

At last, Wilbur Brown said, "All right. All right. I'm coming. You don't have to wake up the kid."

Shafter heard Ellen catch her breath. A lamp sputtered feebly and then the glow touched the window, spilled through.

Wilbur opened the door, hitching suspenders over flannel underwear. His hair was wild, and he chewed at the bad taste in his mouth.

"All right," he said, "what is it — ?"

He saw Young Will then in Shafter's arms. He stared at the child, unable to take his gaze from him. His knees buckled. He said, "Claire . . . Ma." He sagged against the doorjamb. He would have fallen but he dug his hands into the rough planking.

Will stared at them, eyes tortured, and they saw he was waiting for them to say it was all right, and they couldn't speak. There were no words.

Shafter moved past him into the dimly

lighted room. It was poor, but scoured clean, everything in place.

Claire Brown came from the bedroom in a homemade bathrobe. She was tying it at her waist. Her hair was in pigtails. Her mouth trembled. "Will . . . Will baby."

"I'll put him on the couch," Shafter said. "They've gone for the doctor. He'll be here soon."

Wilbur Brown's voice raged from the doorway. He rolled his head back and forth against it. "What happened to him?" he said. "What happened to him?"

Shafter knelt slowly and placed the boy on the couch. Claire brought a basin of water. She wanted to wash the gashes in his forehead but Shafter held her away. He did not want her to touch them. It wouldn't help her any to feel the depth of those cuts.

Wilbur said, "I asked you. What happened to him?"

"A man on a horse," Ellen said. Her voice was very gentle. Shafter thanked God she'd come along. "A man on a horse ran him down."

"A man on a horse?" Brown repeated it. "A man on a horse? Ran a child down? Why? What man?"

"It was Trumbo Gilley," Ellen said.

Wilbur sagged against the doorjamb again.

158

He stared at Ellen, let his gaze move to Shafter and then to young Will.

At last he said, voice dead, "Get out. You. Shafter. Get out of this house."

Ellen stepped toward him. "Please. He tried to help. The doctor will be here in a moment."

"I want you out of this house, Shafter," Brown said.

"You can't blame him," Ellen whispered.

Brown did not hear her. He moved away from the door. Doctor Gaines walked through it. The doctor went directly to the couch and knelt over the boy. He did not speak except once. He said, "Bring that lamp nearer. You got another? A brighter one?"

Brown moaned in his throat, pressed the back of his hand against his mouth, chewing on it. He stepped toward Shafter, swaying like a drunken man.

"Get out," he moaned, throat taut. "I don't want to have to tell you again, Shafter. Get out of my house."

Shafter looked at Brown, nodded. "All right."

He looked once more at young Will, at Claire Brown. He winced, dragging in a deep breath. He moved past Wilbur Brown and went out the door.

Brown stared after Shafter, then reeled out the door.

"Wait a minute, you," he said. He shook his hand toward Shafter. "It means nothing to you, does it? You don't care. Why should you care? What's a kid to you? If it meant anything to you — you'd do something. You hear me? It's your fault, Shafter. Just like you'd killed my boy. It's your fault. If men like Gilley were run out of Pony Wells, or locked in jail as they should be, a child would be safe. Do you understand me, Shafter?"

Shafter did not speak. He stood there in the shaft of light through the doorway with hands at his sides.

Ellen came through the door. Her voice was low. "Mr. Brown," she said. "Will you come in? The doctor wants you."

A sob burst across Brown's mouth. He turned and staggered back through the door. But he could not make it all the way to the couch where the doctor knelt, looking up, awaiting him. He had to lean against the door, panting through his mouth, trying to get up the strength to take him the rest of the way.

SIXTEEN

Zach was sitting behind Shafter's flat desk in the Marshal's office. He was propped back in the chair, legs crossed, boots on the desktop.

Shafter closed the front door. "You look whipped."

Zach sighed. "That Mamie from Laredo. She took more out of me than I reckoned. Else I'm gettin' old."

"You're getting old. You can't stud for the whole valley and not show it."

"Who can't?"

Shafter smiled. He went to the entrance of the cell block. "Is he sober? I want to talk to the son of a bitch before Shad Withers' lawyer gets to him."

He entered the cellblock. Both cells were empty, barred doors hanging open. He wheeled around and strode into his office. His voice burst across the room. "Where is he? Where is that bastard?"

Zach shrugged, yawned. He did not change his position in the chair. "I released him."

"You released him? You? On whose goddamn orders?"

"On mine."

Shafter moved across the room, slapped

161

Zach's boots off the desk.

"I gave you just two orders, Zach. I told you to lock that son of a bitch up, and I told you there was no bond. Now goddamn it, since when do I talk to hear myself?"

Zach stood up slowly. "Cool off, Pop —"

"Cut out that Pop stuff. Right now. I'm ready to slap your pretty teeth down your throat. It won't take much, Zach. I warn you, it won't take much."

"Go easy, old fellow."

"I warn you, Zach."

Zach stood tall, shrugged his shirt up on his shoulders. "I'm not trying to rile you, Bry. I'm trying to make you calm down. It's all right. You and me ain't having any trouble over a thing like this."

Shafter's voice shook. "A thing like this. A drunken, murdering bastard of a killer. You let him go because you want to."

"All right. I decided. Why should I hold him here?"

"Because I told you to. You got that?"

"Yes. Because some kid was hurt, you got excited and said too much down there. I figured you'd cool off."

"That's where you figured wrong. I wanted that killer locked up. You think I haven't known where he belonged all these years? You think I haven't been waiting to get him for something that Shad Withers' money couldn't buy him out of? And I had him. And you figured I'd cool off."

Shafter knotted his fists, paced a tight circle about the office, trying to remain rational enough to speak at all.

"Can't you understand, Zach? That man's a killer. It's written all over him. But Shad Withers needs just a man like him. I couldn't touch Gilley until I got something on him. Something big. With a big stink. That's what I had this time. I let him get away with all kinds of petty things — stealing, cheating, crooked horse deals, because that was one boy I wanted hard. *You* got sense enough to see that?"

Zach's face hardened. "Don't you talk too much, Bry. I'm not taking too much, either. You don't walk over me."

Shafter whirled around. He caught the front of Zach's shirt so abruptly, twisted it so viciously, lifting Zach up on his toes, that the young deputy's face whitened and he swallowed hard, staring into Shafter's murderous gray eyes. For the first time Zach knew what it was to be in grave peril. He winced slightly, tried to pull away.

Shafter held him tightly. "Zach, get some sense. You hear me? You open your mouth smart to me just one more time and so help me God, I'll kick your teeth in. I'm not kidding. You got sense enough to see that?"

He shoved Zach suddenly. The deputy toppled back against the desk, standing straight immediately, adjusting his tie, shrugging up his shirt.

"All right, Shafter. I don't want trouble with you. But don't ever think I ain't right here if you ask for it. So Trumbo Gilley ran down that kid tonight. He'd been drinking some. But it was an accident. It was unavoidable. That's all it was. And all your raging around here won't make anything else out of it."

Shafter exhaled heavily. "Did Shad Withers tell you all this?"

"Nobody tells me what to say, Shafter. Nobody tells me what to think. I just told you the facts. When you cool off you'll know I'm right."

Shafter laughed sharply, without mirth. "I may not cool off. I don't know yet. If that kid's dead, I may go out and kill Trumbo Gilley — and if I can't find him, Zach — why God help you."

"Shafter don't talk to me like this. You been like my old man — or an older brother. I'm trying not to forget that. You been better to me than anybody I ever knew — but nobody walks over me. Not you — or nobody."

"Then if you're smart, you'll get out of here and find Trumbo Gilley."

Zach's mouth twisted into a mocking smile, "Sorry, Shafter, I just went off duty."

Shafter shrugged. He stared at Zach. The deputy's face whitened slightly again and his gaze fell away. Unaccountably, he shivered.

After a moment, more composed, Zach said, "I'll take my chances." Shafter did not answer.

"You and I both know Trumbo Gilley works for Shad Withers. Shad sets a lot of store by Trumbo. He'll stand by him no matter what kind of trouble Trumbo was in."

"I'm not afraid of Shad."

"I didn't say you were. Neither am I. But you aren't kidding anybody. Why pretend that Shad isn't one of the biggest wheels in this part of the country?"

"So?"

"So Trumbo being his assistant kind of makes Trumbo one of the biggest wheels in town. You going to throw him in jail because he accidentally knocked down the Brown kid?"

"That's right. In jail. And in court. And in

a hangtree if I can do it."

"Count me out."

"You're out."

"I'm not making an enemy of Shad Withers because of some nester's kid."

"It could have been anybody's kid."

"It happens to be a friend of Shad Withers involved. That's what cuts cloth with me. Who the hell is Wilbur Brown?"

"Nobody."

"You're damned right. And Shad Withers makes men or breaks them in this valley and if you're fool enough to forget it, all right. But I'm not."

"Why don't you get out of here and go work for him?"

Zach laughed. "I'm right here, and I work for him."

"You're about through working for me."

"Don't threaten me."

"It's no threat, Zach. Don't think I won't fire you for just this kind of talk."

"I not only think you won't fire me — I'm telling you you can't fire me."

Shafter stepped forward and Zach came away from the desk and stood tall, on sure ground now.

"Why don't you get smart, Shafter? They hired you here for a job. That job's over. You're the only one in this town doesn't know it."

"You know it?"

"It's talk, Shafter. Open talk. You think they're talking about the weather down there at the Main Hotel right now? Why you think Jenkins and Pike Vance are meeting with Shad Withers at the bank?"

"I don't know. Maybe you better tell me."

"I don't have to tell you."

Shafter swallowed hard, feeling the emptiness spread from the pit of his stomach. He bit down hard to keep any expression from his face.

"You might as well have it straight, Shafter. They've offered me the job."

Shafter flinched. He did not move a muscle. He forced his mouth into a twisted smile. "You? The new marshal?"

"Not quite. It's a little better, job they offered me. The only one I'd take."

"Yeah?"

"Yes, Shafter. They've already told me. They're making me Sheriff of this county . . . and they're just waiting for one thing — when Bry Shafter goes."

Shafter breathed heavily, face pulled into a mocking smile. The muscles of his face ached. His voice was low. "All right, Zach. That's straight enough. But there's just one thing. You let Trumbo Gilley out of here —

167

against my orders. And I'm still here. And until further notice, I'm still marshal."

SEVENTEEN

The office was too small, too crowded for Shafter suddenly. He hated the sight of the place. And he could not get the Brown child off his mind, any more than he could forget the Hogarty girl. All the rest of it, the way Zach had released Trumbo Gilley, the way the city fathers were trying to ease him out, couldn't matter except as small wounds festering on the rim of a huge one.

He walked out of the office, leaving Zach there. He closed the door behind him and heard someone speak his name. "Marshal Shafter."

It was the winking man. "Hello, Mr. Queen."

The man from Gravehead stepped out of the shadows. "Don't want too many people to see me talking to you like this, Marshal."

"Why not?"

Abel Queen laughed, his face pulling into a wink. "Oh, nothing wrong. I don't want you to think anything's wrong. No. It isn't that. It's just that McHercher and Linnot are over at the Blue Dollar. I slipped away a few moments, hoping to have a private word with you."

"You want to come into the office?"

"Oh, no. I've got to get back. It's just that I wanted to tell you. I wanted to be the one to tell you." He winked twice suddenly. "We've talked it over. The twenty thousand dollars, I mean." His laugh got shaky. "I don't mind telling you, we did a lot of hard talking. But I can tell you, Mr. Shafter, no matter how they squeal, they're going to meet your price."

"Oh?"

"Yes. I want you to remember, Mr. Shafter, I'm your friend in this here deal. I'm not trying to put one over on you. I'm coming right out and telling you. I insisted we meet your price. Well, it never hurts a man to know who his friends are, I always say."

Shafter looked at the winking man, feeling ill, knowing the first obligation that already awaited him a thousand miles west out there in the Utah Territory if he were fool enough to accept the offer to go there.

If he were fool enough.

"I'll remember your kindness, sir."

"Then you — will come out there?"

Shafter shook his head. "I can't say yet. I have to let you know."

Abel Queen winked. "Why, sure, Marshal.

I understand . . . well, I better get back over there to the Blue Dollar before they miss me . . . Like I say, I just want you knowing I'm friendly toward you in every way."

He nodded, watching the little man scurry across Main Street and clop along the boardwalk to the entrance of the Blue Dollar.

For another moment Shafter stood there before the marshal's office, looking along the blue length of Main Street. Somehow, the lights of the saloons seemed brighter, more garish, as if somebody had turned up the oil wicks in all the lamps along Main Street. There were more ponies sagging tired-legged at the hitch rails, there were more men wavering along the walks, going from the saloons to the gambling rooms and down Fourth Avenue to Angie Sefner's boarding house. His gaze crossed the closed, dark doorway of the Baptist Church.

The church people were in bed now, behind locked doors and drawn shades. Their homes were far enough removed from Main Street that they could not hear the click of roulette wheels, shuffling of cards, the sudden spring-out of a switch-blade. These good people could close their eyes to what happened between now and dawn in Pony Wells. They were secure in their knowledge of one fact: if anybody got hurt now, it wouldn't be the good people, and law enforcement officers would protect their property.

The wind in across the fields was suddenly raw, biting through him. It seemed to him the ponies hitched at the rails shivered closer together, huddling against the cold.

Why love this town above another town? Why dread leaving it? He walked slowly across the street, thinking about the three men from Gravehead and the fantastic money they were going to pay him for one year there.

"Papa."

He jerked his head up and there was Maudie and Young Tolliver, walking close together on the boards, headed toward his big house.

"Tolliver still annoying you, girl?"

Young Tolliver shuffled his feet uncomfortably and grinned without lifting his gaze to meet Shafter's. "Evening, Marshal."

"You're keeping my daughter out pretty late," Shafter said, relentlessly prodding the shy boy.

"It is late, sir. I — tried to tell her."

"Oh? It's her fault? You keeping Young Tolliver out like this, Maudie? What kind of girl are you — ?"

"Oh, no sir. It's not her fault. I mean, we were walking. We didn't know what time it was —"

"Do you know what time it is now, Tolliver?"

"Yes, sir. No, sir. What time is it, sir?"

Maudie's voice cut between them. "You stop this teasing, Papa. Right now. And you get a coat on. And you button it up. You'll have the sniffles, for sure."

A man on a horse raced in from the night suddenly riding close to the walk where they stood. Automatically, Shafter wheeled around facing him. The rider swept off his hat and the wind riffled his blond hair. He let out a yell that rattled all the way to the train station.

He prodded his horse, making him race faster and when he reached the Blue Dollar, he jerked viciously on the reins so the pony reared on its hind legs.

The rider leaped from the saddle, tied his pony at the rail, sauntered across the walk to the steps of the Blue Dollar. He paused there a moment with thumbs hooked in belt, staring down the darkened street toward them.

Maudie's voice was empty. "Papa."

Tolliver tried to make his tone casual, "Looks like a stranger in town," he said.

"Nobody I know."

"Yes," Shafter said, watching the wiry young man swagger up the steps and enter the Blue Dollar.

"Somebody looking for a big time," Tolliver said.

"Or trouble."

Tolliver took Maudie's arm suddenly, moving her along the walk with hasty farewells. Shafter stared at their backs. They looked fine together. They went well with each other. They were only children yet, but they were of good stock. That had to count.

All he needed was time. Time was so important. He had a job with Maudie, and it wasn't finished yet. Tolliver loved her, this was clear enough. But Tolliver was a year or two too young to marry. His folks would screech like Pawnees. Suppose I move her away? Suppose I take her a thousand miles out to Gravehead? What happens to her then? Young Tolliver would forget. He was young, he'd swear he would never forget, but memory wasn't what kept the universe moving.

He tried not to think the next logical step, the thought that went: who knew how long he'd stay alive in one more untamed town?

Damn it, it was more than fear for Maudie that made him want to stay here. He looked about, the Main Hotel, the Clarion office, the Home Style Cafe, Wu Sing's Barber Shop, the livery stables, the churches. Why, this was like a town he'd built himself. He wanted to stay here. He wanted Maudie to stay here. He'd buried Hannah here.

It was a good town. Not as good as it could be, but even this was his fault. He'd given the town fathers what they wanted, what they paid for. He didn't like to think it was a town where Gloria Hogarty could be brutally killed, callously buried in a shallow grave, where a child could be run down in the streets by a drunken man.

A man staggered through the batwings at the Blue Dollar. He leaned a moment against a stanchion, moaning to himself, his mouth hanging agape, his neck limp.

The drunk lifted his head enough to locate Shafter. When he recognized the marshal, he tried to straighten his shoulders and stand erect. He stared at Shafter with glassy eyes that refused to focus, and which gave him a hideous imitation smile.

He attempted to take a normal step forward to move past Shafter and lunged crazily against the tie rail so the ponies retreated nervously.

Shafter did not glance at the drunk again. He was too filled with his own thoughts, of what this town was, of what it could be, of what suddenly he wanted it to be.

He moved up the steps of the Blue Dollar. "Marshal."

He half-turned, watching Wilton Jenkins come hurrying from the direction of the bank.

Jenkins gave him a smile as false as a gold tooth. "I was just hoping I'd have a word with you."

"Come on in, buy you a drink." Shafter's mouth twisted because he knew Jenkins didn't drink. Jenkins owned a whorehouse, but Jenkins didn't drink.

"No. I guess not tonight," Jenkins said. "I better be getting on home. I won't take much of your time."

"It's all right."

Jenkins' face pulled with the effort of his continued smiling. "By the way, Marshal, you and I know it's not important but my little woman wanted me to bring word to you. She says she wants to apologize for not speaking earlier tonight. But her glasses are broken — and well, Ada says she just didn't see you. Why, she didn't even know it was you until I told her."

Shafter said, "Why, that's all right."

"Sure. I told her. But you know how women worry." Jenkins laughed emptily,

175

hunched his scrawny shoulders against the rising wind. "What I wanted to speak to you about was that Tom, over at the Main Street bar asked me to speak to you."

Shafter felt a sudden chill that had nothing to do with the night winds. "Yes?"

"He says there was a little trouble over there tonight?"

"A little. A Mexican laborer named Angelo tried to knife me."

"Well, yes, matter of fact, Tom explained that . . . But, well, he says Angelo is a mild man when he's sober."

"So are a lot of killers."

"Oh, I'm not disputing your word. I am opposed to drink. As much as any churchgoer could be. But well, Tom says if you keep the laborers out of town — well, they don't suffer — somebody will bring whisky out to them. Well, Bryant, you and I know who suffers . . . the business men. When they suffer — well, the town suffers."

Shafter wiped his sweated hand hard against his trouser leg. He was remembering the way Angelo had sprung at his face, knife blade gleaming. He remembered two years ago in that office at River Bend, the way this same Wilton Jenkins had wept, begging him to come to Pony Wells "— in the name of all that's humane. Come to Pony

Wells, Mr. Shafter, come at any price."

He exhaled sharply. Come and clean up our town, he thought bitterly, but not too clean, keep the violence there that's profitable, but keep it under wraps, the way you know how, Marshal Shafter, so people in Pony Wells can close their eyes to that violence and open their pocketbooks to its profits.

How sick he suddenly had become of these deals. His voice rasped, striking at the banker. "If that man comes inside town limits in the next two weeks, I'm locking him up. If it costs you and the Main Street bar, I'm sick about it. Right here."

Jenkins' voice sounded injured. "I wasn't trying to tell you what to do, Marshal. I was only making a suggestion. After all, I'm only thinking about what's best for Pony Wells."

EIGHTEEN

He hesitated a moment on the Blue Dollar steps after Jenkins said good night and hurried away along Main Street. When he pulled his gaze from Jenkins' ramrod-stiff back, it settled on the scuffed place where Trumbo had run down the Brown child.

He shifted the weight of his cartridge belt around slightly on his lean hips, thrust open the batwings. The piano player was batter-ing at "Skip to My Lou." The music, the laughter, the gushing talk, the acrid smell of whisky hit him in the face.

He spoke to men and they paused in conversation or cards or drinking as he passed their tables. All glanced up to speak and then covertly to watch him. He chose the same spot on the side of the bar that he'd occupied earlier. A young cowhand tipped his hat, said, "Howdy, Marshal," and slid over, making a place for him.

When the wiry, slow-motion bartender came near he pushed a bottle and shot glass toward Shafter, "On the house, Marshal."

The bartender glanced deep into the crowded room. Shafter followed his gaze. The man standing back there was watching him, studying him. There was owl-hoot written all over the man, dust smeared clothing, trail-weariness in the way he stood, and the defiant stare in his sun-faded eyes.

This one wasn't much over twenty, younger than Zach Adams, twice as ar-rogant. His black slouch hat was pushed up from sweated blond curls, and he coughed slightly when he tossed off his drink. Just a kid, Shafter thought angrily, less than medium-tall, but with a killing in his past so that he's different in his soul, old as murder itself, and no longer afraid of murder.

Shafter sighed, withdrawing his gaze. Cal was watching him, worried. Shafter said, "Cal, I want you to tell me something."

"All right, Marshal. Like the whisky. On the house." Cal tried to keep his glance from touching the gunslinger.

"You knew Glory Hogarty pretty well?"

"Sure. Like all the other girls work here. No better, you understand."

Shafter's smile was wry. "I'm not accusing you of anything, Cal."

"Sure, Marshal. I know that. I just wanted the record straight. Right?" He swiped at the bar with his rag. "What is it you need to know?"

"Maybe I should have kept up with the gossip a little closer, Cal. But I didn't. I want to know . . . from you. Who was Glory's number one love when she worked in here?"

Cal looked at him incredulously at first as though he thought Shafter was joking. Then he saw the marshal was serious; he shook his head and grinned.

Shafter's hand tightened into a fist. He had gotten this same reaction from Angie Sefner earlier tonight. There was something he was supposed to know, some knowledge so common in Pony Wells that no one credited his innocence or ignorance of it. Or was Glory's lover some man so powerful all these people were afraid to talk now that Glory was dead?

"I want to know, Cal. I need to know."

Cal looked uncomfortable and miserable. His mind was working fast. He straightened glasses behind the bar, wiped an imaginary speck from it. He licked his lips.

"Plenty other places for you to find out what you want to know, Marshal, besides me. I mean no offense, Marshal. Lord knows, you know me better than that. It's just — I don't want no trouble, Marshal, with nobody."

Someone tugged at Shafter's sleeve before he could speak again. It was Wally Dewtil. Wally's face was sweated and his pupils distended. He was so excited he was in agony.

"Hello, Marshal."

"Wally."

Wally moved nearer, shielding himself from the view of the gunslinger deep along the bar. He jerked his head in that direction. "That's him down there, Marshal."

"Who?"

"You know. The man I mentioned in Wu Sing's tonight while you were gettin' shaved.

Rio. Guy calls himself Rio Kid."

"That so?"

"He's a bad one, Marshal. He's spoiling for trouble."

"He's just a kid. What's the matter with you?"

Wally's voice was irritatingly high. "Sure. Just a kid. But he's a bad kid. Bad all the way through. And got a price on his head."

Shafter hefted his drink, carefully keeping his head turned away from the Rio Kid. The blond youth was getting louder, laughing too loudly, breaking a glass, snagging at the girls as they passed, purposely trying to rouse the Marshal so he'd look that way. That's all he wants, Shafter thought, just to have me aware of him.

He saw Shad Withers come around the curve of the bar. Shad was smiling, expansive. He wondered what Shad would say if he told him he knew the city fathers had been offering to elect Zach Adams sheriff as soon as Shafter was out of town? There was no doubt about it. Withers would go right on smiling, completely in command of the situation.

"You're letting some pretty unsavory characters in here, Shad."

Shad wasted no time pretending he had no idea whom Shafter meant. He shrugged,

181

smiling. "A man with money is welcome as long as he spends it, Marshal. That's how I stay in business. Surely you're not upset about a kid like that?"

"No. I'm not worried."

"I've some company in my office, Bry. Thought you might be interested. Those three men from Gravehead?"

"Yes?"

"They're worried, Bry. They're afraid perhaps you wouldn't be free to accept their offer to come to Gravehead. I told them we hated to let you go, but naturally we couldn't stand in your way when you could make more money — a great deal more than we could pay."

"They should feel better." Bry's smile was sardonic.

"What does that mean?"

"Just that I didn't know I was working for you, Shad. So help me. Two years and I never knew it, until tonight."

Blood suffused Shad's cheeks but he went on smiling. "You don't have to take that attitude, Bry. That's not what I meant."

"I want to ask you a question."

"All right." Shad was aware the men around them had stopped talking and drinking to hear every word between these two, the biggest men in the valley.

"Where's Trumbo Gilley?"

The smile died on Shad's face then, cold and white. "Out of town, I think."

"You better get in touch with him, Shad. You better tell him to come in and give himself up."

Shad pulled a small cigar from his pocket, pared the end from it. "For what?"

"For several reasons. First, he ran down a child on the street while drunk —"

"An accident. Entirely unavoidable. There were a dozen witnesses. I can get all of them to testify it was the child's fault as much as Trumbo's."

"No doubt you can. No doubt you will. Still. Trumbo Gilley is going to stand trial."

"The child is living. We had word less than thirty minutes ago — from Doc Gaines himself."

Shafter felt the relief flood through him. "Thank God for that. Maybe Trumbo won't hang. Maybe he'll just get a few years in prison."

Shad stared at the cigar in his band, at the sulphur match in his other. He shook out the match.

"Just what are you trying to do, Shafter?"

"What I was paid to do when you brought me here."

"Shafter, there's no sense in our having

183

trouble, you and me. If it rankles you that I told the men from Gravehead you were free to leave Pony Wells, I'll go back in there and amend that — you're free to go as far as I'm concerned. . . . Do you understand?"

"I want you to tell Trumbo Gilley to come in and give himself up to me. . . . Do you understand?"

"I hate to say this, Shafter, especially in front of these men. I think you're getting a little too big for your job. I'll give it to you straight since that's the way you want it. It's time for a change in Pony Wells."

Shafter met his gaze levelly. "You just get word to Gilley. He comes in, or I go out for him. If I go out for him, it might cost him."

"You wrong, Shafter, to take this tone with me."

Shafter straightened. "Maybe you better get it this time. I'm not working for you, Withers. I never was. Any misunderstanding about it — that was your fault."

Shad turned away, then he turned back. His voice was low. "I don't know. Whether it was or not. We'll see. As I said, I've told these men you're free to leave here."

Shafter's voice was chilled. "I'll decide when to leave. It's my job."

Shad had reached the end of the bar. He turned, glanced over his shoulder, letting his gaze move from the tin star on Shafter's chest to his handtooled boots.

"We'll see. I'm afraid you're in for a surprise. You're going to find, Shafter, it's my town. My town and my ten thousand a year."

Shafter's voice lashed after him. "Maybe it is. But meanwhile, unless you want it ripped apart, you better get word to Trumbo Gilley."

NINETEEN

They held their breath around that bar until Shad Withers was gone. Everything seemed suspended until he had reached the door to his private office and stepped through it. Men relaxed then, exhaling but not speaking, not getting too near the marshal who stood, a powerful figure whose rage kept sane men at a distance.

He shoved the bottle from him, turned away from the bar, a tall lonely man. People in the room wanted to speak to him, but had no words.

When he reached the curve of the bar, Rio stepped suddenly from the silent ring of men. His voice rasped through the stillness. Shafter stared at him, seeing the boy's eyes were red-rimmed with weariness, and though he hadn't shaved for two days, his beard looked like faint down on his sallow cheeks.

"You the marshal?" The voice rose. "You the stinking marshal of this stinking little hole?"

Shafter started past him. Rio grabbed his arm, whirling him around. "I ast you a question."

The saloon was silent now, breathless. Men edged nearer, eyes distended, fixed on Shafter's face and the rage there that any man was able to see.

"So help me. Get out of my way, boy."

This last word enraged Rio. He stepped forward. "Why don't you move me?"

Shafter winced, but did not answer. No one expected what happened next. Shafter drove his extended fingers short and hard into Rio's solar plexus.

Rio straightened tall on his boot toes, gasping for breath. His face went chalky white under the faint down of his beard. His eyes for a second rolled up in his head and his mouth flopped open as he tried to gasp in a breath of air. He could not do it and the agony bent him double, slowly, though he grasped out with his left arm for support. Men backed away from him, watching him in a kind of fascinated sickness.

When Rio doubled over, Shafter brought the side of his hand down across the back of his neck in a chopping motion that sprawled the youth on his face.

Rio lay there writhing, retching drily into the sawdust. Shafter stepped around him and walked out of the saloon. He was aware Withers had run out of his office and stared first at Rio on the floor, then stood staring after Shafter as he went through the batwings.

He climbed the steps to the second floor of the Main Hotel. The corridor was dimly lighted with two oil lamps at each end.

At room 218, Shafter stopped and knocked. He waited a few moments, then rapped on the door.

He heard movement from within.

"All right. All right," a voice called. "What can it be, middle of the night like this?"

After a moment the door was opened. The middle-aged Jew was fitting his small, thick-lensed glasses over his bulbous nose. He was not tall, but was very stout, slanting outward from thick neck to belt line.

He stared up at Shafter through his glasses, squinting and smiling. He chewed at his mouth and smoothed his hair along his temples.

"Ah, Marshal Shafter. In the middle of the night?" He spread his hands. "So what terrible thing has happened? Somebody has robbed my jewelry store? Ay, ay, ay. A man can never rest, even in his bed."

"It's nothing like that, Mr. Fortune. I should have come to see you earlier. But I've just got to thinking about Glory Hogarty's rings."

Mr. Fortune nodded. "Ay. Her rings. That girl and her rings. My best customer, Mr. Shafter. My very best customer. Too bad she died like that. Too bad. What a pity."

"Yes. It is. That's why I'm here. I'm trying to find who killed her, Mr. Fortune."

"Ay. I'll help any way I can. But how?"

"I want to know. Did Glory pawn her rings before she left here?"

Mr. Fortune massaged at his moon-belly. "You make a joke, Marshal? That girl. That Glory. She would part first with her soul — oh, more willingly."

"I didn't think she had."

Mr. Fortune sighed. "That girl died — she had her rings with her, you can bet."

"Yes. There's one more thing. Maybe it's even more important."

"What can this be?"

188

"Those rings. You sold most of them to her?"

"I'd say all of them. I ordered them for her. From Kansas City mostly."

"You'd know them if you saw them?"

"Not many people bought rings as she did. And she knew value."

"Have any of these rings turned up, Mr. Fortune?"

"What do you mean?"

"Has anybody tried to pawn them?"

"Oh, no." Mr. Fortune shook his head and light glinted in his spectacles. "If they had, I would have known them. I promise you if such a thing happens, I'll get word to you at once."

"Nobody else in town could pay what those rings were worth?"

"I don't think so. Even if they did lend money on them, they would have brought them to me to be appraised. I mean if they were smart." Mr. Fortune tried to smile. "Smart enough to have money to lend."

"That's good enough for me. We can be pretty sure then those rings haven't turned up yet around here."

"Poor girl. To think somebody would kill a girl that pretty — for her rings." Mr. Fortune shook his head.

189

When Shafter stepped off the stairway into the hotel lobby, the clerk came around the desk. He was a small man in his late forties, tired and discouraged with his failures. There was no memory of the dreams he'd had once. All he was now was night clerk in a Pony Wells hotel, seeing all the things a night clerk sees, and nothing more.

"Marshal."

Shafter stopped, watching the little man dry-wash nervous hands.

"If you'd care to use a side door, Marshal . . . there's some kind of trouble over there across the street at the Blue Dollar. I been watching it all the time you were upstairs. Looks like they're waiting for you to come out."

Shafter stared through the hotel window. A semicircle of men were crowded in the street before the saloon. A few feet in front of them Rio stood, hatless, legs apart, nervously fretting with his thonged-down holster. Rio was staring at the hotel, and the night wind riffled a lock of blond hair on his sweated forehead.

"Thanks, Luke," Shafter said. He walked slowly across the lobby, moving on the balls of his feet through the door and across the

190

deserted veranda.

He walked down the steps, shrugging his shirt up on his shoulders, keeping his arms at his sides.

Rio yelled at him, breathless with hatred. "Draw, Marshal. Draw, damn you."

Shafter did not answer but kept walking forward.

Rio shifted slightly, putting his right foot forward. "Stop where you are, Shafter. Draw."

Shafter spoke loudly. "I'm not going to draw, Rio. You're under arrest."

"You come and take me, you bastard."

"All right, Rio."

Rio's laugh was exultant. "You hear that? He knows me. He's heard of me." He hurled his voice across his shoulder at the men who stirred, silent. "He's afraid to draw."

Shafter walked slowly forward. "Why should I draw, Rio?"

"Because do or don't, I'm going to kill you."

"You're not going to kill anybody, boy."

"Don't call me a boy." Rio spat at him. He tilted his arm slightly. "Draw."

"And kill you? What for? Kill a boy named Rio? For what? For the hundred bucks they offer for you in Dodge?"

Some of the men laughed at that. A hundred dollars dodger was an insult to a man.

Rio screeched, trembling all over. "It'll be more when I leave here. Stop there. Draw." His hand wavered over that thonged-down holster. His arm shook. He made a half-gesture downward, then paused, licking his lips.

Shafter walked forward, warily. He stopped before the boy. "Give me that gun, Rio."

"You take it."

Shafter hit him. He moved so abruptly that Rio was unprepared even this second time. Rio was a gunfighter, and his short experience had trained him to watch only one thing, a man's hand over his gun. When Shafter's left lashed out, smashing against his jaw, Rio reeled backwards so the laughing men had to jump out of his way.

That laughter was like a dozen branding irons against Rio's head. He struck on the hard-packed street and his hand went for his gun. But Shafter had followed, stalking him. As the gun came from the holster, Shafter kicked his wrist so hard the gun flew into the gutter.

Rio whirled over, scrambling toward the gun.

Shafter bent over, caught him by the shoulder and flicked him over on his back. The men who had followed a killer into the street now laughed at a boy sobbing and moaning with rage and indignity. Shafter caught Rio's shirt and jerked him to his feet.

He reached down, ripped loose the cartridge belt so it fell away from Rio and hung by the leather thongs about his legs.

Rio tried to lunge free. Shafter brought his hand back and forth across his face. Shafter said, "Wally."

Dewtil was laughing harder than any of the other men. "Wally, loosen this boy's holster."

Wally laughed louder, cackling at the idea. He opened his knife, ripped the thongs. The holster fell into the street. Rio cried out and again Shafter backhanded him.

"Wally, take his money wallet."

Wally cackled some more, located the boy's wallet. Shafter said, "I'm fining you, Rio, whatever is in that wallet. That or jail. Now, get on that horse and get out of town."

The laughter swelled at that. Tears streamed down Rio's face. "No money? No gun?"

"That's right. And you ever come back in this town, Rio, you'll think you got off easy this time."

Rio's mouth trembled. He seemed to shrink from the laughter that struck against him like rocks. He ran to his horse, pulled himself into the saddle, tearful, agonized, and without his gun, running from the laughter.

Shafter walked silently through the ring of men. He went directly to the Blue Dollar bar, called Cal.

"Cal, I just ran out of patience. Like you said, there might be places I could learn who was Glory Hogarty's lover, but I know you've got that information. I want it, if I have to slap it out of you, and Shad Withers coming out of that office won't stop me."

Cal's blanched face worked. He nodded. "I got that much sense, Marshal. And Mr. Withers ain't here. He's gone to see Mr. Jenkins and Mr. Pike Vance — about you. Lord, Glory don't seem very important to me."

"She's important to me. Was she Shad Withers' woman? Is that what you're afraid to tell me?"

Cal scowled, staring at Shafter. "All right, Mr. Shafter. I reckon you got me."

Shafter knew the bartender was lying, but he also knew he'd go on lying. Whatever the truth was, Cal feared it worse than a coiled rattler.

Tension mounting in him, he turned away. Cal's voice stopped him. "Mr. Marshal, there's something I got to tell you. That crazy loon Albert Tishkin was in here looking for you. I don't usually pay no attention to him, but he was so scared, Marshal, I'm telling you he practically talked sense. He begged me to tell you you had to protect him. I don't know if it means anything, but I promised the loon I'd tell you."

"All right. . . . But remember this, Cal. You lied to me, and I'm not forgetting it."

Cal's gaze fell away. He looked ill in his soul, but he could not force himself to say anything else. He picked up a glass in trembling fingers and polished at it. Shafter met Zach in the batwings. Zach caught his arm. "Just heard about the trouble with the gunslinger," he said. "Came as quick as I could."

"Come to bury me, Zach?"

"Come off it, Bry." Zach led him to a table near the door. "Maybe you feel like joking, but I don't. There's trouble — and you've stirred it up for God's sake. Don't you know Shad Winthers is running around town trying to get Pike Vance and Jenkins and the others together so they can fire you?"

"You worry about Shad. I haven't time."

"Well take time. Being bullheaded is one

thing. But you're being a fool. I've heard what you told Shad. You don't work for him. Good God, you trying to rile him?"

"I just told him the truth."

"This is no time for the truth. It's time for using your head. Shad Withers has passed the word around — to guys like that Rio, that you're out — as far as Shad knows, you're not even marshal here any more."

"Sounds like him."

"That means trouble, Bry. Why don't you find Shad and make peace with him? Whether you like it or not, he runs this valley, the sheriff's office, the county judges, everything. Some gunslinger could shoot you down now and get away with it, because nobody would prosecute him in this valley unless Shad's judges forced them to. And Shad's judges won't lift a finger unless Shad gives the orders. These are facts, Bry, and you know it."

Shafter kept his voice low. "If I were dead, Zach, you'd be marshal, wouldn't you? You'd arrest my killer, wouldn't you?" His tone taunted Zach.

The deputy flushed. "I'd want to, Bry. It would tear me up, and I'd want to, you know that."

"But your hands would be tied, is that it?"

"I got sense enough to know I'm working

for Shad Withers in this valley, no matter how I felt about you gettin' shot in the back."

"You really want to be sheriff, don't you?"

"All right. Why lie about it? Yes, I want to be sheriff. But I don't want you killed sense-lessly . . . I want to do all I can to help you. But I like to stay alive. I ain't mean, Bry. I'm weak enough to know when I'm beat. If I opposed Shad Withers in this valley, how long would I last?"

"But that's it. You're not going to oppose him."

"No." Zach sat perfectly still. "I'm not."

"Like to see me out of here, Zach?"

"Not with a bullet in your back, damn it. You're like a brother. I don't want to slop over. But that's the way it is. We see things eye to toe. Sure. We can't help that. We're not alike. But that don't keep me from knowing you're the best man ever to come down this trail. I try to do things the way you like 'em, try to be like you. I don't want you killed when it don't make sense."

Shafter sat for a moment, looking at Zach. The young deputy's face was taut-drawn, and he spoke between clenched teeth.

Shafter smiled. "All right, kid."

"That's my speech, Shafter. One of the longest I ever made. I'm never going to say it again. You got to have sense enough to come in out of the rain."

Shafter nodded. "You've warned me. I'll try to get along with Withers."

"You mean it?"

Shafter nodded, exhaling. "Right now, I got something else on my mind. Poor Albert Tishkin was in here scared sick. He wants police protection."

"Police protection?" First Zach scowled, then laughed. "Lord, Shafter, you're not taking anything the loon says seriously, are you?"

"Thought I'd ride out to his shack and see what's troubling him."

"No sense in you going. I'll do it."

Shafter shook his head. "No. You stick around here, deputy." He bore down hard on the word. "Remember, I'm still marshal, and until you get the word, you're still working for me."

TWENTY-ONE

Shafter walked out of the saloon to the street and angled across it toward the livery stable.

He could not get Zach out of his mind. It was strange that he had never before realized the extent of passion of Zach Adams' ambitions. Zach wanted to be sheriff. If there was anything else on his mind, it occupied a secondary spot. Looking back over all, the months he'd known Zach, he could see a hundred items that might have tipped him off, the way Zach wanted to learn all there was to know about guns and law enforcement, the way Zach always turned on the charm, ingratiating himself with the influential people of the valley: Jenkins, Pike Vance and Shad Withers. It was never clear before just what Zach wanted, but it was clear now, this impatient way Zach waited, and watched with a mouth-watering kind of impatience.

A light burned in the Home Style Cafe and Shafter paused outside the square frame building, forgetting Zach Adams. For a moment he thought the place was deserted, that Ellen had hurried away and overlooked the lamp. Then he saw them. The lamplight made a glow about Ellen's hair, and the way she held her head made him sure it was she. The man sat across the table from her and was in darkness. Intuition told Shafter it was Amos Cowley. He knew now why the rancher was delaying so long in Pony Wells. He pressed his fist against the emptiness in his solar plexus without even knowing he did it.

He paused for a moment in the street, staring into the cafe. He felt perspiration pop out under the band of his stetson. Hellish, thinking she would see him standing out here. She would think he was spying on her. But for the moment he could not move on along the darkened Street. Ellen and Amos Cowley. It didn't make sense to him, but since when had any woman's choice of a man seemed logical to another man? Ellen needed more than the stodgy, plodding ranchman could give her. How could Ellen be fool enough to marry a roan like Cowley? Sure, there was one thing Cowley could offer her, and she was so badly hurt that it looked more important to her than anything else: Cowley offered Ellen security, security of thousands of acres of cattle land, thousands of cattle, a home and position free of ever-lurking dangers.

He moved toward the cafe door. He had no idea what he would do when he was inside, but he had to do something. Even if he only made Cowley see that Ellen belonged to him, that would help. Surely, Cowley would not want a woman that loved another man. He did not care what kind of scene he made. He didn't care what happened just so Cowley realized the truth.

He paused, remembering the tears in

Ellen's eyes, the tautness in her voice when she told him not to come back. He couldn't hurt Ellen any more, not even if it meant that he lost her. Besides, it was not Cowley who was taking her. He had lost her before Cowley came into town with that watch chain across his vest, his hat precise and square on his head. He had lost her before he ever knew her, he had lost her the first time they pinned a badge on him in some faraway forgotten cattle town.

He turned away from the lighted window of the cafe and hurried, striding toward the livery stable. He was almost to Fourth when the shot rang out from the darkness of an alley and a bullet spun past his head like a crazed hornet.

He fell back into the shadows, shoulders against the siding of a store. He reached for his gun, closed his fist on it, drew it, aware he was shaking all over.

He was afraid. Not even his fist on gun-butt gave him his old sense of confidence. Always before they had angered him when they attacked him, and the anger doubled when the attack came from the dark. Now suddenly he was not thinking about the bushwhacker, he was thinking about Maudie and her need for him, about Ellen, about all the things he had to live for, and his sudden hatred of the idea of dying senselessly in the darkness.

He saw a flicker of movement in the alley and from old habit he sprang toward it, keeping low, staying in the darkness.

The man dodged into the shadows; from there came the orange burst of gunfire. Shafter heard the wail and sing of the bullet, and jerked his gun upward, firing at that brilliant burst of light.

The man yelled, not in agony, but in sudden sense of terror. A rain barrel was pushed over and the man ran, hunched close to the ground.

Shafter straightened, ran after him. He called, "Halt."

The man ran faster. Shafter fired over his head and the man hit the dirt, digging into it, scrambling under the wooden railings of a fence.

For a moment Shafter lost him in shadows, and that sweated emptiness returned. He moved forward cautiously, gun ready, remembering he had fired twice.

He reached the fence, moved to the end of it and started along it, staring into the darkened enclosure. He sprinted from cottonwood to cottonwood, hugging the shadows and waiting for any sound of movement.

He saw the gate ahead and he leaned against the tree trunk a moment, looking about for shadow that would afford protection if he entered the yard.

He held his breath. There was movement on the ground just inside the gate. Shafter pressed hard against the tree, waiting. The gate swung open slowly, whispering drily in the night wind.

The man crawled through it, cautiously, coming up on his knees and rising warily. When he stood up, Shafter saw the gun in his hand.

He said, "Drop that gun."

The man heeled around, mewling in his throat. He jerked his gun up.

Shafter shot him.

He leaned against the tree, watching the man beside the gate. His fingers loosened on the gun and he toppled back against the gatepost. He turned and tried to run back into the yard, but fell. He tried to support himself on the gate but it swung away from him, squeaking.

Even after the man had fallen on his face, half in the yard, half out of it, Shafter did not move. His gaze was fixed on the gun where it had fallen. Shafter pushed his own gun back in its holster. One more man had been shot. Shafter pushed off his hat, wiped his sweated forehead on his sleeve. How much longer would they miss with that first shot? When would he meet some man who would not run?

He walked slowly across the space between them. There was only a faint glimmer of the moon, the unsteady incandescence of starlight. He bent over, picked up the gun, shoved it in his belt.

The man moaned and Shafter tensed, his hand dropping to his own gun. After a moment he stepped nearer, pushed the big man over on his back. He did not have to get nearer to identify his assailant.

It was Trumbo Gilley.

His hatred for Trumbo faded slightly under the thought that Shad Withers had ordered this attack. He amended that. Shad Withers would never hire a gun to attack him; no matter the price paid, it was too risky. What Shad Withers had done was let it be known that he was no longer backing the marshal at Pony Wells, that Bry Shafter was leaving Pony Wells as far as Shad Withers was concerned, leaving one way or another.

Shafter wiped his hand on his trousers. That would be all Shad Withers would need to say. That would recall Trumbo Gilley from whatever hideout he'd sought when

Zach released him from jail.

There was more. Trumbo Gilley would not be the last. Gunmen on the make had ridden out of their way to take a gander at the marshal at Pony Wells. But for the past two years, the marshal had had the solid support of the courts. As Zach had warned him, Shad Withers was pulling that security out from under him. The word would spread. A man might kill Bry Shafter and never even face trial for it, if he did face trial, he would face a weakened prosecution, and friendly judges. That was the word now that would find its way across bars and over campfires and along trails. Marshal Shafter was leaving Pony Wells.

Trumbo Gilley moaned.

"Get up," Shafter said.

"You shot me. I'm on fire. Great God, you killed me."

"I saved you from hanging."

"Get me to a doc, Shafter."

"Is that what you would have done for me, after you shot me from your alley?"

"Help me."

"I told you. Get up. I'm taking you to jail."

"Be human. I'm bleeding to death."

"Either you get up and walk, or I drag you. It's up to you."

205

"I'm in agony, Shafter. I got to have a doctor."

Trumbo moaned, sobbing deep in his distended belly. Shafter went on standing there. He did not get nearer Trumbo to see how badly he was wounded.

"You can bleed to death there, Trumbo, or get a doctor at the jail. It's still up to you."

Trumbo caught the rail fence and pulled himself to his knees. He managed to stand up. He swayed, sweat gleamed on his rutted face.

"Walk ahead of me."

Trumbo staggered toward Main Street. Shafter's curt voice stopped him. He toppled against the fence.

"Not that way. We're going through the alleys. I want you to feel at home."

They moved slowly through the shadowed alleys. It was tortuously slow. Shafter kept them in darkness, made them halt at the sound of a horse or footsteps anywhere near. Trumbo staggered and fell. Shafter stood over him, prodded him until he got to his feet again. For a while Trumbo could not restrain the sobs as he walked. Before they reached the jail he was chewing his mouth, snuffling deep breaths, but he no longer asked for mercy.

The office and cellblock were silent and empty. Shafter supported Trumbo with hand twisted in shirt. He prodded him into a cell and Trumbo sagged to one of the iron cots. It squealed under his weight. He rolled over on his back. He stared up at the ceiling, biting at his mouth, clutching the wound in his side, waiting to die.

Dr. Gaines stood away from Trumbo. "I'm ashamed of you, Bryant. You're not the marksman you were. You only nicked him in the belly. You almost missed him."

"Damn," Shafter said. "Is he going to live?"

"I'm afraid so," Gaines said. "Despite all I can do, I'm afraid I'll have to report this patient will live."

"It's only temporary," Shafter said. "Until I can get a jury to agree on a hangrope."

Trumbo twisted on the cot. "I ain't done nothing."

"You tried to kill me."

"You ain't hurt."

"You almost killed the Brown kid. He may still die."

"It was an accident. You listen to me, Shafter. I want to talk to Shad Withers. I want you to send for him right now."

Dr. Gaines smiled crookedly. "You got a

domineering prisoner here, Marshal. Since he's found out he's not going to die yet, he's suddenly not even afraid of the devil."

"He will be, by the time I'm through with him," Shafter said. He stood over Trumbo. "Listen to me. If you're going to bleed, get off that cot. I got to get away from here for a while. You better pray I get back because I'm taking the key to this cell with me."

"I want to see Shad Withers."

"Maybe tomorrow, Trumbo. . . . Maybe."

From the jail, Shafter walked back with the doctor along Main Street.

"Are you all right, Bry?"

"Why wouldn't I be?"

"Trumbo Gilley shot at you, didn't he?"

"I'm still here."

"He won't be the last."

"He wasn't the first."

Dr. Gaines paused at his gate. "Take care of yourself, Bry. You're a good man. Trouble is, most people don't appreciate a good man until it's too late."

Shafter nodded a curt good night, strode across the street. Doc Gaines was still standing beside his gate watching him when he rode out of the stables and turned his horse out of town.

Albert Tishkin's shack had once belonged

to the line riders on Pike Vance's ranch. They gave it to Albert and he slept there after the last lights were extinguished in Pony Wells and the last door was locked against him.

Shafter ground-tied his horse, walked to the shack door. He called Albert, but there was no answer. He listened, but there was only the sound of the wind flapping a loose sheet of tarpaper roofing, and the distant noises of Pony Wells.

Shafter pushed open the door and stepped inside. The room smelled musty and close as if Albert hated fresh air and plugged all holes, barred all windows against it.

Shafter struck a match. A junk heap erupted in the yellow sputtering flame. He located a glassless lantern on a table. He shook out the match, turned up the lantern wick and lighted it.

He gazed about the room. Albert must have had pack-rat blood in him. He had lugged home almost every discarded item from Pony Wells. He'd repaired none of it, simply found a place for it in the small shack.

He went to Albert's bed, touched it to see if there were any warmth to show that Albert might have been here. There was still excitement in town, but Shafter knew he'd

209

frightened Albert when he caught him robbing sugar from the store. He remembered suddenly Albert's boast that he could be rich if he wanted to, and his sudden need for protection.

Shafter shook his head. There was no reason to put much credence in anything Albert Tishkin said.

He lifted the pillow, shook it and dropped it back on the cot. Something glittered in the light and he lifted the pillow again, thinking it might be a piece of glass or a clean tin can.

He leaned forward, pulling the mattress apart where the glitter showed. They popped out into his hands. He stood there with them, looking about the cluttered room.

He had found Glory Hogarty's rings.

TWENTY-TWO

Shafter looped his reins over the leather-slicked rail outside the Blue Dollar.

He glanced both ways along the street, finding it still alive, still awake as though it existed on some kind of nervous tension it did not itself understand.

He walked up the steps and through the batwings, the rings knotted in a handkerchief in his trouser pocket.

210

He crossed to the bar. Cal saw him coming, tried to appear busy. The bartender didn't want to meet his gaze.

"Cal. You said Albert was looking for me. You seen him since he gave you that message?"

Cal continued polishing a glass. He glanced up once and then jerked his gaze away. "No, Marshal. I haven't. That's the truth."

Shafter watched Cal polish the glass, saw lights glitter in it. "You tell Albert I said to come over to my office as soon as you see him."

"Sure will, Marshal."

Shafter turned away, glanced back across his shoulder, caught Cal watching him. Cal's face was pale.

"You got anything else you want to tell me about Glory, Cal?"

"Nothing, Marshal. I've told you all I know."

Shafter stared at him, shrugged. He moved away from the bar.

"Marshal."

He stopped. Cal was leaning his weight half-across the bar top. "Marshal, I got something else to tell you."

"All right."

He waited. The bartender put a glass and

a bottle on the bar. "Have a drink, Marshal."

Shafter returned to the bar. He stood there with his hands on glass and bottle. Cal leaned close. "I got something you ought to know. Flynn Hawk is back in town, Marshal. He rode back in tonight."

Shafter's laugh was sharp. "Hasn't been very far away, has he?"

"Thought I ought to tell you, Marshal."

"Thanks." He turned from the bar, almost bumped Shad Withers who had come silently from his office and moved between the tables without replying to the people who spoke to him.

Shad gave him a curt smile. "I hear the men from Gravehead made you an attractive offer, Shafter."

"Yes. I told them I was working here."

"A better offer, Bry. We can't stand in your way."

"Maybe I want to stay here."

"I wouldn't advise it." Withers went on smiling.

Shafter held his gaze. "I have a friend of yours in jail. Had to shoot him."

Something flickered in Withers' eyes. "Have you?"

"Don't you want to know who it is, Shad? Or do you know?"

"How would I know?"

Shafter shrugged. "You know everything else. You know I got an attractive offer from Gravehead."

Withers dampened his lips. "Shafter, you must know a town this size can't go on paying a marshal the kind of salary we pay you. You've a chance to better yourself." He cleared his throat, glanced about the room. "I was trying to be your friend."

Shafter closed his hands into fists, trying to control his rising temper. He felt a sudden overwhelming urge to strike Withers in the face and keep striking him until he broke down all the tissues so that Withers could never smile again.

He said, "Don't try so hard, Shad. I told you I had a friend of yours in jail. Worse than that, he's your hired gun. I never knew him to do anything that you didn't order done."

Withers flushed. "What kind of accusation is that?"

"Make what you want out of it, Shad. Trumbo Gilley shot at me tonight from a dark alley. He missed and I chased him down. I had to shoot him. He's in jail now."

Withers stood rigid, face taut. He held Shafter's gaze a moment, looked away. He moved his hand along the roll of the sleek bar, watched a girl laughing with a middle-

213

aged rancher at the rear of the room.

"You've made a bad enemy there, Shafter. He felt you were trying to railroad him. I never gave him any orders concerning you. You should know better. I've nothing but respect and admiration for you, Shafter. I brought you here. You must remember that."

"I remember. But I also know that was two years ago. Now you want me out of here — even worse than you wanted me to come to town."

Withers regarded his hands. He seemed ill. "Shafter, listen to me. You're drawn fine. You're on edge. You're imagining things. Bry, I am more grateful than any other man for what you have done here. I've profited most. I'm not forgetting that. I want the best for you. It looks to me like the best would be another job — at better pay — in another town. Now that's all there is to it. I am remembering our friendship of the past two years. I'm overlooking the things you've said that you're going to regret when you think them over."

Shafter hunched his shirt up on his shoulders. He glanced toward Cal behind the bar. Cal was whitefaced.

Shafter said, "All right, Shad. I'll say that Trumbo bushwhacking me was personal. He's got a right to hate me on his own. I never knew him to do anything you didn't order, but I'll pass that. There's just one thing. I ran a gunslick named Flynn Hawk out of this town over a week ago. I warned him not to come back."

The uprush of blood colored Withers' face to the roots of his hair. "What's that got to do with me?"

"Just this, Shad. If Flynn Hawk takes a shot at me, he'd better not miss, because if I live, I won't hunt him. I'm coming looking for you."

Withers' breath burst across his mouth.

"What kind of talk is this?"

"Sounded plain to me. Flynn Hawk got orders to travel. Evidently he didn't go far. Tonight I heard he was back in town."

Shad's voice cracked. Men glanced around, conversation ceased near them.

"All right, you ought to know that's what I've been telling you. You ought to see now that the only trouble that comes to Pony Wells any more comes looking for you, Shafter."

Shafter breathed deeply. "All right. But remember what I said. If Hawk tries to get me, I'm coming looking for you."

"You're crazy." Withers whispered it.

Shafter looked around the saloon, the gambling tables, the bar, the women, the stock of whisky and beer and everything that went with it, everything Shad Withers owned. Then he looked at Shad Withers one more time.

He turned on his heel and walked out.

TWENTY-THREE

Shafter exhaled heavily when he walked out of the Blue Dollar. He felt a sense of ridding his nostrils of the smell of Shad Withers' saloon, but there was something more. There was the odor of fear all through him, and it was a new sensation. God knew he'd never been a fool and insensitive to danger. But he had never felt the paralyzing effects that fear could exert on nerves and muscles and the very fibers of the human body.

He mounted the horse slowly, pulling its head around and riding slumped in the saddle toward the livery stable. He could not pretend that Shad Withers would back down or warn Flynn Hawk out of town. This was the moment of crisis for Shad Withers, and both of them knew it. He went on being master of the Sage River Valley or he backed down to Shafter. Withers never got where he was by backing down to anybody. He did not go around obstacles, he walked over them.

He glanced over his shoulder toward the lighted saloon, alert although all his thoughts were turned inward. He'd been a trouble marshal for too many years ever to relax.

He rode slowly past the Home Style Cafe. All lights were out now, the building loomed dark and silent and he had the empty feeling of looking at a place lost to him.

He swung down from the saddle and rattled the livery stable door. He heard a grumbling from within, shuffling of feet. The door opened and the night keeper blinked at him in the light of a lantern hung beside the livery door.

"Oh. You back, Marshal."

Shafter's smile was grim. "Didn't you expect me back?"

"Many times when you rode out, Marshal, I never knew if you'd come back or not."

"Is that why you trained this horse to come home alone?"

The stablekeeper came out, took the reins. "Albert Tishkin was around here looking for you, Marshal."

"Is he here now?"

"No. He stayed around here, acting funny, hiding in one of them stalls ever'time somebody came to the door. He said he was going to wait for you, but finally something

217

scared him and he went high-tailin' it down Fourth Avenue there."

"Why didn't you make him stay here?"

"Marshal, I had no idea you wanted to see the loon."

Shafter's laugh was self-deprecating. "Sorry. Sure you didn't. A man gets so wrapped up in his thoughts, he thinks everybody else shares 'em. . . . If he comes back, you keep him here."

He heeled around and walked out of the building. He stared along the dark length of Fourth. Not a light showed in any house down there. Walking in the middle of the street, Shafter strode down the dark avenue. If Albert had been headed home, this was the wrong direction.

He passed the last house, paused and then moved on. He felt impelled by some inner sense that he could not analyze or explain. He didn't know what he was looking for. He almost stumbled over Albert's body before he saw it.

Albert was sprawled on the side of the road with his legs curled up.

Shafter knelt beside him, thinking he was asleep. Albert slept in the open as easily as he did in his airless shack. He shook his head, thinking Albert resembled a bundle of discarded clothes, lying there.

Still there was a sense of elation at having found him. Albert had had Glory's rings. He knew more about her death than anyone else he'd so far located. If he could make him talk coherently, Albert might give him all the answers.

Shafter shook the bony shoulder and spoke his name, voice sharp in the still dark. "Albert."

Albert did not respond. His body quavered limply when Shafter shook his shoulder. He rolled out on his back and his head rolled to the side. He stared at the sky, eyes distended.

Shafter's hand dropped to Albert's chest. His fingers moved into the chilled coagulation of blood. There was no heartbeat. Albert was dead.

Shafter hunkered there for some moments over Albert's body. He stared at Albert's gaunt face, pale and rigid in the faint moonlight.

He lifted his head, glancing at the nearest house. It was several hundred yards distant, but those people could not have missed the sound of gunfire. There was a chance they may have seen two men out here on the road. But they would not have recognized them. There was even a chance they could have heard the gunfire and not stirred from bed. Pony Wells was a quiet town, but late at night there were sounds of violence: a drunken cowboy letting off steam, riding out of town yelling and shooting at the moon. This kind of trouble the people of Pony Wells had learned to sleep through in the past two years.

He considered waking these people and then decided against it. It was clear Albert Tishkin had been killed because of those rings of Glory Hogarty's. The killer had not known until this afternoon that someone had robbed Gloria of her rings. Whoever the killer, robbery had not been the motive. This afternoon, he'd seen her bare hands, and to this killer there had been meaning. Shafter remembered he had been troubled by an elusive something about Gloria's hands: the fact her rings were missing had not struck him as forcibly as it had her killer, because he had not known her so well.

Hunkered there, he recalled the little he knew about Glory. There had been the quiet afternoon when he had come upon her in the yard behind Mrs. Sefner's boarding house. Gloria had been holding the body of a dead kitten, the only living thing she had to love. Somebody had killed it and Gloria had rocked there, crying like a small child. Shafter remembered squatting beside her,

220

trying to console her, looking at the little-girl tears spoiling the whorish make-up of her eyes and cheeks. Her mouth quivered and she seemed young and defenseless, unwilling to let the kitten go even when it was dead, holding its body against her in hands that glittered with her rings. . . .

The next time he had seen her, laughing and talking, too thin, too loud, too bold in Shad Withers' Blue Dollar, it hadn't seemed possible she was the same little girl crying over her kitten. And even then Shafter had felt ill, wondering what Gloria might have been if her father had lived to take care of her.

He lifted Albert's thin body, hefting it across his shoulder. He moved off the road, staying in the darkness. He kept to the shadows, all the way to Dr. Gaines' back door.

Dr. Gaines opened the door, sleep-drugged, angered at being wakened.

"What you want, Shafter? Why do you bring your troubles to me? Isn't Doc Swilner good enough for you?"

"Not this time." Shafter unloaded Albert's body on Gaines' kitchen table. This was not unusual. He'd brought men to this table before so the doctor could cut bullets from them or sew up knife cuts.

Shafter closed the back door. When he returned to the table, Gaines was staring at him, brow tilted, mouth pulled. "This your idea of a joke, Shafter?"

"It's no joke. I want you to do what you can for him."

"You crazy? Tishkin is dead. Not even Doe Swilner could save him. He's been shot in the heart."

"That's what you think, Doc. You better look again."

Gaines didn't even glance toward the body on the table. He leaned against it, never taking his gaze from Shafter's face. He waited, without speaking.

Shafter pulled the cloth packet of rings from his pocket, showed them to Gaines quickly and replaced them.

Gaines continued to study him, did not speak.

"So help me. Don't you get it, Doc? These are Gloria Hogarty's rings. That's the reason Albert is dead."

"He didn't kill her?" It was practically no question the way Gaines said it. Neither of them believed Albert capable of murder.

"No. But he robbed her. Don't you see it? Glory collected rings. Put every penny she ever got into buying rings. Went hungry for them. Some kind of desire —"

"Maybe it fulfilled her desire for security."

Shafter shrugged. "She bought rings. Out there this afternoon, I noticed something wrong about her hands, but didn't realize I was seeing them without rings —"

"Naked, eh?"

Shafter nodded, smile grim. "Mrs. Sefner said she took all her rings. The jeweler said she didn't pawn any of them. But — out there she had no rings."

"So?"

"So help me, Doc. Don't you see? The killer was out there, too."

"Half the town was out there."

"That's right. Half the town. That makes it that much easier. The killer was there. He saw the same things I did. Her rings were gone. He had not killed her for those rings, and that meant somebody must have seen him kill her, even seen him bury her, and had robbed her — after she was dead."

Gaines smiled, nodding. "I admire you, Shafter. I admire any man good at his profession. You're tops. Too bad you're no longer appreciated around here. Pony Wells will never get another man to replace you."

"They're going to try."

"Yes. They're going to try." Gaines glanced at Albert's body. "So now you know this much more. The killer did not rob Gloria, he buried her at night out there. And when he saw those rings were gone, he spent all the hours since then finding out who saw him bury her, and he killed this witness because only then would he feel truly safe."

Shafter stared at Albert's body. "Too bad he missed."

"What?"

"I said, it's too bad he missed. Poor Albert, lying there while you probe for that bullet, wavering between life and death."

Gaines nodded. "Yes. That's what we've got to do, isn't it? Spread the word, let half the town know that the man who shot Albert Tishkin missed in the darkness, and poor Albert is going to live after all."

Shafter said, "That's right. And I admire you, Doc. You're a pretty fair country doctor."

"Oh, we're great people, Shafter. You and I."

Twenty-Four

He left the doctor's house, going out the front door and walking to the street. He stood for a moment at the gate. He listened for sounds he could not explain but which would be an instant warning. He couldn't say what he expected to hear, or even if the truth were that perhaps something he would *not* hear might be meaningful. Wind slipped through the cottonwood trees in front yards along the street, hardly rousing the leaves and sending down nothing more than a sibilant whisper.

He was at the corner of Main Street when he saw someone move out of the darkness near the Home Style Café.

Shafter sidestepped into a shadow and standing tall, hand resting on gun butt, he waited. This was the sort of thing that killed a man, he thought, tension, and he did not see how he could endure a hundred nights of it in a place called Gravehead.

He recognized Ellen Thomson and exhaled heavily. He stepped out of the shadows, relaxed his hand at his side. His palm was sweated and he wiped it on his trousers.

"Yes, Ellen."

"Are you all right?"

"I am now that you're here."

He heard her abrupt inhalation, impatience at his gentle tone.

"I've been looking for you, Bry."

"Is the child all right?"

"The child?"

"The Brown boy. Is he all right?"

"I believe he is. He was resting when I left him. He had regained consciousness."

"Thank God."

"It's you I'm worried about, Bry. I'm deathly afraid for you."

"You do love me. Why don't you just say that?"

"Whether I love you or not — I have loved you — you're no stranger. I don't want you hurt."

"This is my job. Remember? You told me. It's the chance I take."

"There's no sense in being a fool. You've done all you can for Pony Wells. I want you to leave."

His mouth twisted into a smile. "You, too?"

She frowned in the darkness, taking an involuntary step nearer. "What do you mean, Bry? I didn't know anyone wanted you to leave."

His voice was bitter. "Didn't you? Who wants a trouble marshal in Pony Wells any more? There's no trouble here. There's no place for Bry Shafter. You haven't heard that one?"

"Whether I have or not, that isn't why I came to see you."

"You came to say you were sorry for all the unkind things you said. You do love me. You will marry me."

Her voice was forlorn. "Please, Bry, listen.

I heard tonight a killer named Flynn Hawk is back in town and says he is going to kill you."

"What kind of company you keeping?"

"Never mind. Be glad I heard it. I want you to leave town, Bry. At least until he gets tired waiting."

His laugh was cold. "A marshal should run when a killer comes to town?"

"You're not a marshal. Not as far as Flynn Hawk is concerned. You're — just another man with a fast gun. It's that personal. That terrible. He came here looking for you. He means to kill you."

"Who told you all this?"

She touched his arm. "What does it matter who told me? It's the truth, Bry. It's nothing you have to face." She waited, staring at him. "Amos Cowley told me. Tonight. He said gunmen have come here before looking for you, but none as dangerous as Hawk."

"They're all dangerous. Any man with a gun in his hand is dangerous — the less he knows about it, the more dangerous. Still, I can't run because Amos Cowley thinks it might be a good idea."

"Stop, Bry. Amos has nothing to do with it. You've got to think about Maudie. You've no right to place yourself in this peril."

"No. No more right than I have to run from it."

Her fingers closed on his arm. "What foolish reason can you give yourself for facing a man like Hawk? It's not part of your job. He wants to prove he's a great gunman — and you've got to kill him, or let him kill you. His game. His rules. And you've nothing to gain — everything to lose."

His voice was dead. "Even if you're right, what else can I do?"

"What else? Get out of it while you're still alive. Get out of town."

He looked down at her. His voice was gentle. "Will you go with me, Ellen?"

She was silent a long time. He had no idea what she was thinking or remembering or what battle she was fighting within herself. At last she lifted her head. "Yes."

He felt the sharp surge of exultance. He caught her arms, pulled her against him. It felt good to laugh, good to have her close again.

But she held herself rigid. He sensed the chill. His voice was low. "Because you love me, Ellen? Or because you think you should try to save my life?"

"What difference does it make? I said I'd go."

He released her. She did not move. She

228

did not lift her gaze to meet his. "Wouldn't you think I was a coward, running away?"

"Why would I think you were a coward? I don't think anyone should face a man that has turned into a stalking animal."

"And it would never bother you that I ran away?"

"I would only think you a fool to face a killer when you don't have to."

"I was hired to protect the people of this town."

"You've done that, Bry. Nobody can say you haven't done that. This has nothing to do with your job."

"Still, I'll have to go on doing what I think is my job whether I like it or not — until it's not my job any more."

Her voice lashed at him. "Or until you're dead."

He closed his hands on her arms. "I love you, Ellen. I don't want to hurt you. When this is over — if you'll have me, I'll — try to find something else . . . though God knows what it would be."

"No." She pulled away. "I've heard your promises before. I won't be here, Bry. I'm sorry. Amos has asked me to marry him . . . and I have told him I would."

She stepped away from him but he caught her arm roughly and dragged her back, pulling her off balance so she toppled against him.

His arms slid about her, his hands huge against the small of her back. He held her helpless, pressed his mouth against hers until she stopped struggling. . . .

Abruptly, he released her. His voice was cold. "Marry him — and you'll lie in his bed remembering me."

He walked away from her, taking long strides toward the brightest lights of the saloons on Main Street.

TWENTY-FIVE

Bry Shafter had the sensation of walking toward a rushing avalanche, as though the sounds of the avalanche obscured all other sounds. He didn't know whether this was caused by the pounding of his heart and racing of his blood, or if the sounds were external as they seemed to be.

He paused near the Main Street Bar, for the moment feeling as though this was two years ago after midnight in Pony Wells.

There was the same sudden and concentrated kind of sounds. It was as if all bonds had suddenly burst. If he walked into the Main Street, he'd find Angelo drunk and gambling and armed with knives. Or if he

230

moved on to the Blue Dollar, the gunslicks would stand awaiting him, eyes watchful, mouths contemptuous, daring him to make his play.

Drunken men argued and shouted outside the Blue Dollar. It was as if all the violence Bry Shafter had kept tamped down for two years, controlled and beneath the surface had erupted.

Bry stepped off the walk, started across the street toward the saloon. This was nightmarish. There were more people on the walks and on the hotel veranda than ordinarily were out at seven in the evening. It was after midnight now, and some people he recognized as townfolk who'd gone to bed hours ago were now up, drawn to Main Street by some promised excitement.

It was like the recurring nightmare that brought him out of restless sleep.

These people were out here to see Bry Shafter driven away from Pony Wells. The trouble marshal had stayed too long. They no longer needed him, but did not know how to get rid of him. Tonight they had the answer.

Shafter shook this thought from his mind. This was a nightmare thought. Most of the people in this valley respected him for what he'd done; the ones who wanted him to

231

leave Pony Wells were the ones who'd profit by his going.

He could not escape the thought that the town was crowded and noisy; the people were drawn here for some reason that nobody bothered to explain to him.

He glanced over his shoulder toward the Home Style Cafe. Ellen stood near its door, watching him. Again he had the nightmare sense of her being there watching him, but at the same time beyond his reach, beyond the sound of his voice. If he shouted at her, she would no longer hear him.

He looked about. The streets were crowded, loud with people, but he was alone, more alone than he had been in all his life. They stared at him, and at the gun at his side and the gun made him different from them, a man apart, a different breed. They had tolerated him as long as they needed him; the need was gone, and he remained. But they withdrew from him, watching him standing alone in the noisy street.

The batwings of the Blue Dollar were thrust open and Flynn Hawk strode through. Shafter exhaled sharply. This was what brought people back to Main Street. His arms felt weak and a laxness numbed his hand as though he could not grip the butt of his gun.

He glared around, seeing the faces and forms withdrawn in darkness, standing in shadows of hotel veranda, the stores, watching. Perspiration broke out across his forehead. If he were to ask for help, they would laugh: they would as soon see him vanquished as killed. Either way they were rid of him.

"Shafter."

Hawk's voice was cold as night wind. It chilled him. "I'm telling you to draw, Shafter."

Shafter kept his gaze fixed on Flynn Hawk. The lean gunman came down the steps and paused on the boardwalk with the light at his back. Shafter was staring into the garish glare from the saloon, and stood illumined in its light with the night at his back. Everything favored Hawk. It was as though this were something prearranged.

Shafter raised his leaden arm to his side, knowing that even if he lived through this gunfight, he was through. His nerves and his heart would never stand this tension again. Whatever it was that had driven and sustained him through the last sixteen years as a trouble marshal was dried up and gone, the way a spring creek dries up and disappears.

It might even be better if Hawk killed him here in the street. What was left for him when he took off his gun? How would he make a living? Where would he go? What would he do?

He breathed deeply, holding it. He knew now what killed men in gunfights. It was not the man they faced, it was what was inside them, the worrying and tensions knotting their muscles and weakening their wills. The other gunman didn't need to be faster. All he needed was to have better nerves.

He spoke, keeping his voice level. "I told you to stay out of this town, Hawk."

"And I told you to draw."

Flynn's hand streaked toward the thonged-down holster. He watched with a terrible kind of fascination, knowing he had not reached for his gun. He had given his mind the order, but there was a block, it was not obeying. He heard a gasp that smoked through the crowded street, keenly aware of everything. He knew he was reaching for his gun but it was taking too long, he was moving in slow motion. He would never clear leather.

A gun cracked from the darkness at Shafter's right. There was the blurred flare of orange. Shafter stood with gun in hand.

He watched Hawk step back under the impact of the bullet. Hawk stumbled backward. He dropped the gun and closed his hands over the bullet hole in his chest. His knees sagged, buckled, and he fell.

The people ran out from the shadows, walked down from the hotel veranda and stared at the man crumpled on the street. His mouth stretched back in a grimace from his teeth.

Zach stepped up beside Shafter, replacing his gun. "It's all right, old man," Zach said.

He heard the murmur of people near them. Young Zach Adams had stepped in in time to kill the gunman. If it had not been for Zach, the marshal would be dead.

Ellen ran across the street, hand pressed against her throat. She stood behind Shafter, staring up at him, unmoving.

Shafter's voice was low. "Why did you do it, Zach?"

Zach smiled. "Somebody had to, old fellow. Why let a gunslinger kill you?"

"It was my fight."

There was the sharp sound of protest from people near them. They spoke aloud. Some said the marshal didn't know how fortunate he was to be alive, he had no gratitude toward the man who'd saved his life.

Shafter was aware that Amos Cowley had

walked out into the street from the hotel veranda. Cowley walked close to Ellen, put his arm about her. He spoke to her, something Shafter could not hear above the muttering and talking about him. Ellen nodded, looked toward Shafter one more time. She walked away into the darkness with Cowley's arm about her. The night wind was colder than ever, raw cold.

Shafter pulled his gaze back to Dr. Gaines who knelt beside Flynn Hawk. Gaines glanced meaningfully at Shafter, then spoke loudly. "This man is dead. Second shooting tonight, Marshal."

Shafter forced himself to speak. "That so, Doctor? Who is the other one?"

"Poor Albert Tishkin. He fared better than this one. Staggered into my kitchen with a bullet in him. At least, he's still alive."

TWENTY-SIX

Shafter walked beside Dr. Gaines toward the doctor's house. At the Main Street Bar, they paused, glanced back at the crowd.

Shafter said, "Thanks, Doc."

"It's all right. Least I could do. You still got to face him."

"Yes."

"Are you all right, Bry?"

"Just getting old. I froze tonight, Doc. It was like being scared in the guts. I didn't want to kill that man. I didn't want to be killed."

Gaines shrugged. "I'd say it's a kind of hangover, Bry. You've been a marshal a long time. You've had to use your gun, whether you wanted to or not. It's caught up with you."

"A hellish time for it to happen."

Gaines shook his head. "We can't tell our nerves when to go bad, or our conscience when it is convenient to paralyze our will. I don't know how it happens, Shafter, just that it does. I suppose it's a kind of compensation. A man cannot go on doing what he innately feels is wrong forever without paying for it. Perhaps in my own brilliant way I have just explained sin and atonement to you."

Shafter wiped sweat from his face. "This is my job, Doc."

"Then you better change jobs."

"You know better than that."

"I'm not telling you what to do. I'm only telling you what to do if you want to stay alive. . . . Come in and have a drink with me."

"I can't."

"Sometimes one drink is better than two pills."

"I've got to get to your place. He'll be looking for Albert, if he was there and heard what you said about him being alive."

"You better give Zach that job."

"No. I'm going down to your place. You better stay away for a while, Doc."

"And if you freeze up again when the killer gets there?"

"Make 'em shave me before they bury me, Doc."

The doctor entered the lighted bar. Shafter walked down the street and then hurried around the block, entering the doctor's yard from the rear as he had carried in Albert's body earlier.

Inside the house, he placed a chair in the darkness, sat down to wait with his gun on his lap. He pushed the chair back on two legs, pressed his head against the wall. Through his mind passed lazy pictures of his life, and then tantalizing scenes of what might be. The way it would be to turn in this star and work around the cafe. What could he do? Learn to cook? Make change? Loiter around telling people the way it had been when he was a trouble marshal? He shivered. He could walk down to the depot, board the train and arrive one day in a town called Gravehead. He would not live long. He had that premonition, because from this moment forward, he would never kill any man without that increasing sickness, that moment of paralysis. He did not know what he would do. He stared about in the darkness, thinking he would decide that in the daylight, there were still hours of darkness, and somehow he had to ride them out.

"Albert."

The word was a sharp whisper from the darkness of the front room. Shafter's heart constricted. His hand closed on the gun. Someone had entered the house and he had not heard him.

"Albert — do you hear me, Albert?"

Bry let the chair down easily. Even so, there was the click as legs touched flooring. He heard sharp intake of breath from the other room.

Bry spoke loudly, holding the gun leveled, waiting. "No, Zach. It's me."

There was a long space of stillness, a breathless time. At last Zach spoke. "Where is Albert, Bry?"

"He's dead, Zach."

Zach caught his breath. At last he spoke. "You conned me, Shafter."

"Yes."

"I got nobody to blame. I fell for it."

"Yes."

"What you plan to do, Shafter?"

"That's up to you, Zach. You want to throw your gun in here, quiet, I'll take you to jail."

"You know I couldn't do that, Bry."

"No. I didn't figure you'd want to."

"You knew it was going to be me?"

"It had to be, Zach. Somebody close to me who was playing around with Glory so people thought I knew about it. You wanted to be sheriff. You wanted to marry Pike Vance's daughter. Glory was in your way. Tried to scare her out of town, and when she wouldn't go . . . You wanted to be sheriff pretty bad, Zach."

"I still do."

"No, Zach. It's all over. This town ain't going to be the way you and Shad want it. I'm sick of deals. It's going to be a clean town."

"I could have let you lay dead on Main Street, Shafter. Don't forget that."

"No. I ain't forgetting. You were telling me and the town you'd saved my life, and I ought to move on to Gravehead."

"It's a fact, Shafter. Nobody but you knows about this. I hate it all to hell. But you ain't going to tell nobody. I hate this, Bry. I really got a feeling for you. But when it's you or me. . . ."

"You better draw, Zach."

"I'm ready, old fellow. I got you. Over there against the wall in the dark. I followed your voice. If you reach for your gun, you're dead. Get smart. Go on to Gravehead. Nobody's hurt but a moron named Tishkin and a tramp named Gloria Hogarty."

"I ain't going, Zach."

"Then draw."

"My gun is waiting, boy. There are a lot of tricks better than being fast on the draw."

He heard Zach's sharp inhalation. He heard the whisper of movement, saw the flicker of shadow as Zach moved across the doorway. At the precise instant the shadow was framed squarely, Shafter pressed the trigger, fired. Zach was still moving and his gun blazed an instant later. The bullet struck the wall where Shafter would have been if he'd been standing.

The shadow was gone from the doorway and Shafter stood up slowly.

He stood there waiting. Sweat oozed from his pores in single cold droplets and slid along his ribs.

He said, "Zach."

There was another silence and then the sound of a chair scraping the floor, of thighs striking, and then the sound of metal against wood.

Shafter kept to the shadows, moved around the room, paused at the doorway.

He stepped out into it. Zach was on the floor in a patch of the first dawn through an east window. Zach was twisted, legs up under him, an arm crushed against the pain in him, and then Shafter saw the gun in Zach's hand, upraised, waiting. Zach's face was rutted with the effort of raising the gun.

Outside in the dawn, Shafter heard the townspeople running toward the sound of gunfire in Doc Gaines' house. He stared at Zach, saw the gun tilt. He raised his own, fired.

The gun toppled from Zach's fist and Zach fell forward, his body stretching tall and straight.

The front door was thrown open and Dr. Gaines hurried in. He stared at Zach.

"My God, Bry. It's Zach. You've killed young Adams."

Shafter knew the agony showed in his eyes. He felt his mouth tighten. He shoved the gun back in its holster, knowing suddenly why he used it; he killed because he had to, because of the times and his job; it was what he had to do, and he was free again. He could go where he wanted to, he could make of his life whatever he wanted. He was not a breed apart, a man alone. He was a man who had faithfully done his job, right to the end. He glanced toward Zach's body stretched long in the dawn-light, felt an ache of hurt and pity. He dragged in a deep breath, tried to shrug it off. He was the marshal at Pony Wells and this was his job.

He did not look at the doctor.

"Yes," he said. "Somebody had to do it."

The doctor nodded, understanding. But Bry Shafter did not glance at him again. He walked out of the house and down the steps through the growing crowd, watching the bright place where the sun was just coming up over the roof of the Home Style Cafe.

CROSS THE RED CREEK

BY HARRY WHITTINGTON

CROSS THE
RED CREEK

BY HARRY WHITTINGTON

ONE

He heard the fast-riding horsemen some minutes before he saw them, as he remained hunkered close over his greasewood fire, too numbed with cold and his own woes to worry about riders who were no concern of his, but reading frantic urgency in the pound of hoofs, and thinking, *Trouble for somebody.*

Trouble for somebody. He shivered. He was riding away from trouble as steadily as his tired mount could carry him, and out in the darkness somebody else was racing toward it.

He had come west out of the hills, feeling the chill of winter at his back as he picked his way through a piñon copse and crossed this creek an hour before dusk.

He waded the gray cautiously because the country and creek were strange to him. Yet, it wasn't really strange. He'd herded cattle once through Kiowa Valley, more than ten years ago when he was a teenager working for Will Allbrand.

He looked about, thinking what a lovely fertile valley it was, and the way its beauty had stuck in his mind all these years. And four days ago when he'd climbed into his saddle at Winter Sage, he'd headed the gray this way after all these years, not even admitting aloud at the time where he was going.

Emerging from the creek through a sorry clump of willows in thick, orange clay banks, he'd made night camp.

The testy chattering of a blue jay down the creek bed had cut into his consciousness through the layers of weariness, and for some reason he could not name, he had grown wary enough to stake the gray across the creek in the piñon, wade back, build a small fire, and hunker over it shivering.

He felt cold clawing like a lynx at his neck out of the jagged, purple shadows of the foothills behind him. Up and over the hogbacks, higher peaks cast long shadows, enveloping him and darkening the sweet-cactus and sage-dotted alkali flats below.

He'd stayed hugging the fire longer than made good sense. But the chill inside wouldn't release him; it was in his bone marrow, and with darkness came the sense of uneasiness. And though he tried to tell himself it was just that he was saddle tired and worried about Eualie alone back at Winter Sage, he couldn't shake either the cold or the sense of wrong.

He gave up hoping the fire would ever warm him, and stood up, a winter-lean man over six-feet tall and baked leather-dark, fur-collared jacket streaked gray with alkali, battered Stetson torn at the crown. When he stood up, his much-washed salt-gray levis peeled from his flesh, sweat-stained and stiff.

He got his saddle blanket, returned to the fire and crouched over it again, thinking he should make coffee and eat the last of his biscuits. His stomach growled with hunger, but he spread his hands over the flame and did nothing about fixing another meal that hadn't been appetizing four days ago.

Yawning with weariness, he sagged to the ground, placed two branches across the fire, and worked off his boots, upending them and emptying soiled creek water.

Heating his toes at the fire, he wriggled the ones showing through woolen socks, and whispered aloud, "Don't fret, Eualie, it's going to work out. This time I'm going to make it work."

Then he told himself he was crazy to be

here at all like this, damp and chilled with cold, a hundred miles from Eualie, looking for something he'd never found even among his neighbors back at Winter Sage.

He yawned again, knowing he wouldn't sleep, worrying the way he was about Eualie. Lean, sweated, unshaven, he crossed the blanket on his arms over his chest.

Now, with the fire crackling, chewing on the new wood, he heard the pound of hooves, and remembered the cry of the jay, and the premonition of wrong he'd been too tired to investigate.

Knowing his fire could be seen for miles from this shelf on the hillside, he sat tense, listening to the thunder of the hooves in the earth, hoping they wouldn't come near. He was too tired to talk to anybody.

He waited a long time, and the hoofbeats died away — maybe disappearing too abruptly, but his senses were dulled by fatigue. And he did not care. He thought, *Whoever it is that's got trouble, I don't need it. I got enough for all of us.*

The silence settled in heavy again, spreading with the darkness. He felt his toes growing warm at the rim of the fire, and he counted them, grinning tautly, pleased that he could feel even this faint stirring of warmth and life in him again.

Fire flung feeble yellow shafts across his lean face. He pushed his feet against the near side of warming stones and let his mind slide again to Eualie and his ranch back in the Winter Sage country.

"I'm going to find us a new place to live, Eualie," he had told her, thinking maybe it would be better for them, maybe over another hill, across the next creek. God knew, it couldn't be any worse, the way the people he'd counted as friends had started their lies and gossip about Eualie.

Jim felt a chill wrack him in his loins, a tremor that had nothing to do with cold. Sure, it was lies. Gossip. But what could you say to people who whispered behind your back, about your wife because she was pretty and young, people you'd known always?

He heard a twig break in the darkness, and he rolled on his side, glancing around, but still too cold and tired to do anything else.

After a moment, he breathed again, feeling the anger and the hurt because of the way things were back at Winter Sage. Ranch going down through no fault of his. Needing medicine for the stock, a new hay-cutter, hell, even food for the pantry. And what could you do about those ugly whispers that seemed grounded nowhere, yet wouldn't stop?

"You wait, Eualie," he had said. "I'll find a place where we can start over, on our own, depending on nobody — and away from these liars."

A few yards down creek from him, a horse whickered, disturbed.

Jim sat bolt upright, half-drugged with sleep, and began pulling on his steaming, soggy boots.

He tried to tell himself he was edgy, drawn fine with cold and hunger, jumping at shadows, but he knew better. *Something was wrong, bad wrong, and it made it worse, not knowing what it was in this strange dark country.*

"You got to take a look-see," he told himself aloud, thinking this showed how crazy-tired and lonely he was, talking to himself. But suddenly he liked the sound of his own voice in this dark silence, and if he could have thought of anything else to say, he would have said it.

Only there were no words for what he suddenly feared.

Not even waiting to get boots on, he shrugged off the blanket and moved to stand up.

But he was already too late.

They were ringed around him before he could get up, before he could reach for his gun. His firelight winked at them, barely touching their set, cold faces.

Eyes blinking, Jim sank back on the clay and stared up at them, a silent, tight ring of men trailing their mounts, slack-reined. He didn't know how many of them there were, but he knew it didn't matter; they were trouble, and trouble had trailed him west down out of the hills and caught him, just across this creek, somewhere in the Kiowa Valley, a land so beautiful a man could remember it for ten long years.

Two

Still pulling at his heat-shrunken boot, Jim watched the man nearest him, watched the thin firelight winking on a badge.

"What you fellows want?" Jim said. "You'll have to step closer, gents, to share my fire."

He was thinking with cold agony that the words were fine, but his stomach was tied in knots that shook his voice.

Presently the man with the badge stepped closer, and Jim Gilmore, still struggling with his boot, held his breath, waiting. In moving, the big man kicked a clump of clay into Jim's fire and it sputtered wetly, smoking.

Jim watched the quivering fire and its smoke a moment, then returned his gaze to the gun the lawman carried in the crook of his arm.

"What's your name?" the lawman asked, cold eyes suspicious under thick brows. He was a medium-height man, thick in belly, chest, shoulders, and head. At least, Jim felt he read this in the slow way the heavy-set man spoke. He was a dangerous man because he did think slowly and distrusted abrupt movement around him. He was a man who would kill once his mind condemned; once he made up his mind, it was slow and hard to change him.

His gaze moved in that slow-plodding way across Jim, and then he glanced over his shoulder at his posse, and they stepped closer into the light.

Waiting for Jim to answer him, the lawman worked his animal closer to where Jim was sprawled. Jim saw that the sorrel was lathered, slobbering with fatigue. A man as heavy as this law officer could ride even a big animal to death.

"I ask you. Civil," the lawman said, angered when Jim continued working with his boot, watching him. "What's your name? Make up your mind. Talk while you can."

Jim worked his foot into one boot and

stood up, still holding the other one. Jim spoke tiredly after a second bitter pause, "What's the idea, mister?"

The lawman stepped forward abruptly, tired as his lathered horse, his patience gone. He pushed Jim around hard, hand thrust against Jim's shoulder.

With abrupt savagery, Jim batted the hand down with the heel of the boot he still held in his band.

He heard the intake of breath around him. The posse stirred nervously, glancing at each other.

"Where is it?" the sheriff said.

For a moment he and Jim stared at each other, the incredible rage in the sheriff's face slamming against the bitter weariness in Jim's.

The posse remained, unmoving, waiting.

Dropping his boot, Jim worked his foot into it.

Catching him unbalanced, the sheriff drove his leather-gloved fist into Jim's face. For a stout man, the lawman moved fast, and anyhow Jim was off balance, waltzing into that boot.

Jim sprawled out backward, stumbling and falling across the fire, toppling heavily into the clay beyond it. Some of the horses pranced, disturbed, but the men didn't move, watching him.

The sheriff, across the small fire now, leveled the rifle at Jim's belly.

Too sickly angered and too despairingly tired to get up, Jim raised himself to his elbows, hat gone, lank dark hair falling over his forehead. His mouth pulled in bitter disgust.

"Where is it?" the sheriff said again.

'Where is what?"

"I done told you, boy. You best talk while you can." Jim stared up at the sheriff, seeing the impatience — the rage in the stranger. It burned hot, seething in his eyes and face.

"All right," Jim said after a long wait. "What is it I have done to you fellows?"

Some of the men in the posse growled, but the sheriff jerked his head, silencing them. The fat-bellied lawman was boss here; he would handle this.

"We tailed you all day," the sheriff said. "None of us is in any mood to fool with you. You robbed the bank at Kiowa City last night." He exhaled, as if he were a just man, willing to give even a criminal a break if it was possible. "Turn that money over to us, and might be I can keep these here men from hanging you."

"You hang people here — for bank-robbing?"

Somebody laughed coldly. "You oughta asked around before you tried it."

But the sheriff gestured downward sharply. "Not for bank-robbing. And you know it, just like you know you robbed that bank. What they been talking rope-tying you for is for murdering poor Ed Keller."

Jim shook his head slowly. "I don't know any Ed Keller. I don't know you people. I didn't rob your bank."

"Look, mister!" The sheriff's voice rasped, his store of patience abruptly exhausted. "I'm telling you. We been trailing you all day. You. I been trying to tell you. You cooperate with me — maybe I can talk these men out of hanging you — until after your trial."

Jim moved his head again from one side to the other, "My name is Jim Gilmore, mister. I didn't rob your bank."

There was just a shred of restraint in the sheriff's voice, "You want to git hung? That it? We trailed you all day."

Jim saw there was little chance of convincing this sheriff of anything. It was already too late for that. The sheriff had made up his mind. Chances were, there was nothing he could say to any of these other tired men, either.

He moved his gaze, looking at those men, trying to find one among them who might believe him. He didn't find one.

He said. "Not me. You didn't trail me. Kiowa City is west of here. Right?"

"Like you know," the sheriff said.

Jim licked his mouth. "I crossed this creek at dusk, heading that way." He lifted his arm, gesturing toward the valley lost in the black night below them. "Your man has given you the slip, mister."

He got up slowly, anger pulling his mouth down. He moved his gaze across their faces, a hot resentment burning in him. He'd said just about what they'd expected him to say, and they were just waiting anyhow for him to speak his piece before they hung him. They didn't care what he said; their minds were closed against him, and they barely listened.

He brought his gaze back across their set faces. He saw he had kicked his fire to pieces when he fell across it. True, it hadn't been much of a fire, but he thought in rage, *they had no right, coming in on a man like this.*

"I didn't do it," he said again, but there was nothing in his voice now but helpless rage.

The sheriff laughed at him, something

258

ugly and final about the sound. As far as the sheriff was concerned, he had led a successful hunt. A bank had been robbed; evidently some bank clerk, somebody named Ed Keller, had been killed, and they'd ridden hard and relentlessly all day. Jim saw he'd already been tried and convicted. Months later, perhaps, when they learned his true identity and their own mistake, they would be sorry, but it would be too late then. *Maybe it was already too late,* he thought.

It seemed to him that against the fact that they were convinced of his guilt was the other fact that he didn't have the stolen money on him. This didn't rouse any hope in him. He was grimly aware that they would search for the money before they hung him, but not finding it would fan their tempers, not soothe them.

The sheriff stepped across the broken-backed fire, close to Jim Gilmore. "Where is that money?"

"I don't know. I didn't get it."

He saw the thick fist coming this time and slapped it aside with his left hand.

Before a member of the tired posse could react, Jim drove his own right fist straight and short and hard into the sheriff's face, feeling the shock of it all the way to his elbow.

They gasped, seeing the sheriff's legs buckle, and they paused one instant and then lunged toward him.

Jim heeled around in the clay. For a moment he stared at the tilted bank, slanted downward toward that creek in the black dark. The first hands grabbed for him as he sprang for the sluice ramp. The hands missed him and he was gone. Slipping and sliding, he ran along the bank, one boot splashing in the creek.

Running, he tried to place in his mind the exact spot where he'd staked the gray to graze. A pistol cracked behind him, and he crouched lower in the darkness, hearing the sharp, sickening whistle of lead.

THREE

The posse was like a crazed animal flailing out in the darkness behind Jim Gilmore.

Running, he heard the men shouting and other men firing their rifles at shadows. Then the sheriff recovered his senses enough to pull all those writhing arms together. In the night, his voice throbbed with fury and frustration, but at the same time, he was a man taking control. Like every slow-witted man, the sheriff would despise ridicule, and the fact that he'd had his hands on this man and let him get away would gall him for months to come. It was something that maybe he would never forget, and it would make him frantic to find the fugitive now.

"Stop all that shooting before you kill each other!" the sheriff yelled, and the shooting stopped. And then he was yelling orders at them, spreading them thin in the darkness, fanning them out so that they could run Jim Gilmore down in the timber. "And no more shooting!" he yelled. "Not till you know what you're shooting at."

Jim Gilmore struck across the creek without slowing down. Unless the creak of their own saddle-leather, their own movements, covered the sound of his splashing across the creek, they would hear him. It did not matter; they knew he was out here, but maybe they hadn't located the gray.

He heard his mustang whicker, fretting, and he ran toward it, arms outstretched.

There was no time for his saddle, no chance to get the rifle from its scabbard. He caught up the lines and the ground-tied little quarter horse lunged away from him. The gray threw its head high, spooked, eyes distended. It skittered away as Jim flung himself across its bare back.

Fighting the lines across the pony's mane, Jim listened in the darkness. The posse was silent, with deadly silence, not speaking and not shooting any more. They were fanned out on the sheriff's orders, pursuing him, guns held ready but wary now of shooting each other.

He touched his heels to his tired animal's flanks. The gray quivered, moving uncertainly in the thick piñon grove. He rode cautiously, knowing his chance of survival was gone now that he'd hit that sheriff. It had been bad enough before — hopeless — but now they'd swarm over him and hang him, guilty or innocent, money recovered or not.

He set the small horse moving upslope, climbing toward the rocky foothills. This was his pursuers' country; they knew it a lot better than he did, and his only chance to survive was to get out of it, going back the way he'd come, from the wintry plateaus and ranges-lost-in-ranges above him.

He was jarred, riding bareback, clinging to the horse, knowing that if he was thrown he'd lose the horse in the dark. His mount was tired and frightened, ready to bolt. Well, he'd existed a hell of a lot of years without much to go on — and up to now, he'd stayed alive.

Up to now, he thought, clinging to the horse.

He felt the bright bursting flare of rage that told him he wasn't going to make it this time. Bareback, cold, and lost in this alien country, surrounded by armed men who wanted him dead — he'd had it.

After this first crazed moment of realization, he felt a sudden exultance. It was all over. He had gone as far as he could go. The hills were thick with gun-bearing lawmen and the trap was closing on him. It was just a matter of when it would snap.

All right, so it was over. It had been crazy from the start, running away from something; now he was running away from something else. He had fought and tried as long as he could, and now it was over. *Damn it. Eualie. I'm sorry, but it's done.*

A rifle cracked suddenly in the darkness behind him and he thrust his boots into the gray, spurring her onward, even when he had no hope left at all.

The gray lurched forward with Jim fighting to hang on. Fighting to hang on. Hell, that was all you ever did, wasn't it?

When the wail of gunfire had echoed and bounced around in the hills and died, the silence was deeper than ever. But it had started Jim moving again, and as long as he was moving he was alive, and the hell with them.

He pushed upward through the screening growth of timber, thankful he was leaving no easy trail for his pursuers in the thick carpet of pine needles.

He heard the labored breathing of the gray and knew time was running out for both of them. It had been an endless day moving west, and the quarter horse was game, but he was beat. They both were.

Pulling the mustang around through a stunted clump of tamarack, he slid off, landing silently on the rocky ground.

The gray was blowing, spooked up and nervous, trembling with exhaustion. It seemed to him that anyone listening could hear the horse's labored breathing ten miles below in the valley.

He stayed close to her, and gradually felt her gentle and quiet under his arm.

Clenching his teeth together to force himself to breathe through his nose, he sagged against the pony, trying to pick out the sound of the nearest hunters off in the timber.

A dislodged rock was loud in the dark. There was the muffled whisper of cursing, and then there was silence, and tension in the cold night wind.

Jim stayed where he was, knowing both he and his horse had to rest. If they found him here that was too bad; he would face that when it came. If they came upon him suddenly, he would fight as long as he could breathe. He did not mean to hang for something he had not done.

He closed his fist on the butt of his gun, waiting.

He stared through the darkness, thinking with fierce bitterness how loco he'd been to believe a new place would be better. That was the king of all fool ideas, and he knew that now, because as bad as things were at Winter Sage, he was a stranger here in this strange country, and these men hunting him meant to hang him.

As if to blur out what was happening in the darkness as the posse closed in on him, Jim's mind leaped away to a moment almost as bitter, that day in Will Allbrand's office at the National Bank in Winter Sage.

"Hell," he had said to Will Allbrand, "I know those stories about Eualie. All of them are lies, but lies hurt a girl like Eualie."

"She's got to be strong. She's got to stand up to them. You can't let a liar hurt you, Jim. You got to tell Eualie that."

Jim clenched his fists against the trembling. "Yeah. Tell me more about not letting lies hurt you. She can't go on living among them, Will, the way they are treating her. She says they act like she's a bad woman — and not fit to associate with them that's good women."

"Good women being the ones that peddle lies about her?" Will Allbrand asked with some irony.

"That's what I tried to tell Eualie. But she's sick about it. Don't want to go to church. She's convinced she's bad."

Will Allbrand shook his head. "You got to understand, Jim. Women are no different out here in Wyoming than they are back east. Men treat them special out here — like they was different — because females are so scarce out here. Pretty ones like Eualie are downright rare. But a woman that's shallow and empty here in Wyoming would be shallow and empty in New York, say. That's why you got nothing to worry about Eualie — she's a good, strong girl. When this bad time is past, she'll be all right."

"No." Jim shook his head. "I'm moving on. Things are as bad at the ranch as can be. I could face that. And the debts I've got with you —"

"What's a friend for?" Will Allbrand said. Jim watched the big man chewing on his expensive cigar.

Jim trembled, hungry for a smoke, but no longer willing to accept any more charity from Allbrand or anybody else. "I'm tired depending on people," Jim said, raging suddenly. "I'm going to sell out my ranch. You said you had a buyer. Cough him up, Will, I'm moving on."

"I don't want to see you do that, Jim. Screw worms and drought. That happens to the best of men. Your trouble at the ranch ain't your fault. Hang on. You'll make it."

"No, I made up my mind. I'm going to find a new place. I don't rightly know just where yet, but it's going to be where Eualie and I can be happy."

And now he was here, crouching hidden in shadows on the side of a winter hill, hunted and lost.

He raised himself slightly, trying to think ahead. He couldn't go on sitting here while the circle of men closed in on him.

He studied the steadily rising slope of rocky land above him, thinking that he could find a place to hide among the boulders that wouldn't dissolve when the sun came up.

He glanced upward, checking the stars, cold and sharp in the deep night sky. He had no idea what time it was. Perhaps only minutes had passed, maybe hours.

He turned again, slowly, and the horse-man was almost at his back before Jim was aware of him, or the rider knew he was walking over the fugitive.

He heard the boy's sharp intake of breath.

For one hellish moment, they stared at each other. The youth on the horse threw back his head to yowl, and Jim sprang at him like a panther.

FOUR

Jim landed high, thrusting his cupped hand outward toward the youth's opened mouth.

He struck against the rider, dragging him from his saddle. The horse skittered away, whinnying.

From the darkness somebody yelled, "Kip. You over there, Kip?"

Jim felt the breath explode from both himself and the youth who struck the stones beneath him. He clamped his hand hard over the boy's mouth, digging fingers into his cheeks, pressing as if to crush the face in his fist.

"Kip?" The man off to the left yelled again, farther away now, but troubled.

The youth on the ground reared upward, putting all his muscle into his lower legs and hips. Jim clipped him hard and put his arm across his throat, pressing his head back. The boy sucked breath through Jim's clenched fingers.

"Hate to do this, kid," Jim whispered close against the boyish face. "But you can yell me into a noose just as fast as a grown man."

The youth's distended eyes worked. Jim had cut off his oxygen supply; he was suffocating, but inside him he was yelling his head off.

"Listen to me." Jim's mouth was taut, hard with the bitterness spilling out of him. "I ain't stole money, see. I ain't killed anybody."

The boy fought him, trying to work free.

Jim cursed him. "I don't want to have to kill you. But if I have to to save my neck, I will."

The boy lunged around, trying to work free, jerking his head and not even caring that he was striking the stones every time he moved.

"Damn you," Jim said. "Stay where you are. I don't want to have to kill you."

He pulled away and when the boy turned, drove his fist short and direct against his jaw. He felt the youth's body go lax beneath him. The boy's head sagged back, roiling against the small stones. He was out cold.

Poised, waiting, taking no chances and

trusting nobody, Jim watched for signs that the kid was faking. The youth didn't move. Breathing shallowly, Jim released him and got to his feet.

In the rock pasture above him, rocks were loosed and rolled in an avalanche past him. There was somebody above him, but in the darkness Jim could see nothing.

He could no longer stay where he was. He loosed the cinch, jerked the saddle off the youth's horse. It wasn't even in his mind, yet he was taking the saddle rather than the horse for two reasons: he hadn't committed any crime yet, and anyway he trusted his own gray, tired as she was, over any strange mount.

He whispered to the gray, laying blanket and saddle across her back. She stirred, nervous as a coot nestling, and he stroked her neck, barely daring to breathe.

He removed the unconscious deputy's gun, thinking wearily he was making things worse at every turn. He was a stranger, accused of murder; he had slugged a sheriff and fled. Now he was robbing an unconscious deputy.

"Hell," he said, whispering it. "But I'm still alive."

He swung into the saddle, breathing deeply of the cold night air just to prove he

270

was alive. The saddle leather creaked under him, and he thought it was going to be easier to ride fast when the moment came for it.

There was a canteen of water thonged to the saddle, and Jim drank thirstily. It was good, sweet water, with no trace of alkali. *Good water from a good land,* he thought bitterly.

"Good or bad, they don't want you here," he told himself and headed the gray east and into the hills for no better reason than that Winter Sage and home lay that way — across a hundred endless Wyoming miles.

He glanced once more at the unconscious deputy sprawled on the ground and moved on through the rocks.

He had gone less than twenty feet when the rock slide started above him, and he reined in hard and jerked his gun free from its holster.

"Ceal?" A tense, frightened voice yelled from above Jim. "Ceal Sistrunk!" The voice was frantic now. "That you, Ceal?"

Jim put the boots to the gray, angling away from the frantic voice and the rolling pebbles, and shouted across his shoulder, "Yeah."

"Don't sound like —" and then there was the breathless silence as the roan caught on.

Suddenly he was yelling in a voice that carried and reverberated through the hills, "Hey! It's him! I found him!"

From the rocks above Jim, a rifle cracked. He jerked the gray around, springing from the saddle, and running with her downward in the darkness.

The man above him was yelling like a Ute. "He's heading down hill. Heading down hill."

A rifle from below Jim spoke now, snapping in the darkness, bullets whistling.

Jim pulled up, spooked pony nuzzling at his back. The rifle above him cracked, and the one below was like its echo.

Now another rifle blazed far below Jim, winking like a firefly in the dark.

Crouching, jerking the gray's head down, Jim turned once more, angling upward, still moving away from the crossfire.

From the darkness, a man screamed, the sound ripped out of him. Somebody had creased one of his possemen, and from far off, the sheriff was yelling to cut out that damned shooting, and others took it up, like bounds baying the moon across a hillside.

Listening to them, mouth taut and cold, Jim pulled into the saddle and started riding upward in the chilled night, leaving the sounds of the posse behind him.

Suddenly he knew this was good. *Funny thing about traps, he thought, once one of them snaps, if it doesn't close on you, you can get away from it.*

He lifted his head, breathing the good winter chill, good because it was free open air above him, and he could keep riding over this hill, and the next hill, and keep riding and they would never overtake him now.

The last shout of the posse reached him, a distant sound in the night. Touching the pony with his heels he urged her upward, sending her faster into the hills.

FIVE

In the breathless morning heat of the settlement, Isabel Bowne watched Stan Mills come toward her chair in the crowded lobby of the Kiowa Hotel.

Until the moment his searching gaze had found her in the room full of women, old men, and children, she had been depressed, feeling more than ever the sense of being caged.

Sighing, she hid her inner excitement from the people around her. A bosomy, honey-blonde girl with wide, artless eyes, she had learned that the settlement of Kiowa City had created an "image" of her. It angered, and flattered her at the same time. In the eyes of the settlement, she was the embodiment of fresh, young purity; she had been their schoolteacher, and though she no longer taught the school, she was treated — by the roughest men — as something special.

She knotted her fists in the lap of her gingham dress. These people had put her on a pedestal, and she despised being there almost as much as she hated living in Kiowa City.

She felt stifled! She was only twenty-one years old, and she was pretty, she wanted the fun that belonged to a lovely girl of her age. But instead, she had to behave as if butter wouldn't melt in her mouth!

She stared through the wide double window in the lobby front. From here she could see the whole length of Kiowa City's main Street. It was depressing, and boring, and ugly — the frazzled end of the world. A town set down for no good reason in a ranching valley in western Wyoming. Western Wyoming — God knew you couldn't get much closer to nowhere than this.

Earlier this morning she had walked along the main street, joining the tide of people flowing toward the Kiowa Hotel to await news of the posse. There was so little to see — the livery stable, the general store and post office, the tall false front of Stan Mills' Bright Star saloon.

She felt her mouth pull. Sure, there was life and excitement and toe-tapping piano music over there, but the town would be scandalized at the thought of her entering such a place. Not that she hadn't thought about it, plenty, lying alone on her bed in the afternoons. In the lazy silence, she could see herself being toasted, and courted, and danced with — and kissed — by those men who had all the fun at the Bright Star. And the ultimate excitement was the idea of being in Stan Mills' arms, being held close, closer, tight, tighter — until she couldn't breathe, until the way he held her hurt her, and still she didn't want him to stop.

Feeling her face grow faintly warm with rising blood, Isabel shook this thought from her mind, surveying the hot, mid-morning street out there — this stultifying village that was her cage. There was the frame house that Dr. Knoblock now used as living quarters and office, and next to it the similarly constructed frame cottage that Rosemary Meade had converted into a restaurant. There were a few more buildings, the bank, the county building where court was held and elections executed and where the sheriff had his office with the jail in the rear. There was the stage-coach office, because naturally, Kiowa City was eighty miles north of the Union Pacific railroad and the stage was the only connecting link.

She stirred, restless and impatient with this world of hers that was like a cell in Sheriff Walker's jail.

Now, watching Stan Mills walk toward her, she felt she would have died of boredom if it had not been for Stan Mills.

She tipped her tongue across her mouth. Of course, there was nothing between them — except the vibrant charge of static electricity that shot through her every time he was near. But knowing there was a man like Stan Mills in this town made it somehow more bearable for her.

A woman near Isabel said, "I think the posse is coming in."

Another woman said, sighing with her relief, "I pray so. I've been waiting here since three o'clock this morning. I do pray they've come back safe, don't you, Isabel?"

Secretly swearing inside, where she had learned to swear so that the townspeople would never suspect, Isabel answered the woman in the saccharine tone they'd come to demand of her. "Oh, I've been praying constantly."

The woman patted her hand, smiling at her, eyes brimmed with abrupt tears. "Don't worry, Angel. Your Kip is all right."

"Thank you," Isabel said, glancing once more at Stan Mills, pushing his way through the throng of women toward her, then casting her eyes demurely downward.

Some of the children ran out of the hotel veranda, and the women followed. There was a tense feeling of expectancy in the air. A thirteen-year-old youth, riding a mule, had ridden in from the west road.

"I seen the dust!" the boy yelled. "Won't be more'n a few minutes. They'll be back in here."

"Some excitement," Stan Mills said.

Isabel glanced up, not daring to smile as Stan Mills bowed over her. She was thinking, *A posse coming home from a foot hunt, and that is the most excitement in months.* Aloud she said, "It was a terrible thing — about Mr. Ed Keller."

"Yes, wasn't it?" There was no more interest in Stan Mills' voice than there was in her own heart.

Her head jerked up suddenly. She was afraid he was laughing at her, but his face was calm, with just the correct touch of sadness. She felt suddenly like laughing.

She wanted to giggle at him, tell him what she knew to be the truth: Stan Mills didn't care about the posse, or Ed Keller, or the bank, or the money, or any of the rest of it. No more than she did.

But she lowered her eyes, feeling that burst of static excitement in her that Stan Mills always aroused. He was in his early thirties, but seemed younger to her. Most men in their thirties seemed ancient, over-worked, over-married, overage to Isabel, but not Stan Mills. Stan was just right, hand-some in the tailored wool suit that he had bought in Cheyenne and that heightened the muscled bulge of his chest, the width of his shoulders.

"I rode out with the posse," he said to her. "But when it degenerated into a purpose-less ride — like a dog chasing its own tail — I gave it up."

She glanced at him, thinking that if he'd returned tired and saddle-weary from night riding, shower, shave and fresh clothing in his suite over his Bright Star saloon had erased all traces.

"Don't you believe they'll find the man that robbed that bank, Mr. Mills?" she asked.

"Do you?" he inquired.

His question caught her off guard. It was so direct, so full of laughing contempt, she had to bite her under-lip to keep from smiling.

Aloud she said, in the soft sweet voice, "Why, I *hope* they do."

"Well, we all hope so," he said in a tone that suggested they all hoped for rain in August, too.

She heard shouting in the street. The posse had reached the western limits of the settlement, probably passing Lon Person's Livery.

She did not move. It was hot out there, and Stan Mills was standing over her chair, and it was pleasant to feel the charge of excitement he roused in her.

"Here they come," Stan Mills said.

She glanced up, letting him look for a moment into her bared eyes — the lobby was almost deserted. The hotel clerk was behind his desk, but he was straining up on his toes, staring through the lobby window at the dust-glinting street.

For a second their gazes locked.

Isabel felt herself tremble. The least Stan Mills could do was smile, But he never did what you expected. He stared into her as if he could see *everything,* her deepest secrets.

She flushed, lowering her eyes. His blue

eyes behind those rimless glasses were clear and cold in a disturbing, mysterious way.

She felt her fingers tingling. Most men in glasses looked bookish, but Stan was more distinguished. She had never seen him without those glasses except once a couple of years ago when he had broken a lens and had to wait for a replacement all the way from Cheyenne. But she liked him, tall, distinguished, with that air of danger and strength about him.

"Kip not back yet?" Stan Mills inquired with a faint twisted smile.

Isabel showed her sudden exasperation, then slanted her eyes up at him. "Kip was with the posse. You know he'll be the last man home. Kip always puts his heart and soul into everything he does."

"How nice for you," he said.

She gasped faintly, didn't speak. Her neck feeling warm, she sensed those pale disturbing eyes on her. "I can't see how Kip remains so devoted to duty," Stan Mills said, "with a wife like you waiting at home."

She let her demure eyes thank him. She said what anyone would expect her to say, "If every deputy were as devoted to duty as Kip, heaven help the thieves —"

"And the wives?" Stan Mills persisted.

She let her gaze fall away. "And the wives."

It was a taut whisper.

After a brief, tense moment, Stan Mills said, "Kip's a very fortunate man."

The people on the veranda had spilled down the steps to boardwalk and street. Through the window they could see the posse breaking up out in front of the hotel.

Women crowded around them to hear the news. But the men straggling in were tired and humorless, faces bearded and gaunt with need for sleep. Some of them found wives and children in the crowd and dragged them, silent, away home.

Isabel and Stan watched idly through the window. One man out there was shot in the hand. He was yelling for Doc Knoblock, and holding his hand up, blood streaking down his wrist and forearm.

"Five to one he shot himself," Stan Mills said.

Isabel stifled back her laughter.

Sheriff Tom Walker bulled his way through the ring of people at the hotel steps, moved into the shade at the double doors of the lobby entrance.

He saw Isabel and Stan Mills. He nodded at Isabel, tired, but remembering what a sweet, brave little woman she was. Besides he had bad news for her, though he could not bring himself to speak it at the moment.

Instead he gave Stan Mills a gruff nod.

"You run him down, sheriff?" Stan Mills asked.

Isabel felt only she understood Stan Mills well enough to see that the big man was needling the sheriff. The slow-witted Tom Walker took him perfectly seriously, and gave him a serious answer,

"Ran him right down," Walker said. "Caught him. Red-handed."

Stan Mills looked almost as startled as Isabel felt. Stan Mills said, "Good for you, sheriff. It would be hellish to let Ed Keller's killer get away."

The sheriff swore, and then apologized to Isabel. She nodded, forgiving him under these strained circumstances.

The sheriff came tiredly across the lobby to them. He said, "Had my hands on him, Stan. Ran him to ground. But he got away."

"Got away! All you men, and he got away."

"I can't explain it. No more than I can forgive myself for what happened."

"That's too bad, Tom. We all know you did your best." Stan Mills towered two inches above the heavy-set, six-foot lawman.

Looking at them, Isabel sighed, no longer listening to them discuss the chase and the failure last night. It was what she'd expected, and seeing Stan compared to men like the sheriff always stirred her. It was a man like Stan Mills that Isabel had dreamed of when she'd come out here to Kiowa City to teach school. A big man, a wealthy man who traveled and spent money freely. With such a man you'd never be tied down to a hole like this. You could go when you felt like it. You could really live. A man other women would envy you. A man with power and strength. Stan Mills had all that, owned the biggest saloon, the stage line, a mining operation, one of the valley's largest ranches, and every time there was anything showing a profit, Stan Mills was somewhere behind it.

She shook her head impatiently. She'd been rushed into marriage with Kip, that was all there was to it. It was just the perfect romance, according to everybody in the valley, and like an empty-headed fool she had listened to them!

She glanced up at Stan Mills. Beside Stan, Kip Bowne was like a half-grown boy. Kip was twenty-three, but looked like a teenager with that mop of unruly hair, that open, smiling face. Oh, what a fool she'd been. In such a rush to get married, and blinded by what everybody was saying about her and Kip. Well, whatever the romance was, it was soon gone, it hadn't lasted —

not for her anyhow. And it was almost impossible trying to exist on a town marshal's salary. And always, in the back of her mind was the disturbing picture of this big man, the wealthy, powerful Stan Mills.

The sheriff was saying something to her, and she saw in his dull face that he was very morose about it. She had no idea in the world what he had said, but naturally she couldn't ask him to repeat it.

She felt Stan Mills watching her. She took her cue from the sad look in Tom Walker's face and murmured, "Thank you, sheriff."

Both the sheriff and Stan Mills stared at her oddly, and she wondered what was wrong. But before she had a chance to say anything else, Abel Tornet joined them and she sat back in her chair.

"What you got to report, Tom?" Abel Tornet's big voice boomed in the room. He'd been a rancher, but now owned the bank. He spoke loudly, wore a ten-gallon hat, and smoked strong black cigars that made Isabel ill when she was in the same room with him. She hated Abel Tornet.

"Just that I haven't got him," Tom Walker said. "But also that I'm going to get him — sure."

"How?" Stan Mills asked.

Isabel heard Tom Walker saying, "I can

describe him. I've sent a telegraph on him to every sheriff within a hundred miles any direction."

Isabel thought with some irony; that wouldn't take many telegrams in this country.

But the men were listening to Tom Walker's plodding voice, "Why, I'd know him, I was standing as near to him as I am to you, Stan, when he slugged me and run. Well, I can tell you. It ain't going to be easy for him when I do get him."

The crowd in the lobby was swelling again, because the town leaders had gathered in here. Doc Knoblock brought the wounded Ceal Sistrunk up on the veranda to dress his gunshot tear. The slender young cowhand yelled and cursed so violently that women clapped their hands over the ears of their children.

Everybody was chattering about the way the sheriff had had his hands on Ed Keller's murderer.

For this moment, Isabel felt almost as if she were alone with Stan Mills — even in this crowded lobby. She knew he was looking at her, in an odd way, and though she kept her face averted, her heart was slugging.

A woman touched her arm, "Oh, my dear

Isabel, I'm so sorry to hear about Kip."

Isabel went icy cold. Kip. She jerked her head up, looking around. Then she remembered. Sheriff Walker had said something to her — something she hadn't heard. What was it? Was Kip dead?

She only nodded at the woman, unable to speak.

And then she saw Stan Mills' mouth was pulled into a taunting smile. He was laughing at her. He knew what was inside her, and he was laughing at her.

She looked about, frantic and helpless. She had no idea what had happened to Kip, but she couldn't ask now.

She felt stinging beads of perspiration break out across her forehead.

The sheriff was saying, "And that Kip Bowne. Bravest young boy ever lived. It was a brave thing what he done."

The men in the crowd chanted agreement. Even Stan Mills said, "If anybody could bring in that killer, it would be Kip Bowne all right."

Isabel felt ill. She only half listened as the women crowding around her chair offered their sympathy, some even saying, "Don't you worry, Isabel. Don't you worry."

If she was not to worry, didn't that mean Kip was alive? She stirred, overheated, feeling the women pressing too closely around her. She could barely breathe. She jerked her head up, looking at Stan Mills. Damn him. He knew, and he was enjoying himself, laughing at her.

There was an exultant shout from the street. The crowd turned, hastening like sheep from the lobby. She was glad. They would leave her alone. She saw that Stan Mills had not moved from her side. She was glad she would be alone a moment longer with him. At least with him alone she could admit she hadn't been listening to the sheriff. She could make Stan tell her what had happened to Kip.

She smiled up at him, warily, but letting her deep eyes linger on his.

Stan Mills grinned at her, tongue in cheek, "Didn't you hear what that shouting was about?"

"No," she said, watching him.

He shook his head. "Don't you think it would look better if you ran out there with them?"

"Why?"

"My God, girl, that's your husband everybody is running out there to meet."

Isabel felt blood surging hot to the roots of her honey-blonde hair. She came up to her feet, full skirts rustling about her ankles as she ran toward the door. She could feel Stan Mills watching her, laughing at her, Damn him. She hated him.

SIX

Isabel Bowne ran through the wall of chattering women on the hotel porch, going out into the sun-blasted street.

When she reached the boardwalk, she stopped, feeling her heart lurch. She went sick all over. Kip Bowne disappointed her in every way possible. Now he was adding ridicule to all her other woes.

"Kip," she whispered. "Oh, Kip."

"There comes that boy," somebody yelled, laughing.

Isabel looked around, frantic, wishing the street would open and swallow her. In turning her bead, she nudged her gaze an instant against Stan Mills who had casually sauntered out to the walk. His taunting gaze was fixed on her from behind those rimless glasses.

She jerked her head back around. Some of the children ran forward to meet Kip. Others, grown men, called to him. He looked like a fool to Isabel, but she knew how this settlement loved him.

"The conquering hero returns," Stan

Mills said at her back.

"Oh, my God," Isabel said aloud, passionately, forgetting herself.

But the women around her misread her sickness. They never truly saw Isabel Bowne anyway, she knew, they saw only their own image of her. The women patted her arm, and some of them said, "Never mind, honey, he's alive anyhow."

"And that's the important thing," she heard Stan Mills saying against the top of her head.

She trembled. The important thing. She wished Kip Bowne dead. With all her heart, she wished him dead. At least then he would have *looked* like a hero, instead of a clown.

Her eyes brimmed with angry tears. The rest of the posse, at least, had returned to the settlement, riding their horses. But not Kip. *Oh, please, earth, open up, swallow me!*

She stared along that sun-whitened street. Somewhere, somehow, Kip Bowne, the pride of Kiowa Valley, the young marshal everybody said would be sheriff someday when Tom Walker got too old to work — somewhere Kip Bowne had lost the saddle to his horse.

Isabel stood stock still in the sun, staring.

Kip was walking toward her, leading his mount, and Kip's feet were killing him in his high-heeled boots that were never meant for walking any further than from hitching rail to sheriff's office. But Kip was making a joke — telling the kids when he tried to ride bareback, he slicked off and fell on his tail in the dust.

The children laughed, pleased with Kip's clowning. She saw he was searching for her in the crowd. He was always looking for her, hobbling toward her on his burning feet. How she despised him. She tried to dissolve backward into the crowd, but only bumped against the wall of Stan Mills.

"He's really had a bad time," she heard somebody say. "Wonder he can laugh about it at all."

"That boy Kip will find something funny in his own funeral oration," another man said, chuckling.

Isabel pressed her eyes tightly shut for a moment. When she opened them, Kip was nearer, exaggerating the way he hobbled to the delight of the crowd. That was when Isabel saw that Kip's gun was gone from its holster.

For a terrible moment her gaze was riveted on that empty holster. He'd gone out, mounted and armed. Who else could come hobbling home without his gun?

Her mortified gaze lifted slowly to his

face, and then she saw the purple welts, the swollen black eye, the bloody cut around Kip's mouth. There was a swollen purple welt along his left jaw, a bright orange bruise on his right cheekbone.

Nobody had to tell Isabel now. In this miserable second she knew the truth, Kip had chased down the thief, all right. And to prove it, here he came toward her, looking, despite his twenty-three years and marshal's badge crooked on his vest, like a small boy who'd foolishly fought the town bully and not known when to stop after all was lost.

She felt she had to turn around and run. She could never go near him again. But she knew she could not budge. Her marriage to Kip Bowne was the ideal romance of the whole valley.

She had to struggle to keep her upper lip from curling disdainfully as Kip moved, hurrying on tortured feet the last few steps to her. She saw the smiling people step aside making a path for him.

"Oh, lord, I missed you," Kip said. "I hurried back — fast as I could, sweetheart — under the circumstances."

Everybody laughed — except Isabel Bowne. She heard her practiced voice cooing, "Darling. Darling, what on earth happened to you?"

"The damnedest thing," Kip said, grinning. The grin hurt his torn mouth and welted face, but he grinned anyway. It was a habit, "I caught Mr. Robber. By the tail. And that's what it was, just like getting me a bull by the tail. I got him and I couldn't let go. I tried to yell for help and that younker was all over me." He shook his head, laughing ruefully again, "I give it all I had, but what he done to me was plain hell . . . And I woke up with the sun in my face — and all alone."

Thank God, Isabel thought, the way Kip laughs at himself, the town would never laugh at him. They'd be on his side. The way they were always, in everything he did.

Isabel touched at the long welt raised along his jaw. "Does it hurt, darling?" she cooed.

Kip winced, then smiled. "Not now," he said, laughing. "Not with your hand on it." Doctor Knoblock had pushed through the crowd to where Kip stood. Kip glanced at him, shaking his head. "Won't need you now, Doc. I got me better medicine right here than you ever heard of."

The townspeople laughed in warm approval.

Kip put his arm about Isabel. He was so sweated and grimy, Isabel wanted to draw away. But she stayed where she was, smile pasted on her mouth.

People were questioning Kip. Where was the robber headed? Kip admitted he didn't know. "When he left me, I was getting the best night's sleep I've had in months," Kip said.

Where had he come upon him? Kip shook his head, but reckoned the meeting took place somewhere near the crest of Conifer Ridge.

Listening to them questioning Kip, feeling his arm tight and uncomfortably possessive at her waist, Isabel let her eyes stray for a moment. She found Stan Mills as if her gaze were drawn, magnetized to him. But it was always easy, finding Stan Mills in any mob, because Stan towered head and shoulders above other men.

Seeing Stan Mills, Isabel hated having to stand, dutifully inside Kip's arm, tenderly touching at his bruises, the perfect wife.

From the corner of her eye, Isabel saw some woman speak to Stan Mills, and he turned from his amused watching of her playing the loving spouse.

Isabel jerked her head around to see who the woman was. It was Rosemary Meade.

Isabel felt the blood seep out of her face. Rosemary. In her twenties. Too lovely to be a widow, too young, and yet she was. Red-gold hair catching the sunlight, worn in loose curls about her face, and caught in a soft bun at the nape of her neck.

Isabel despised Rosemary without being able to say why. They were nothing alike. Isabel knew she was cuddly, and small, and had to watch herself or she'd get fat — but that wasn't going to happen for years. Tall for a woman, Rosemary Meade was everything Isabel Bowne was not, and everything, Isabel told herself hotly, that she never wanted to be.

Seven

"Both the sheriff and me got a close look at that killer," Kip Bowne was saying. "Don't you folks worry. He won't stay loose."

Isabel, watching Stan Mills' face, caught her breath abruptly.

She saw the sun glinting on Stan's rimless glasses. But more than that, she saw something she recognized, and something twisted inside her.

She saw the way Stan Mills looked at Rosemary Meade. *He never looked at me like that, Isabel thought. Damn him, why should he want a woman like her?*

She forced herself to turn back to Kip,

feeling helpless and wild with a jealousy she could never let out of her. It was like dynamite tamped down hard inside her, and ready to explode.

She glanced with concealed distaste at Kip close beside her. He looked so young, so much younger than he was. The top of his head didn't reach Stan's shoulder. He was such a boy — and she wanted a man — that man.

She glanced back at the way Stan was looking down at Rosemary, allowing Kip to lead her away through the crowd toward their small cottage on a side street.

She said, softly to Kip, "That Rosemary. I hate her."

Kip's bruised mouth sagged. "Why? Honey, how could you hate a wonderful woman like Rosemary?"

"I don't know how, but it's easy . . . She's — so brazen . . . Did you see the way she walked up to Stan Mills on the street back there?"

Kip smiled, hugging her close. "Well, sure, that's something you couldn't do, honey. But that's because you're a sweet little housewife. You're not like Rosemary Meade."

"Thank God."

"Rosemary feels like she's one of the business men by now, Isabel. Right along with Abel Tornet, Stan Mills, and the rest."

"She doesn't act like a man."

Kip laughed, then winced when the pain struck his mouth. "No. She don't look like one, either. But she ain't had it easy since Randal Meade was killed. You got to give her credit. The way she turned that old house next to Doc Knoblock's into a restaurant. And she's made it pay, too."

Isabel said, sharply, "I wonder how? I wonder what else she serves to all those men — besides just hot meals?"

Kip stopped walking on his aching feet. He stood stock still in the middle of the thoroughfare. His eyes were shocked and he stared at Isabel as if she were a stranger.

"Good lord! Isabel, don't ever say such things about her. She's a wonderful woman. She's had a tough time. I don't ever want to hear you say anything like that again."

Isabel shrugged, thinking she'd bet Rosemary Meade was no better than she had to be. Five to one — as Stan Mills said — she got lonely at night, her a widow and so young, all this lonely time since Randal's death.

They moved forward again. She did not glance back at where Rosemary stood talking with Stan Mills. She walked straight in the sun beside her hobbling young husband, feeling the heat of the sun, but none of its warmth.

Her hands were clenched at her side.

Kip heard something west on the road, and paused, staring that way. He stood as if rooted to the ground.

She saw his eyes widen, saw the disbelief fill them, saw his torn mouth droop open.

He turned, yelling across his shoulder, his awed voice ascending in wonderment. "Good lord a-mercy! Sheriff! Sheriff! Look who's coming yonder!"

Kip's hand fumbled for his gun before he remembered his holster was empty.

The townspeople, led by Sheriff Tom Walker, surged forward, running toward where Isabel and Kip Bowne stood watching a man ride a lathered gray horse slowly toward them.

Isabel stared, but saw nothing very exciting. A tall man, timber-tall and coyote-thin, rode painfully slowly toward them, sagging in his saddle. She saw the man was as tall as Stan Mills, but rail-thin, dusty, ragged, and unshaven.

When he got near where Kip and Isabel stood, he slid from the saddle, walked forward, wide shoulders slumped round. In the dark face was a look of incredible weariness.

"It's him," Kip whispered, awed. "It's the man robbed the bank, killed Ed Keller. It's him that slugged me."

Recognition now smote the members of the posse who'd ringed Jim Gilmore's fire beside Kiowa Creek last night. A whisper rattled back across the crowd.

Sheriff Tom Walker plowed forward, swearing. His voice boomed in the hot street.

"What you doing here?" Walker said. "Why in God's name would any man do a fool thing like this?"

Drawing his gun, the sheriff advanced past Kip and Isabel. The tall man didn't pause, but came forward slowly until Isabel recognized Kip's gun in his holster, and saw Kip's saddle on the lathered gray pony.

The townspeople stopped talking, staring at the stranger, still unable to believe what they saw.

The tall man paused before Sheriff Walker, drew the gun from his holster in a cautious way so that no one in the crowd could doubt his intentions.

"Here's my gun, sheriff."

The sheriff met Gilmore ten feet in front of the crowd. The two men cast squat shadows in the white dust.

Isabel felt a faint stirring of unwilling admiration for the stranger. There was incredible courage in the slow way he walked forward into this town that despised him, meant to hang him.

The sheriff took the gun. They faced each other, the sheriff wary, the tall stranger tired, wincing with the weariness in him.

The sheriff said, "You got plumb away, stranger. Why did you come back?"

Jim Gilmore shook his head. "Maybe you won't ever understand it," he said, voice hoarse with fatigue, "But I do. That's all that matters, I've run as far as I'm going to."

EIGHT

Judge Wilbur Griffin rapped a gavel on top of the pine table that served as his bench, and the overflow courtroom gradually grew silent.

"This here court is in session," the judge said.

Jim Gilmore sat, legs stretched out before him, in a long slant of sunlight through a tall window. He felt the eyes of all the people in the room on him, merciless and unblinking.

Jim felt chilled, even in the sunlight.

"Well, first I'll now select the jury to hear this case," Judge Griffin said.

There was stirring in the room, and the judge struck with the gavel. "There'll be some silence in here if I have to clear the place. Now we pledged this here man as fair a trial as we can give him under the circumstances. And I mean to see he gets every bit of that."

The undercurrent of whispering rose and died away.

The judge stared out across the tense faces before him. He began selecting the jury by pointing to a man, calling his name and ordering him to step up and take a seat in the jury box.

"Aren't you going to ask them any questions?" Jim said.

"What kind of questions, boy?"

Jim shrugged. "I don't know. You're the lawyer. You're a judge. You should ask them how they feel about hanging — about the man that was killed . . ."

"I don't need to ask 'em. I know these here people. Know just how they feel. Knowed most of them all their life. Why don't you let me handle this, boy?"

Jim shrugged again, and sighed.

The next person the judge selected for jury duty was a woman. Jim felt himself go tense. Before the judge was through there were seven men and five women on the jury.

Jim hitched his shirt up on his shoulders. This was Wyoming, and Wyoming was his home, and women on juries, or voting, was nothing new to him. Wyoming had passed the woman suffrage law eight years ago.

Still, it was his life. And women on a jury just didn't look right. He'd spent most of his life among animals, and he'd learned one thing — often to his sorrow — and that was: the female of the species is always more dangerous than the male.

The mouths of those women were set; their eyes were hard. And, he would have gambled, their minds were already made up.

Jim felt his stomach tying in knots. After sixteen hours of sleep in a jail cell, a warm meal brought in from the restaurant, he had begun to feel better, almost human. He began to believe he had a chance. These people would see how wrong they were. Now, he began to lose that hope.

He stared at the small stack of his belongings on the front of the judge's long pine table. There was the five hundred dollars he'd had left from the sale of his small ranch to Will Allbrand back in Winter Sage. He'd left some money with Eualie to tide her over until he could send for her, and that money was to have been used to make a payment on their new home. His gun and belt — which had been brought in from his creek camp along with his saddle, and battered hat — were on the table beside the money. Almost, he felt, as if that gun were placed there as a constant reminder that he packed a gun. He would say he wore it because he was traveling in strange country. But they would say it was a tool of his trade — robbing and murder.

"Well, the trial is now ready to open," the judge said.

The judge touched the big Frontier model .44 at his right hand, adjusting it to suit him on the table top.

"Now," he said. "Since I am not only the judge here in the settlement of Kiowa City, Kiowa County, Wyoming, but also the only practicing attorney within sixty miles in any direction, I will conduct this trial as I see best. I will represent you citizens as judge and prosecutor — and I will, with all the fairness at my command, attempt to place before the jury this young defendant's side of the case."

He stroked his handlebar moustaches and stared down at Jim Gilmore, waiting.

Jim exhaled heavily, but didn't even bother

302

to protest.

He watched the judge's moustache quiver as the big man in rust suit and string tie pondered the best way to get the trial moving.

"Reckon I'll call Abel Tornet to the stand first," he said.

Jim Gilmore sat forward when the foreman of the jury had to step out of the jury box and sit down in the kitchen chair beside the pine table that served as witness stand.

"Men in the jury going to testify?" he said.

"Son, you got to realize. This here is just a Wyoming settlement. We ain't got enough land-owning, responsible citizens that we don't have to double up. I'm sorry about Abel being on the jury — but several of the men that rode in the posse that trailed you — pardon, trailed the John Doe that robbed our bank and killed Ed Keller — are sitting on the jury."

Jim Gilmore sagged back in his chair as the men and women in the room chattered, whispering among themselves until Judge Griffin restored order by rapping the table sharply with the gavel.

"Will you tell us just what happened, Abel?"

Abel Tornet nodded; a pot-bellied man who'd gotten rich and soft in banking, real estate, and mortgage loans, he stared hard at Jim.

"Ed Keller and me was alone in the bank. It was after banking hours. We had closed the front door, but didn't lock it. After all, folks drop in. Well, this fellow came through the door —"

"Now, just a minute, Abel," the judge protested. "You sure it was this here fellow?"

"Sure as I'm sitting here."

The room buzzed loudly, the tension growing. "Why are you so sure?"

Abel licked his mouth. "I seen him kill Ed Keller. Seen him steal a gold shipment. It was him all right."

"Was he alone?"

Abel Tornet shook his head. "No. He wasn't. But he come in the bank alone. Another fellow outside held the horses and watched for anybody coming into the bank — but I didn't get no good look at him."

"Thank you, Abel." The judge waited until Tornet returned to the first chair in the jury box.

"What you got to say to that, young fellow?" the judge asked Jim.

Jim shook his head. "Only that he's lying. He never saw me. I never saw him before."

Abel started forward in his chair, and a

growl rolled through the crowd. The judge rapped with gavel, let his other hand cover the .44 on his desk.

"Never mind now, Abel," the judge said. "This here is a court of law. You had your say. The young fellow had his. We'll let the jury decide who's telling the truth."

"But he's on the jury!" Jim said, leaning forward so that Sheriff Walker beside him put a thick hand on his shoulder, restraining him.

The judge gave him a pitying look. "It wouldn't matter no-how, boy. Can't you see that? Who on a jury in this town would accept your word against that of the banker's? You got to come up with something better than that anyway."

The judge then called Bertha Keller. The wife of the slain bank teller was a stout woman, eyes swollen, wearing funereal black.

She told how she had walked to the bank to meet her Ed. She heard gunfire and stood petrified as the robber ran out past her.

"Was it this here man?" the judge asked her.

She stared at Jim, eyes blurred with tears. She was a good, grief-stricken woman. She bowed her head, speaking reluctantly, "I think so. I stood there petrified with fear when he ran past me. Then when I saw Ed — bleeding, dying, everything else went out of my mind . . . It seemed it was a smaller man — but I — don't know."

"You wouldn't swear under oath it was this man?"

"I couldn't do that," she said.

The next witness was Ceal Sistrunk, a cow hand on a locally owned ranch. He had ridden with the posse.

"When you and the posse come up on this fellow beside the Kiowa Creek, was you convinced you had found the right man?" the judge asked young Sistrunk.

"I didn't doubt it."

"Why not?"

"We'd trailed him all day. Going in circles part of the time. Once or twice I tell you honestly, I figured maybe we was following our own tracks, but I didn't say anything. We lost the trail a couple times. But when we picked it up — it led straight toward Conifer Ridge, and we found this fellow tuckered out, so tired he could barely move at all."

"Why was he so tired?"

Ceal Sistrunk laughed, "He never told me. But I can tell you why I *think* he was tired. Because he had robbed the bank — and him and his partner separated and he spent the whole day — a stranger lost — trying to get out of the valley."

The judge glanced at Jim, slumped in his chair beside Tom Walker. "What you say to that, stranger?"

"I say I'd run a hell of a long time in one place if I didn't get any further than Kiowa Creek in a whole day," Jim said.

"How about that, Ceal?"

Sistrunk shrugged. "We covered a lot of ground. Went in a lot of circles. A man don't know this country might spend a lot of time running lost."

Suddenly, Abel Tornet jumped up in the jury box.

Tornet's face was livid, his eyes distended. "Why go on wasting our time like this, Wilbur? Make him tell where my money is — *my money?* Why, it's your money, Judge. And yours, Tom Walker, and yours Stan Mills. It belongs to all the people of this settlement!"

There was a cry of assent in the courtroom. The grumbling grew loud. The judge smote the pine table with the butt of the .44.

"I'll run my court my own way!" the judge told them, his handlebar moustache quivering. "Now, if you want to hang this man, you'll have to wait until I'm through with him."

It was some moments before order could be restored. The people ignored the judge's gavel and his threats to clear the room. It wasn't until Stan Mills stood up in the jury box, punching his rimless glasses tighter on the bridge of his nose, that the room quieted. A room always quieted to hear Stan Mills.

"As Abel says, Judge, it is my money — as well as anyone else's that's been stolen. But I agree with you, this man is entitled to his moment in court — his fair trial — as fair as we can give him."

Stan sat down amid a smattering of approving applause from women in the room, including lady jurors.

The judge rapped once more for order. The doors at the rear of the room were thrust open. "Ho!" a man yelled. Three dust-streaked men, wearing sack-masks over their faces shoved through the spectators, guns drawn. "All right, Gilmore," the leader yelled. "Let's go, buddy. Let's get out of here!"

NINE

Women screamed. Grown men scrambled to get out of the path of the men with the guns.

The masked men wore hats pulled low over their sack-masks, their collars were turned up. They moved forward, jerking their guns back and forth to keep the people in their places.

"Just don't get excited," the leader said. "And nobody gets hurt. Let's go, Jim boy."

The sheriff leaped to his feet after the first stunned moment of disbelief. It had never occurred to Tom Walker a thing like this would happen, and it had taken his mind a few seconds to credit it.

He drew his gun and faced the men at the rear of the room.

Jim pushed his chair back out of his way, staring across the frightened crowd at the three strangers hailing him as one of them.

"What's the meaning of this?" Judge Griffin stood up with the gavel instead of the .44 in his hand.

The man at the back of the room laughed. "Just means we're taking Jim Gilmore out of here."

Tom Walker shook his head. "Nobody is taking this man out of here, 'cept over my dead body."

"Don't be a fool, Tom!" Stan Mills spoke, leaping up in the jury box so suddenly all three gunmen heeled to face him. "Tom. Don't shoot. Can't shoot in here. Innocent people will be killed."

The sheriff hesitated, stunned by Stan Mills' common sense.

The crowd stampeded at Stan Mills' suggestion that the innocent would be slain in exchange of gunfire. Men and women cowered, moving toward walls and windows, sliding off benches and to the floor.

Tom Walker stood, undecided. If he did not fire, those men would take his prisoner. If he did shoot, some of his friends might accidentally die. His face worked as be wrestled with the problem.

Suddenly Jim Gilmore stiff-armed Tom Walker aside and leaped forward, landing against the judge's pine table.

The judge stood petrified, watching Jim scoop up the .44 and heel around, standing beside Sheriff Walker.

Jim's voice shook with rage. "I don't know who you men are," he said. "Or who's behind this. Or why you're trying to get me out of here . . . But you'll have to kill me to do it . . . I didn't give myself up to pull a fool caper like this . . . You gents want

310

me . . . come and get me."

"Well, I'm damned," the sheriff said aloud. He brought up his own gun again, standing at Jim's side.

The three masked men wavered at the rear of the room. They stared at Jim and the sheriff and the guns in their hands. They looked at each other, uncertainly. Now Kip Bowne stood up in the first row, face battered, gun drawn.

The masked man nearest the door was already backing toward it. Hesitantly, still waving their guns menacingly, the other two followed.

They slammed the door behind them. Their boots rattled on the boardwalk outside, and then their horses were loud, going along the road out of town.

"Kip Bowne!" The sheriff's voice boomed. He tried to thrust his way through the people who now stood like a solid wall between him and the rear of the room. "Kip! Get after them devils."

Kip pushed his way through the shouting milling people. But by the time he reached the rear doors of the courtroom, both he and the sheriff knew it was too late ever to overtake the fleeing gunmen.

The judge, face gray, moustache drooping suddenly with sweat, pounded on his table.

"Order," he yelled. "Order. Let's get on."

Jim turned slowly, extending the .44 butt first toward the judge.

It took some time to restore any semblance of order in that room, but finally Kip Bowne was put on the stand. The judge said, "Kip, I reckon the best thing is just to have you tell what you know about this here case."

Kip nodded, gingerly touching at the welt along his jaw. "Seems to me sometimes I know quite a lot about it — I was in the middle of it, all right." The people laughed mildly. "Then when I think about it, I'm not sure. There are a few things I feel bound to say, though."

"Let's hear them."

The young marshal stared for a moment at Jim Gilmore, face troubled. "Well, first, this fellow took the time to tell me he wasn't guilty — that was before he cold-cocked me, and left me sleeping up on Conifer."

He waited until the laughter subsided. Then he said, in a serious tone, "The bad part of it is, I believed him — even when he hit me. Because he could have killed me, as easily."

"Gunfire would have brought help," the judge protested.

"There was plenty of rocks at hand big enough to finish me if that had been this gent's idea. He said all along he come from the east into Kiowa Valley — and we ain't found the money, we ain't proved he didn't."

"Abel Tornet says he positively saw this man in his bank," the judge reminded him.

"That there's another funny thing," young Kip Bowne said, scowling. He glanced toward the banker in the jury box. "I hate telling this, Abel, but I'm bound to tell the truth."

Abel opened his mouth to speak, closed it. His face was flushed.

"What you got to tell, Kip?" the judge said.

"Well, I was the first one in the bank after the shooting. When I got in there, Abel — Mr. Tornet was crouched down under his desk with his arms over his head." People tittered reluctantly, but Kip jerked his head up. "Now, wait a minute. I don't blame Abel Tornet one bit for what he done. The bank robber had a gun, and we know he used it — on Ed Keller . . . Abel saved his own life by crouching under his desk. No, sir, I don't blame him one bit. But — there's this, he couldn't identify the man who killed Ed — the one that robbed the bank."

Abel Tornet leaped to his feet. "I saw him. I tell you, I saw him. It was this man." He shook his finger, pointing at Jim.

Kip shook his head, eyes troubled. "Just a minute, Abel. I'm sure you're telling what you think is true. We arrested a man, and you want to believe he killed Ed and robbed you . . . But when the bank was robbed, and I got you out from under that desk, the first thing I asked you was if you could identify the robber. You said no. You said you ducked under your desk and let Ed face him the minute you saw he had a gun — and a mask."

"I don't care what I said," Abel shouted. "I know it was this man."

"Sit down, Abel," the judge said. Fuming, Abel Tornet sat down, still shaking his head. The judge glanced at Gilmore. "I now call Jim Gilmore to the stand — that your name, ain't it, stranger? That what you said, Jim Gilmore?"

Jim nodded, taking his place in the stand.

The judge said, "You base your claim of innocence on the fact that you was coming here — from the east and hadn't yet been in Kiowa City — right?" When Jim nodded, he said, "Well, tell us where you're from?"

Jim hesitated. He had been debating this in his mind since the moment he decided to return here and stand trial. If he told them where he was from, they could prove who he was, when he left Winter Sage. But if word that he was on trial — for robbery and murder — got to Eualie, she would be alone, worried about him.

He wiped his hand across his mouth. It was a hundred rugged miles east to Winter Sage. News traveled slow. But wireless would have the news that Jim Gilmore was accused of murder across that hundred miles in seconds. But if he didn't prove who he was, where he was from, they would hang him — whether they recovered the money or not.

"Well, come on, boy, speak up," the judge said.

Jim nodded. But he was thinking that Eualie was alone, and scared enough without getting this kind of bad news. He didn't want word getting back to her until this trouble was over — one way or the other.

He said, "Exactly where I'm from don't enter into it."

"Might mean the difference between you staying alive — and hanging," the judge said, and the people nodded.

"I'm guilty of no crime," Jim said, voice flat. "I came back — of my own will and surrendered to the sheriff. Maybe you folks will hang me, but you won't ever prove I'm guilty."

315

"Why'd you come back?"

"I told you, I'm innocent. And I'm tired running away from trouble."

The judge touched at his sagging moustache ends. "Seems to me," he said, staring at the jury, "that if this man was guilty of any crime — even robbery without murder in the bargain — he would never have done two things he has already done. First, he never would of walked into Kiowa City and surrendered to the sheriff. Second, he wouldn't of passed up this chance to escape. But now he don't want to tell us where he's from. Why, mister?"

"It don't matter. I got people — back there. They would worry if they heard about this trouble."

"But, man, you need them friends right now. The sheriff could wire and they could certify to the honesty of your character."

Jim breathed in deeply, held it. Sure, they could wire to Will Allbrand at the National Bank at Winter Sage. Will was always helping him, seemed to him sometime he lived off Will Allbrand's charity. Will even took the ranch off his hands when he was impatient to get away and start over.

He shook his head. He was through leaning on Will Allbrand, too, and besides Will would carry the word of his trouble straight to Eualie.

"No," he said, exhaling. "You'll have to take my word."

"There you are!" Abel Tornet leaped to his feet. "This man is lying. This proves it."

The judge stared at Tornet. "Yet, a few minutes ago you said you stood and looked at this man in your bank, Abel. But that ain't strictly true, either, is it?"

Tornet looked wild with rage, but he sat down again.

"Seems to me, we've reached the point where it's up to me and the jury to go quiet in the jury room and decide this thing. A man has a right to his silence. According to law — we got to prove him *guilty* — he don't have to prove hisself innocent. And the only money on his person he says come to him from sale of land and stock —"

"He says!" Tornet's words burst across his mouth.

The judge nodded. "He says . . . Yet, there ain't no proof this paper money ever belonged to the Kiowa Bank. As I been led to understand, only two bags of gold, used to pay off the miners was missing. Wasn't that true, Abel?"

The banker nodded, face gray. "We took an accounting. That's all that was missing . . . But them bags was worth thousands of —"

"True," Judge Griffin said. "And the life of brother Ed Keller was sacrificed. All this is extremely serious. But this man knew — from the moment he was found on the creek bank — if not before — a hang rope waited for him here, yet he come back to us, trusting our decency to give him a fair trial. Ladies and gentlemen of the jury, I have tried to do that. And now, I want you to come with me into the jury room, and we'll ponder the facts we know. And I direct you to look past your hatreds into your hearts."

An angry murmur washed back through the crowd. Jim sat in his chair, feeling their hatred eating at him like acid.

The jury marched out, faces set, shoulders rigid. The people remaining in the courtroom waited, whispering, tense. Occasionally from the jury room came angry shouts, wrangling. In two hours they were back. Abel Tornet was no longer jury foreman, having been deposed by the judge for violently ignoring facts. Dr. Knoblock, the new jury foreman, stood up, faced Jim Gilmore. "Your honor," Knoblock said, "We find the defendant not guilty, for one reason — that reason is for lack of evidence."

TEN

The courtroom emptied slowly, people leaving unwillingly as if disappointed. There had been no guilty sentence, no hanging. What had happened to justice?

Outside people stood in groups on the boardwalk, discussing the outrageous verdict.

Jim waited in his chair, feeling a weakness and a sense of relief at the same time. He was still alive.

Beside him, the sheriff sat withdrawn and silent.

Kip Bowne let Isabel leave the courtroom without him. He leaned against the judge's pine table before the sheriff and Jim.

"I'm glad it went this way, Gilmore," Kip said. "I believe you're innocent. Though ask me why I do, and I couldn't tell you."

"You're young," the sheriff said, staring up at Kip, "easy swayed."

"I don't think so," Kip said. "Nobody proved Gilmore guilty."

"Or innocent," Walker said. He stared at Jim. "You're free."

Then the sheriff got up and stalked from the room without looking back.

Kip smiled. "Once Tom makes up his mind, it's hard to change."

Dr. Knoblock came forward. He was a thin, scholarly appearing man almost as tall as Jim. He smelled of antiseptic and peppermint. He said, "Well, young fellow, now you're free, what you expect to do?"

Jim stood up, exhaling. "Look for a place to live."

The doctor scowled, "Here?"

"I got to live somewhere."

"My lord," Dr. Knoblock said. "You got to live among people that hate you — people who think you're guilty of murder?"

Jim spread his hands. "What would they think if it suddenly left here?"

"Just what they think now . . . that you are guilty," the doctor said and walked away.

Kip grinned sheepishly. "From the way these folks act, you wouldn't think they're the salt of the earth, would you?"

"I know how they feel about me."

"And you're staying?"

Jim got his money, buckled on his gunbelt. "Until I know what I'm going to do."

Kip Bowne shook his head. "Man, I'm like Doc Knoblock. I'd hit the road out of here." He saw the set look in Jim's face, shrugged. "Come on, get your horse and saddle from the jail."

Jim counted his money, pocketed it. This was all he had to show for years of sweat and labor in the Winter Sage country. What would it buy him here? Yet, what would it buy him anywhere? You were always running away from something, and it never worked. One place looked as good as another right now.

He followed Kip Bowne toward the doors. The courtroom was empty, hotly silent in midday heat. Flies buzzed at the window and talk floated in, tense and angry, from the street.

When they came down the steps to the boardwalk, the knots of people fell silent, staring at Jim.

He set his battered Stetson on his head and walked through them. He could hear the whispers start behind his back. Whispers. God knew it was no wonder Eualie had been so miserable at the way folks lied about her back in Winter Sage.

A tall girl with red-gold hair stopped them on the walk.

"I don't want you to think all of us are like Abel Tornet," she said. "Some of us wish you well."

Frowning, Jim looked at her. "Everything's crazy. First, three men I never saw tried to save me from that trial. Now the prettiest lady in town says she's on my side." His grin was weak, crooked, "Thank you, ma'm."

"This is Mrs. Meade, Jim Gilmore," Kip said. "Her husband was killed little more than a year ago."

"It's all right, Kip." Rosemary's voice was cool, her lips no longer smiling. "If Mr. Gilmore doesn't need friends, I'm sorry I spoke —"

"I meant no offense," Jim said.

She shrugged. "If you're going to be in town, Mr. Gilmore, I serve hot meals. There. The restaurant in that house next door to Dr. Knoblock's office."

Jim glanced about at the set faces of the townspeople, watching. "Even to me?"

"You're determined to be unfriendly, aren't you?" she said.

"I'm trying to be friendly," he said in a helpless way. "I reckon I've just forgot how."

"I sell meals," she said. "To anybody. I need the business."

She heeled about, walking away from them, her heels loud on the boardwalk.

For a moment, Jim and young Bowne stared after her. She was beautifully made; not even the cheap, ankle-length cotton dress could conceal this.

Kip said, "Come on over to the Bright Star first. What we need is a drink. I'll buy."

Jim nodded, and they stepped off the walk, angling across the hard-packed street toward the Bright Star Saloon.

"She's a touchy redhead," Jim said, turning to look for Rosemary Meade, but not finding her in the street.

"She wanted to be friendly, but you acted edgy. People are fine in this town. If you're innocent, they'll like you."

"If I'm innocent?" Jim paused, staring at the marshal. "Thought you believed me."

Kip shrugged. "I do. But hell, Rosemary and me. We're a small minority. Hell, what do I know? I think you're innocent, but my wife Isabel says I spend half my time being wrong, the other half apologizing for it."

They crossed the boardwalk, moved up the steps to the Bright Star entrance.

Stan Mills pushed through the batwings as they reached the stoop. He stood barring their way.

At Stan Mills' back stood a towheaded man with flat, soulless eyes and thonged gun.

"Sorry, Gilmore," Mills smiled, but his voice was chilled. "You'll have to do your drinking somewhere else."

"Come on now, Stan," Kip said. "Where else? You got the only saloon in town."

Mills shrugged. "And I'm in business for

money. Plenty of people in town feel you missed hanging today, Gilmore, because of that grandstand play you pulled with your friends. Plenty feel you ought to hang. Me, I don't care one way or the other. But I'd have to close up if I went against the people in town."

Kip frowned, looking from Gilmore to Mills. The two big men's gazes met, levelly, clashing.

Kip spoke at last, voice hollow. "O.K. Stan. We'll see you again sometime."

But Stan caught his arm, smiling. Light glinted on his glasses. "You come in here, Kip. I didn't mean you."

Kip licked his mouth. "Reckon not this time, Stan. I got to turn over Gilmore's saddle and horse to him."

"You riding out?" Stan said, staring at Jim.

Jim shook his head. Stan Mills patted Kip on the shoulder, turned and went through the batwings.

The towheaded gent remained standing, staring through Jim.

Jim felt the sudden twist of rage. "Better follow your boss," he told the gunslick. "I saw a speck of dirt on his boot. He'll be looking for you to lick it off."

The thin gunman's hand quivered toward his holster.

But Kip caught Jim's arm, pulling him away. "Forget it, Fisher. Jim's just edgy — after that trial."

The gunman's voice was strident, but flat. "Be careful what you say to me, mister. My temper — almost as fast as my gun."

Jim grinned tautly at him, across his shoulder. "My back will make an easier target."

Still pulling him away, Kip led Jim to the street. "Good lord," the marshal said, "you attract trouble like this all the time?"

"All the time," Jim said. "It's easy. I use a magnet."

ELEVEN

Lon Persons started shaking his head from side to side before Jim even reached the livery stables on his gray.

Jim rode slowly along the main street when he came from the stables behind the jail. He felt the noon sun against his shoulders and the eyes of the townspeople on him. There was a satisfaction in their faces, a look of relief when they saw him ride past. They thought he was quitting the settlement.

"I'm sorry. I'm sorry." Lon Persons was a thin, angular man with a prominent Adam's apple and unruly brown hair. He was up off his chair in front of his livery stable, walking out to meet Jim.

Lon Persons attempted to smile, and he stroked the gray along the nose. "Fine little quarter horse, mister. Like the breed. This one looks almighty smart."

"Just want to bed her down until I figure what to do."

Lon Persons looked up at him, squinting against the sun. "That shouldn't take you no long period of time, mister . . . In your place, I know what I'd do."

"You don't know anything about what I'd do," Jim said.

Lon shook his head. "Please sir, maybe not, but I do know what I got to do. I got to refuse your horse here. Folks would be down on me if I took your horse here —"

"They think if they make it tough enough on me, I'll leave?"

"I don't know about that. I just know I don't want any trouble. Now, I can't take your little pony, much as I'd like to, but if you're in town a day or so, the sheriff will let you stall her down behind the jail. He won't like it, but he'll have to do it — long as you pay for her feed."

Jim stared at the livery owner a moment, then nodded, and turned the gray about in the street.

There was new tension in the faces of the watching people when they saw him coming back toward them, and they drew together, whispering in knots and staring at him across their shoulders.

Jim paused in the middle of the sun-struck street, feeling an emptiness in his stomach. Why stay where they hated you so bad? And yet — why go on running when running wasn't the answer, and he'd already proved that? He saw a small sign tacked on a frame cottage: HOT MEALS.

Jim tied the gray to the hitch rail outside the cottage.

Jim paused just inside the front door of the young widow Meade's small house. She'd removed partitions along the center, turning the front rooms and one side to the rear of the cottage into a serving room. He heard bustling in the kitchen.

Almost every table was occupied. Of course, it was a court day, and that made a difference; but this place with its white tablecloths and steaming dishes, had a look of moderate success.

There was an odd silence and a sudden charge of tension in the room when Jim entered.

Rosemary Meade, face pinkly flushed,

bright hair netted away from forehead, saw him and indicated a small vacant table near a window.

"We're serving roast beef today," she told him when he sat down. "With mashed potatoes and garden greens. There's fresh vegetables. But if I bring them, you must eat them."

He smiled. "I'm different from cowhands you know; I eat vegetables."

She nodded, left him. The silence was intensified, there was no longer even the sound of service against plates.

Suddenly, as if gauging the temper of the room, Abel Tornet stood up.

"Must we now *eat* in the same room with a thief and killer?"

He stared along his nose at Jim. Jim remained unmoving, feeling blood mount in his cheeks.

Tornet's voice hardened. "Sure, they let him go in court. What could we do? What a showy trick — refusing to let his partners spring him! Well, he may have fooled the judge — and some of you people — but reading character is my business. I know a guilty man when I see one, and this man is a murderer."

Kip Bowne spoke from across the room, with Isabel pulling at his arm to restrain him. "If he'd been guilty he'd never have come back here to the trial."

"Why not?" Now Tornet stared at Kip Bowne. "Maybe there are other places ripe for picking in this valley. Maybe Stan Mills' mine's next — the payroll is considerable. A rich little town. Why move on when the people are so gullible?"

A woman spoke shrilly, leaning forward across her plate. "We don't want you here. Why don't you leave?"

"Maybe he's waiting for us to run him out," a man said from across the room.

"Well, he can have that, too."

Chairs scraped, men got to their feet.

"Killer!" the woman screamed at Jim. "Murderer!"

"Stop it!"

The woman sat back suddenly; the men paused where they stood.

Jim saw Rosemary coming through the door from her kitchen. There was a rifle across her arms.

The men grumbled, but subsided.

"What possesses you people?" Rosemary said. "You're people I've known for years. But you're acting like wild animals. Why? Because he's a stranger — that's the only thing you know against him that you can prove . . . Now, I've seen enough violence to last me forever . . . . I won't have any in here. You people can eat or leave. I serve everybody who comes in. If you don't like that, leave. But you might as well eat what you ordered because you're all going to pay for it, anyway."

Jim spent the afternoon riding about the valley outside the town. He felt better in the open, and he cooled off. When he thought about Rosemary, he grinned, admiring her.

The valley was lovely, even with the touch of winter in the afternoon air, the sun going chill before three; despite everything, he felt again the urge to live here, to make a homestead for himself and Eualie, to call this place home.

He rode back into town before dark, bedded the gray down behind the jail, and walked toward the hotel, tension building in him. He had to be rejected just about one more time and he was going to strike back whether he wanted to or not; he was ready to buck.

He strode up the hotel steps, across the veranda, and into the lobby, looking neither left nor right.

He saw the way the hotel clerk's face got gray when he recognized him. Jim's fists clenched, and he took longer steps, jaw set, daring that clerk to refuse him a room.

The clerk's shoulders sagged, and Jim was ready to hear a polite but definite refusal. When the clerk instead merely turned the register and handed him a pen, Jim was so surprised he almost spoke in rage anyhow.

"How long will you be with us?" the clerk said.

Jim scratched his name on the ledger. "I don't know." He didn't mean to be abrupt, but the rage was in him.

The clerk shrugged, found a key, handed it across the desk. Jim waited, but the clerk did not speak. Jim read the room number on his key, exhaled heavily, and went to the stairs.

He slowed, going up the stairs. He even grinned as he went slowly along the upper corridor looking for his room. He was pleased to find that it was a corner room with cross ventilation and looked down on main street — the Bright Star, the doctor's cottage, and Rosemary Meade's restaurant beyond it. Maybe these people weren't so bad, once they got to know you, once you got to know them — once there was a little mutual trust.

He had not realized he was so tired. He locked his door, undressed in the fading daylight, and fell across the bed. He ached with weariness, and fell asleep, and dreamed of Eualie and home — wherever that was.

TWELVE

Three days later, Rosemary walked with Jim along the sun-baked street to Judge Griffin's office.

The judge bowed Rosemary to a chair in a courtly manner. He said, "Hear Rosemary has been showing you the places around the valley you might buy?"

"Yes."

"Rosemary's a real chamber of commerce," the judge said. He waited expectantly behind his desk. He handled most real estate transactions in the valley. "You found a place you want to buy?"

Jim described the place he'd chosen. Rosemary sat at the front window, watching the street.

"Sounds like the old Brumby place," the judge said, glancing at Rosemary. She nodded. The judge shook his head. " 'Bad Luck Brumby Place' folks around here call it, Gilmore, you sure it's what you want? The house was almost burned away."

"It's what I want." Jim nodded. "Parts standing have good lumber. Be a repair job that I can handle myself. There's a good well, and water, and natural winter shelter. Good graze. It's what I want."

The judge stared at Rosemary. "Haven't you shown Gilmore any of the good places around here?"

Rosemary flushed. "It's what he wants. He kept going back to it."

"It ain't the best a man could buy," the judge said.

"It's his choice," Rosemary said. "I was only trying to be friendly showing him around. Seems our people have been everything else."

"Maybe a man's a fool to stay where he isn't wanted," Jim said. "But I can't keep moving until folks rush out with open arms."

"Well." The judge considered, staring at the ceiling. "Three hundred dollars seems to me a reasonable price for the Brumby place. As you say, good graze, good water?"

"It's too much," Rosemary stood up. "Two hundred and fifty —"

"No," Jim spoke hastily. He shoved his hand in his pocket. "Three hundred is fair. Fix up the papers, judge. I want to buy it."

When they were on the street again, Rosemary looked at him, frowning. "Why did you pay more than you had to?" she said. "He knew that was high —"

"I've got to let them take me for a while," Jim said. "They don't like me, Rosemary. I've got to make them like me, or move on. I've had enough of moving. This is going to be my home."

She nodded and smiled as if pleased about something. She left him, going into her restaurant.

Jim rode the gray out to the Brumby place. The barn was gone; half the house stood charred and black.

He turned the gray out to the rich pasture and set to work. It was the kind of house Eualie would like. He was anxious to have her follow him from Winter Sage. Something bad had happened to them back there, gossip, his own doubting, loss of faith, on top of his woes with the ranch. Here in the Kiowa Valley they could start over, and things would be as they were at first between them.

He worked feverishly. The sun seemed to race him, spinning downward beyond the Witch Broom hills. When night fell, he cursed because he could not see anything he'd accomplished.

He whistled in the gray, rode in to Rosemary Meade's and ate supper. He felt her eyes on him as he ate, but she merely asked if he liked his meal.

At the hotel, he turned up a lamp, sat figuring the lumber he would have to buy, the cost of shipping Eualie's things here from Winter Sage, a few head of cattle to get started on. He felt himself sweating. But be was too tired to do much worrying. He toppled across the bed, asleep in the midst of his figuring.

Kip Bowne awaited him at the Brumby place the next morning.

When Jim rode up, Kip was walking around inspecting the work Jim had done the day before.

"Hear you're building," Kip said. "Thought you might need hired help."

"You a carpenter?" Jim said. "Thought you were town marshal?"

"That's mostly nighthawking," Kip said, "Keeping down trouble in the saloon and the streets. People know I don't make much — they expect me to take other jobs when I can find them . . . Besides," his young eyes clouded, "it's tough on Isabel, trying to live on what I make."

Jim nodded. There was much the marshal wasn't saying, but he didn't question him further. He did some quick figuring: the cost of a man by the day, the things he needed. But hiring Kip would speed the work. With Kip helping, he could see the end of work on the house. He could send for Eualie to come at once.

They worked well, and when Kip quit at four that afternoon, they could see the house taking shape, becoming livable.

Jim was working alone by lantern light when he heard a horse ride into the yard a little past eight that night. He walked to the front door of the house.

In the light from behind him, he recognized Rosemary. She carried a covered basket of lunch.

"You didn't stop for supper," she said. "I knew you'd be hungry."

"Thanks, Rosemary."

Her smile was wry. "It's all right." She looked at him in a direct way. "I have a feeling about you coming here. A good feeling. Don't ask me to explain that. I couldn't." She smiled. "I wanted to come out."

He said, "As the house gets nearer being ready, I get more excited about having Eualie out here."

Rosemary spread the lunch on the front porch, sat across from Jim as he ate fried chicken. "What's she like, Jim?"

He frowned, trying to picture Eualie for her. "Eualie? Well, not like you. More like Kip's wife Isabel, I reckon. She's a lovely girl, but maybe her folks spoiled her some.

They had money. They didn't want us to marry because I had none — and steadily got worse . . . Eualie and I weren't happy at Winter Sage . . . Maybe we will be here."

"I hope so," she said. "I really do. Nobody knows how terrible it is to lose the one you love — until you've lost them. I know. If people knew what a precious thing happiness was, they'd hang on like it was — gold."

"How did your husband die, Rosemary?"

She lifted her shoulders, brown eyes meeting his directly. "He was in — our house. Where I have the restaurant now. He was — shot in the back, from the dark. Over a year ago."

"Why?"

"I don't know."

"Didn't they find who did it?"

"No."

"But you must have some idea?"

"I said I don't know!" For the first time since he'd known her, Jim Gilmore saw a shadow of fear flicker across Rosemary's face. After a long moment in which she seemed to be holding her breath, she said, "Randal had discovered a gold vein, there — in the Witch Broom hills. He registered it, swearing we were going to be rich . . . He never got to work it."

"What happened to it?"

337

"I had to sell it." Again he saw the shadows swirl in her eyes, as if she feared even discussing the mine.

"To Abel Tornet, I suppose?"

"No." She shook her head, "Abel wanted me to hang on." She shook her head again, her chin tilting, and sighed. "But it takes money to get gold out of the earth. I didn't have it. I sold the rights to Stan Mills."

He waited, but she had said all she would say. She glanced about the dark yard as if suddenly afraid of the shadows. There was so much unsaid, so much she wouldn't even discuss that Jim just looked at her, scowling. When he saw she would not talk further about herself, he changed the subject. She sat and watched him as he worked an hour longer, and then they rode back together in her carriage, trailing the gray. . . .

THIRTEEN

Jim Gilmore looked up from the inside finishing work on his house three days later. He and Kip had been working in silence for three hours. Silence wasn't part of Kip's natural self.

"What's eating you?" Jim asked.

Kip went on working a moment, then looked up. "Who me? Nothing." He glanced

338

around. "Place about ready to live in."

Jim nodded. "Thanks to you. But that's not what's on your mind."

Kip Bowne shrugged. But Jim persisted. "Is it about me — about that bank robbery?"

"No. I don't think you robbed the bank."

"Find any trace of the three jaspers that tried to spring me from the trial?"

"No." Kip spoke reluctantly, working. Something was eating at him, all right. "I trailed them west. They headed toward the Witch Brooms. But I lost the trail. We got no idea who they were."

"Lot of men at the mine not too well known in town. And those sacks covered their faces."

"Sure. It *could* have been somebody at the mine. But why would they do it?"

Jim straightened, feeling the muscles in his back protest. "Because somebody was afraid I wouldn't get hung — but I might get shot and killed making a break."

Kip stared at him as if he were insane, "But who?"

"You're the marshal."

"Yeah," Kip said. "That's right." His young face darkened, and he went back to work. He worked steadily, with no pleasure in it, no willingness to talk.

Finally, Jim said, "I thought you were my friend, Kip."

"Well, I work for you."

"Look. You got a burr in your tail. Speak up."

They faced each other. Kip's young face flushed, then his jaw set in a hard line. He took a deep breath. "You going in to Rosemary's to eat lunch?"

Jim nodded. "Why?"

Kip shrugged. "Reckon you know what you're doing, Gilmore. But — well, figure I ought to warn you, people are talking."

Gilmore swore in a hard, taut voice. "People are always talking. That's one thing you can take odds on."

Kip glanced at sunlight bright on the dusty floor. "They say Rosemary spends all her time talking to you when you're in there — and rides out here to visit you."

Jim stared at him, remembering the gossip that had poisoned things between him and Eualie at Winter Sage. "Don't they know I'm building this house so I can bring my wife here?"

Kip shook his head. "They don't care. They only go by what they see."

"What they see! What do they see?"

"What they can see is that you and Rosemary spend a lot of time together."

"She was the first friend I had in this town — not counting you."

"Well, I like Rosemary. She's had a raw deal. I don't like to see her hurt."

They left the house, saddled up, and rode silently along the road into town.

Kip stared across the valley, deep in his own thoughts, and Jim was thinking: in Winter Sage they talked about Eualie — here they've started on me. Out of frying pan into hot coals.

His fists tightened on the reins. Damn them; they hated him. Rosemary was friendly. But they wouldn't tolerate that.

He glanced at Kip's set face. He was glad in a way this stupid mistake had occurred. It showed clearly that gossips were all alike, Winter Sage or Kiowa City. People didn't change much from one place to another, and you were a fool to think you could run away from trouble. But all this made him feel better about the whispers that had swirled around him about Eualie. It helped renew lost faith. Gossip could hurt you only if you let it hurt.

Kip went to his cottage to eat lunch with Isabel. Jim rode to the restaurant, found it half-filled with people who were silent or barely civil when he entered.

He found himself hoping Rosemary would

not be too friendly today, but she smiled when she brought his order, asking how work was progressing, brought her own lunch, and sat at his table by the window to eat with him.

He frowned faintly, seeing that she was oblivious to whispers.

He sighed. "Looks like you're going to lose a star customer, or a lot of others," he told Rosemary.

Her head jerked up, face going gray under the golden flesh-tint. She'd heard those whispers, too, even if she had tried to ignore them.

"What do you mean?" But her voice was too casual.

He stared at her, trying to force her to meet his gaze.

"Kip says there is a lot of gossip about us."

"I suppose so. No man can ever be friendly with any woman without somebody talking."

"I don't like to see you hurt."

She shrugged. "It should be over when Eualie arrives."

"Yes. I hope so. For your sake."

She glanced about the room, meeting directly as many gazes as would remain fixed on her. She laughed. "Stop being so serious. You're a happily married man. Your wife will be here tomorrow. I know how rare happiness is. I wouldn't come between a man and his wife — even if I wanted to. What have you got to worry about?"

He tried to smile. "You're good people."

"Sure I am. And nothing anybody can whisper about me will change it." She shook her head. "People have got to have something to talk about. Don't let it bother you. As for me, I'm a big girl. I can take care of myself." Her brown eyes darkened. "Are you worried about what it might do — to you and Eualie?"

"No." His jaw was set tautly. "They gossiped about Eualie, back home. So the tune's the same — just the words are changed."

FOURTEEN

Eualie's stage was delayed four hours, and it was 1 a.m. when it arrived at the stage depot in Kiowa City.

The whole town, except for the lights at Stan Mills' Bright Star, had been dark for more than three hours when the stage creaked and jangled to a stop, the driver cursing the horses.

Jim stood in the shadows under the over-

343

hang with Isabel and Kip Bowne. They'd insisted upon waiting up with him to meet Eualie.

Jim felt his stomach go empty. He was glad Kip and Isabel were with him. It felt strange, waiting here for Eualie to step off that stage. It was as if she were a stranger to him. Things had been so rough. Now they had to be better.

He took a step forward, watching for the first sight of Eualie when she stepped out of the Concord. He paused, seeing her, feeling elation, excitement, and a sense of dread he could not explain even to himself.

He watched Eualie step out of the stage, giving her hand to the driver who helped her alight. She moved in a tired, half-drugged way, like a child wakened from sleep.

He saw she wore a new traveling suit, and small pert hat on Indian-dark hair that lay in soft waves about her face and roiled in a smart bun at the nape of her neck. She was wearing her hair differently, he thought. He saw the tilt of her tiny nose, the squared look to her fine-cut jaw.

She stood a moment, looking around before she saw him.

In her face there was a look of utter desolation.

Jim stepped forward in long strides, going toward Eualie. Never mind the look of despair. She was tired after the long rough ride. He would make it all up to her. He had promised her things were going to be all right, and this was a promise he could keep. Doubt had made an ugly wall of tense silence between them back at Winter Sage. But everything was new here.

He said, "Eualie." He put out his arms.

She came slowly toward him, fatigued, dusty, and ready to cry. "Oh, Jim," she said. "It's so dark . . . It's like I stepped off the end of the world."

He pulled her against him for a moment before the other passengers, and smiling Kip and Isabel. Over Eualie's head he saw Isabel was studying Eualie narrowly in the light from the stage office. He grinned to himself. Nobody could find anything wrong with Eualie — even tired out, she was lovely.

"It's going to be all right, Eualie," he said, holding her. "Give it a chance."

Her voice had the hard flint in it that he remembered. "I don't like it. I want to go back home, Jim."

He tried to laugh it off. "This is home," he told her.

He turned, leading her with his arm about her to where Isabel and Kip Bowne stood in the lighted shaft from the stage windows.

"These are my friends, Isabel and Kip Bowne," Jim said to Eualie. "Kip helped me fix up the house — and Isabel says she wants to help you fix your things so it will seem like home to you."

Isabel said, "It's not much of a town, Eualie. But you'll get used to it, dear."

Kip laughed. "It's not the end of the world. Really. It just looks like it."

"Sure," Isabel said. "It's not the end of the world. The world ended miles back there."

"A hundred miles," Eualie said in a tired, chilled voice.

Jim and Kip set Eualie's trunk and valise in the rear of the surrey Jim had rented from Lon Persons' livery for the evening.

He put out his hand to help Eualie into the carriage, changed his mind, and swung her up in his arms.

She protested, voice sharp. "Jim, stop that. Put me down. What will people think?"

"Lord knows," Jim said, depositing her in the surrey seat and swinging up beside her. "But you're here now, and I got no time to worry about that."

Isabel and Kip stood in the rectangle of wan saffron light and waved good night.

He felt Eualie sitting stiff and withdrawn

from him on the seat. He told himself everything was strange to her, and she'd feel better when they got home where her things were — or tomorrow, sure, things would look brighter.

As he rode past Rosemary Meade's restaurant he saw a light in the front windows. For a moment he was almost certain he saw Rosemary standing tall and alone in the doorway.

"Will Allbrand says to tell you if you need anything, Jim, you can always call on him," Eualie said after a brief silence.

"Forget Will Allbrand," Jim said. He closed his hand on hers, clenched in her lap. "This is our home, Eualie. We're not leaning on Will Allbrand, not on anybody."

"I'm sure he was only trying to be friendly," she said in a chilled away.

"He always has been. Until people talked about the way he was always at the ranch."

"My God, Jim," she burst out, "That's the worst thing I ever heard you say. Will Allbrand is old enough to be my father — and bald besides. My goodness, the way you talk."

He exhaled. "This is our home, Eualie. There's no Will Allbrand around to make things easier. We're going to live here, and we're going to try to be happy together —

the way we were once."

"We could have been happy at home," she said, staring out into the darkness and silence, "if you hadn't been so jealous."

"I never said anything to you —"

She laughed at him, "You didn't have to. It was in your face. You think I didn't see it? Even Will Allbrand when he tried to help us. Just because his wife died, and he was widowed. He tried to be nice — but all you wanted was to get us away. You've been a fool, Jim."

"All right," he said at last, "I was a fool. But that's all past. Come here."

She tried to protest, but he pulled her against him, letting the bay run with the carriage. His mouth covered hers, his arm closed on her tightly. First, her mouth lay flat under his, but slowly he felt her grow warm, responding. She sighed, her arms stealing around his back, closing her nails into his shoulders in the way she had. "I love you," she whispered against his mouth, "Really I do, Jim. It's just that — we've had so much trouble."

"We're going to be all right."

"Maybe it was my fault, Jim. I wanted so much that you could never give me — but I couldn't help that."

He thought about that the next day when

he and Kip started to work rebuilding the barn. So much he couldn't give her.

He pounded nails furiously. That old feeling of emptiness and insufficiency had settled in his stomach since the moment Eualie had stepped off the stagecoach. The old doubt had returned to sit like unmalleable stone in his chest. When Eualie was in his arms, he felt alone, as if she were not really there — as if her mind and her heart were somewhere else.

"Hey," Kip laughed. "You trying to get this thing done in five minutes?"

Jim looked up, hardly knowing what Kip had said. Kip shook his head, "You can kill yourself working that fast in this sun if you want to, Jim. I'm not going to try to keep up with you."

"All right," Jim said. "All right. Don't. I guess something is in me. I got to work it out of me."

He heard Isabel and Eualie laughing and talking together as they worked setting up furniture, placing curtains inside the house.

His jaw set harder. What was the matter with him? He should be glad they got along so well, shouldn't he? He wanted Eualie to make friends, didn't he? Then what was eating at him? Why did he keep thinking their laughter sounded so empty and foolish.

He worked faster, trying to drown the sound in the banging of his hammer. He searched his mind, unable to say why the very sound of their laughter exasperated him. Maybe there was nothing wrong with their laughter; maybe something was wrong with him.

He wanted something. Looked as if he would never have it, as if he wasn't even sure what it was.

In two days the barn was up, and he and Kip moved out to build a feed lean-to and set out a pole corral.

His mind was chewing over the sick, empty longing inside him, the wrong that had trailed him, like something Eualie had brought in her trunk, from Winter Sage.

Kip said something to him, and he jerked his head up, not even hearing him. "What?"

Kip's voice was flat. "Trade has fallen off at Rosemary's. Sharp."

Jim felt his heart lurch. Damn them, they had no right to treat Rosemary like that. They ought to know her by now, even if they didn't know him.

"You — think it's my fault?" he asked, straightening.

"Hell no. It's just a fool idea them people have got," Kip said.

But Jim felt the sense of wrong spreading

inside him. There was nothing he could do about what was happening to Rosemary in town, but he felt there ought to be. Too bad a man couldn't fight gossip with fists and guns.

A few days later, he and Kip were finishing up work in the barnyard when Eualie put her head out the kitchen door and called to him. "Jim. There's a friend of yours here to visit you."

Rosemary was in the living room when he and Kip entered. The first thing Jim saw was the way Isabel and Eualie exchanged meaningful glances and smiles behind Rosemary's back.

It was the first time Rosemary had met Eualie, and the young widow felt a sense of shock because Eualie was not at all what she'd expected to see.

She looked from Eualie to Isabel and back. From all Jim Gilmore had told her, she'd expected a small, cuddly, and helpless-appearing girl like Isabel Bowne.

She sighed. Though Eualie was small, she was dark, and there was a look of strength and steel about her; she appeared to be a willful, headstrong, stubborn young woman. As Gilmore had admitted, maybe her parents had spoiled her, but Eualie had a stubborn set to her jaw. She looked strong enough to get anything she wanted.

Eualie glanced at Isabel, exchanging a secret smile. It was plain she and Isabel had discussed Rosemary and Jim's friendship for her in detail. She said to Jim in a sweet tone, "Rosemary came out to see you, Jim dear — on business. Isn't that what you said, Mrs. Meade?"

Rosemary remained cool. "Yes. But I came partly to meet you. I've heard so much about you."

"I'll bet you have," Eualie said, glancing at Isabel again.

Jim said, "What was it you wanted to see me about, Rosemary?"

Rosemary bit her lip. "I'm afraid it's — not anything I could talk about here, after all."

Eualie and Isabel were exchanging glances.

"Maybe some other time," Rosemary said.

"Let me walk you to your carriage," Jim offered.

They walked silently out to where Rosemary had left her carriage in the front yard. He helped Rosemary into the front seat; still she had not spoken. He saw that her face was rigid.

"What is it?"

"It's nothing I can tell you here," she said.

352

"Maybe I've changed my mind, anyhow. I've no right —"

"What is it, Rosemary? You helped me, I want to help you."

"You don't owe me anything."

"I didn't say I did. I want to help you."

Something was troubling Rosemary so terribly that she looked about, as if lost. She did not know where to turn. He saw that she had reached the end of her rope, or she would never have come out here.

"You got to tell me, Rosemary, I'll just keep hounding you until you do."

She tried to smile. "You don't think we're being talked about enough?"

"The hell with that. What is it?"

She shook her head. "I couldn't tell you here. Will you come to — my back door — late tonight, I'll wait up for you. When I hear you outside, turn off the lights and you can come in. I wouldn't ask you to do this, Jim, but I don't know what to do — I don't know where to turn."

FIFTEEN

Jim tied his gray in a thicket some hundred yards behind Rosemary Meade's cottage about ten-thirty that night.

He moved stealthily through the under-

353

growth to the rear of her yard. The settlement had not yet spread in this direction. It was easy to come stealthily upon the house from here. Jim could see how a man could wait in ambush, shoot Rosemary's husband through a window, and escape without leaving a trace.

Most of the lights were out in the town. He glanced around, thinking about Eualie and Isabel at his house. They'd been almost pleased to see him go. He'd never seen women with so much to talk about. Kip was night-hawking on his marshal's job. How Kip worked all day and most of the night, Jim didn't know. Kip had one aim in life — to make enough money to keep Isabel happy. Jim wondered how much that would be. Then he thought emptily of what Eualie had said that first night she arrived here: he could never give her the things she wanted.

He shook these thoughts from his mind, crouching close to dark shadows around a stunted tamarack. Nearer to Rosemary's back door were young cottonwood trees, looking to be three years old, something her husband had probably set out as a windbreak. Until the Chinook blew in from those hills, winter blizzards out here were Alaska cold.

He whistled once, and almost instantly

the lamp in the kitchen was turned down, extinguished.

She was waiting for him. He went hurriedly across the yard.

Rosemary held the door open. She closed it behind him and they stood a moment in the darkened kitchen. Jim realized he was breathless.

"This wouldn't do you any good, if anyone found out," he said.

"What I have to tell you — is more important than any fear of silly gossip," Rosemary answered. She went about the room, pulled the blinds tight so no light leaked around the windows or sills when she set a match to the lamp again.

The wan light filled the room.

Jim said, "What is it, Rosemary? What is it we couldn't have discussed right out in front of God and everybody?"

She sighed, "Maybe I shouldn't tell you about it — even here. But I could never talk about it where anyone might overhear me. I'm — almost afraid to think about it."

"All right," Jim said. "I'm glad you sent for me then."

She spread her hands. "I've no right to burden you with it. Yet, all I really want is some advice . . . You see, Jim, I've been thinking ever since you came here — ever since you had the courage to stand up against these people when you were right, and knew you were right, against great odds. I've no right to be afraid."

"I never said I wasn't scared."

"But you did what you knew was right." She pressed the back of her hand against her mouth a moment. "That's the kind of courage I haven't had. But lately, I knew I had to do something, or I couldn't live with myself. Then — because you're the first man I've met that I trust enough, I knew I had to ask you what I ought to do . . . I know something, Jim. I'm sure I do. I'll go to the sheriff with it if you think I ought to."

"About your husband? About who killed your husband?"

She nodded, staring about the lighted room, shadows in her eyes. "Yes. First, I better tell you that it has been told to me that a lot of gossip against me — and you — has come from Stan Mills, of all people."

"Stan Mills. I thought he was your friend."

"Oh, no. I'm afraid of him. I always have been. You'll see why. But I couldn't understand why he would start ugly whispers about me, try to drive me away . . . But I can't let him do that."

"All right," Jim said. "I'm with you. What

is it you know about Stan Mills?"

Her face muscles were rigid. Her eyes were stark. She held her right fist clenched before them a moment, then opened it slowly, the lamplight winking in two slices of glass in her palm.

"This is what I had to show you," she said. "I was afraid if I showed it to you in the restaurant somebody might see it — know I have it — and I never trusted anyone enough before to show this to them."

Jim was staring at the two slivers of glass. He pushed them together on her whitened palm. When they fitted, he saw that they were the lens from a pair of glasses.

"Stan Mills wears rimless glasses," he said.

She nodded. "Randal was shot. In this room. Through that window from the back yard. Late at night. I was wild with grief at first, and then the sheriff came — and they searched the grounds out there — and found nothing. But the next day, I went out, as if drawn out there to find something — anything. And under a tree with a low hanging limb — I found this broken lens."

"You didn't take it to the sheriff?"

"I knew it belonged to Stan Mills. I knew when I saw it. But suppose Stan had been out there with the sheriff when he was looking for a trace of the killer — or suppose he'd lost it before when he was out there talking with Randal?"

Jim nodded. "And you were alone, and you were afraid for Stan Mills to know you had this. If he had killed Randall, he'd also kill you."

Rosemary nodded. "He was too powerful. Even more powerful now. Suppose Tom Walker told him I had this lens, and he had broken it that night? Then in the next weeks, Stan was good to me. He bought the rights to Randall's gold claim. As Abel Tornet and everybody said, all it was was a claim, and yet Stan paid me a fair price. I could live — even without this restaurant. Yet, all this time I've been afraid of Stan. I was afraid of him before, and it got worse. I even thought of destroying these pieces of his glasses. But now, I know I can't."

Jim sighed, "You still can't go to the sheriff, either. One way or another Stan Mills would hear you've got this lens. It may be evidence against him, or not. But you can't take a chance. He might be afraid to let you live if he worried about it."

She paced the room, as if caged, "What can I do?"

"Can you just trust me to look around a few days?"

"I do trust you, I would never have shown

you this except I trust you — but I've no right to drag you into my fight."

"Maybe it isn't just your fight. Maybe it's everybody's fight — against a man who would kill a friend to get something he wanted. . . . Anyhow, it won't hurt to let me look around . . . just let me see what I can find out."

"You think Stan Mills might have lost it there — that night?" Rosemary turned and looked at him, her face gray.

"I think he might have shot your husband through that window, turned to run, banged into one of those young trees that your husband set out —"

"The cottonwoods," Rosemary whispered.

Jim nodded. "If he broke his glasses as he ran, he wouldn't dare stop to find them. He might have joined the posse in the search out there. But all this time he hasn't known for sure what happened to them. It makes sense to me. Stan Mills wants to own everything that makes money in this valley. Let me check it."

She sighed heavily as if a terrible burden had been removed from her shoulders, and after a moment, eyes blurred with tears, she nodded.

SIXTEEN

Jim lay sleepless, staring at the dark ceiling. It was almost 2 a.m. He moved restlessly, wondering if he would ever sleep.

"Jim?"

"Yes. I thought you were asleep."

"I can't sleep," Eualie said. "Isabel told me of all the trouble you had when you first came here, Jim. . . . You should have told me. . . . I don't think it was very fair of you to bring me here — to face what people think of you."

"The hell with what people think about me," he said. "I haven't done anything wrong."

"Isabel said nobody wanted you to stay here. She said it seemed almost that you stayed to — to defy them."

"I ran away from Winter Sage, Eualie, because people were talking about you —"

"Lies. All lies."

"What they said about me were, too. Lies. We had to have a home somewhere. If people were going to lie — I'd rather it be about me than you."

"Are they all lies, Jim? Even what they say about you — and that widow?"

He sat up in the bed, staring at Eualie in the filmy darkness. "My God, Eualie, she was trying to be kind."

"So was Will Allbrand!"

"All right! We've got to live somewhere, I chose to live here. It's good land. We can make something — if you'll just give us a chance."

They stopped talking, hearing the sound of galloping horses in the yard. A moment later there was a pound of heavy knuckles at the front door.

Jim got up, dressed in the darkness.

He got his gun from its holster without knowing why he did it.

"What's the matter?" Eualie said.

"Stay there," he told her. "Nothing is wrong."

But in the darkness he was scowling. There had been a sense of wrong in the very atmosphere since he'd left Rosemary's house, stealing across her yard and returning here a little after eleven. Isabel and Eualie had been gaily discussing clothes. They got along wonderfully: both hated Kiowa Valley, both loved fancy clothes, each wanted a great deal more than she possessed.

He moved out of the room in the darkness. When he returned from Rosemary's, Kip had been here to take Isabel home. Kip had not mentioned anything unusual going on in town. He had not asked Jim where he'd been. Eualie had been full of life while Kip and Isabel were in the house, but when they were gone, she'd fallen silent, and they'd gone silently to bed, each lying there sleepless in the dark.

The pounding on his door was louder, like thunder. "All right," he called. He crossed the small hall, pulled open the door.

Sheriff Tom Walker stood in the doorway. Behind him, Jim saw a dozen mounted men. He recognized another of Tom Walker's posses.

"What do you want?" Jim said.

"Step outside," the sheriff said.

Some of the men stirred when they saw the gun in Jim's hand. Jim closed the front door, feeling the chill of night wind, the prickling of wrong.

"I'll take that gun," Walker said, "No sense nobody getting hurt."

"What do you want?" Jim said again.

"I don't know," Walker said, staring at him in the gray dark. "Depends on what you tell us."

"About what?"

"Payroll has been robbed from the mining office," Walker said.

Jim felt himself go tense. "What's that got to do with me?"

The sheriff turned, said, "Light that lantern. All right, Lucas. You come up here."

Somebody handed the sheriff a lighted lantern. Walker raised it aloft beside Jim's face.

The sheriff spoke to the man named Lucas. "This look like the man that robbed you?"

The mining company guard stepped forward, staring with squinted eyes into Jim's face. Jim smelled the strong fumes of whisky. Lucas was more than half drunk. But there was a bloody gash, untended, along his right temple, and this posse took him seriously.

His gaze struck against Jim's, then fell away.

His voice was a whine. He shook his head uncertainly. "I got hit pretty hard."

"Think, man, for God's sake," the sheriff said.

"I'm not sure," Lucas said. "I think so. But there was two of them. I'm not sure."

"Where was you tonight, Gilmore?" The sheriff tilted the lantern, staring into Jim's face.

Jim breathed deeply. "I — was home," he said. "Most of the night."

He heard a sharp intake of breath. He realized it came from inside his front door.

Eualie was standing there listening.

He felt an abrupt surge of rage against these men who came galloping into his yard at the first sign of trouble.

At that moment, three posse members ran across the yard from the barn. They were afoot, their lanterns swinging, long beams of light licking upward and breaking against the thick night.

"We found part of the loot," one of the men panted. "Out there, sheriff. It was planted nice and neat under this gent's nice new barn."

There was a moment of silence. Jim was hardly aware of the men on horseback, or the man waving the sack of payroll money. He was listening for Eualie to move inside that front door. But it was as if she were standing there, tense, and not breathing.

"Reckon that just about does it," the sheriff said in a flat voice, looking at Jim in the lantern light. "You better come in to town with us, Gilmore."

SEVENTEEN

Jim Gilmore sat in a chair beside Tom Walker's cluttered desk. The sheriff's office was crowded. The men who'd formed his hastily gathered posse now sat in chairs or lounged against the bare walls.

Jim moved his gaze across their faces. There was a look of grim satisfaction about these men: they had believed Gilmore a crook from the first; now they were proved right.

Tom Walker fingered the recovered payroll money.

"Now, no sense fooling around no longer, Gilmore. No sense keeping these here men up rest of the night. This came from under your barn. You can save yourself a lot of grief by telling us where the rest of the money is."

Men in the room growled in agreement.

Jim shook his head. "I don't know."

"We don't want to stay here," Walker said. "But we will."

"I still don't know how that money got there."

Tom Walker leaned toward him across his desk. "If you got some idea you're going to get into Griffin's court again, and get away when I got the goods on you cold, you're dead wrong, Gilmore."

Jim met his gaze but did not say anything.

The sheriff shrugged as if his patience were exhausted. He twisted around in his chair, motioned two men forward from the wall. "Looks like we got to reason with this gent," he said. "You, Padgett and Johnson. Hold him. We'll get a confession before Griffin even hears we've caught the thief."

The posse expressed growling satisfaction with this plan.

Jim set himself. As Padgett and Johnson advanced warily toward him, Jim abruptly kicked his chair back, coming up to his feet.

Two men lunged forward behind him, grabbed his arms and bore him downward. Jim fought to free himself, but Padgett and Johnson were on him before he could writhe free.

The four men wrestled Jim around until Walker could snap handcuffs on his wrists behind his back. They shoved him into a chair then.

"Where's the rest of the money?" Walker said.

Jim shook his head.

He saw Walker's fist coming toward him this time, but was helpless to protect himself. Walker's knuckles struck him in the temple, and his head rocked.

Walker waited for Jim to sit up straight again before he spoke. "Where's that money, Gilmore?"

Jim shook his head. Walker hit him in the face again. Jim felt the blood spurting hot in his mouth and seeping from the corner of his lip.

The room wheeled and skidded around him.

As if from the top of a distant hill, he heard Walker's voice. "Who was in this with you?"

He tried to shake his head; he was not sure if he made it or not.

He must have shaken his head. Walker hit him in the right temple, and it was if an avalanche gushed downward through Jim's body. The pain was all down through him rather than only in his head.

He did not even hear Walker speak again, but the lawman must have spoken, because Jim was hit again on the other side of the head, the big fists slugging him. He did not even know if it were minutes, or hours, later.

From some far mountain crest somebody yelled something at him, but he had no idea what they said. The winds battered the voice to bits, and anyway it was as if there was a violent rumbling inside his head.

He sagged forward in the chair. He waited for something, and finally it was clear to him what he was waiting for. He was waiting for the sheriff to hit him again.

But nothing happened. They must have stopped hitting him, or he no longer felt the pain. He stayed slumped in the chair for a long time. Finally, he heard voices, the noises scrambled inside his head.

He felt cold water strike him in the face, and he jerked his head up. Wan daylight streaked through the office window, painful in his eyes.

He put his head back, and through a thick fog obscuring everything before him, he saw Kip Bowne leaning over him.

He pressed his eyes closed tightly, slowly opened them, and Kip was still there.

"You fool, Walker," Kip said over his shoulders. "You stupid fool. Why didn't you wait until you questioned somebody on a thing like this?"

"Don't tell me how to run this office, Bowne. We found this here money under his barn."

"Sure. And all that means is somebody put it there."

"We got a good idea it was this younker, boy. The trail led pretty clear to his place — and we found this money."

"Only Lucas has told you twenty times the mine was robbed between eleven and midnight last night. Gilmore couldn't have been out there in the Witch Broom hills. He was at his own house. He has witnesses. His own wife. Me."

"We found this here money under his

barn," Walker said again.

"How much better proof we got to get?" one of the possemen said.

Kip didn't even look at him. He stared at the sheriff. "The robbery was happening while Jim was at his house. With me."

Walker looked at the money he'd found at Jim's place, at Jim's bruised face, at Kip Bowne staring at him, at the silent ring of men who'd ridden with him last night. At last, he said, "Before you get too mighty, Mr. Marshal, where was you before eleven o'clock?"

Kip laughed, despite his rage. "Before eleven? What's that got to do with it?"

"Maybe Lucas was wrong about when that robbery took place."

Kip laughed again, shaking his head. "He's told you a dozen times he wasn't wrong. But say he was — what's it got to do with me?"

"Maybe plenty."

Kip's voice was cold. His young face was set and dangerous. Jim saw then why Kip was a respected marshal. Nobody pushed him very far.

"Go on, sheriff." Kip's voice was tense.

The sheriff blustered. "You been thicker'n — you been mighty thick with Gilmore ever since he come to town."

Kip wavered a moment between rage and laughter, but laughter won because he could not take it seriously. "Why, you fat old fool," Kip said. "So now I helped rob that mine."

"I didn't say that," Walker said. "I just asked where you was."

"Well, I can tell you where I was. I was making my rounds. But I happen to have a witness. Pop Mauser has been hearing noises in the rear of his mercantile. I was over there with him, since eight, sitting in the dark, listening. And we caught the culprit."

"Yeah?" The sheriff waited.

Kip nodded. "It was one of your brothers, Tom . . . Biggest skunk you ever saw."

Every member of the posse laughed, the tension in the room dissolving. The sheriff went gray with rage, but he was a fair man where Kip Bowne was concerned. Kip was a smart young fellow, and the sheriff admitted he'd pushed him a little too far.

He heard the nervous laughter that washed across the office.

Jim glanced at Kip whose jaw was set in a hard line, though he was smiling. Kip had the power to sway these men who knew him well. He was a good-hearted kid, a conscientious lawman. None could doubt that.

The sheriff grinned ruefully at last. "I got

my job to do, Kip. Can't help it if it makes me look bad."

"It was the *smell* I mentioned," Kip said grinning.

A man stepped forward from near the street door. Jim saw that the banker had come to the office sometime in the past few hours. "The money was under Gilmore's barn," Abel Tornet said.

Kip said, "Let us handle this, Mr. Tornet."

Jim spoke slowly, through bloodied lips. "It was another try to frame me, Kip. Same as when those jaspers tried to get me out of that courtroom."

"We found that money on your place," Walker said.

"Sure. And if I'd run from court that day, I'd of looked guilty then, too. . . . Somebody sure wants me to look guilty."

Kip nodded. "Somebody's pulling some slick work."

Kip moved away from Jim, pacing the office. He glanced at Abel Tornet, at the men in the posse, but he spoke to the sheriff as if they were alone in the office.

"It's slick work, Tom. Somebody who knows when there's a gold shipment in the bank, when there is a payroll at the mines. That needs to be somebody that lives here in this town, Tom. No stranger — like Jim

371

Gilmore — could have rode into Kiowa City at just the right time to walk off with two bags of gold. . . . Sure, it's easy for such a gent to make Jim Gilmore look guilty. The good lord knows all you jaspers want to believe the worst about him."

As Kip talked, Doc Knoblock came through the front door.

"You sent for me, Kip?" he said.

Kip nodded toward Jim's bloodied, bruised face. "See if you can patch him up, Doc."

Doc Knoblock looked at Jim with a contempt that puzzled Gilmore. But he opened his kit and set to work. Jim felt the sting of strong antiseptic, but he was too bitter to feel any physical pain.

Tom Walker said, "All right. You was home at eleven. Lucas can be wrong about the time of that robbery. So where was you before eleven? Was you at Mills' saloon?"

Stan Mills spoke with a tone of regret. "He wasn't there."

Tom Walker straightened with a look of satisfaction in his face, "Any you other men see Gilmore tonight between nine and eleven?"

Jim felt Knoblock's eyes probing into his as the doctor worked over his face, hands rough. Each man in the room spoke quietly, definitely. None had seen Gilmore.

"Where were you?" Walker said.

"You was some place, that's sure to hell," Kip said. He grinned, "No matter what Tom keeps saying, Lucas has said the robbery happened around midnight, but clear it up, Jim. Go ahead. Tell him where you was — and I'll get witnesses to back your story if it takes the rest of the day."

Jim glanced up at Kip standing beyond Doc Knoblock's shoulder.

The young marshal's face was pulled in an expectant smile.

Jim breathed deeply, feeling the sting of antiseptic, the rough way Knoblock probed at his bruises. "I'm sorry, Kip," Jim said. "I won't say."

Kip's mouth sagged. "You *won't* say! Lord a-mighty, Jim. You want more beating? This is just the kind of thing they can use against you — no matter what Lucas says about time. They can even prove he was wrong, you give them something like this to hold against you. You got to say where you was."

Jim stared at him, shook his head.

Doc Knoblock stepped back from Jim. His face was gray and strained. His thin hand, clenched on the poison-labeled bottle, shook.

"I'll tell you where Gilmore was," the doctor said, "And I'll tell you why he won't speak. . . . I dare say, he is innocent of robbing the mine. I suppose he is, no matter where you found that money, Sheriff. The reason he won't speak is he thinks he's protecting a fair lady's name. But if that's what he thinks, he's dead wrong. He should have thought of that before he went sneaking into the widow Meade's back door last night. I saw him. I was sitting out on my back stoop, alone. He thought he was clever, sneaking in unseen. But I saw him clear, and that's where he was."

Some of the men guffawed suddenly, voices harsh.

Other men stared at Jim, white-lipped, narrow-eyed. In their faces he could see clearly what they thought of him. This had been a good town until he came along, and Rosemary Meade had been one of its most respected women — until he came along to foul it all.

Jim, face gray under the raw bruises left by Sheriff Walker's fists, turned to look at those men.

He saw Stan Mills' eyes behind rimless glasses were stricken and dark. Stan Mills was staring at Jim, and after a moment, he stepped quietly to the street door, and went through it, closing it after him without a word of farewell.

Walker stood rigid beside his desk. He moved his gaze from Kip Bowne to Doc Knoblock and back to Jim Gilmore.

"You brought nothing but trouble to this town since the day you come," Walker said, "Now, you ain't got trouble enough, you got to flaunt your own wife's good name, and the good name of a fine woman of this town."

Jim shook his head, but said nothing.

Walker got his keys, unlocked the handcuffs, removed them from Jim's wrists. Jim sat a moment, massaging his forearms.

Walker said, "Go on. Get out, Gilmore. I found that money at your place, but I'm letting you go. . . . I ain't holding you. I can't stand the sight of you."

He turned away and went around his desk. He sat down heavily in his swivel chair so it squealed in protest.

Jim got up slowly. He looked at Kip Bowne. The young marshal's smile was gone. Kip's face was gray, eyes pained. Jim started to speak to him, but Kip only shook his head, and turned away. . . .

EIGHTEEN

Isabel Bowne was washing breakfast dishes, watching the street that ran in front of her small cottage.

She saw Stan Mills ride to her front gate on his big palomino. For a moment she stood staring at him through the window.

Hastily, she dried her hands on the dish towel, ripped off her apron and hurried through the house to her bedroom mirror. She patted her hair into place, dabbed the perspiration from her forehead.

She was smoothing color on her cheeks when she heard his knock at her door. The sound of his rapping, asking to come in, made her heart pound faster.

She called out, "Just a minute."

Holding her breath, she made a rapid last minute inspection and then went running through the cottage to the front door. Reaching it, she slowed down, tipped her tongue across her lips.

Stan followed her into the parlor. He was so tall she felt smaller than ever beside him. He was so tall the room seemed to shrink to form-fitting size when he entered it. It wasn't large, and even a large room seemed smaller when Stan Mills was in it.

She saw the way he glanced at the cheap

furnishings, and nervously she dusted at the center table with her handkerchief, wondering why he had come here like this in broad daylight, wondering what the neighbors would say, wondering what she would find to say to him.

"You look mighty fetching this morning," he said.

"Why, I've been doing my house work."

She felt his disturbing gaze moving over her unhurriedly. "Mighty pretty," he said. "Pretty enough to eat. Pretty enough to kiss."

"Do I?" she said with an arch smile. Then she spoke from habit. "Such a way to talk — to an old married lady."

"We're alone in here, Isabel, let's not pretend with each other," Stan said.

She felt empty. "Why, Stanley Mills, whatever do you mean?"

"You know what I mean. Don't you, Isabel?"

She felt the smile falter on her mouth. She knew what he meant; she had always known what he meant when he looked at her in that upsetting way. But then she remembered the way he had looked at Rosemary Meade, too. In a needing way he'd never looked at her.

She inhaled deeply, turning away. Looked

as if all the men wanted Rosemary. She thought of the whispers she'd heard about Rosemary and Jim Gilmore. Well, you certainly never could tell by looking at a woman what she was.

She said, coolly, "I think you find a lot of women who affect you that way, Mr. Mills."

He laughed. "What's this *Mr. Mills* stuff?"

"Isn't that your name?"

"Stan," he corrected her. After a moment he laughed and nodded. "And I do find women I love to look at. I enjoy looking at a lovely woman. That's why I was glad of this opportunity to ride over this morning."

"Oh?" she said, relenting. She turned, looking at him again.

"Yes," Stan said. "I wanted to see Kip. Is he around?"

Isabel felt the surge of chilled disappointment. "No," she said. She waited, but he did not speak. She moved toward the front door ahead of him. "I'll tell him you were here."

"What's the hurry?" He caught her arm, "Can't you and I talk?"

"Whatever would we talk about?" she said. But she paused, smiling up at him.

"Let me stay a moment?"

She nodded. She sat on the lumpy divan. He walked over and sat beside her. He was too near, but she did not move away. She did not move at all. There was a scent about him, maybe soap, maybe something indefinably male. She couldn't say, but knew only it excited her.

"Yes," Stan was saying. "Tell Kip I was here. Ask him to come over to my office."

"All right." She sat waiting for his hand to cover hers.

"I think I might have a daytime job for him."

"How nice," she said, barely listening.

"Out at my ranch," Stan said.

"Your ranch?" Now she frowned faintly, meeting his gaze. "Won't that keep him away from home all day?"

He smiled faintly.

She met his gaze, feeling the color creeping up from her throat.

"It might," Stan said in a low voice. "He'd have to be out there all day."

"Oh."

"I won't think of offering him such a job, Isabel, if you'll be lonely with him gone —"

"I — I might be lonely at first," she said. Her gaze lowered under him. "But Kip has to take any job he can get."

"I'll pay him well," Stan said, watching her.

She smiled, nodding. "We do need all the

money we can get."

She felt his big hand close on her icy fingers.

"The only thing is," Stan said, "I wouldn't want you to be lonely. I wouldn't ever want a pretty young girl like you to be lonely."

"Oh, Kip ought to take the job," Isabel said. "I — want him to."

Stan's hands slid up her arms. She felt herself trembling. She had dreamed about his touching her like this. She'd lain awake in the night thinking how it would be. But she knew it was an excitement she'd never even been able to imagine.

She tipped her tongue across her lips. She wanted him to kiss her, wanted to feel his arms crushing her against him.

She felt his hands close on her, and abruptly she thought in a cold way, someday — I might want to marry Stan Mills.

She felt the chill go through her. She wanted more than a stolen moment like this. She always had. Stan Mills represented more than just a lover. He had money, power. And suddenly she knew she could never make Stan Mills marry her unless she could make him want her.

She knew suddenly the surest way to lose a man like Stan Mills was to give him what he wanted.

Somehow she had to make him believe there was just one way he could ever have her. In that moment she saw she had her own kind of power — and it lay in the image of goodness and purity and innocence that the valley had created about her.

Now, calm and watchful, Isabel allowed herself to be carried closer and closer until her face was only inches from Stan's parted mouth. She could feel his warm, whisky-tainted breath against her cheeks. Then at the last instant, she twisted free, pulling away from him.

"Don't be a little fool." His voice was rough.

"I'm trying not to," she whispered.

"Stop it." His hands closed on her, tighter. "You want this. As much as I do."

"More," she agreed in a tremulous whisper, eyes starry. "You know that."

"Then stop fighting."

"I can't, Stan. Much as I want to. I mustn't."

"Now you are being a fool."

"I'm married, Stan. Why, what would you think of me?"

He released her, and she fell back against the divan.

She smiled in a rueful way, completely cool now. She gave him a twisted smile, her fingers moving across the hairs on the back of his hand. "You — you're used to your kind of women, Stan," she reproved him. "The kind you meet in town — the kind you hire at the Bright Star. I'm not like that."

His mouth twisted into a grin. "Aren't you?"

She was shocked, and her sagging mouth showed it.

She drew away. "You wouldn't want me if I were."

He moved his shoulders. "Way I see it, the man who wants any other kind of woman is a damn fool."

"Why, Stan. What a terrible thing to say."

"There are all kinds of women, Isabel, just as there are all kinds of men. The man who gets a good one is blessed. That's true out here — or anywhere else."

"Why, I don't know what you mean," she said.

"Don't you?" He stood up. He shrugged his coat up on his shoulders, dismissing her from his mind. His fingers touched automatically at the bridge-bar of his rimless glasses, pressing them tighter on his nose. "Well, you tell Kip what I said. Now that he won't be working for Gilmore, he might want to work for me."

When he was gone from her, Isabel felt chilled.

She nodded without speaking. She watched him leave the room, bending his head slightly as he went through the front door. She stayed there on the divan until she heard the sound of his horse going away toward main street. Then she got up and stood at the window. She pinked the shade back in her fingers, watching him ride, erect in his saddle. After a moment, a satisfied smile played across her lips. . . .

NINETEEN

Jim was building stalls inside his barn when he became aware of Eualie's standing behind him.

He stopped hammering, glanced over his shoulder. "My mind was all busy," he said. "You been standing there long?"

She did not smile.

"What sort of trouble are you in here in this town?" Her voice was cold.

He straightened and turned, looking down at her. Her eyes were chilled, and her squared jaw was set.

He tried to smile through his battered face. "It's just what I told you. I got started off in this town on the wrong foot. First, they thought I robbed their bank just because I happened to arrive in their valley the night it happened."

"But last night it was something else."

"Yes." He shook his head. "Last night a payroll was robbed."

She drew in a sharp breath. "And they thought you did it?" Her voice rose. "They came in the night and dragged you out of bed —"

"I'm a stranger here. They just don't know me —"

"They don't trust you. Why, Jim? That's what I want to know. . . . I heard you tell them last night that you were home all evening. . . . You lied to them. . . . Where were you, Jim?"

"I had to see somebody."

"Somebody like Rosemary Meade?"

After a long moment, he nodded. There was no point in going on lying to Eualie. "There was nothing wrong in it."

"Oh, I'm sure there wasn't," she said in sarcasm. "And then they come and arrest you for robbery. How nice. My husband. Dragged off in the middle of the night. Coming home beaten like a common criminal."

"It's all a bad mistake, Eualie."

"Yes. Coming here was a bad mistake."

"We're going to live here, Eualie."

Her voice was sharp in irony. "Oh, yes, this town is so much better than Winter Sage —"

"No," he admitted. He sighed heavily, looking around the barn, at the place where the posse men had dug up part of the payroll last night. "No. It's no better. It's the same. The people are the same. Different names. Same wants. Same fears. It's just that I've learned something I didn't know when I pulled stakes and ran away from Winter Sage. I had to learn. The hard way. People are the same everywhere . . . There's no use running any more. We can settle down here, and make our home here — no place is any better just because it's far away from where you are."

"If you've sense enough to realize that, at last, why do we stay here? Why can't we go back to Winter Sage?"

He shook his head. "I can beat this, Eualie."

"But I don't want to."

"It's me they talk about here, Eualie. I can take that. I'm not going to run away. I'm going to stay here —"

"Until they hang you?"

"Until I prove they're wrong in the things

385

they say — in the things they believe about me."

"Stay then!" Her voice rasped at him. "You stay. But I better tell you this. I'm not going to stay, Jim."

"Eualie. It will be all right. Just give me a chance."

"I've given you a chance. You're only making things worse. I hate it in this place, and I don't know how much longer I can stand it."

He strode across to her. Her face was white. He pulled her to him. "They won't go on treating me like this, Eualie. I promise. And when they accept me, they'll love you."

She laughed at him, but it was a hard, chilled sound.

She pulled away from him. "Let me alone."

Eualie writhed free of Jim's arms and ran from the barn. He took two steps after her, then stopped.

He stood in the doorway and watched her dark head tilted as she crossed the sunlit yard to the house. At last, he turned slowly, staring at the hole the posse men had dug in the sod-flooring of his barn. Eualie was right; they couldn't go on with people feeling as they did toward him. It was too much to ask of Eualie. He had to do something to prove these people wrong once and for all in their estimation of him. Eualie had a right to happiness, and she was not happy here as things were.

He stared at that excavation. There had to be something he could do. And then it was as if he saw an answer in that upturned earth. Maybe it wasn't the answer, but it might change everything if he chased it down.

His mouth pulled into a taut, hard grin. The movement spread the cuts in his lips, but he went on grinning coldly. He buckled on his gunbelt, threw his saddle across the gray.

He rode the little horse at an angle across the yard, yelling in the house to Eualie. "Going to town to talk to Kip Bowne. Be back soon."

He saw Eualie standing in the kitchen doorway staring at him. She did not say anything.

Jim saw Kip coming down the steps out of the Bright Star saloon. Jim reined the gray in, tied her at the leather-slicked rail.

Kip's face was dark and thoughtful.

"Kip."

Kip glanced up, saw Jim. Kip's mouth set,

and he paused on the boardwalk but kept his gaze averted.

Jim laughed sharply. "Now you're treating me the way all the others do," he said.

"Am I?"

"Come on, Kip, I haven't done anything wrong."

Kip met his gaze then, mouth twisted. "Oh, I don't think you're a robber," he said sourly. "But I told you a long time ago. I like Rosemary Meade."

"I know."

"She's been hurt enough. Why don't you let her alone?"

Jim glanced both ways along the street. He could not mention what he and Rosemary had talked about, and until he could there was no sense trying to explain to Kip why he'd gone to her house last night to visit her.

Kip turned away. "Well, I've got to go," Kip said. "I'm going to take a job with Stan Mills. Out at his ranch."

"Thought you were working for me. I still need you."

Kip shook his head. "No. This pays better. Anyhow, I'm not working for you."

Jim looked down at his hands. "Hate to lose you for a friend, Kip. Can't you trust me a little longer?"

"Looks like I've trusted you past the call of anything already."

"Yes. Reckon you have. Too bad you don't play it out."

Kip flung the words at him. "Well, I can't." He exhaled heavily. "Let's drop it, huh?"

"All right. Will you tell me one thing?"

"If I can."

"I been thinking about that money they found buried in my barn."

"Yeah?"

"You got any idea who told the sheriff there would be money under my barn?"

Kip stared at him, impatience in his taut face. But after he gave it some thought, his face muscles relaxed and he shook his head. "No. Tom never did say. Not to me. It never occurred to me to ask. They just found the money, and I let it go at that."

"So did I. But it couldn't be like that. They wouldn't just go out to my barn and start digging."

"No. Somebody must have told him it would be there," Kip agreed. He nodded, "Why don't you ask Tom Walker?"

"O.K., Kip. I will. I hoped maybe, though, you'd go along with me on this."

Kip hesitated, then shook his head. "No. Far as I'm concerned, you never robbed the

389

payroll. That ends it with me. You couldn't have robbed it. You were sneaking in a back door. That ends it with me, too."

Their gazes clashed a moment, and then Kip turned on his heel and stalked away along the boardwalk.

TWENTY

Sheriff Tom Walker was alone in his office. He glanced up across his desk when Jim entered.

When he saw what he had done to Gilmore's face, and saw the look in Gilmore's eyes, the sheriff's mouth went slack, eyes revealing his thoughts. He looked around quickly for his gun belt. It was on a small table beside his desk, an impossible distance from him.

He spoke loudly, blustering. "You think to come in here and catch me alone, Gilmore, you watch yourself."

"I want to talk to you."

"I'm the law here. What I do is done in the performance of my duty. I warn you, Gilmore. I'm the law here." He was inching his chair toward his gunbelt on the table. "You touch me, Gilmore, and you'll land yourself under the jail."

"I don't want to touch you."

The sheriff hesitated, considering this in his slow burner mind. He decided Gilmore was telling the truth and he relaxed, shrugging his denim shirt up on his thick shoulders. "What do you want?"

"I want some information." Jim stood across the desk from the stout lawman. When Tom Walker nodded, Jim said, "I want to know who told you there'd be money buried inside my barn."

He watched Tom Walker's whiskered face screw into a scowl as he thought about this. He said, "Yeah. I see what you're driving at."

"Somebody had to tell you there was money in that barn."

Walker nodded. He scratched his chin, getting up. He paced the room, staring at Gilmore. "Let's see now, there was a powerful lot of excitement. I had a lot to see to. You don't know. A lawman always has a lot to do when he's trying to work with a posse of men he's picked up off the street."

"Still, somebody had to say to you —"

"I know. I know. I'm thinking about it. I'm trying to figure the way it happened. Way it had to happen. When I finally got me a posse and we got out to the mine office, the guard was lyin' there unconscious. I brought him around. Then I had to question him —"

"But he didn't say anything to you about where the money might be hidden. There would be no way for him to know anything like that."

The sheriff waved his arm. "Let me figure. This here could be powerful important."

"It's important to me," Jim said. "It's my barn. Somebody framed me. Good lord, sheriff, you must know who told you you could find money in my barn?"

The sheriff walked to the window, stood staring into main street with his back to Jim. Finally he turned, nodding slowly, "I think it was Lon Persons. Yep. That was it. When we come out of the mine office and was saddling up. It was Lon, all right. He said we ought to search your place — search your barn is what he said. But my lord, Jim, Lon's too dumb to be crooked."

Jim Gilmore nodded. He felt suddenly let down at what the sheriff had told him. He did not know what he expected to hear. But Lon Persons was the last name he was prepared for. Still, he'd dealt himself the hand, and he was going to play it out.

Lon Persons was haying the horses in the livery stables when Jim entered the big red barn. There was the smell of horses, of nitrogen, of leather, and of hay in the dim-lighted interior of the stables.

Lon was singing to himself as he worked. Jim said, "Lon."

The thin man started and jerked around.

"My lord, don't walk up behind a body like that," he said. Then he saw Jim's bruised face, and he grinned.

"Sheriff did a pretty good job on me," Jim said.

Lon whistled. "You keep running into trouble all the time way you do, mister, and pretty soon you're bound to start looking just — the way you do now."

"I want you to answer me a question, Lon."

Lon shrugged. "All right. If I can."

"The sheriff just told me that you suggested he look in my barn for that payroll money."

Lon's Adam's apple worked in his leathery neck. "Yeah," he admitted at last, scowling. "Reckon I did, at that."

"Why?" Jim said. "Just because you hate me?"

"Now, just a minute. I don't hate you. You seem nice enough a young fellow to me. I don't want trouble."

"Yet you told the sheriff to search my barn. How did you happen to think of something like that?"

Lon's slumped, thin shoulders straightened.

"By golly, that's a good question you asked me there," he said. "Now, I reckon on it, why would I say a thing like that there?"

"You must have had a reason, Lon."

"Maybe somebody else in the crowd said it to me. You know there was a lot of confusion. It must have been that somebody said it to me — and I repeated it to the sheriff."

"Well, who said it to you?"

Lon Persons screwed up his brows, trying to puzzle that one out. "There was so much confusion and all."

"Think, man! Think."

"Well, lord knows I'm trying. I was out there in the crowd. I volunteered to ride with the posse, you know. Sheriff swore us in. Kind of hasty, seemed to me. Appears to me, a man gettin' deputized, they ought to be more serious about it —"

"Who spoke to you? Who mentioned my barn?"

Lon mopped his forehead with his bandana. "Like I say, it was dark, and there was all this milling around. Some gent was standing next to me in the crowd. I recollect I could smell whisky on his breath, and it was makin' me thirsty. Now, you take some people, they don't like the smell of whisky. But me, it always makes me thirsty —"

"Lon, please." Jim felt himself sweating. But he knew the man didn't live who could get the livery-stable man to hurry.

"All right. All right. It appears to me that it was young Ceal Sistrunk that was standing next to me. He had been drinking at the Bright Star and —"

"What did he say about my barn?"

"Well, Ceal says to me it would be a good idea to search your barn, and why didn't I mention it to the sheriff?"

It was mid afternoon when Jim rode his way to the far reaches of the valley where Ceal Sistrunk was line-riding.

They had told him at the ranch that Ceal would be somewhere east of the Witch Brooms checking fences. Jim, feeling impatient and sweated, rode for what seemed hours, finding no trace of the young cowhand.

As he crested a knoll that looked down on a waterhole in a willow-ringed sump, he heard the whickering of a pony.

He turned the gray and moved down the incline to the sump. The first thing he saw was the riderless horse, saddled, ground-tied in a square of sweet grass.

When he came near the sump, he saw Ceal Sistrunk lying asleep under a cottonwood near the waterhole. His hat was over his face. The raucous chatter of a blue jay wakened him, and he sat up, blinking when he saw Jim swing down out of his saddle.

Ceal whistled at the bruises on Jim's face.

"Like to talk to you," Jim said. Ceal walked with him to the edge of the water. Jim let the gray stretch her neck over the shadowy pool and drink.

"Lon says you told him the posse ought to search my barn last night."

Ceal nodded. "Yeah. That's right. But don't go giving me credit for that. It wasn't my idea. You see, Splinter Wilcox was along. He had a bottle, and he and I were hitting it pretty heavy — tell you the truth, it's been hard for me to take Tom's posses very much to heart since we rode in circles that day and found you by that creek."

"This Splinter Wilcox. What about him? Did he think you people ought to search my place?"

Ceal nodded. "Yeah. That's right. As we was drinking, I recollect Splinter says to me this time they ought to search Jim Gilmore's barn. Them very words. Like I say, I was getting liquored up, but it seemed a good idea to me. But I didn't want to be the one to suggest it to Tom Walker, so —"

"Splinter Wilcox?" Jim shook his head. "I don't know him."

"Sure you do. He's the little dried-up bartender at Stan Mills' Bright Star. The one that can fix any drink you name. Come out here from New York. Some kinda trouble back there." Then Ceal shook his head, remembering, "That's right, you don't get in the Bright Star much, do you? Stan Mills still won't let you drink in there?"

"He'll let me in this time," Jim said.

It was full dark when Jim rode into Kiowa City. A wan moon hung low in a faded night sky. The darkness seemed to swirl about the unlighted false fronts. The yellow-glowing windows at the Bright Star seemed unnaturally bright. The noise had an exaggerated loudness in Jim's ears as he rode near.

He was sagging with weariness, but he was not even thinking about stopping now. He had run this thing down this far, and it had brought him to Stan Mills' place — just as had those broken bits of glass in Rosemary's hand.

Jim looped his reins over the slicked tie-rail and walked up the steps. He pushed open the batwings, feeling the music and laughter of women wash out around him. He felt the slow unnatural thud of his heart as he crossed the room to the long, crowded bar.

Splinter Wilcox was working at the end of the bar. Jim shook his head at the stout bartender who spoke to him, and moved along the line of drinkers to where Wilcox was at work.

Wilcox was a small man who spoke from the corner of his mouth. He wore a large bow tie and arm garters on his brightly colored shirt. Jim remembered, now, seeing him among the posse members in the sheriff's office.

Wilcox smiled. "Yeah, friend? What's your little drink going to be?" He spoke from the edge of his mouth, and nothing in his face revealed he had ever seen Jim Gilmore before.

"Whisky, straight," Jim said. When the little man pushed the bottle across the bar, Jim said, watching him, "My name is Jim Gilmore."

The little bartender smiled. "Oh? So that's how your face got like that? Thought you'd been arguing with a freight train."

"I heard you know something that might be important to me. Will you talk to me?"

"I talk to everybody, friend. What's eating you?"

"Not here. It's about what happened — out in my barn." He stared at the little man.

The oddly twisted mouth stopped smiling. "I got nothing to talk about."

"I'm willing to buy what you know," Jim persisted.

The hard eyes seemed to glaze over. "You're all wrong, friend."

"A hundred dollars," Jim spoke hollowly, naming the last cent he had in the world.

The little man hesitated. "You'd want a lot for that kind of money."

"Not much. Just a name."

The man stared at him. "What's the name?"

Jim shook his head. "Not here. You know better than that. I'll give you the hundred — if you'll meet me — down behind the jail. When you get off here."

The little man liked the sound of this. Jim watched the idea of an easy hundred dollars war with the fears inside the bartender. Finally, Wilcox nodded. "What can I lose? You got the hundred with you, friend?"

Jim nodded. At that moment, he felt a hand touch his shoulder. He heeled around, saw the man at his back was Stan Mills.

He shrugged Stan's hand off his shoulder,

placed his back against the bar.

"You must of forgot what I told you," Mills said quietly.

Jim shook his head. "I haven't forgotten."

"What you doing in here?"

"I came in for a drink."

But Stan Mills was staring across Jim's shoulder at the bartender. "What'd this gee want, Splinter?"

Stiffening, Jim stared straight ahead, waiting.

He heard Wilcox's nasal twang. "Just a drink, boss."

Jim breathed out then. At least the little man hadn't betrayed him yet. Maybe he wouldn't — at least until after he'd collected that hundred dollars. . . .

Fisher followed a few paces behind Jim all the way across the saloon.

Jim passed through the batwings, then stepped quickly to one side, pressed his body against the wall.

He held his breath. A moment later the towheaded gunslick pushed open the batwings and stepped through. He stood there, looking around in the darkness.

Jim pulled his gun and jabbed it hard into the gunman's kidney.

"You looking for somebody, Fisher?"

The gunslick moved to heel around, but

Jim thrust the gun harder. "Just hold what you got," Jim told him.

Fisher relaxed. "You're just buying yourself trouble, man," Fisher said.

Jim took his gun from the thonged-down holster. "Maybe so. But you can collect this gun from the sheriff's office in the morning."

Fisher drew in his breath sharply. "What you talking about? Mills would fire me if I went back in that saloon without my gun."

"That's your problem," Jim told him. "I'm tired fooling with you and Stan Mills, and he might as well know it." He thrust the gun into Fisher's side so suddenly the gunslick gasped. "Turn around. Face those doors."

Fisher turned slowly. When he faced the batwings, Jim put his boot high against Fisher's back and thrust. The man went sprawling forward through the batwings.

Jim stood a moment holding Fisher's gun; then he turned, crossed the boardwalk, and mounted his gray.

He rode slowly and warily along the middle of the street, watching the doorway of the lighted saloon. But nothing happened over there.

He saw there was a light in Rosemary Meade's cottage, but he moved past. There was nothing new to tell her. And Kip was right. Gossip could only hurt her.

Even when Rosemary called his name from the darkness, he pretended he had not heard. Then she was running after him along the boardwalk.

He pulled the horse around, waiting.

"You love to be talked about, don't you?" he asked.

"When I haven't done anything wrong, I don't care what people say." Her voice was defiant.

He nodded, smiling down at her.

Rosemary stared up at his battered face. "I'm sorry about what happened to you."

"It didn't have anything to do with you."

"You wouldn't tell them you were at my place."

"It wouldn't have made any difference," he said. "And it won't help if somebody suspects what you have, Rosemary. I want to help you if I can. What Walker did to my face doesn't matter."

"It matters to me," she said. "I don't want to make any more trouble for you. Please forget about what I told you, Jim."

"I can't do that."

"But — what difference does it make? It won't bring Randal back, no matter what we might prove. . . . It'll only make more trouble for you."

"Thanks, Rosemary. But I'm in it now. Let me play it out the best way I can." He nodded to her, turned the gray and rode away along the street.

Jim went to the stables behind the jail, tied the gray in a stall, watered her, and hung his saddle off the stall rail.

Kip Bowne was in the sheriff's office when Jim came in. Jim turned over Fisher's gun to him, explained what had happened at the Bright Star. He did not mention Splinter Wilcox because Kip had said he wanted out of this investigation. When Kip asked what he'd learned about the payroll money, Jim only shrugged.

When Kip left to make his early rounds, Jim asked if he could wait in the darkened office. Kip agreed, and Jim sat near the main street window, waiting as the minutes ticked away.

At a few minutes past midnight, he let himself out of the street door.

He went soundlessly to the end of the building, moved along it in the shadows to the stables at the rear.

From the stables he could hear the restless stirring of the horses. From the rest of the town there was a thickened silence.

He stood for a moment at the edge of the

stables, staring around in the shadows. Wilcox wasn't coming. Maybe Stan Mills had gotten to him, suspicious after Jim talked to him in the saloon.

He moved around the corner of the stable and his foot struck something.

Jim stumbled, caught himself. He stopped, staring down. In the faint winking of moonlight he saw the gleam of knife blade and handle. The knife was thrust deeply into a man's back.

Jim knelt beside him, but even before he turned him over, he knew the dead man. It was the little bartender. Somebody had gotten to Splinter Wilcox — and left him dead here behind the jail.

TWENTY-ONE

A chilled night wind dried the sweat on Jim's face. He stood up slowly, still stunned at the sight of the little bartender sprawled dead at his feet.

He looked about, but the only sound was the whisper of the wind, and the only movement the limber shadows. He retreated into the darkness, hearing the restless stirring of animals in the jail stalls.

He moved in the shadows, going the way he had come around the building.

He heard a horse on the main street, and he paused, leaning against the building. The horse sounded tired, and after a moment the sound of its hoofbeats died in the darkness.

At the rim of the sheriff's office, Jim paused, looking both ways along the silent street. A tumbleweed rolled on the wind. He'd pushed his luck past the breaking point; he knew he could not be caught anywhere around here.

He stepped away from the building and moved along the street, feeling as if he wore a target painted large on his back.

He kept walking, not even sure where he was going. If he found Kip Bowne, he might make the young marshal believe he had stumbled on Wilcox's body after he was dead. But he didn't even really believe this.

He saw no sign of Kip along the dark street. He kept moving, increasing his pace. When he reached the corner of the side street on which the sheriff lived, he admitted he must have been headed this way from the first.

He turned off main street, feeling the chill of the wind go through him. He paused. Every light in Tom Walker's frame cottage was turned up, full wick. Light spilled out around it. He went up the front steps, rapped on the door.

The door was jerked open at once. Tom Walker's mouth sagged open when he recognized Jim Gilmore. He stepped aside, and Jim moved into the sheriff's front room.

Stan Mills heeled around across the parlor, staring at Jim. Jim shook his head, feeling as if he were in a nightmare. He watched Stan Mills punch his glasses tighter on the bridge of his nose.

For a moment there was a tense silence in this room, and Jim had the certain knowledge the two men had been talking about him.

Jim pulled his gaze away from Stan Mills. He said, "I found a man, sheriff. He was dead. He's been knifed. He was dead."

The sheriff stared at him, without speaking. Jim heard Stan Mills breathe in sharply across the room.

"Who was it?" Stan Mills said.

"It was Splinter Wilcox," Jim said.

Stan said, "You're crazy, Gilmore. I left Splinter Wilcox, at the Bright Star. Less than an hour ago."

Jim kept his gaze on the sheriff's face. "It was Wilcox. I stumbled over his body. I didn't want any more trouble. I came straight here."

Mills moved toward them. "How'd you

just *happen* to find that body, Gilmore? What were you doing around the jail this time of night?"

Jim felt as if someone had struck him in the pit of the stomach. He turned slowly — and stared at Mills. "Who said I found him at the jail?"

Mills caught his breath. "Didn't you?"

Jim nodded. "That's where I found him, mister. But I never said so. How did you know where I found him?"

Light glinted against Mills' glasses. He stared along his nose at Jim. "That's where Splinter said he was going when he left the saloon. . . . He said he — had something he wanted to talk over with the law, and — I might as well tell you why I'm here — the Bright Star was robbed tonight . . . Maybe you know something about that, too?"

Both men were watching him. Jim hunched his shirt up on his shoulders. They had been talking about him. The Bright Star had been robbed, and Stan Mills had come running over here — to mention one name. Jim Gilmore.

"I don't know anything about the saloon," Jim said. He almost mentioned he was sitting in the sheriff's office after Kip went on his rounds. Then he remembered he'd been sitting in the dark. If he tried to explain that, he would lead next to what he had learned today. He said, "I left my horse in your jail stables tonight, Sheriff. I — was back there to collect it. That's when I stumbled over Splinter Wilcox's body."

"What you doing in town until now, Gilmore?" Walker said.

"Unless he was sneaking into Rosemary Meade's house again, he was probably sneaking in my office window behind the Bright Star. Somebody knew where I kept my safe."

Jim had clenched his fists and moved toward Stan Mills. Tom Walker caught his arm roughly. "You're in enough trouble, fellow, without making yourself any more."

Jim exhaled heavily, stepped back. Stan Mills continued staring at him.

"Why don't you just give me your gun?" Tom said to Jim. "And we three will go down to the jail and see about Splinter's body."

Jim hesitated, then handed over his gun. "You arresting me?"

"I don't know," Tom Walker said tiredly. "Let's walk down to the jail and see what we find out. Nothing more we can do here."

They walked in silence through the night street.

When they came around the stables, the

sheriff held a lantern and stood looking down at Wilcox's body. He jerked his head, and Jim and Mills carried the dead man around the building and put the body on a cot in one of the cells.

The street door of the sheriff's office stood open. They heard the pound of boots on the boardwalk, and then Kip Bowne was yelling in the darkness, "Sheriff —"

Jim heeled around, ran through the door.

Stan Mills yelled, "Sheriff! He's making a break."

Tom Walker came running forward from the cell. He and Stan Mills hesitated a moment, and then came through the office door, Tom's gun drawn.

Jim was standing on the boardwalk watching Kip run toward him. The young marshal's hat was gone. His clothes were disheveled. He was wild-eyed.

"Sheriff, where's the sheriff?" Kip said.

"What's the matter?" Jim caught his arm.

"Damnedest thing," Kip said. "Stan Mills offered me a thousand dollars — to kill Splinter Wilcox for him. I told him he was crazy. Then Fisher hit me from the back — and I woke up tied in a room behind the bar —"

At that moment Walker and Stan Mills came through the street door.

The sheriff came down the steps, but Stan stopped where he was in the doorway. For a moment, Stan and Kip Bowne stared at each other, eyes distended.

Kip shook his head, lifting his arm, pointing at Stan.

A rifle crackled at an angle across the street. There was the sickening thud of lead slammed into flesh. Kip was punched forward, struck in the back. His knees caved in, and he toppled against Jim.

Kip caught at Jim's shoulders to support himself and then sank heavily upon him.

Jim made two quick moves. He stepped aside, letting Kip go down slowly to the walk, and in the same movement pulled Kip's gun from its holster.

He leaped past Kip then, going across the street.

Both Stan Mills and the sheriff yelled at him, but Jim did not slow down, or glance back at where they stood.

His gaze was fixed on that place where he'd seen the burst of gunfire.

He struck the boardwalk, and went around the corner of the building. He heard running footsteps ahead of him in the darkness. Somebody had hung around too long this time, thinking the shock of Kip Bowne's being shot would stall pursuit.

With Kip's gun in his hand, Jim ran through the darkened alley. He heard the steps ahead of him slow and then stop out in the darkness.

Jim stopped running, pressing himself against the rough wall in the deep shadows. He came warily to the corner of the building, peered around it.

The first thing he saw was the horse, ground-tied a few yards away in the shadows. And then he saw movement, a hatless man running toward the horse.

Jim stepped out into the open field behind the building. He said, "Hold it."

The man still facing the horse, and only feet from it, paused, shoulders tensed, the rifle held across his chest.

The winking moonlight touched the top of the towhead out there.

"Fisher," Jim said.

Jim saw the way Fisher's shoulders tensed as he brought up the rifle, setting himself to fire as he whirled around.

Jim stepped hard right into the shadow of the building and fired as he moved.

He felt his finger closing on that trigger, saw the orange spurt of gunfire. Fisher had turned when the bullet struck him in the chest. The rifle went upward from his arms — Fisher folded forward and struck on his knees. The second time Jim shot him, it knocked him half around and he fell face down, twisted on the ground.

Jim hesitated only the space of a breath, staring at the gunslick.

He ran back along the alley, his boots striking hard against the earth. He came out of the buildings, staring at the lights across the street at the sheriff's office.

The gunfire had wakened the town. Lights were flashing on all along the main street. But Jim was staring at that office over there.

Kip Bowne's body was sprawled on the walk. The sheriff was hunkered over him.

Jim ran across the street, looking for Stan Mills. But Mills was gone from the stoop before the office.

"Where is he?" Jim said.

The sheriff looked up, crouched over Kip's body. "He's dead," the sheriff said. He was stunned. "Young Kip. He's dead."

"I know he's dead!" Jim raged at him, the agony roiling inside him. "Where's Stan Mills? He's the man I want to see. Where is he? Where is he?"

The sheriff looked up slowly, moving his head in the darkness. "He was here," he said.

"And now he's gone," Jim said. "Where'd he go? Which way did he go?"

The sheriff looked up at him, shaking his head.

Jim took one last look at young Kip Bowne. Kip was the first friend he'd had here, maybe the only one. And Kip had been hurt by what he believed about Jim and Rosemary. Jim felt chilled because Kip was dead, and now he could never make him see the truth.

His mouth pulled in a hard, mirthless grin. There was one thing he could do for him. In that moment he vowed he would do it. He heeled about, running on the board-walk toward the Bright Star. People passed him, yelling at him in the suddenly lighted street. But he did not even look at them.

He struck against the batwings at the Bright Star. The inner doors were barred.

He looked both ways along the street and then ran to the corner of the building.

As he came around the corner, a gun barked from the rear of the building.

Jim flattened himself against the wall. "Mills!" he yelled.

There was a breathless moment of silence. Jim waited, with Kip's gun poised for movement in the alley behind the saloon.

Suddenly he heard the galloping of hooves back there as a man rode away in the darkness.

Jim ran between the buildings, cursing himself. Mills' gunfire had stopped him just long enough to let the big man get away on a horse.

He saw the rider going fast in the darkness, gone out of gun range. He spent only a moment feeling the rage eating at him. Then he turned and ran toward the stables at the rear of the jail.

TWENTY-TWO

Jim moved into the stables and tossed blanket and saddle over the back of his gray. He worked with fevered anxiety, and yet it seemed that everything moved with agonizing slowness.

He was making too much noise, but the gray had chosen this moment to become spooked in the strange stall, in the darkness. Or maybe she was reacting to his own frantic breathing and sweated panic.

The jail and sheriff's office was brightly lighted, and he heard men shouting in there.

He made no effort to hear what they were saying. It no longer mattered to him. Very likely they were yelling his name at the sheriff. It would take this valley a long time to believe the truth about Stan Mills. Stan Mills was behind all this trouble, and had been from the first. But the valley people would be hard to convince. Stan had been smart. One thing Jim felt was sure — by now the sheriff must be ill with what he had to know about Stan Mills.

Jim led the quarter horse to the alley, swung up into the saddle. He rode swiftly into the darkness back to the place where Stan Mills had raced away from behind the Bright Star.

He swung down then and crouched low on the ground trying to find some marking left by the shoe of Mills' horse. There had to be something he could follow.

Slowed like this, he felt less panic; his mind began to work clearer, and it seemed to him that Stan Mills would be looking for him now.

He nodded to himself, straightening and swinging into the saddle. Fisher the gunman was dead. Kip Bowne had been killed before he ever got to tell the sheriff the truth about Mills. Splinter Wilcox was dead. So far, Stan Mills did not suspect that Rosemary Meade had evidence against him.

"It's just me now," Jim told himself, turning the horse from the alley, moving out toward his own place. To stay alive now, he would have to stay alert. But he did not have to go looking for Stan Mills. Stan Mills would be somewhere in the dark, looking for him. Jim Gilmore was the only person who stood in Stan Mills' way now — he would have everything he wanted, because with Gilmore dead, Mills could lie fast enough, and the sheriff would believe his lies. Stan had been a powerful leader in this valley for a long time.

Jim rode warily on the narrow roadway to his place. He told himself that Stan Mills was full of panic, too, right now and wouldn't be thinking clearly. Stan would be looking for him, all right, but it would not occur to Mills that Jim would be headed for home. Stan might even believe that the sheriff would have already arrested Jim. Mills might even hang around town in the darkness, trying to find out what had happened.

All the lights were burning in Jim's cottage when he came in sight of his place. He went cold. Stan Mills was a brutal man if anybody stood in his way. Jim felt ill, thinking that Mills might strike at him through Eualie.

He urged the horse forward, jumped his gate, and went racing across the yard. He jumped down from the saddle, ran across the porch and, drawing his gun, threw open the front door.

With the door flung open, Jim stopped cold, feeling as if he'd been struck in the face.

Will Allbrand released Eualie from his arms, and both turned to face Jim in the doorway.

Jim went wild with the nightmarish agony whirling through him. This didn't make sense. It wasn't real. Will Allbrand was in Winter Sage, a hundred miles east.

He pushed the door closed behind him, hardly knowing what he was doing. Face gray, he stared at Eualie and Will Allbrand, remembering the whispers at Winter Sage, the things he had branded as lies. He had worked for Will Allbrand, felt as if Will were like an older brother. People had been talking about Eualie. And other people asked why Will Allbrand was so friendly. But Jim had trusted only two people, Will and Eualie. Sure, Will was trying to help him get started, then to keep going when things went bad on that ranch. He'd given them presents, a registered bull. And often when Jim came in from working his ranges, Will Allbrand would be there, talking with Eualie. But there was always a reason for Will's visits. Allbrand was helpful, good to them. What could you say to a man like that? You had to say the gossip was lies, didn't you?

Will was a widower, but he was twice as old as Eualie.

Now it looked like the difference in age didn't matter.

Eualie stared at Jim. Her face was pale, but her squared jaw was set. She was in gown and bathrobe, her dark hair done in two braids down the side of her head.

"Will's here because I sent for him." She spoke defiantly, tilting her head. "You were carrying on with that Meade woman. You were in trouble with the law, I sent for Will."

"Why?"

"I didn't know anyone else could help me."

Jim shook his head, staring at them. "All the things they said about you — and Will — back in Winter Sage. They were true. They weren't lies at all."

"Don't act so holy," Eualie said, mouth pulling. "I know all about you and your widow."

Jim stared at her a moment, shaking his head. Then he stared at Allbrand. "Why'd you come here, Will?"

"I thought I could help," Allbrand said.

"He's come to take me back home," Eualie said.

"Take you home?"

"Will and I are going to be married," Eualie said.

"Now wait a minute," Will Allbrand said. His face flushed. "We don't want trouble. We're all upset."

"What do you want?" Jim said.

"Why, I came to see what I could do."

Jim's laugh was flat. "Only you don't want to take her back with you."

"Why, Eualie is married to you."

"Will," Eualie cried. "You know you want me. You've always wanted me. You said so."

Will wiped the back of his hand across his mouth. "See here now," he said. "I never wanted this kind of trouble."

"I'll get a divorce, Will," Eualie said, voice frantic. "Take me back with you, and —"

"Now, just a minute," Will said. He mopped at his face with his handkerchief. "I didn't expect anything like this."

"You've got to take me," Eualie said, grabbing his arm.

Sweating, Will stepped away from her. "We're all upset," he said. "I'll — come back — and we'll talk about it in the morning."

Jim shook his head.

"I don't want to talk about it." His voice was dead. He pushed the gun back in his holster. "Don't come back here, Will. . . . If she wants you, she can go to you."

Will Allbrand looked ill. He glanced at

Eualie, but then turned, face gray. He started to speak, but something in Jim's face stopped him. He nodded and walked slowly past Jim. He went out the front door and closed it behind him.

Eualie stared at the closed door, her face rigid and pale. Then she sank on the divan, staring up at Jim, eyes blurred with tears.

Jim did not speak. When he dragged the gun from his holster, she gasped.

"Jim. What are you going to do?"

He looked at her, his mouth pulled in disgust. He snapped open the chamber, ejected the spent shells, and refilled it. He shook his head. "To you? Nothing. Maybe I loved you once, Eualie. But I don't love you now."

"I don't care. I hate it here. I hate you. I'm going back home."

He shrugged. He was amazed that he felt nothing inside, just the sense of being dead, of no longer caring about Eualie, about anything.

He stood there a long time after he heard Will Allbrand drive away in his carriage.

"What's the matter with you?" Eualie said, but he did not answer her. He did not know how much time passed. He heard the sound of movement in the yard. He moved quickly across to the center table, turned down the lamp, and blew it out.

Eualie said, "What's the matter? What kind of trouble are you in now?"

"Keep your voice down," he said in the darkness.

She spoke petulantly. "Why must you turn off the light like this? Why are you afraid? What have you done now?"

Jim moved to the window in the darkened room. He closed his eyes tightly for a moment, then opened them. He spoke in a tense whisper across his shoulder. "Shut up, Eualie."

He leaned close to the window pane, peered through.

He saw moonlight glint on the golden coat of Stan Mills' big palomino. The horse pranced, ground-tied in the shadows.

Jim held his breath, waiting. After a moment, he saw Stan Mills, gun in hand, break from the shadows and run across the yard.

Jim sank to his knees. Cautiously, he raised the window an inch, leveled the gun on the sill, but before he could fire, Stan Mills was lost in deeper shadows, running around the side of the house.

"I won't stay in this darkness," Eualie said. "I'm frightened."

"You'll be a hell of a lot more frightened with a lamp on," Jim told her. "Shut up,

Eualie, and stay still."

"I won't have you talking to me like that," she wailed aloud.

"If I have to slap you, I'll have you quiet," Jim whispered. "I'm trying to save your life."

"What a fool you are!" she cried. "Just because these people hate you. It doesn't mean they hate me."

Jim caught his breath, watching first flames lick up in the hay stalls across the yard in his barn. "That man out there hates me enough to want to hit at me in every way he can, Eualie," he whispered, standing up. "First, he tried to frame me to hide his own guilt. Now he wants to kill me because I've learned the truth —"

He was moving across the room.

Eualie cried out, "That's your fight."

He paused, hearing her gasp when the lamp chimney burned her fingers.

He heeled about as she lighted the wick and, with a look of smug triumph, set the smoke chimney in place. Light sprang upward, blazing in the room.

Before Jim could reach her, or the lamp, the crack of a pistol broke the night still. Simultaneously, the pane in the window was smashed, and, in the same breath, Eualie went staggering away from the table under the impact of the bullet.

She fell against the wall, crying out, a look of agony and puzzlement twisting her face. She was holding her left breast, and blood leaked between her fingers. She stared at Jim, and her lips worked, pulled taut and bared from her teeth.

The pistol cracked again from the night. Jim lunged forward on his knees, raking the lamp from the center table as he fell, blowing into the chimney. The room was plunged into darkness.

"Eualie," he said. He set the lamp aside, crawled toward her. Light from the burning barn illuminated the room now in a strange red glow, flickering with weird shadows.

"Eualie."

He touched her, lifted her in his arms. Her head sagged back on her shoulders. He crouched there, feeling the illness surge through him. Things were going to be better for him and Eualie? He had brought her here. He had caused her death.

TWENTY-THREE

The fire crackled, raging through the dry wood and hay in the barn. Jim ran across the room to the opposite side of the house from the fire. He thrust up a window and slid through it to the ground.

He ran along the house, paused at the rear, and then stepped around it.

Mills, out near the burning barn, was waiting for him. It was as if Jim had made the move Mills anticipated.

As Jim stepped around the rear corner of the house, Stan Mills fired again.

The bullet splatted into the frame house-edging, splintering away a slice of wood near Jim's shoulder.

Instead of going back toward the house, Jim threw himself hard to his right, hitting the ground.

In the brilliant illumination of the fire he saw Mills plainly. Mills was to the right of the barn, in a section not yet burning.

Jim held the gun out before him, putting both hands on the butt to steady it. He fired, and Mills faded deeper into the shadow at the dark side of the barn. Mills fired again, and Jim rolled away into the yard.

In the vague light on the dark side of the barn, he saw Mills sliding away from him in the shadows, back against the wall.

Jim came up on his knees, firing the gun at the movement in the shadows. He pressed the trigger, feeling the agony singing in his mind, feeling the rage shaking his hand and arm.

Under his firing, Mills moved faster, going backward along the side of the barn.

Jim threw himself behind the trunk of a cottonwood tree, gasping through his mouth as he reloaded.

When Mills saw his chance, he leaped away from the barn and at that moment, Jim fired at him again.

Mills lunged back into the shadows at the barn.

The fire licked outward behind him. Mills tried to run forward. Jim fired and the big man, heeling around, hurled himself against the barn again. Mills had trapped himself. The wall of fire spread rapidly at his back, and Jim's gun blazed when he moved away from the barn.

Suddenly, Mills laughed in a wild way, and Jim fired toward the sound.

And then Mills was gone. Jim came slowly around the tree, but there was no trace of the big man against the barn wall.

Jim stayed warily there beside the cottonwood, staring at that wall of fire. There was only one way Mills could have gone, and that was to leap past the spreading flames.

Jim ran forward, seeing what Mills was attempting. It was the crazy sort of thing that would pay off if it worked. Mills was trying to run across the inside of the burning barn, hoping to leap to safety on the other side.

Jim ran toward the swiftly burning side of the wall. He moved coldly, watching that burning barn, waiting for Mills to show himself outside it. There was nothing on his mind now but killing this man.

He waited. He held his breath, waiting, trying to figure in his mind how Mills could have tricked him. Mills didn't come through that sheet of flame. The fire over here was a red sheet of certain death.

Suddenly, from inside the barn, he heard Mills' scream of terror.

Jim's heart slugged against his ribs. Mills had run into the fire, thinking it had burned down enough on one side so that he could leap through it. But instead, now all four walls were burning and Mills was trapped inside.

Burn, damn you, Jim thought. He couldn't think of a more fitting way for Stan Mills to die. He hoped that the fire was intense in that barn — as intense as the hell inside Jim Gilmore. If it were, Stan Mills didn't have a chance.

Mills screamed again. Voice wild with pleading and terror, he begged Jim to save him, get him out of that inferno.

His pleading voice rose to a wail.

Jim stood rooted, watching that fire. He

felt cold. The pleading voice roiled out above the crackling flames.

Suddenly he was moving toward the double doorway of the barn. This screaming was more than he could stand. There had to be another, saner kind of justice, even for a man like Stan Mills.

Jim thrust his gun into his holster, running through the doorway.

When he ran past the first sheet of flame, he paused in an open place much as if finding himself in the eye of a hurricane. The heat was intense, but the fire was crackling around the open stalls after consuming the pole separations.

Mills crouched in a haystall where the fire had eaten out the hay, scorched the ground, and moved on. Mills' face was seared, blackened. His screams poured out, one after the other, as if all that was left in Mills' mind was the screaming.

Jim yelled at him. Mills twisted on the blackened earth, still screaming. Jim moved toward him. Mills brought up the gun suddenly, pressing the trigger, firing point blank at Jim Gilmore.

TWENTY-FOUR

Jim Gilmore swam up from painful sleep to the agony of waking, feeling the searing burning all through his body. When he breathed, he was aware that all the fire was concentrated in his chest. He could breathe only shallowly, and even this caused sharp thrusts of pain.

He tried to move his body but couldn't. He turned his head, gradually becoming aware of the choking grip of thongs about his ankles.

He fought, trying to free his ankles. He pulled his arms upward, and realized they too were bound out on each side of him.

He opened his fevered eyes, and they throbbed painfully in sunlight. The whole room was a fiery haze, and at first he thought he was in the burning barn, and then after a long time some of the haze cleared away, and Jim found Tom Walker bending over him.

Gilmore turned his head away from the whiskered face above him.

"Jim," Tom Walker's voice sounded gentle, and distant.

Jim was staring at his wrists. His wrists were thonged with buffalo leather, and the other end of the long strap was nailed into the wall with a squareheaded peg.

Above the bed was a window. Jim could see the light streaming through the panes. He closed his eyes, opened them again, trying to find something familiar inside this room, or beyond that window.

Doc Knoblock moved between Jim and the window. "Sorry, Jim. But we had to stake you out like an Indian. You were loco — you knew no one — and hated all of us."

Gilmore closed his eyes, hearing the crackling of fire, remembering the point-blank firing. He cried out, writhing against the thongs. He heard voices above him, but they were not the sheriff, nor the doctor; he heard Kip's voice, and knew better because Kip had been killed, and then there was a softer voice and he recognized Eualie's voice, and he twisted, crying out that Eualie was dead.

He twisted his head, trying to escape the sound of those voices. He realized his body was caked with grease; the bed on which he lay was slippery with it.

From somewhere he heard Doc Knoblock speak. "At least we got the lead out while he was unconscious. That part is over."

Gilmore kept his head turned toward the wall. He heard a voice that sounded like Eualie's voice asking the doctor if he were going to live. He strained, listening, but it was no good, he could not hear the doctor's answer. Eualie's voice was screaming inside his head suddenly. He had no right to bring her here. She hated him.

He writhed, fighting the thongs. Eualie was right, He should never have brought her to this place. He knew that now, when it was too late.

The voices faded, grew nearer, and when he heard Eualie crying inside his mind, the sickness swept over him. He rolled his head back and forth on the wet pillow. He heard the voices, rising, fading, growing and growing until they were shouting inside his head, and then abruptly it was terribly still, and he lay there waiting to hear the crackling of the fire around him.

When he opened his eyes, they were gone, and it was dark beyond that opened window. He moved his head slowly, feeling the soft glow of lamplight touch at his eyes.

In the lamplight, he found Rosemary's face, and thought he was dreaming again. His gaze moved past her to the fire in the lamp, and a shudder wracked his whole body.

He pulled his gaze back to Rosemary.

She leaned toward him in her rocking chair. Her eyes were troubled. Then her gaze met his, and he watched her uncertain smile. Her hand on his forehead was cool.

"Your fever," she said. "It's all gone."

He drew his gaze from her lamp-tinted face and looked for the others, Knoblock and the sheriff.

"Where are they?" he said.

"The doctor?" She stared at him, and in her eyes he read deep pity, and turned angrily from it. "He and the sheriff?"

Jim nodded. "Where are they?"

"They haven't been here for three days, Jim."

He winced, startled and shocked. He moved his head, looking about uncomfortably.

He moved his hands, the restraining thongs were gone; so was the leather from his wrists and ankles. The bed was dry, the sheets fresh smelling and clean. A bright Indian blanket was doubled back at his waist. Above this, he saw he was tightly bandaged across stomach and chest to his armpits. Where Mills' bullet had struck in his belly was a hump of gauze.

"Where am I?" he said, frowning.

"They brought you to me," Rosemary said.

"I've been loco," he said.

"You've been out of your head. You had a

terrible time."

"I seem to bring you a lot of trouble."

"We wanted you here. We're close to Dr. Knoblock. You'll be safe here."

Jim frowned at the way Rosemary phrased this, but he did not speak.

"If you feel better," Rosemary said. "They want to talk to you. They're waiting outside. They've been here every night asking about you."

He scowled, then after a moment, nodded. He waited, breathing shallowly. Walker, Dr. Knoblock and Abel Tornet trooped into the room on tiptoe.

Walker bent over him, spoke gruffly. "How are you, boy?"

Jim shrugged.

Abel Tornet said, "We made you suffer more than was your due. Nothing can change what we've done to you."

Jim glanced up at the banker's gray face.

"When I'm well," Jim said, "I'm moving on."

"You can't move on," Dr. Knoblock said, "After what you've done for the valley. It would be a selfish thing." When Jim glared up at him, Knoblock said, "If you can make more money elsewhere, own better land, forget your sadness, and the inhumanity of people who knew you were a stranger and

432

didn't probe any deeper, then go. Then you should go, Jim. But I still say we need men like you, Jim."

Jim frowned, looking at their strained gray faces in the lamplight. Walker who had beaten him, Tornet who had accused him, and the doctor who had slandered him.

"You can't ever forgive us," Walker said, "and I can understand how you feel about that."

Abel Tornet nodded. "You needed us once. We failed you. You had pride and loneliness — we mistook them for evil."

"We'd like you to try to forgive us," Knoblock said.

Walker scowled. "Would you stay on, Jim — if it wasn't for Stan Mills."

Jim stared at them. He felt all the sickness and rage congeal in the pit of his stomach. "Mills is dead," he whispered.

Knoblock shook his head. "No."

"We got no proof he's dead," Abel Tornet said.

"If he is dead — we never found his body in the fire," Tom Walker said. "You talked plenty while you were raving, Jim. We figured it. He let you come in and try to save his carcass from the fire — then tried to blow your insides out."

Gilmore pulled himself up on his elbows.

He almost passed out. He bit down on his teeth, hanging on to consciousness. The room spun and skidded wildly before his eyes.

"If he's alive . . . I've got to get up."

"Take it easy, boy," Knoblock said.

"He had Kip shot in the back," Jim said, shaking. "He bushwhacked Randal Meade. Took his claim for a few dollars. And he killed Eualie . . ."

"We know all that, Jim," Walker said. "It took us too long to see it. But we know it now."

"I've got to get up," Jim cried, "I can't rest — as long as he lives."

"You've done your part," Tornet said. "More than your part."

Walker nodded. "It's up to us now."

"Where is he?" Jim whispered.

Walker shrugged. "We don't know. We came on you only a minute or so after you were shot. The impact of his bullet knocked you all the way back out the door of that barn — it saved your life. . . . We knew Mills had been there. . . . We trailed him, but we had wasted too much time when we found you raving, burned, almost dead. . . . We lost him."

"He may be dead," Knoblock said. "He must be bad burned."

"There must be some sign," Jim cried. "His golden horse — he couldn't just disappear."

"We'll find him," Walker said. "We're not smart — like you and young Kip Bowne . . . But we'll find him."

Knoblock nodded. "Rosemary has shown us those pieces of the lens Mills must have lost the night he shot her husband. The robberies. The murders. They were all Mills'. He was bleeding us white. Robbing us all . . . But — how were we to believe a man would rob himself?"

Tornet said, "I should have guessed. Of all of us, I was the one in the position to know — at the bank. But I couldn't believe a man who stood to be rich, if he worked hard, and saved — was too impatient to wait for it that way. . . . Mills overreached himself. Trying to work a mine, run a ranch, a saloon, and at the same time live high and like a king. He overspent. The robberies were his way of finding an out —"

"I say he's run out of the valley," Tom Walker said. "He'll never come back here now."

Gilmore's gaze raked across the three men. "But he will. He's too much at stake. What if you people do hate him? What proof do any of you have? My word against his?

Those lenses that he lost the night he killed Rosemary's husband — he will tell you, they only prove that he was out there, sometime — and not the night Randal Meade was killed."

"Let him come back then," Tom Walker said. His face was grim.

"We're ready for him now."

When the three men were gone, Jim lay watching Rosemary move about the room. She went to the wall, took down a single-shot rifle from its peg on the wall. He smiled, remembering the day she had stepped into her café with this rifle in her arms to quiet the townspeople who were going to run him out of the valley.

She placed the rifle near him on a chair beside his bed.

He shook his head. "I couldn't shoot it," he said. "It would tear me apart."

Rosemary smiled. "But I know you by now. You'll feel better, knowing it's there."

"Yes." He nodded. "If he's alive, he's coming back. You know that, too, don't you, Rosemary?"

She moved her shoulders, but kept her gaze averted.

"You know he will," Gilmore persisted. "And if he's heard about the lens from his broken glasses — he'll come here. You know he will."

"I'm not afraid," she said. "Tom has men on guard."

He exhaled heavily, wondering if she really trusted any of Tom Walker's guards against Stan Mills.

His gaze strayed to the open window, the dark beyond it. "How long have I been here, Rosemary?"

"A little over a week, Jim."

"A week," he whispered, awed. His voice lowered. "Where is he? A week — where has he been hiding?"

She shook her head, looking at him. Their gazes touched. He remembered in that moment the first time he saw her, all that had passed between them.

"He may be dead," she said.

"You know better."

"No one has seen him. No one has heard of him."

"But I know better. He's alive. Over a week I've been here — a week, lying helpless. Why didn't he come in the night?"

"I don't know. If he's out there, he may be worse off than you."

He scowled. "If he does come, Rosemary. What will you do?"

She looked at him with a sober smile. She

went around the bed, let the window fall. She placed a stake to bar it.

"There, is that better?" she asked.

"He'll be looking for you, Rosemary . . . as well as for me."

"I know that." She shook her head. "I told you, I'm not afraid."

"You need somebody in this house — besides me."

"I told you. Tom has men staked out — watching for Stan — day or night. And I'm not afraid." She paused at the door, hand on the knob. She smiled. "Anyway, I'm not afraid with you here."

"I'm helpless."

She shrugged, smiling, held his gaze for a moment. "Still, I'm not afraid. And I'm not lonely."

She closed the door behind her, and he lay there, hearing her at work in the other part of the house.

TWENTY-FIVE

Isabel Bowne moved aimlessly about the front room of her cottage. She turned up the lamp wick, putting more light in the corners of the room.

She shivered with the chill of loneliness that went through her. Kip had been dead over a week. She had thought for so long she despised him; she had never thought she would miss him so terribly.

She sat down in a chair, but was too nervous and restless to stay there. She should leave this place, get out of this house and out of this valley. There was nothing to keep her chained in this dispiriting place any more. She did not know what kept her here.

She was free. She could go anywhere.

She caught a glimpse of herself in the wall mirror, and trembled. She hated widow's black, but she had to wear it for a while anyhow. She felt that when she removed this miserable mourning dress, her marriage to Kip would truly and finally be over. A mistake. Though she missed his laughter, and the way he insisted on making love to her, even when she was tired and tried to put him off — even though she missed Kip in a hundred little ways, she admitted he had not been what she wanted.

She shuddered. Even at Kip's grave some of her tears had been shed in sheer relief.

She forced herself to sit down in a chair and take up a book, again. Now Kip was dead, she would have to go back to teaching. If only she had married Stan Mills.

She laid the book aside, thinking about

Stan. No one in the valley had seen him since the night Kip had been killed. But she could not believe a big, vital man like Stan Mills was dead. He couldn't be dead. He owned most of this valley — and even if he owned only the Bright Star, he would be rich enough. . . . Rich enough for what?

She felt her face grow warm. She remembered the whispers she'd heard that Stan Mills had hired somebody to kill Kip. But they couldn't prove that. She didn't believe it. Why would a big man like Stan Mills care whether a boy like Kip lived or died?

She thought instead of the way Stan had come by and offered Kip a job at his ranch. Wasn't he trying to help Kip?

She smiled, knowing Stan had really come to see her. But in aiding Kip, he was doing good for her, too. She wondered where he was, and when he would be coming back. She would no longer have to deny what she felt when Stan came back. Just the same, she wanted to be Mrs. Stan Mills, and she was glad now she'd resisted when Stan had tried to make love to her that morning.

The first time she heard the rattling sound at the rear of the cottage, she frowned, thinking a breeze was banging a limb against the roof.

There was a surreptitious knock at her

back door. It was sharp, hard. There was silence. Frowning, she got up, carrying the lamp from her center table and went through to the small kitchen.

She said, "Who's there?"

There was a tense pause, then a male voice said, "Let me in."

Her heart pounded faster. The voice was Stan Mills'. She was sure of that. Stan had come back to town. The first place he came was to her.

She set the lamp on the kitchen table, unlocked the door. When she opened it, and saw Stan, she stepped back, eyes distended in her pale, rigid face.

"Stan," she whispered.

He pushed past her into the kitchen. His tailored clothing was gone. His glasses were lost somewhere and he squinted lashless, browless eyes to see her at all. One side of his face was seared and twisted, blistered in long welts.

"Don't stare at me," he snarled, "I was almost burned to death, I'm lucky to be alive at all."

"Stan. The sheriff. He has men out looking for you."

"The hell with that." He glanced around the kitchen, "You here alone?"

"Yes, Stan."

"Listen to me. There's something I've got to know."

"They'll shoot you if they find you." Her gaze touched his face again, and she felt ill, revolted, "You need a doctor."

"The hell with that. The hell with Tom Walker. He knows nothing about me that he can prove. I've been thinking about that for a week. But there's something I've got to know."

"Where have you been, Stan?"

He squinted, his burned lids looking odd in his welted face, "What difference does it make? I've been safe. I've been hiding up at my mine. Plenty of men up there who know I'm boss. Know they better do what I tell them."

"I — I'm glad you're safe," she said, shivering.

"That's just it. I'm not safe. Not yet. I killed him. I know I killed him. I shot him. Point blank. As close as I am to you."

"Who, Stan?" She knew whom he meant, but she also knew that Tom Walker had sworn the town to secrecy about Jim Gilmore's being alive, or his whereabouts.

"Jim Gilmore!" Stan's voice broke with the bitterness in it.

Isabel licked her lips, "Stan, you must let me get a doctor for you."

"Hell with that. He'd turn me in. That quick. Shut up chattering. I've got to know, I sent men from the mines. They asked everywhere — they can't find out. No one will tell them anything. Everybody in the valley is lying. Jim Gilmore is alive — and I've got to know where he is."

"You're sick, Stan. You can hardly stand there." She shook her head, fighting back the illness inside her. "You need a doctor."

"I'm crazy," Stan growled, "I've got to be. I killed him. I saw him go plunging back when I hit him. He fell in the flames. He toppled through them. I've got to know. I thought he was dead."

"I could take care of you," she said without much conviction, her desire for him slowly dissipating. "We could go away. You could sell what you have here, Stan —"

"Sell what I have! It's mortgaged past its value. I know what I've got to do. I've got to kill Jim Gilmore. I've got to get back — where I was."

"You said you wanted me," she said, frowning.

"Where is he?"

She bit her lip. Suddenly, she saw that Stan Mills had shot Jim, had probably paid to have Kip killed. She saw the hell in his seared face. She no longer trusted him.

"I don't know, Stan," Isabel said, "Why don't we go away? You could take me away from here!"

His seared face twisted, pulling one eye wide. She shuddered.

"Why would I do that?" he demanded.

"You said you — wanted me."

For a moment, he stood in the middle of the room, staring at her. "Sure, I wanted you. Just as I'd want any faithless little baggage throwing herself at me. Stan Mills. You wanted my money. You were willing to see your husband dead to get it. . . . But get one thing straight . . . I don't want you now. I hire women like you, every night at the Bright Star."

She caught her breath, going ill with rage, "Liar! You said you loved me."

He laughed at her, "Once I wanted you — for one reason — and nothing very wonderful about that — Horses want the same thing."

She ran at him, hands in claws. But he caught her wrists, twisting, staring down at her, one eye distended in his burned flesh.

"I only want one thing from you. And make up your mind. I'll make you wish you were dead — unless you tell me."

"I hate you," she cried, trying to writhe free. "I can see why this whole valley hates

you — why they love Jim Gilmore for expos-
ing you —"

"He is alive!" Stan twisted her wrists
again. She cried out.

Isabel kept fighting, but Stan twisted her
wrists until she was too agonized even to
scream any more. She sank slowly to her
knees on the floor before him. "They're hiding him," Stan said to her. "Where are they
hiding him?"

She shook her head. Her hair fell loose,
spilling about her shoulders. She could
hardly see his face any more through the
pain swirling across her eyes.

"Where is he?" Stan said.

He twisted her wrists until she thought
they'd break, until she hoped they would
and he would stop hurting her, until she
lost all control of her body, sagging, unable
to faint and escape the torment. He twisted
until finally she whispered the word he
wanted from her, "Rosemary . . ."

When he was gone, closing the door softly
behind him, she sprawled on the kitchen
floor, her hair wild, eyes distended, sobbing
and staring at her bruised, useless hands. . . .

TWENTY-SIX

Jim lay on the bed, listening to Rosemary move about the house beyond the closed door.

She had turned his lamp low; the room was bathed in a wan orange light that glinted on the window pane. The time passed slowly; the town quieted so that every sound was magnified in the night, the crickets, the faraway screech owl, the distant whine of a cable in the wind.

He turned, staring at that barred window. His grin pulled at his mouth. Did they really believe that that stake would restrain a growing boy who wanted to enter that window?

The light glinted on the pane. He sighed. He'd asked Rosemary what she would do when Stan Mills came back. Now he wondered, *What will I do when Stan Mills returns? What could I do? What better moment could Stan Mills seek than now, tonight, here? I could never be more helpless than I am lying here tonight. Why has he delayed this long?*

Sooner or later, he had to prepare for the moment when he faced Stan Mills again.

He stirred on the bed. Holding tightly

against the gauze pack on his belly wound. Gilmore struggled to a sitting position.

He gasped aloud. Pain set him afire in every inch of his body. He bit down on his mouth until he tasted blood to keep from screaming. He forced himself to keep his eyes open, but the room would not stop skidding and wheeling about his head, and the fires blazed inside him.

Sweated, he sank back.

Well, now he knew just how helpless he was. He reached out his hand toward the rifle Rosemary had placed on the chair beside him. It might as well be on the moon.

He breathed in short, shallow drafts.

He lay there, eyes tightly closed. He heard Rosemary moving about in the next room. There was the soft, sharp sound of a door closing quickly, stealthily.

He heard Rosemary's sharp exclamation.

He heard scuffling movement and then the jumble of urgent whispering.

He sweated, straining forward to hear those whispers. He struggled to pull himself up again. He pressed his fist against the gauze wad.

The whispers continued in that room. He held his breath, straining to catch the tone of those voices.

The thudding of his own heart was deafening thunder in his ears. He pressed forward, trying to rise, fell back, sweated on the pillow.

His head rolled; he strained to hear those voices. His head ached, and his eyes felt as if they would burst from their sockets. The whispering went on for an eternity, harsh and urgent, with long pauses.

He couldn't go on lying there.

Laboriously, he struggled upward, feeling the stabbing of agony. His senses reeled. Blindly he put both arms out for support but stayed where he was, sitting up in bed. Slowly he swung his legs around, sliding them off the side of the bed. He was breathing through his parted mouth.

He stayed there a long time, finally reached out, closed his trembling hand on the single-shot rifle. With his other hand he thumbed back the hammer. It took an eternity and left him shaken and breathless.

Poised there on the side of the bed, he listened to the whispers, growing louder, more violent. Slowly he stood up, bracing the backs of his legs against the side of the bed. He heard something that was like a fist against a face, and the whispers started again, furious beyond that closed door.

He took one careful step away from the bed. The room wheeled and skidded out from under him. He faltered, and reached behind him, for support against the bed.

The weight of the rifle pulled him forward, and he wavered, his legs trembling and no longer able to support him. He plunged forward, the floor slamming against him. The rifle struck the floor beside him. Mixed with the sound of the rifle striking the floor was Rosemary's scream. Somehow he pulled himself up, caught the rifle in his fist.

The door was flung open. The light was brighter in that other room.

Through blood-blurred eyes, Jim saw Stan Mills looming in the doorway, filling it, his shadow falling across Jim on the floor. Mills' face was smoke blackened, scarred.

He saw the gun come up in Mills' hand.

He heard Rosemary scream behind Stan Mills. He saw Mills waver there, wondering why he didn't shoot him. Then he saw that Mills' glasses were gone.

The big man squinted, seeking him on the bed and finally finding him sprawled on the floor. Mills' roar of pleasure and rage rattled against the wall.

But Jim had pulled the rifle upward. His finger tightened on the trigger. There was one shot in it. One shell had to settle it all between him and Stan Mills. He saw Mills' .45 swing down, fixed on him. And then Jim pressed the rifle trigger. He lay prone watching the lead punch upward through the big man's solar plexus, striking him mortally. The impact drove Mills back a step across the threshold. The gun bucked in Stan's seared hand. Gilmore saw Stan Mills crumpling, watched the .45 slip in his weakening fingers and topple from his hand. It struck the floor and Mills seemed to be reaching for it when he landed on his knees, but he twisted away from it at the last moment and sprawled on the floor. Jim didn't attempt to move. He saw Rosemary come through the door and run toward him, and he was content.

■ ■ ■ ■

DESERT STAKE-OUT

BY HARRY WHITTINGTON

■ ■ ■ ■

To Harry Joe Brown

ONE

Less than a mile from the water hole were the bleached bones of a horse. They remained, ash-white and petrified, no longer yielding up anything to the pitiless sun. If the horse had had a rider, there was no trace of him, no memory. There was only the water hole, hidden, secret — named Patchee Wells by the few men who knew, had heard or dreamed frantically of it as throat tightened, tongue swelled. It was the only water within forty miles in a forsaken, rectilinear area of parched waste.

For days, sometimes for weeks, the water hole lay silent with its terrible, infinite stillness. A buzzard traced a high arc in the cloudless sky. A coyote sniffed, trembling; it drank, darted into the mesquite and greasewood, lost. A sidewinder slid through the rocks, and the water made a cool sound, spilling on a worn stone, and the stillness was magnified by the soft cool whisper of the water.

Stretching away from the rock-walled sump all the way to the heat-shimmering horizon lay flat gray alkali and sage wastes. Beyond, the hills were as dry as the flats, burned, shunned. In the mountains, three days' ride, were water and grass and shade, but between, the badlands lay like hot spikes, reflecting the brass of the sun.

Infrequently, a white man or a roving band of Indians came to the water hole that was a living thing upon this warped and festered scab of earth, calling to a man like the faint, tormenting whisper of a bawd. But the man passed, and the Indians; the silence settled again, breathless and unbroken.

Only the water hole remained forever.

For an hour now he had felt the brassy bite of his old chest scar and he rubbed at it with the back of his hand. Watchful, tense, he had not yet seen or heard anything, but the itch of that scar told him as plainly as though someone had spoken the words, "Apache trouble."

He glanced over his shoulder but did not speed the ponderous gait of the two army dray horses. He recognized that upon this limitless *playa,* the army wagon and himself, alone on its boot, were the only movement, and were almost lost in the gray land of heat and silence.

He was a day and a half south of Fort Ambush, still two days north of the mission at San Carlos. *The Apache strikes first and asks questions later, and that puts me in a bad spot,* he thought, and then he loosed another button of his gray shirt and mopped at his face with a bandana, thinking, *A bad spot, that's about the story of my life.*

Ahead of him was a rise, stubbled with mesquite and rock, and beyond the rise, the land fell away into a treeless valley. Behind him were a few stunted piñon and more boulders, offering as much danger as concealment. He figured ahead the hours to Patchee Wells. No way to escape trouble there, but at least a man could get a cold drink of water.

He touched the rifle on the boot beside him, glanced once more around the gray canvas wagon covering. He grinned faintly. The trouble wasn't behind him; it was ahead. When there was trouble, he was always riding into it, not away from it.

He felt a faint rise of anger that he'd allowed himself to be pushed into a position like this where he could not even run, couldn't even put his back against a wall. He'd had enough trouble with the Apache to last him a lifetime. It had been six years now, but he remembered that trouble, relived it in nightmares two and three times a week. He thought about it now, and even thinking about it was a torment. He mopped his sweated face again, thinking about cold water for himself and the horses, just out of reach ahead there at Patchee Wells.

He was a tall man, lean in the belly, wide in the shoulders, with hair faded by desert suns, eyes bleached blue and shadowed with old hurts. Tragedy drew bitter lines about his eyes and mouth, so even when he smiled it was an acid caricature of a smile. There was about him the kind of wariness that grows in a man who lives alone and stays alive by being alert to everything, the crying scold of a jaybird, the whisper of wind in a pine, the clatter of a small stone on a hillside.

He was almost to the top of the knoll. The midmorning silence was broken by distant gunfire, the scream of Apaches. He rubbed at his chest with the back of his hand. He'd been right all the time. The trouble was ahead of him.

A day and a half ago in Major Ralph Brackett's quarters at Fort Ambush, he'd wanted to say no, and it seemed to him the Major had read his mind and talked fast so he didn't have a chance to say anything.

"Sure, Blade, I could send a cavalry company," the Major said, answering the question that had been bothering Merrick. "You ask why I don't send a cavalry company —"

"I'd like to ask it, if I got a chance to ask anything."

"It's a good question." Major Brackett's voice increased in speed. "It's the surest way I know to guarantee those supplies would never get to the mission at San Carlos." He strode about the room. "Now, Blade, you and I are old hands out here. We respect the Apache. No company in this fort could stand up against a dozen Apaches in their own backyard and you know it."

Blade Merrick gave the Major one of his bitter smiles. "I know if the Confederacy had had a few troops of Mescaleros, that war wouldn't be over yet."

The Major stood with his back to Merrick. He stared out the window at the red parade grounds where a company marched in the sun.

"Merrick, it's an epidemic at San Carlos. I won't minimize the terror those people are going through. Fever. They have doctors, a couple of them, and the nuns at the mission are doing the nursing. They don't ask me for doctors or nurses. All they want are drugs and medical supplies. The need is urgent. I haven't slept, trying to figure it. Suddenly this morning, you ride into the fort, and the whole answer comes to me. You could take a wagon of supplies down there to the mission at San Carlos. Blade Merrick. I almost laughed aloud because the whole thing was so simple. I've already ordered the wagon loaded. You can get out of here inside an hour."

"That's just fine," Blade said. "And what are you going to do when I start out of here with a wagon of medical supplies all by myself?"

"Well, first thing I'm going to do is hit the sack and get some sleep. Man, I been up all night."

Hardhead Charley Clinton stood up cautiously when the six redskin raiders suddenly jerked the heads of their ponies around and raced toward the hills west at the mouth of this valley.

He cursed, forgetting the woman crouched near him. But he would have cursed if he'd remembered her. This was no time to think about social niceties, and oaths were the major part of his vocabulary. And what else was there to do but curse helplessly at the fate that had put him down here at this moment — four dead horses, a burning wagon, a wounded man, a woman, and a thousand square miles of hostile land, hot and dry and endless? Perch and young Billy were unhurt, but with dead horses they were as helpless as he was.

He was a big man, standing with legs apart, his hat knocked off during the attack and forgotten. Hardhead Charley had Nordic ancestors. He looked like a Viking pirate.

His hand tightened on his rifle. He had blue eyes with a squinted, snow-blind look to them. He had the twisted mouth, the scraggly beard of the blond Viking. He had been placed in the desert country by some whim of addled fate, out of time, out of place.

He cursed at the top of his bass voice, hurling curses after the plume of dust. He always talked loudly, accustomed to the wild places where wind dashed a timid man's voice to atoms. And a man had to be heard to be obeyed. Hardhead Charley Clinton intended to be obeyed when he spoke. A man must be obeyed, to be a man.

He drew in a breath through distended nostrils and his pirate face twisted into a scowl.

He heeled around, staring at the burning

wagon, reduced now almost to charred ashes. The Indians were gone and they were going to return, five people afoot in these wastes. Him, with riches in his grasp, and no chance to get out of this bind alive. Suddenly, the matter that offended Hardhead Charley the most was the burning stench from the body of that overturned wagon.

"Name of God, woman, what in goodbilly hell you toting in that wagon to stink thataway?"

Valerie Butler cradled Jeff's head in her lap and stared up at the loud, foul-mouthed man. He looked to her to be about fifty, but it didn't seem possible a man could become so evil-tongued in only half a century.

"I don't know what it is," she answered him. Her red hair trembled about her shoulders and her green eyes impaled him. "Why don't you go look and see?"

Hardly knowing what she did, she soothed Jeff's brow with her smoke-blackened hands. All she knew was that everything she owned was in that wagon, burned now to ashes. And she had to endure sarcasm from that rotten old man.

"Let the little lady alone, Hardhead Charley," Perch Fisher said.

Hardhead glanced around at Perch, thinking that every day Perch got a little smarter, a little harder to handle. He thought about settling the matter right now. A man like Perch, you had to show him; every once in a while you had to show him that you were the boss and that Perch was taking orders. He wanted to put Perch in his place, relieve some of his anger and rage at being left afoot in this waste by chewing Perch out so bad he rocked on his heels. But at the moment, Perch's stepping out of line didn't seem to pull much leather.

Perch slapped around his pockets, seeking a cigarette, his face pulled crooked with a contemptuous smile. Old Man Clinton better not push it, not in this heat, not after what they'd been through, not in front of this woman.

Perch turned his back on Hardhead Charley, looking the woman over again. Hot damn. He'd thought that the first time he saw her on the trail this morning. He still thought that. Hot smoking damn. This was the kind of woman a man walked barefoot through broken glass for. A man didn't meet her kind every day, not even in the hook-joints at Laredo. She was in her early twenties, tall and lush. Even with her hair loose on her shoulders, her face streaked with soot, a blue welt along the squared planes of her jaw, it was plain a man called her a lady — but she knew better, too.

She was in a state of shock, that was clear enough. But she wasn't so far gone she couldn't hand back to old Hardhead Charley better than he could give her.

Perch looked at the wounded man stretched out with his head in the woman's lap. It hadn't taken them long to learn today there wasn't much to her husband. It took an Indian bullet to shut him up. He had leaked a lot of blood, but the woman wasn't looking at it, as if as long as she didn't see it, she wouldn't have to believe her husband was dying with a bullet in his belly.

"Anything I can do for you, ma'am?" Perch said. He'd found a cigarette he'd rolled while waiting for the Apaches to come into rifle range this morning. He thumbed fire from a sulphur match and lighted up, watching her through a curl of smoke.

"He's dying," she said. Her voice was low, flat.

"Yes, ma'am, looks like he is." Perch gave her a rancid smile. He would have liked to look unhappy, but, seemed to him, a thing like this called for a drink. Slightly taller than Hardhead Charley, Perch Fisher weighed two hundred pounds, and pain never bothered him, certainly not another man's pain.

He batted dust from his blue trousers and black vest. He took off his flat-brimmed hat, inspected a bullet-rent in its crown.

"Man out here," he said, "chances dying every day. It ain't good for a lady like you to think about, but that's the way it is."

Young Billy Clinton emitted a fluted laugh. He sat on the ground a few feet from Valerie and her husband. He backhanded his hat from his head and began to work at his thick black hair with a pocket comb.

Not yet twenty, Billy had a sharp face, sharp features and soulless eyes, bluer than his father's and somehow much older. He wore an expensive white silk shirt with a string tie, a corduroy vest and whipcord trousers he'd had tailored for himself. His holster was handtooled, as were his high-heeled boots. He wore a gold chain across his vest and his belt buckle showed a carved long-horn head.

"That's right, ma'am. But don't you worry none. Men without women are plentiful out here."

Valerie heard him through the shock. She turned and stared at Billy, agony roiling in her green eyes.

"Please." She looked at them. "Can't you help him? Can't you do something for him?"

Hardhead Charley laughed coldly. "Looks

like we'd be doing him a favor, not cutting that bullet out of him."

"What are you talking about?"

"About them Apaches, ma'am. Seems to me your husband wasn't the bravest critter I ever laid eyes on the first time they attacked — and our horses were alive then. When they come back next time, looks like he'd be happy to be already dead."

She slapped the back of her hand against her mouth, chewed at it, staring at him.

Hardhead's voice was loud in the silent valley. "You don't think they're through with us, do you? They'll be back. But if they'd knowed what a looker you are, they'd be back even quicker."

She looked around helplessly, her face muscles rigid. "We — can't just let him die," she whispered.

Hardhead Charley pumped an empty cartridge from his rifle chamber.

"Maybe you can't, ma'am," he said. "We ain't got time for fool things. We got to get ready for company. Because don't ever think we ain't going to have it."

Young Billy Clinton stopped combing his hair. He stood up, tall, lean and dandy. He set his hat crookedly on his head, staring toward the ridge to the north.

"Pa. Somebody's coming."

"Looks like an army wagon," Perch said, moving beside Billy. "Got red crosses on the side — see that from here."

"Army wagon." Hardhead Charley laughed. "That means the army is coming."

Young Billy shook his head. "I don't think so, Pa. That wagon is all by itself."

"Army wagon, out here alone? Don't be a jackass, boy."

"Might sound crazy to you, Pa. But that's what it is. One wagon, traveling slow. All by itself."

"And just one man," Perch said in weary disgust, "riding the boot. Don't look like this is the day for miracles, Hardhead."

Two

Blade Merrick closed his fists, tightening the reins so the plodding army horses stopped near the burning wagon, shying slightly at the odor and the dead animals.

He had taken in the tragic picture all the way down the incline, with only the shoes of his horses as they cracked the alkali crust giving any sound to the whole world.

He saw the woman crouched in the sun with the man's head in her lap. From the distance, she was just a woman, and his gaze moved quickly from her to the three hardcases who had stepped around the charred remains of the wagon and stood waiting for him, squinting.

He gave a final scrape at his shirt front with his thumb.

"You folks making camp?" he inquired. His mouth was twisted into a bitter smile.

The teenager's eyes blazed, and he stiffened. Before he could speak, the older man caught his arm.

"A man stops where he has to." His voice was soft. "Where's the rest of the army?"

"Not more than two days' ride," Merrick said. "That way." He jerked his head in the direction he had come. He let his gaze move over the dead horses. "Might take you a mite longer afoot."

"Oh, well, we got plenty of time," Hardhead Charley said. But the tensions in his face belied his tone. "You hate people, ridin' alone out here this way?"

"I don't hate people," Merrick said. "But seems they just can't stand having *me* around."

"Where you heading?"

"South. Mission at San Carlos. You folks come from that way?"

"Yes," Perch Fisher said.

Anger showed under the surface of the older man's mild voice. "Well, we come

466

from that direction. Like you can see, mister, we can stand jawing with you in this here sun the rest of the day. But we'd take it most kindly if you'd help get us to hell out of here."

"Them Apaches ain't gone far," Billy Clinton said.

"Anyway, not far enough," Perch Fisher said. "So let's cut the jawing."

"Just a minute, boys," Hardhead Charley Clinton said. "We'd be mighty beholden to this gentleman for help. But this is kind of a tough spot. We want him to make up his own mind if'n he cares to pause here long enough to aid us."

The big man's polite tone may have deceived the other men, but Blade Merrick wasn't fooled. He realized that the bearded man knew they were doing their talking below the surface banter. They had scarcely pulled their gazes apart since they first had locked in that moment of low-voiced greeting.

Merrick drew the back of his hand across his mouth. This man wasn't the polite type — not unless the hostiles had improved his disposition by scaring religion into him. Merrick doubted this. The big man wanted help, wanted to get out of this inferno, but he was stepping cautiously, a barefoot man in a patch of sidewinders.

Merrick frowned faintly. The big man's face was the kind seen on reward posters. He'd seen him somewhere before, but couldn't place him for the moment.

He waited, licking his parched lips. He was being weighed, too. The big man had lived a long time. Indian attack was not his only worry — trouble awaited him in the civilized spots of this territory. He wanted to know how much Merrick knew about him before he made his next move. One thing sure, the big man would kill him in a second. He was already considering it.

He saw Clinton nod almost imperceptibly at the other big man. Perch walked with elaborate casualness around the horses, as if admiring horseflesh. This put Perch on one side of the wagon, the Clintons, father and son, on the other.

"Better just hold what you got," Merrick said to Perch. "Right there."

Perch looked wounded. "Why? What's the matter?"

Merrick shrugged. He moved deliberately, taking his Colt from its holster and laying it on the seat beside him, his hand covering it. He said, "I'd just like to say a couple things to you men." He stared at old Clinton.

"Why, feel free to say anything you like,"

Clinton said.

"It's about these army horses," Merrick said. "They'll pull far. But not fast. I figure three men could take turns doubling on one horse. They might get quite a ways — if they wasn't chased by Indians. Like I said, these horses couldn't outrun a little old lady, empty-saddled."

Clinton was silent a moment. His mouth pulled into a grimace. He was thinking, hard.

"The other thing is," Merrick said very softly, "if three men were to draw on me — all at once — wouldn't be but two of them left needing horses, and I'd figure to get the older one — the leader. You see how that would be."

Clinton licked his whiskered mouth. "Whatever give you them inhospitable thoughts we might attack you?"

Merrick exhaled. "Maybe I wasn't thinking about you folks at all," he said, keeping his voice very low. "Maybe I was considering what I might be tempted to do if I was alone out on a wilderness with a woman and a wounded man — and some loner came along with a couple horses."

"Don't know what ever gave you that thought," Clinton said.

"Of course if this lady is your daughter,"

Merrick said. "I'm wrong right from the start."

"We never saw 'em before," Billy said.

"Shut up, Billy," Clinton said. He was looking at the heavy-shod army horses, at the wagon, and at the pink-plumed dust where the Indians rode.

Perch had moved again, so it was difficult for Merrick to see him at all and watch either of the men on the other side of the wagon.

He kept his voice friendly. "I'll have to ask you to stop right where you are. In fact," he stared hard at Clinton, "I think you better ask your friend to come back around there with you. I mean if you want to keep this whole thing friendly."

"Perch." Clinton spoke the word sharply. Perch laughed and walked slowly back to him, trailing the flat of his hand along the horse's flank as he walked.

Merrick sighed, shoving the gun back in its holster.

"See you got a casualty there for yourself," Merrick said, glancing at the man sprawled on the ground.

"It's nothing," Hardhead Charley Clinton told him. "Just a belly wound. Won't hurt him much if'n he don't laugh sudden."

"Or drink any hot coffee," Billy Clinton

470

said. He tilted his hat slightly.

"Shut up, Billy." The older man's voice had iron in it.

Merrick pulled his gaze to the boy, and to the heavy-set jasper siding him. Nothing in their faces gave him anything to cheer about. The teenager had followed somebody too far along the owl-hoot trail. There was nothing in his mind now but self-indulgence, and a reputation he was going to build with the gun thonged at his thigh.

The cold stare of the other young man gave Merrick a slight chill at the nape of his neck. Here was a man who pulled wings off flies to watch them die, slowly.

"Like you can see," Old Clinton said, "the Indians have burned our wagon, killed all our horses."

"Probably plan to eat them when they come back," Merrick said.

"Please. Please help me."

The woman's voice had agony in it, and the fevered terrors of all she'd endured.

"Please help me."

Merrick said to Clinton, "Pardon me?"

"Shore," Clinton said. He and the other two stepped back enough so Merrick could spring to the ground beside them.

For a moment he faced them, hat pushed back on his forehead. In dark trousers and sweated gray shirt, he appeared slender beside the two big men, but his leanness was corded muscle, and they saw this. They stepped back, watching him stride to the woman.

She looked up, and Merrick paused, catching his breath. Men always did this the first time they saw Valerie Butler, whether it was on a crowded dance floor, or out in the middle of the wastes.

Merrick breathed deeply. Once, a long time ago, he'd gone head-on into the butt of an army rifle. It was something like that now. He could have staggered under the impact of her. Not even the desert sun could spoil the soft smoothness of her skin or dull the fire of her hair.

He frowned. What was a woman like this doing with men like these hardcases?

She stared up at him. "My husband is dying."

He knelt beside her, pushing the looks of her and the smell of her out of his mind. He kept the wounded man's prostrate body between him and the three gunslingers, glancing up at them frequently. He pulled away the man's shirt and stared at the raw tear made by the bullet. He heard the woman's intake of breath.

"Got himself a nasty one," Merrick said.

"Deep, too."

"Can you help him?"

"Might. If I could cut the bullet out."

"Please —"

"That would take some time."

"Hell with that," Old Clinton said. "Let's get out of here before we all croak of lead poisoning."

The girl's eyes had filled with tears. She was staring into Merrick's face, silently pleading.

He kept his voice level. "Your friend has got a good point there, ma'am. If we can keep this fellow alive until we get to a safer spot, we'd all be a lot better off."

"Let's get out of here," Perch Fisher said.

Merrick stood up, facing the three men across the girl and her prostrate husband.

"That's up to her," he said. "This here is her husband. It's up to her. She better know — it might kill him to move him."

"Going to kill us all not to move," Clinton said.

Perch Fisher's hand flexed, inches from his holster. "Ain't no question about it. We say we're moving out. That about settles it. She can get another husband — ain't many of us can grow a new scalp."

Merrick said, "Move your hand away from your gun, mister. And keep it away from it.

473

If I hadn't come along, you people would've got scalp treatments anyhow."

"But now you brought horses, mister," Perch said. "That changes things."

"They're my horses."

"Three of us got guns, though, say them horses belong to us."

"You move an inch nearer that gun, mister, we're going to have to cut lead out of you," Merrick said. His temper had blazed suddenly; his face grew hot and his eyes were dry, fixed on Perch Fisher and his poised gunhand.

Old Clinton spoke loudly. "Perch, don't be a fool." After a moment, he said, lowering his voice, "Now, Mrs. Butler. It ain't reasonable to stay here in this place and wait to be killed. If we can get to some kind of shelter, we can get that bullet out of your husband."

The wounded man's lips parted. He tried to speak. She knelt close. Then she looked up, eyes stricken.

"Water. He wants some water."

Clinton stared at Merrick. "You got any water?"

"I'm out. Water hole up the way is a stop I planned to make."

"I got a canteen of water," Billy Clinton said. "We can give him some of that — if it ain't too far to the water hole."

"It's not far," Merrick said. "Patchee Wells. Few miles off the trail. Only water I know during the dry spell." Billy brought a canteen from the saddle of one of the dead horses. He knelt beside Valerie and tilted Butler's head while she held the canteen against his lips.

"Good you know this country," Clinton said. "We wouldn't last long without water. Drank up all ours during today's hot spell."

Merrick glanced at him over his shoulder. "You know Patchee Wells?"

"Can't say we do," Clinton said, voice loud.

Merrick knelt beside the wounded man again. "If he can hold on until we can get to the water hole, ma'am, we can fix him."

"All right," she said. Still dazed and unaware of what she was doing, she gave him young Clinton's canteen and stood up.

Merrick stood up, too. He extended the canteen toward the boy, then drew it back. "Mind if I have a drink?"

"You know how far it is to that water hole, mister," the boy said. "Help yourself."

Merrick took one long drink of the water. He removed the canteen from his mouth, touched his tongue along his lips. He replaced the cap, handed it back to the boy.

He frowned, staring at the canteen, but he did not say anything.

"We best get to goodbilly hell out of here," Hardhead Charley said, staring across the sun-baked flats.

Valerie Butler was staring at Merrick's canvas-covered wagon with the red crosses smeared hastily on its side. She shook her head, her voice still awed. "But you are alone," she said.

"That's right, ma'am."

She looked at him, puzzled. "Why were we attacked?" She looked at the three hard-cases, at her husband, brought her gaze back to Merrick. "Yet you can travel alone across this Indian country and not be attacked?"

A shadow flickered across Merrick's face. He felt the gazes of the three men on him, saw the swirling lights in the girl's eyes.

His mouth tightened. It was a long story. He didn't have time for it now.

He kept his tone light, his voice level as he let his glance touch the dead animals. "Maybe the Apaches figure army horses ain't fit to eat."

THREE

A hot wind blew east across the valley, carrying a thin film of alkali dust stirred by the Indians. The sun had slid west of its apex, but none of its heat had lessened.

Merrick glanced at the woman, wondering when she would break. She was only holding herself together through some hidden will.

He frowned. It would be a lot better if she had a screaming, raging cry for herself. Merrick had seen what bottled agony could do to human beings.

He squinted west, searching for the Indians. The land lay flat and gray and silent, touched faintly with settling dust, glistening in the sun. The Apaches had disappeared. There was no sign of them. But he knew them too well. As far as he was concerned they were the smartest warriors the world had ever known. Just because you didn't see them didn't mean much.

He wasted no time. He vaulted into the rear of the wagon. It smelled like an overheated hospital ward under the canvas. At that, the woman's husband would be better off in here than broiling in that sun. He cleared away as many boxes as possible, stacking them against the support ribbing.

He spread a blanket on the bed of the wagon, got down from the rear.

"All right," he said. "You men can move him into the wagon."

Billy Clinton moved to obey without question. He paused only long enough to toss one glance toward the distant dust. After a slight hesitation, Old Clinton moved to the wounded man's boots.

Perch Fisher did not move. He stood watching Merrick with a twisted smile.

"Get your arms under his back, fellow," Merrick said. "Don't get him bleeding any worse."

Clinton spoke sharply. "Perch. Get to hell here and give us a hand."

Perch wasted just enough time to strike his gaze hard against Merrick's.

Merrick shrugged. *It's your scalp, mister.*

He led the woman to the front of the wagon, helped her into the seat. He looked around, but all of her belongings had been consumed in the wagon fire.

The three men lifted Jeff Butler carefully into the wagon bed with Merrick watching them.

His voice was sardonic. "Makes you feel good to be able to do something for a man, don't it, men?"

Old Clinton laughed, but Perch stepped

away from the wagon, eyes cold.

Clinton backhanded Perch across the bicep. "Come on, Perch. Get your saddle bag."

They moved hurriedly then, cutting their thick saddle bags free from their dead mounts. Carrying their rifles and the tightly-buckled saddle bags, they returned to the wagon.

Billy clambered up on the front seat beside Valerie. Perch watched them, face expressionless.

"All right, mister," Old Clinton said. "Turn them horses around and let's get out of here."

Merrick had started toward the front of the wagon. He stopped, turned. He jerked his head south. "Water hole's that way — and that's the way we're going."

Perch sprang forward. "Now you get this. I'm getting sick of you telling us —"

He stopped in midair, facing Merrick's drawn gun. Merrick held it low, waiting.

Perch Fisher paled slightly.

Clinton laughed again, loudly. "All right, Perch. In the wagon. We can discuss our route later. Like the gentleman says, the important thing is gettin' to the water hole and gettin' the lead out of that poor wounded man."

Billy Clinton laughed. "The important thing is that gun in his hand, ain't it, Pa?"

Fisher shrugged his shirt up on his thick-slab shoulders. He backed away, never taking his gaze from Merrick's face.

Clinton waited until Perch had swung into the rear of the wagon. His voice was tea-party polite. "We're mighty beholden to you for all you're doing for us, mister. Uh, I don't believe I caught your name."

"Blade Merrick."

There was an odd tightening about Clinton's mouth so that his scraggly beard wiggled slightly.

"You heard of me?" Merrick asked.

Clinton had not stopped smiling. "No, sir. Not that I recall."

He hoisted himself into the rear of the wagon beside Perch Fisher.

Merrick glanced once more toward the boulders west of them and then swung up beside Valerie Butler.

She sat rigidly, her gaze fixed on something deep inside her own mind. Merrick glanced across her at Billy Clinton. Billy shook his head. She was pretty far gone.

Merrick took up the reins, slapped them across the rumps of the horses.

The animals strained forward. They were only slightly faster than army mules would have been, though Major Brackett had given him horses to help speed him south.

"Can't these critters move any faster?" Billy Clinton said.

"Not built for speed," Merrick said. Valerie Butler had sagged slightly. He felt the pressure of her shoulder against his arm. Even though he realized she was unaware of what she was doing, he felt the warmth of her against him.

His mouth pulled into its bitter semblance of a smile. *It has been a long time. Never one so lovely as this.*

Billy was watching the west end of the valley, but he did not mention the Indians. He didn't have to. They were in both their minds.

"Blade Merrick," the boy said. "My name's Billy Clinton. The bearded old goat is my pa. Hardhead Charley Clinton. Maybe you've heard of him."

Merrick nodded without turning his gaze from the way south. He'd been right again — Hardhead Charley's face was on reward posters back at Fort Ambush.

The silence, broken only by the crackling earth crunching under the horses' hooves, deepened. Billy said, "You an army man, Merrick? I mean, you got the wagon, and I seen army supplies. But no uniform."

481

"Working for them right now. Sometimes I scout. But mostly, I work for myself. I'm a hunter."

"That so? What do you hunt?"

Merrick did not answer. Billy Clinton caught his breath just faintly, shrugged his shirt up on his shoulders. Valerie Butler swayed slightly between them.

"Watch her," Merrick told Billy. "She might faint."

"I'm all right," the woman said. "How far is it to this water hole?"

"Not far, ma'am. Just hope the Indians didn't circle around this way."

"I don't think so," Billy answered him. "I been watching. I seen no sign."

Merrick's laugh was short. "You pretty good at reading Indian signs, boy?"

"I'm good enough. Pa and Perch and me have moved around right under their noses when we had to. We used the same water holes. And it was me that knew where they were, and what they was doing."

"Takes a smart man."

"I'm smart enough."

"I wasn't ribbing you, boy. I meant it. I admire a man can live in Indian country and keep his scalp."

Billy laughed, pleased at the praise. "Wasn't real good living. No gunfire, no fires. You don't have things real comfortable."

They plodded forward some moments in silence. Merrick told himself to forget the smell of the woman, the warmth of her touching him. She was ill with shock. If she fell into his arms, it would mean nothing. Just the same his heart slugged faster at the warm scent of her hair.

He spoke to Billy. "You know this country, eh?"

Billy opened his mouth to speak, closed it. After a moment, he said, "We were just passing through."

"But you get this way — often?"

"Any man who'd travel this country when he didn't have to is crazy."

Merrick stared across the girl's red hair at the boy. "But sometimes a man has to, eh?"

Billy's gaze met his levelly. As plainly as words, the boy's eyes told him he was pushing it, that he might as well save his breath.

Billy shrugged.

After a moment, Billy said, "You been in Tucson lately? Lordsburg?"

"Few weeks ago."

"Man. I miss them spots. We been down on the border, but it ain't the same. They tell you a woman is a woman. But I like Tucson. I like noise. I like excitement.

What's new up that way?"

"Depends on how long you been away," Merrick said. A small muscle worked in the hard line of his jaw. " 'Bout a month ago, bank was robbed at Tucson."

Billy laughed, staring at him. He shrugged his shirt up on his shoulders again. He said, "I don't mean that kind of news, I mean, any new women up there, anything like that."

"I don't know. You'll have to wait until you get up there and see."

"Man. I will." He let his gaze graze unhurriedly over Valerie Butler. "Mrs. Butler here is the first white woman I've seen in — a long time. Too long. A man can get mighty thirsty, you know, Merrick?"

The jolt of the wagon thrust her hard against him again. Merrick's hand tightened on the reins. He slapped them across the horses. "Yeah," he said.

Billy Clinton laughed. "Her husband. He's a real dude. They got lost, he told us, couple days ago. Here they were, alone in that wagon, and Apaches trailing them. That's when we caught up with them this morning."

The woman made a sound deep in her throat. Both of them stared at her, but her gaze was fixed on nothingness. She seemed unaware of them.

Billy said, "I'd been seeing Indian sign for hours. They ain't too smart — if you're smart. My old woman was part Mescalero. Them Apaches were after anything that moved. Like you said, they're eatin' horses this summer. They were after us, too. It was a question there. We didn't know what to do. Traveling with the wagon would slow us down —"

"They could catch you anyway — if they decided to."

Billy nodded, shrugged. "We considered that. And the Butlers' wagon offered the only shield in case they did attack. They had it loaded. Mrs. Butler said it was everything she owned — man, that husband of hers hadn't bought her much. So — anyhow, we threw in with them. It was just as well. We stumbled into an Apache ambush just before noon. We outran them into the valley — and that was a mistake. We got out there in the open, and the first thing they did was to shoot our horses and burn the wagon."

Merrick nodded. "Makes sense. They could always come back for you people."

FOUR

Merrick slowed the horses to a walk and then halted them on the rise above Patchee Wells.

"How about it?" he said to Billy. "You smell Apache?"

"Think we better scout before we ride in?"

"If they're here, they knew we were coming. They've had time to bake us a cake."

Billy Clinton stood up on the wagon. He gave his hat a rakish tilt, caught his thumbs in his belt, moving his head slowly.

The water holes called Patchee Wells were in a depression, with the bubbling water against a wall making a short fall to a second level and then a drop into the sump. From the lowest part of the ground the earth rose upward forming a broken cup with the water at its bottom. Above the rim were twisted piñon, gnarled Joshua trees, a beard of mesquite that petered out into the barren hills and flatland so a man could pass within a mile of the water hole and die of thirst without even knowing it was there.

A soothing balm of cool rose from the sump and the silence deepened inside it. The largest pool was clear and deep with rock formations misshapen through the water.

"Let's go in," Billy said.

Merrick nodded, slapped the reins. The horses cleared the rise and then he drove the wagon downslope to within a few feet of the lower pool.

Clinton and Perch Fisher leaped from the wagon. Fisher flopped to the water's edge, buried his face in it, came up blowing.

"Let's get this man out of the wagon," Merrick said, swinging down.

He saw Billy helping the woman from the seat, watched the boy's hands travel swiftly, hungrily over her body.

He climbed into the wagon bed, lifted Butler's shoulders. Billy and Old Clinton took the wounded man's legs. Carefully, taking their time, they lifted him out to the ground.

Merrick spread a blanket and they placed Butler on it. Merrick tore away his shirt.

Valerie knelt at the head of the blanket, staring at her youthful husband's bloodless face.

Merrick felt a sharp twist in his solar plexus. This Jeff Butler was a handsome devil, with straight, even features and curly hair. No doubt he was a devil with the

women. Plainly enough, his wife was en-
slaved.

Merrick's voice was sharper than he'd
intended. "Billy, loose those horses, water
them and stake them in that grass patch."

"Sure, mister," Billy said. Merrick didn't
look around.

Hardhead Charley said, "It's an uphill
climb for them horses, in case we have to
get out of here in a hurry."

"Don't get yourself in a bind, Clinton,"
Merrick said. "That wagon could be seen
from miles on the ridge. Put it in the
mesquite and it's too far away from us.
Them Apaches come back, likely we won't
have time to get in the wagon."

Valerie said, "Is he alive?"

Merrick tested Butler's pulse, found it
weak. "He's hanging on," he told her. He
glanced up at Clinton. "There's antiseptic
in that wagon, some gauze and bandages.
Would you get it?"

Clinton moved to the wagon, pawed
around inside it.

"You, Fisher, build a fire," Merrick said.
He removed his knife, tested it against his
cheek. Finding a smooth boulder, he began
working the blade against it.

"You build the goddam fire yourself,"
Fisher said. "Clinton's can take orders from

you if they want to."

With the knife in his hand, Merrick came up to his feet. His heart was slugging, the blood congealed in the pit of his stomach. He felt the rage from the backs of his knees upward. It would take very little to make him attack any one of these three. Nobody had to tell him Old Clinton and Fisher had plotted his death all the way across the badlands.

Clinton swung around from the wagon. His voice struck the sump walls, rebounded. "Damn you to goodbilly hell, Perch. I warned you. You simmer your pot, fast, boy. You build that fire like he says."

For an instant, everything in the silent world of the water hole seemed holding its breath. Perch Fisher kept his hand clawed out over his gun. His sunscorched face was paled, and a pulse worked in his throat.

Merrick stood there gripping the knife. He had seen Fisher's kind in every saloon west of El Paso. A man on the prod, carrying a chip on his shoulder, feeling degraded the moment some man didn't share his own high estimate of himself. He could take a beating easier than he could take orders. And there was more. He was a man who notched his guns, thonged them down, and got almost a sexual excitement from using them. But he was a big man, too, and he got another thrill from inflicting physical pain. He would beat a man's face in in a fist fight, and few cowmen cared for that kind of combat. But then, Merrick knew he had not for a moment considered Perch Fisher a cowman.

Fisher looked Merrick over, laughed. "Sure, friend."

"You can gather some greasewood sticks," Merrick said, aware his voice reflected his own inner rage, though he kept it low. "Makes a faster fire."

He knelt beside Butler again, whetting his knife on the stone.

Butler was rolling his head slowly back and forth. His eyes were closed, and though he was burning with fever, his flesh was dry and his clothes were not sweated. He was talking swiftly, but his words were unintelligible.

Her head bent, Valerie was watching her husband. She tried to smooth his hair back from his forehead, but he twisted away from her, speaking in that fevered monotone. Fisher tossed some greasewood sticks to the ground near them, and slapped his shirt, seeking matches.

"Don't build that fire in the open," Merrick said.

490

"Why not?"

"How have you stayed alive this long?"

Fisher laughed. "By being just a little better than the next man I meet, Merrick."

"You got to be smarter than the Apaches to get out of this one."

"You think they don't know we're at this water hole?"

Merrick kept his voice low. "There's still a chance they don't know. They know they left you at that wagon, without horses. They might not know you got this far."

"Them horses of yours left shoe tracks."

"They'll find them — when they get back to your dead horses. Meantime, no sense telling them we're here. This water hole is known to mighty few white men."

Clinton stood there with the medical supplies and bandages.

"Right," he said. "That might give us a little time. If they think we don't know about this place."

Merrick jerked his head toward the overhanging boulder and the sheltered place beneath it. "Build a small fire over there."

Fisher and Billy Clinton built a fire. By that time Merrick had spread out the medicines and supplies he would need on the blanket beside Butler.

He got up then, crossed to the fire. Perch

was whispering to Billy as he approached. Perch stopped talking and looked up, grinning.

Merrick stared at the thick-jowled man. *Fine. I have less to fear from the Apaches than from these hardcases.*

He jabbed the knife into the hottest part of the fire, and held it there.

They watched him walk back to the blanket.

Valerie cradled her husband's head against her breasts.

"You better not watch," Merrick said.

She stared up at him. "I'm all right."

Old Clinton pressed his weight against Butler's shoulders and upper arms. Sweat popped out across the old pirate's forehead as he watched Merrick's knife probe deeper and deeper through the layers of Butler's flesh.

Blood spurted suddenly, erupting from the man's side. He heard Valerie gasp, saw her tighten her hands about her husband's head.

Butler stiffened, and then sagged, unconscious.

"That's fine," Clinton said.

Using gauze wrapped around his fingers, Merrick worked the bullet out against the knife blade.

He dropped the knife, the pellet of lead and the strings of blood on the blanket.

Valerie was rocking back and forth, pressing Butler's head against her breasts, crooning something unintelligible.

Merrick glanced up at Clinton. "Too bad she won't join him."

"I could clip her on the jaw," Clinton stated, matter-of-factly. "I got nothing against hittin' a woman."

Merrick was pouring the antiseptic over the wound, reaching for the dressing. He glanced up briefly, his mouth twisted. "In her condition, you'd be taking a chance. If you didn't knock her out first time, she might beat hell out of you."

Clinton laughed, twisting Butler's inert body so that Merrick could bandage it. "Wouldn't be the first time some woman belted me. I've had me a mite of trouble with women in my time. Never met one yet that would fight fair."

With Butler bandaged and laid out in the shade of the wagon, there was nothing to do but wait for him to regain consciousness or die from shock.

Clinton replaced the medical supplies in the wagon and went to the overhang. He kicked out the fire, tromping the ashes under his boot.

Merrick cleaned the knife blade by thrusting it into the sand several times. He picked up the small lead pellet, studying it. It was blunted and shapeless. He dropped it on the blanket beside Butler. He might like a souvenir.

He walked down to the pool, washed up.

Hunkered beside the clear pool, he stared at himself for a moment, seeing the reflected piñon, the boulders, and the sky. He moved his gaze to the three men under the overhang. Hardhead Charley was propped against the stone wall with Perch lounging on his left and young Billy flat on his back to Clinton's right.

He stared at them for a long time, his mouth taut. Then he looked at Valerie Butler and her husband. Butler was still unconscious. Valerie was leaning against a wagon wheel, motionless.

He sighed, washing the blood from between his fingers, immersing his hands and then shaking them dry.

Clinton said, "Merrick."

Merrick walked up the slight incline and stood under the rock overhang. The three men stared up at him, old Clinton openly, Perch through hooded eyes, and Billy with a faint grin from beneath his hat.

"You done a fine job, Merrick." Clinton

nodded toward Butler. "That shore ain't the first bullet you ever dug out of a man."

"No."

"We figure now the bullet is out, it's time to hightail it out of here."

"Apaches," Billy said, grinning. "Remember?"

Merrick waited.

Clinton said, "Way I figure it, once them Apaches come back to eat our horses, won't take them a coon's age to trail us here."

Merrick scraped his thumb joint against his shirtfront.

"So, if we want to get to Fort Ambush with our scalps, we best hit the road," Clinton said.

Merrick let his gaze move from one to the other, and finally back to Hardhead Charley.

"I thought I told you men. I'm not headed to Fort Ambush. I came from there."

"Just where do you plan to go?" Clinton kept his voice level.

"I'm on my way to the mission at San Carlos. There's a fever epidemic. They need these medicines. That's where I'm going. You men want to go with me, you're welcome."

Clinton glanced at Billy and then at Perch. Suddenly Perch burst out laughing. Billy pulled the hat over his face and Clinton stared up at Merrick, grinning.

FIVE

Old Charley drew in a deep breath, staring at Merrick. But before he could speak Billy sat up, his hat toppling forward. Billy touched Old Charley's arm and shook his head at him, warningly.

"What's the matter, boy?" Hardhead said.

Billy whispered, "Apaches, Pa. I smell 'em."

Merrick saw the tensions swirl in the older man's eyes. Obviously, Hardhead Charley and Perch Fisher stayed alive in the Indian country by trusting young Billy's keen senses.

Merrick moved from the overhang, forgetting the veiled threat of the Clintons in the more urgent matter of the Apaches having found them already. He'd hoped for more time. He'd thought he had the situation pretty well figured: the Apaches had pulled away from the attack back there in the valley to let the surviving white people stew in sun and fear while they prepared themselves through soul-cleansing ceremonies for a feast of roast horse, and for the warrior's pleasure of torturing white prisoners and enjoying the white man's woman before they killed her, or she died. Of course, he had been certain they would return after those ceremonies to the scene of the attack: their victims wouldn't get far on foot in that waste. He had believed that when they returned to the valley and found their victims had eluded them, they would pause to eat the horses. He was hoping he and the others had that many hours before the Apaches trailed them here to the Wells. There was no reason to hope they had that much time any more . . . not if Billy Clinton's instincts spoke truly.

Billy came forward to his knees, tapped his hat rakishly and got silently to his feet. Merrick watched, amazed at the Indian-stealth of the boy. There was not a creak of boot leather, rattle of spur or bump of gun against leather.

Billy glanced over his shoulder at his father and Perch Fisher.

"Stay right there. Don't breathe," he said. He turned his mocking gaze on Blade. "All right, Merrick. You know how to handle Indians, let's go handle them."

Billy crept up the incline and Merrick matched his cautious steps. They moved silently; any sounds in the dry breathless afternoon came from the camp behind them, the water below in the sump.

They crouched behind the boulders at the rim of the knoll above the water hole. For a long time they watched the piñon and mesquite tangled woods before them. Not even a breeze stirred in the underbrush. If there were men out there, they breathed as shallowly as Billy and Merrick.

They might have missed the Apache hidden in the underbrush, but his pony switched its tail at a fly. In that immense expanse of stillness this slight movement grabbed their gazes.

"There," Billy whispered. "Right in that underbrush."

"Probably got a rifle trained on us right now."

"One of us could stay here, other try to go around him."

"What makes you think he's alone?"

"What do you think?"

"As you do. He's likely a scout, sent up here to find out we're here. That case he's alone. Or it might be three or four."

"Either way I get impatient just sitting here waiting."

"Wait a minute. We got two chances. One is that even if he's got a rifle, he won't be as expert with it as with arrows or knives, if we can draw his fire, maybe we can disarm him."

"Disarm him?" Billy stared at him as if he were insane. "We'll kill him."

"Won't buy us much. I'd rather risk letting him have one shot."

"You said we had two chances." There was lack of enthusiasm in Billy's voice. "What's the other one?"

"The other one is that maybe he is a scout and is alone. If he's alone, he's scouting for the raiders. Maybe he don't want to fight. If he's a scout, his job is to find out about us and get back to report. If we let him get away — nobody has to get killed."

"You an Injun lover, Merrick?"

"No. I don't mind staying alive, though."

"I'm not about to let him go back and tell them where we are."

"Now you're loco. It's only a matter of time until they find us anyhow — without him. Our only hope is that we can get Butler out of here before then."

"That's your idea, mister. I say if it's a scout, let's try to outfox — and kill him — then get out of here, whether Butler enjoys the trip or not."

Merrick glanced at Billy. There was lust in young Clinton's eyes, more urgent now than when he had looked at Butler's wife. He had the lust to kill; you saw in that moment in his face what he had become, what he would be if he lived fifty years or if this Indian killed him. He was a gun killer. He wanted another notch on his gun butt; an Indian made as good-looking a notch as a white man.

Merrick's mouth tightened. No sense in attempting to argue with Hardhead Charley's only whelp. If he could get Billy to moving away from him, hiding and running in an entrapment try that wouldn't deceive an Apache eight-year-old, it would give Merrick his only chance to work out something; a dead Indian would be dangerous to wear around their necks right now.

"Okay," he said. "I'll go around this boulder far enough so the Indian can see me. You move out to the right there — keep moving way around. If he comes out enough to get a shot at me, maybe you can get him."

Billy nodded. Then his mouth twisted. "You trusting me pretty far, Merrick. You must know how bad we want you dead if you won't head north."

"Hell," Merrick said with a casualness he did not feel. "You don't want an Indian to kill me, Billy. That wouldn't put any notches in your gun."

Billy looked him over, grudging admiration in his gaze.

"Okay," Billy said. He slithered to another boulder. "Take care of yourself."

Merrick moved around the boulder. He glanced at Billy, hoping he got a moment for palaver with the Indian. If he did maybe he could keep Billy from shooting. He didn't count on it.

Merrick gave a low call. Behind him he heard Billy stop, tensed. He was watching the underbrush, did not turn his head. He saw the brush rattle some yards away in a line between himself and the pony. There was a rocky clearing between the rim of the boulder and the edge of the mesquite beard.

Merrick said, "Friend." He repeated the word in the Mescalero dialect.

He showed himself, tense, ready to dive back to the concealment of the boulder.

He waited, holding his breath. The brush parted and the Apache warrior stood up, face streaked with white and yellow paint-patterns, a rifle in his left hand.

Merrick stepped away from the boulder, showing himself. There was another breath-less wait, the kind that rips a man's nerves to shreds, and then the Apache stepped forward.

Merrick squinted, staring at the Apache. There was something familiar about the warrior's face, but the hell of it was, he could not recall the Apache's name.

The Apache looked him over, standing tense, ready to spring back into the brush.

Merrick saw the look of recognition light the Apache's eyes. His faint smile was a fantastic thing in the painted face. Thank God, Merrick thought, this one knows me. This is the answer, the way out.

The Apache lifted his right hand in a gesture of friendliness, palm outward. His widening smile pulled at the yellow lines in his cheeks. He stepped forward, and at that moment Billy Clinton's forty-four cracked from behind the boulder to Merrick's right.

The Indian never even got a chance to stop smiling. Billy Clinton was a dead shot as well as a fast draw. The bullet struck the Apache in the chest and spun him around. The rifle toppled from his grasp. The Indian struck the ground on his knee, then turned to move away, trying to sprint toward his startled pony. He was already as good as dead, but Billy shot him again.

"Good work, Merrick," Billy shouted. "God knows you really pulled him right out in the open."

Merrick stared at Billy, eyes cold. Not even hidden from God in the night could Billy ever say he had not seen the rifle in the Indian's left hand, his upraised palm. He turned on his heel and ran across the rocky ground to the place where the Indian had fallen.

He knelt on one knee, turned the Indian over. All the rest of his life he would wish he had not done it. A moment more and the Indian would have been dead, and he would not have had to see the look of hatred and contempt on his painted face. Maybe the Apache didn't know the name Judas, but that was what the look in his black eyes named Merrick.

Perch Fisher and Hardhead Charley climbed the incline, ran out to where the Indian had been shot. He was dead by the time they got there.

Billy stood looking down at the Apache, still holding his forty-four.

"I killed him, Pa," Billy said.

Merrick stared up at Billy. "What you've done, boy, is just bought us a part of hell none of us will get out of."

Then, forgetting the Clintons, Merrick jerked his head around. He and Billy spoke simultaneously. "The pony."

"Grab that pony," Merrick said, staring toward the underbrush where they'd sighted it.

He jumped to his feet. Billy ran forward

beside him, and then both stopped.

Standing side by side they watched the pony race north in the flatland, pounding dust balls from the earth, trailing its single-strand hair-bridle.

Merrick pulled his gaze around. But it didn't seem to matter which way he turned, all he saw was trouble. The dead Indian lay contorted in the sun. Whatever chance they'd had to get out of here alive had died with him. Whatever tortures the Apaches had had in mind this morning would be intensified twenty times when they found the murdered scout.

"We got to get out of here," Billy Clinton said.

Merrick's laugh was cold. "You begin to see what you've done, boy?"

"Hell. You pulled him out so I could kill him, and I killed him."

"He had his hand raised, friendly. You recognized it."

"Maybe I know enough Indians I don't trust them."

Merrick shrugged. "Or maybe you got just enough white blood in you to make you mistrust everybody. But it ain't buying us anything to worry about that now. When those Indians find that pony, they might even delay that feast of roast horse to come avenge this buck." He glanced at the insignia on the Indian's wristlet. "A well-born warrior — and that won't help, either."

"All right," Perch said. "You got sense enough to know that, let's go."

"Running won't help you — or me, now. If we run, we'll kill Butler, and we still won't escape them. What we had was one chance in a thousand, and Billy-boy just shot that to hell." He paced back and forth, his boots harsh against the outcroppings of rock. "Billy, there are army spades in the back of that wagon. Bring 'em. Maybe we still got one chance — if we can bury your mistake."

When Billy brought the sharp-bladed spades, Merrick led them into the wooded area. He chose a mesquite bush and began digging about three feet out from its base. After a moment Old Clinton and Billy, seeing that he intended removing the bush in a solid clump of roots and earth, fell to digging.

They dug deeply under the roots. They didn't pause to breathe. Loosening a large clod of earth they carefully put their backs to it, lifted it from the hole and set it aside. The four of them dug then, excavating a five-foot rectangle, piling each spadeful of earth in neat piles at the rim of the open grave.

They lifted the Indian, lowered him into the earth, buried him with his rifle.

"Them Apaches won't like a white man burial for this buck any better than they'll like us killing their scout," Clinton said. That was his prayer and epitaph uttered over the open grave.

"I'm hoping we get out of here before they find him." Merrick mopped sweat from his face. They replaced the earth in the hole, stamping it down so that all the brown-colored underearth could be replaced. Finally, they lifted the mesquite bush, set it in place and repaired the scarred earth surface around it.

Merrick carefully scraped up all the telltale underearth remaining. He walked twenty paces into the forest, scattering it in the underbrush.

He returned, and with mesquite limbs they swept around the bush until there was no sign of their digging, no trace of their bootmarks. They walked on the balls of their feet back to the rock outcropping, dragging the brush after them.

They toppled to the shade of the overhang. Billy lay face down, panting. They stared at the water hole, at the sky, at each other. For a long time none of them spoke.

Billy sat up, flicking the chamber of his

gun, reloading. "What now?"

"You tell me," Merrick said.

"Let's get out of here." Perch Fisher gathered up his gear and the tightly-stuffed saddle bags.

"Not a chance," Merrick said. "All we can do now is wait until either Butler gets well enough to travel, or the Apache finds us. If they don't learn we've killed the scout, we got one chance of leaving here alive."

"Hell." Perch laughed. "You wait, mister. But you wait by yourself." His voice rose, his taunting laughter striking at Merrick.

Six

Hardhead Charley picked up a burnt stick and traced lines along the ground beside him. Suddenly Perch Fisher stopped laughing, the sound ending abruptly. His face was chilled as though he'd never laughed, would never laugh again. It grew quiet under the overhang.

"I think you're wrong," Hardhead Charley said at last. "I don't like to dispute a smart young fellow like you, Mister Merrick, but there don't seem to me but one thing to do — and that is to head north out of here and run like our tails was afire."

Perch got up on his haunches. His voice

was blunt. "I can give it to you straighter than that, Merrick. A lot straighter. Now, we three don't intend going back to San Carlos. It's up to you after that. If you don't want to walk, you better change your mind."

Merrick stared at the pulse working in the stout man's throat. He sighed. The way the rages built in him at the sound of these men's voices was bad. It was as though he'd come to them with a built-in hate. It was hell when you stood there almost wishing that a man would go for his gun, or make a play.

He tightened his fists. He had to shake thoughts like these. He knew what made him hate these men all right, but intuition and instinct was not enough — if they were the men he sought, he'd been looking for them for a long time, and he had to have proof.

"Perch, do yourself a favor." He kept his voice low, hoping the inner rages didn't show. "Don't threaten me."

Perch came upward, standing with his back against the wall of the overhang. "There ain't no sense you and me delayin' any more, mister. You turn it to clabber with me — so if you don't like what I say, I'm more than anxious for you to make anything you want to out of it."

Merrick kept his voice low. "No use to kill each other yet, Perch. Butler is still too ill to travel. So unless he dies in the next couple hours, nobody's going anywhere."

Perch put his hand out at his side.

"You don't get the message. I'm not staying in this place until them Apaches scalp me."

The pulse throbbed in Fisher's neck. His gaze darted against the walls of the sump, to the wagon, and to the boulders and the rim of stunted trees beyond. Clearly, this depression was a trap as far as Perch Fisher was concerned, and they were in the deepest cranny of it.

"You got that clear, Merrick?" Fisher's voice shook. "We're clearing out."

Merrick's face changed too, in that moment. The cold hatred that contorted it when he looked at Perch Fisher became something hot and livid when he stared at this water hole. Perch scowled at what he saw in Merrick's face. Young Billy sat up and tilted his hat back on his head. Hardhead Charley's eyes narrowed. The look in Merrick's face named this spot a hell, and his searing hatred included every grain of sand around it.

His voice quavered slightly when he spoke. "I got no wish to stay in this place one minute longer than I have to."

He exhaled, watching them. For a moment there was deep silence. They read it in his face — a man hates a place so it is agony to return to it: a place associated with deep hurt, or fear, or horror — maybe compounded of all of it. And they saw this in Blade Merrick's face. Until this moment they may not have considered him capable of fear. Now they knew better. Fear and hatred and horror, that was what this water hole meant to Blade Merrick.

Merrick turned and walked away from them. He stepped out of the shadowed overhang, squinting suddenly at the brassy brilliance of the sunlight.

Perch stepped away from the wall and his hand moved to his gun.

Merrick spun on his heel, crouching and stepping to the left. It all happened so abruptly they were hardly aware his gun was in one hand and his other was spread above its hammer, ready to fan a spray of six rounds under that overhang.

Young Billy Clinton gasped. He had seen Merrick draw fast earlier, but it was nothing like this. Billy had watched trick-gun artists work for drinks along the border, but their speed was not this kind of speed.

Ed Clinton's laugh was falsely hearty.

"Why, man. Man," he said, "you got to trust us better than this, Mister Merrick. Why, which one of us would draw on you when your back was turned?"

Billy Clinton laughed. "After what I just seen, Pa, that's the only way I'm ever going to draw on him." He pushed off his hat and worked at his hair with a comb, grinning at his father and Perch Fisher.

Perch Fisher's face was white, and it was an effort for him to move his hand away from the butt of his gun. He let it slide back. He had not cleared leather, and for a moment he was almost paralyzed, realizing how close he'd come to dying. He managed to move his hand away and to breathe out slowly.

Merrick's face, too, was pale. His voice was cold. He ignored old Clinton, staring at Perch. "You breathe too loud, Fisher. You telegraph it. You give yourself away — you give yourself away, even when you mean to shoot a man in the back. Sometime, that's going to cost you your life."

Perch tried to laugh. His voice was loud. "If you're going to shoot, why didn't you shoot?"

Billy laughed. "I can tell you, Perch, if you're too stupid to know. He don't want to kill you — unless he has to. Not with a gun.

Them Apaches ain't deaf."

"Go to hell, you little bastard."

Billy laughed again. "Pa, you gonna let him talk about your only son like that? Go on, Pa. Tell him. Tell him how you was married to Ma — by a full-blooded chief — with a gun in your back. Tell him."

"Shut up, Billy." Clinton walked out of the shadow. "Put away your gun, Mister Merrick. Perch meant nothing. We're all upset here. But Perch ain't going to shoot you. Not unless he gets the order from me . . . and I ain't going to give it."

Merrick shoved his gun back into its holster. He was trembling, and to hide it, he closed his fists. He stared at Hardhead Charley, let his gaze move to Billy and to Perch.

He turned on his heel and walked away then, going down the incline. Valerie Butler looked up, eyes dull, watching him stride past. His shadow lunged along the ground, and as he passed, she watched his shadow. He glanced at Jeff Butler only long enough to see he was breathing shallowly and that his eyes were closed. The bleeding had stopped; his outer bandage was not stained.

They watched him reach the ridge, and then he walked to the left and was out of sight.

He moved slower now, going down the incline.

He stayed alert, listening. He had seen in the faces of the Clintons and Perch what they meant to do. Within minutes after arriving at the place where the Indian attack had left them horseless, he'd known Clinton was weighing the chances of killing him, taking the army horses and abandoning the Butlers to the Apaches. He had stopped them there. But there had been more than that: Clinton had known the Indians would come back. The army dray horses were slow and plodding; the three of them couldn't hope to escape the attackers on two mounts, in the desert, without water. It had seemed better sense to keep Merrick alive, another gun against the raiders. They had let him live because they had been sure they could kill him when they found it convenient.

He gave a short hard laugh. Wasn't that moment going to come the first time he closed his eyes to sleep?

His fists clenched at his sides. Well, he wasn't going to sleep, because they were not the only men out here looking for something.

He paused beside a mound of earth. The earth turned up here was so fresh the plants hadn't covered it yet, a few blades of grass, the prickled head of a sweet cactus. He knew how fresh this mound was — he'd turned it up making a grave deep enough to foil the digging coyotes. The only marker he'd left was a small cross formed with stones. They were untouched.

This grave was one month old.

Merrick knelt beside the mound, fists knotted at his sides. His mouth was a taut line.

He braced himself suddenly at the sharp sound of Billy's laughter down in the sump.

SEVEN

A month ago he had ridden expectantly into this hidden water hole.

"Ab!" He had called even before he swung out of the saddle. Only a month, but it seemed longer. He felt so much older now, full of urgent hatred where before there had been only the day's troubles and the hurt of a loss, that, great as it was, was old and at least covered with scar tissue. He felt old now. Older than the devil himself.

"Ab!"

He was still calling his brother when he dismounted and ground-tied his mount in the grass clump. He had even laughed a little. Ab trusted nobody any more. Still, it

514

didn't make sense that he would hide around here until he was certain Blade was alone.

He almost stumbled on Ab's body.

He stared down at the body and first there was nothing but disbelief. It couldn't be Ab, and Ab couldn't be dead. But it was Ab, and his death was brutal and senseless. Somebody had emptied a six-shooter into him, willfully and crazily, firing after Ab was already dead because whoever he was, he got a sensual pleasure from slamming bullets into a human body.

After the first wild grief passed, a chill went through Blade Merrick's body. He walked slowly about the water hole, going over it carefully, with deadly purpose.

The day was dry and breathless. The sun glittered in the clear pool and something skittered through the mesquite. Ab was sprawled near the largest pool, and the blood had made a round dark place in the sand where it ran from his mouth. He had been kicked repeatedly.

Blade had stood there, trembling. Had they kicked him before he died or after? Knowing Ab, he was sure it must have been after they'd put bullets into him. Somebody had gotten a lot of pleasure from this killing.

Blade stood rigid. They'd pulled off Ab's boots, ripped his shirt away, left his body to the sun and the ants.

That was when Blade made the next discovery. Though they'd ripped away his clothes and kicked him, filled him with lead, it was all a senseless killing. They had not robbed him. They hadn't even taken the change from his pockets.

Why had they killed Ab?

To this day Blade Merrick did not know.

He had stood there in the clearing beside Ab's body trying to find the answer to the meaningless killing. He had stared at the coppery sky, demanding to know. He had searched the rocks, the water, the wooded places. There was no answer.

It had been a reasonless, senseless killing. In this long month Merrick had tried to think out some reason for it. Only one occurred to him: these three men had come unexpectedly upon Ab; they had been spoiling with the need and pleasure of killing, and they had told themselves they did not want to leave a witness to their trail south from Patchee Wells.

He had strode about the place, a man mad with his anger. If there had been a reason for killing, they would have robbed him. They would have taken time to search him.

It was sure they didn't know Ab. There was nothing personal in the killing. It was something done hurriedly and without profit. They had killed Ab as they would kill a tarantula on a hot rock, and then had ridden hurriedly on after they'd watered their horses and filled their canteens.

Blade had removed his brother's belongings from his pockets and piled them on a handkerchief: a wallet, a Mexican gold piece, some silver money, and Blade's letter that had tortuously searched him out on the border.

Hunkered beside the body, Blade read the letter he'd written to Ab. It had taken a long time for that letter to find Ab. It had been a much longer time before Blade received his reply.

Dear Ab:

I'm writing you this letter because I've good news. At least it is good to me, and it will be to you if you'll pocket your crazy stubborn Virginia pride and admit the war between the Confederacy and the Union is over — and has been over for years.

I better tell you, Ab, that despite the fact the war is over, the United States considers you a pretty formidable enemy.

They've a list of crimes charged against you longer than my arm, starting with your escape from the Yankee prison in Ohio. It's hard for them to forgive the robberies charged to you along the border because a lot of them have been against the government.

But I've a good record with them, Ab. After the war, I came back out here and worked with the Indian agency, and with the army. I've made some good friends, and I've used every one of them trying to square things so you can go back home a free man.

Anyhow, there's a full pardon awaiting you at Tucson. You have only to report, take an oath of loyalty to the United States, and it's yours.

Don't be a fool any longer, Ab. The bloodshed and the bitterness have done enough hurt. I know you love home, and want to go back there. Your wife is waiting for you. This is your chance, Ab. I'll meet you in Tucson. Don't fail me, and don't fail yourself.

Always,
Blade

He had scribbled the address of a Tucson hotel where Ab could get in touch with him.

Weeks drifted by and he had almost given up hope. A Mexican, with trail dust powdery on his clothes, brought him Ab's answer one day at the hotel.

Ab stated first that he didn't trust the United States of America any more now than he did the day they blockaded the Confederacy. Ab trusted one person, and that was Blade. He agreed to meet Blade, alone, at the Patchee Wells. He named the date.

That same afternoon, Blade left Tucson, riding south and east. Ab had not promised to go to Tucson. He wanted to hear more about that pardon, and any conditions. If it all sounded good to him when Blade met him at Patchee Wells, he would accompany him north, where he'd make his peace with the government.

The ride into the badlands was hot and slow. For hours the land seemed changeless. The wind was like the breath of a blast furnace. But Blade Merrick had been deep in his memories, and most of them were pleasant. He was remembering when he and Ab were boys on the Virginia farm. It was no plantation with slaves — those huge, feudal estates were few enough all through the South; less than one fourth of the people in the South owned slaves.

Blade had found Virginia too crowded, too sweet-smelling for his liking. He went west, met a girl named Mary Beth and married her. When the war broke out he took Mary Beth to Dallas and joined a company of Texas volunteers. He had belonged to the Arizona–New Mexico territory, and the war was not his. But the anger against outside oppression was bred into him.

He had met Ab in Tennessee. It was the first time he'd seen his younger brother in over ten years. They had a week together. Blade was a sergeant and young Ab was a captain. Ab swore he'd move heaven and the Confederate capital to get Blade a commission. The next Blade heard, Ab had been taken prisoner.

He hadn't seen Ab again. After the war he heard that Ab had escaped the Yankee prison and made his way to the Mexican border. Ab had left a wife and a farm in Virginia, but was afraid to return.

Then the Federal government had agreed to a full pardon.

Ab had had a chance at happiness right within his reach for the first time in ten years. Then somebody killed him at Patchee Wells and left his body to the ants.

Blade had covered every inch of the water hole. He figured how it must have been. Ab had been at Patchee Wells waiting for him. Three men had ridden in, and Ab, mistrustful, had grabbed his horse and hidden in the mesquite.

There were tracks, heel prints around the spring. Somebody had lain long, drinking, with his face in the pool. A man had smoked cigarettes. One of them had read a sign, or heard the slightest flicker of sound. They had dragged Ab out, gunned him down, ripped off his shirt and boots. They had ridden away then, going fast, and heading south.

That had been a month ago.

Merrick had tracked those men for three days and lost them in rock croppings far to the south. They'd known he was on their trail by then, and they moved on the slate stones, picking up their feet, but hurrying.

He had made his way back to Fort Ambush. He had questioned everyone about men headed south. Once he had worked; now he did nothing but hunt, obsessed with his hunting.

Something about these three men had filled him with the urgent fever to kill, the moment he saw them beside the burning wagon.

At first, the sight of the woman with the three hard-cases had misled him. Then he learned that they'd picked up the pilgrims on the trail just a few hours before they were ambushed. Riding to the water hole, he had baited the boy about the bank robbery a month ago at Tucson, but the kid was wily. He had played with the bait, spit it out.

He stood up slowly, looking down at the mound of earth covering his brother's body. He remembered the way he'd found him, the brutal, senseless slaying.

Blood throbbed in his temples. He told himself to move slowly. Anger and instinctive, murderous hatred were not enough. He had to have proof.

He tried to walk away from it. Hatred like this seared out a man's insides.

EIGHT

When he heard the woman scream he spun around and ran up the incline. He had been away for only a few minutes; it didn't make sense that there'd been time for anything to happen in the camp. Perhaps her husband had died. He didn't think so. It wasn't that kind of screaming.

He drew his gun as he ran.

Perch Fisher still had her in his arms when Merrick came over the lip of land and raced down the incline toward the wagon. Her head was back and her hair flailed like flames in the wind.

Perch had one arm about her waist and a hand caught in the front of her dress. Her hands were free and she was clawing at him. Perch didn't even know she was striking him, scratching or clawing at his eyes. He knew only one thing, he had her body close against his body.

Merrick spun the gun around, catching it by the barrel to use as a club. But the Clintons were around the pool before he could reach the wagon.

Old Clinton reached across Fisher's shoulder, caught two fingers in his nostrils and yanked backwards. Perch screamed gutturally and fell back. Billy Clinton pinioned the man's arms at his side.

The girl staggered and toppled against the wagon, breathing wildly, staring at Perch and the Clintons.

"Christ," Perch yelled. "Christ, don't stop me!"

The Clintons were wrestling him toward the overhang.

"Next time I'll yank your head plumb off, boy," Hardhead Charley told him.

"Did you ever see a body like that, Charley?" Perch raged, struggling as they danced him along.

"Ain't you got troubles enough without spoilin' that dyin' man's woman?" Clinton shouted into his ear.

"Spoiling?" Perch was yelling, his voice quavering. "That's what's the matter now, for God's sake. She's spoiling. She needs a man. Let me go, for Christ's sake!"

They fought him to the overhang. Suddenly Clinton caught Perch in a bear hug, lifted his two hundred pounds off the ground, spun him around three times and hurled him with all his strength against the wall under the overhang.

Perch struck against the wall, flat, and the sound was like a goatskin tight with water dropped on stones. The breath was slammed out of him, but he came up on his knees crying and yelling. "Get out of my way, Charley. Get out of my way."

Clinton stepped forward and kicked Perch in the throat. He gasped, sobbing for air, and sprawled forward on the ground.

Across the pool at the wagon, Valerie was pressed back against the wheel, breathless. Her green eyes were swimming in tears.

Suddenly her head went back and laughter poured from her mouth, raging and spilling like water in a flash flood.

Merrick stared at her. The sound of her crazy laughter filled the sump, spilled out of it, spinning and racing in the afternoon silence.

He stepped forward. It had to come out of her. He thought bitterly, she was a woman who put everything she was into everything she did. When she had hysterics, she had them like no other woman ever had.

In the midst of her raging laughter the sobs would build and break. She had her head back, staring straight into the cloudless sky. Her mouth was pulled open with her sobbing and laughing. The sound vibrated in everything, seeming to congeal in the pit of Merrick's stomach and boil there.

Perch Fisher was sprawled on the ground, but both the Clintons had turned their backs on him and were staring openmouthed at the laughing woman.

Merrick stepped forward. He brought the back of his hand across her face, hard.

She half fell under the impact. She pulled herself back up then, one last sob gulped back into her throat.

He stared at the livid marks of his hand against her cheek. Her eyes were wild, but the swirling shadows were dying in them.

She kept her gaze locked on his face. Her cheek muscles were rigid and her color was a paleness of death. She whimpered once, then her breathing quieted. She closed her lips and sagged against the wagon wheel, still watching him.

He heard footsteps behind him, turned. He was aware he still carried the gun and was holding it by the barrel.

"You won't need that on me," Hardhead Charley said. He nodded toward the gun. Merrick shoved it back into his holster. Clinton let his gaze move to the girl crouched on the blanket beside the wagon. "Though it wouldn't take much to make me as loco as Perch."

Merrick exhaled, did not answer. He didn't look at Valerie Butler, either. This was a strange land out here, and it hadn't taken him fifteen years to learn that. Women in the territories were revered, put on a pedestal and regarded as the Puritans regarded their women. But this was a hot land. Women were scarce. Sometimes it got so that ten thousand head of cattle, a pure vein of gold, a hundred square miles of ranchland didn't mean much. A man got a hunger that at only a woman and violence could appease.

"What happened to him," Clinton said after a moment, "is that the woman called one of us over here to look at her husband. Perch came. Husband was all right. Perch dug around in the wagon, found some alcohol in a medicine bottle. He went back over there, drank it. You can't blame the alcohol entirely though. He's had his eye on her since the first minute he saw her."

Merrick looked at the wounded husband, sprawled on the blanket. He shook his head.

"The wonder is," Clinton said, also looking at Jeff Butler, "that he ain't had her taken away from him long before this."

Merrick did not answer.

Perch called to Clinton. The huge old pirate went back around the water hole to the overhang. Perch said something Merrick could not hear. Clinton nodded and squatted against the wall.

About twenty feet around the pool from the wagon and directly across the water from the overhang where the Clintons were, was a ten-foot boulder. Merrick carried a blanket from the wagon and staked out the boulder for his own. The boulder gave him a wall to put his back against. He fought better that way when he was crowded.

He sat down with his back against the boulder. He wanted a cigarette, but when he lit one, he found it tasteless. He ground it out. There was only one thing wrong with him. He could feel the gaze of Valerie Butler on him from one point of this strange triangle, and from the other point, the

Clintons and Perch Fisher were watching him and whispering. The Clintons were bad enough, but having that girl there, a torment just out of reach, another man's wife, that was worse.

He thought about Mary Beth, remembering the goodness and the excitement of her, and then recalling in anguish the way she had died six years ago. There hadn't been any other women after Mary Beth was killed. There never would be. The hurt had gone too deep. For a long time there had been madness that had taken her place.

He stared at the men across the pool. He would be all right, once he got out of here. If they made it to San Carlos, the Butler woman and her husband could go their way. He'd be all right again, left alone with his loneliness.

His mouth twisted into an acid smile. *What makes you think you'll ever get south to San Carlos? What makes you think those three men can't take your wagon and horses away from you? What are the odds that you won't end up dead right here at Patchee Wells, the way Ab died?* Three men had ridden into this watering place and left Ab dead. Three men stared at him across that pool right now. Hardhead Charley Clinton had considered killing him within the first five minutes, back there in the valley. He must have gone over it a hundred times by now.

He shook his head. Even if they killed him, they would not get far. Those Apaches would be looking for them, soon. The trail led clearly from the valley to these Wells.

He shivered. His gaze pulled around again to Valerie Butler, the smooth skin of her face and throat, the full ripe body, ready for living. What a hell of a thing if the Apaches got her.

Perch was a gentlemanly choice, as against the warriors in that raiding party.

He cursed. No matter where he tried to take his thoughts, they came back to the Apaches, and what they could do to a woman. *It's hell, Mary Beth,* he thought. *It's a grim hot hell when you can't forget.*

"Mr. Merrick." The girl was kneeling over her husband. Her voice was frantic.

Merrick sprang to his feet, aware the men across the pool had stopped whispering and were watching him. He walked around the pool, for a moment caught by the reflections in it.

She looked up at him.

"Fever," she said. "He's burning up."

He knelt beside her, laid his hand over Butler's forehead. His fever was high, the heat penetrating Merrick's palm. Butler whimpered and twisted away from him.

"This is it," Merrick said to the girl across her husband. "This is the bad time. Either this fever will burn the poison out of him or —" He did not finish it.

She held his gaze levelly. Her face paled just slightly and she bit at her underlip. She did not say anything. He could see the marks of his fingers fading on her cheeks. A small desert animal skittered through the mesquite. The horses flickered from the grass clump.

He walked to the wagon, turned back the rear flaps. Inside were boxes, piled high, and they awaited them in San Carlos. He found the drug he wanted, returned to Butler. He held his head in his hand, forced the liquid between his lips.

"One thing we can fight," Merrick told her with a wry smile, "is fever."

"I — want to thank you for all you've done."

Mouth twisted into a bitter smile, he stared at her.

She colored slightly, touched her cheek with the backs of her fingers.

"For everything," she told him.

He exhaled. One thing, those marks were fading. He would not have to go on looking at them. He got up, aware she was watching him, and replaced the medicine in the wagon. He turned then, glancing at her, walked toward the boulder he'd staked out as his own.

"Mr. Merrick."

He returned to the blanket.

"We're in your debt."

"Don't thank me. We're not out of this yet."

"But you stopped for us. You should be on your way somewhere — and it worries you."

"Nothing pressing. A fever epidemic at San Carlos. They should have had these drugs a week ago — a couple days' delay won't matter much."

"I'm sorry. . . . Is there someone there you care for very much?"

His mouth tightened. "There's no one I care for — anywhere."

"You're — not married?"

"I was."

"No woman ever left a man like you, Mr. Merrick."

"I don't know. Maybe she would have. She died before she got a chance." He breathed deeply. "Seems when I think back she hadn't even time to make up her mind about me one way or the other."

"I am sorry. I can understand now why you look so — unhappy."

"I'm just naturally a sour-looking cuss."

"No. It hurts deeply to lose the one you love."

He nodded toward her husband between them. "He's going to be all right, Mrs. Butler."

"Yes." She felt his forehead. The fever had not yet subsided. "I'm sure he will be."

He shook his head tiredly, looking at her husband and then at Valerie. "It's none of my business. But what's a girl like you — and a man like him — doing out here? From your voice, I'd say you're from Georgia —"

"South Carolina." She looked at the backs of her hands. "We came out here after the war. If you weren't there — in the South, after the surrender — you can't know what it was like."

"I was there for a while. I got back out as quickly as could."

She nodded. "That's the way it was with Jeff and me. . . . I met him after the war. The — man I'd loved — he was killed. Jeff was gay and charming — despite all the misery around us. And that's what I needed then — just to laugh."

"You should have stayed there, done your laughing in your own country."

She nodded. "We know that now. Jeff got along well — even with the people who overran our land after the war. He — can be very ingratiating when he wants to — or needs to."

"There are worse talents."

"We were married. We would have gotten along all right, even there. But Jeff was unhappy. He had fought all during the war. Despite the fact he was friendly with the Yankees after the surrender, he had been fighting for his freedom — and he had lost that. He was restless, too. And — well, he got deeper and deeper in debt."

"So he thought it would be easier out here?"

"There were all kinds of glowing stories, Mr. Merrick, about the land, the fortunes to be made in cattle. Jeff wasn't really running away. Not entirely. He was in debt, he was restless, but his family had owned a huge place before the war. It was gone. He wanted a sprawling place of his own, like the old estates had been. He believed he could buy land cheaply out here, raise cattle — and find the freedom and peace he was looking for."

His eyes held hers levelly. "And you? What did you want?"

She spoke to the backs of her hands.

"What I want now. What I always wanted — a home and a family. We were losing everything back there — even each other. I didn't believe it could be any worse out here."

His mouth pulled down.

"Nobody ever does."

"Yes. It was too terrible. Too lonely — and too brutal. We — didn't have enough money to begin with. We were beaten from the start. We sold out, bought a wagon, loaded it up and headed back east — and got lost."

The sun was gone; the sky was a saffron color. It was still an hour to full dark.

Merrick climbed the knoll, seeking the highest spot near the water hole. He could not discern a moving thing on the plains around him. This did not satisfy him, but he figured they had until morning before the Apaches found them. Even if they'd already found the wagon tracks, they would not move in tonight.

His laugh was bitter. Good to tell himself that, anyway. A fine fairy story it was, too. The Apache struck at the moment most advantageous to him.

He walked down to the boulder telling himself this was a pleasant thought to live with through the night.

The Clintons and Perch Fisher were almost lost in the shadowed overhang.

Hardhead Charley's bass voice struck at him as he sank to his blanket.

"We could put a lot of miles between us and this place tonight. Push them horses, we might make Fort Ambush by noon tomorrow. We three vote to pull out of here."

Merrick kept his voice level.

"I told you when we would travel," he said. He waited a moment. "I also told you where."

The only answer was a derisive laugh from Perch Fisher. Merrick stepped back, putting his shoulders against the boulder. He could not see Perch Fisher under that overhang, and he didn't trust him where he could see him.

He heard a footstep near him and turned, his hand striking the butt of his gun.

"It's me," Valerie Butler said. "Would you come up with me to Jeff?"

He followed her around the pool edge, and up the slight incline. Terrible how taut tension could draw you. Here he was breathing through his mouth, jumpy, his heart slugging.

She knelt beside her husband. She touched his forehead. "His fever has subsided," she said.

He felt Butler's forehead, found it cool, checked his pulse. It was stronger, and Butler's breathing was more regular, less ragged. *He's breathing a lot better than I am,* Merrick told himself.

"I'll get him some water," Valerie whispered.

He remained on his knees, watching her move through the deepening dusk to the water hole. Not even the dusk could conceal what she was. He saw her kneel beside the water, fill his canteen and return up the incline.

Merrick lifted Jeff Butler's head, Valerie held the canteen to his lips. Jeff accepted some of it, moistening his parched lips. Most of the water ran down his chin, splotching his shirt.

She sat back. She poured water into her hands, patted it across her eyes and forehead, letting the beads trickle down her cheeks. "Cool," she whispered. "It's so cool."

She pressed the canteen to her mouth and drank greedily. "First water I've had," she said, gasping for breath. "I hadn't — even thought about water."

She extended the canteen. Merrick shook his head.

"It's so sweet and good," she said, voice awed.

Merrick nodded. "Sweet clear water is scarce in this country. Lot of it has a coppery taste. Some has an alkali taste. This water is good. It's funny. You've been out here as long as I have, you can tell where water comes from, by its taste. No matter where I tasted this water, I'd know it came from Patchee Wells."

She took another deep drink from the canteen. Merrick stood up, watching her head tilt back, her hair fall away from her shoulders, her throat moving.

She sighed. "I'll always remember the taste of this water, too," she said. Her voice was soft.

"Yes." His voice was chilled. "It's good water."

He turned and walked away.

"Mr. Merrick?"

He glanced over his shoulder. Why didn't she let him alone? Did she really think he was any less human than Perch Fisher? Wasn't he worse, because he didn't need medicinal alcohol to start his pulses pounding? A man can stand only so much loneliness — so little loneliness.

"Yes?"

"I heard — the Clintons asking you to

take them to Fort Ambush."

"Yes."

"When can we travel?"

"As soon as your husband can be moved."

"You will take us — to Fort Ambush?"

He breathed deeply. "No. You heard them, then you heard me tell them I wouldn't."

"I beg you. Please. We were on our way to Tucson. We — we're so far from there now — I don't think we could make it — not from San Carlos."

"I'm sorry. You could head east from San Carlos — across New Mexico to Texas."

"We've friends in Tucson, Mr. Merrick. They'd help us. We've no money. We lost everything when the wagon burned."

"I can't turn back."

She reached out her hand toward him. He looked at her hand, lifted his gaze to her face. His mouth twisted.

"All I want," she whispered, "is a chance to get Jeff back east. We'd have a chance there — and we don't have any in this terrible, lawless place."

His gaze held hers for a moment. At last he said, "I'll fix some grub. You — you'll feel better after you've had something to eat."

NINE

The night came on cool and wind-touched. It deepened all the shadows about the water hole. The sky was the impenetrable black of a bottomless void. As the wind rose, it keened around the boulders, cried in the lost, dark places. It gave movement to immobile things, and brushed a limb against your face where no limb ought to reach. You might feel a man standing close at your shoulder, and by the time you heeled around, you knew it wasn't a man at all, it was the wind, lonely and cold.

Merrick found himself straining to listen in those moments when the wind died. Somewhere in the dark there was a lonely cry, and no matter how long you'd been out here, sometimes it was hard to convince yourself it was the crying of the wind.

He had built fire enough to warm beans, sidemeat and coffee. Valerie sat with them under the overhang. The fire flickered in their faces, was reflected in their eyes. They drank coffee from tin cups.

Merrick poured his fifth cup, drank it black. He had to stay awake. He couldn't remember ever having been so tired. The hatred that had chewed at him all day had squeezed out his strength. The fact that if he slept he would never wake up worked against him, too. His nerves were drawn taut, and having Valerie beside him in the firelight, seeing the way Billy and Perch licked at her with their eyes, didn't help any either.

Valerie was listening to the cry in the wind. Her voice was hollow. "You get so you wish for any sound," she said. "Because except for the wind there isn't anything." She shivered. "I hate it. I don't see how anyone would willingly stay out here."

Hardhead Charley Clinton's laugh rattled under the overhang. "Why, ma'am, loneliness ain't the worst thing that can happen to a man."

Merrick's laugh was sharp and cold. He stared at Clinton beside him in the flickering firelight.

"No," he said. "There's always the hangrope."

Though Merrick expected another response, Clinton only laughed again, louder.

"I'm not a man as would lie to you, Merrick. I've had myself some brushes with the law. Like I was telling the little lady, there's been many times when I welcomed a lonely spot like this where I could hide."

"How about this one?" Merrick said. "You ever hide out here?"

He heard Billy Clinton's lazy laugh. "I bet every one of us has had a turn, Merrick, telling you we didn't know this place. What's the matter? You own it or something?"

"No. I don't own it."

Clinton laughed again. "Seems to me this afternoon I seen a look in your face that said right plain you don't even like this place."

"I could live without it."

"So could we," Billy said across the fire. "So quit pushing it, Merrick."

Merrick looked at them, slowly. "My brother was killed here."

"Say, I'm mighty saddened to hear a thing like that," Clinton said.

"Are you?"

"I said I was. I know what a man's kin means to him. My boy Billy, there. He's all I got. Whatever I do, on whatever side of the law I am, I do it so I can give my boy Billy better than I ever had."

Merrick's voice remained expressionless. "Whoever killed my brother never gave him a chance. Shot him in the back. Then filled him with lead. It was a willful, senseless killing."

"Lots of killings don't make sense when you look back on them," Clinton said.

Merrick was aware that Perch Fisher had

541

straightened up against the wall. His eyes did not blink as he watched Merrick. Beside him, Valerie had forgotten her coffee, had almost forgotten to breathe.

"They ripped off his boots, and his shirt — left him lying in the sun."

"Sounds like Indians," Clinton said.

"After a man's dead, he don't care much where he's laid out, is the way I look at it," Billy Clinton said.

"It wasn't Indians." Merrick ignored Billy. "They would have robbed him."

Clinton swigged down a gulp of coffee, then poured himself another cup, watching the steam.

"You've had a rugged time, Merrick. A man would have to be mighty heartless to deny that. But let me tell you, Charley Clinton never had it easy. I took to living by the gun. I admit that to you people. But I never done it from choice. It was forced on me — back when my boy Billy was just a lad. I had steaded me some land, lived on it with my woman and my boy. When they deprived me of my lands, I figured somebody had to pay for it." He slapped his leg and laughed. "And I been making them pay for it ever since. Perch and my Billy and me. We learned from them stinkin' Apaches.

We strike and we run. Ain't that right, Perch?"

"We take what we want, all right." Perch was staring at Valerie.

"We hit these badlands when we have to. And we cross the border. But living ain't as good down that way, and my boy Billy gets kind of restless down there. That's why we're heading north again."

As he talked, his voice filling the darkness around the sump, Merrick stared at the big man thinking that his ancestors had roamed the north seas, plundering and pillaging. Clinton was a pirate, too, roving the wastelands and striking at the towns.

"I was cheated. Cheated out of my lands. My woman died. But I'm going to have myself a stake one of these days. A big stake. The name of Clinton will be respected in the towns."

"They already respect my name in the towns," Billy said. He laughed.

"Son, you ain't going to have to shoot your way into towns — and out of them. I still mean to buy lands, and raise cattle. My boy is going to be a big man in this territory — respected, admired —"

Perch laughed. "I'm gettin' sick of your jawing, Hardhead. I heard a lot of versions about your ranching days. Heard you used the running-iron mighty free — even in your most honest days."

Clinton nodded. "We all did. When we rounded-up, we couldn't stop to count out a man's strays. I reckon I lost as many as I branded for my own."

"I doubt it." Perch's laugh was derisive. "That just don't sound like you, Hardhead."

Clinton's voice was wounded, cold, "A man has got to look out for hisself — and his own."

Perch was watching Valerie, pleased with the ribbing he was giving old Clinton. "You ever shoot a man in the back, Hardhead, when he stayed overnight at your place?"

Clinton said, "A man looks after his own."

Perch sniggered. "Why, don't take offense, Hardhead. It's just that I say you were as treacherous and ornery during them ranching days as you are right now." He gave the old man a mocking nod of the head. "No offense intended, of course."

Clinton turned, looking at Merrick with a false smile. "Merrick, I have admired you much today. *Mucho,* like they say down south of the border. You're the sort of *hombre* what makes a fine friend and a *muy malo* man to have for an enemy. I know we have had some things to disagree about today, but in the long run, there's one thing both of us are."

Merrick waited.

"Yes sir, I will say that we both are reasonable men. You figure yourself a reasonable man, Merrick?"

Merrick stared at him, waiting.

Clinton laughed falsely again. "Why, sure goodbilly hell you do. That's why I can talk to you reasonable. Like a reasonable man."

Clinton waited, but Merrick did not say anything. "It's about gettin' a fast running start toward Fort Ambush —"

"I already told you."

"Wait now. Wait. Hear me out. The boys and me understand you got a real burr under your tail to get down there to San Carlos. We figure maybe there's money in it for you — something like that. But I never met a man in my life that wouldn't change his plans if the price was right. You found that to be true, Merrick — I mean if the man was reasonable?"

"I reckon every man's got his price."

"Well now, there you are. To show you we are friendly, we'll tell you right out — them saddle bags are poked full of spending money. Yes sir, we got three bags full of money."

"Yours?" Merrick's smile was bland.

The look on Clinton's face matched his.

He slapped his leg and laughed. "It is now. And that's what the boys and me talked over. We're willing to offer you a firm one thousand dollars in Federal money to turn them horses around — tonight — and hightail it north to Fort Ambush."

"A thousand dollars," Merrick said.

"That's right. A whale of a lot more'n you'd make in a year going the other way. True?"

Merrick nodded. "A thousand dollars would buy a lot of beefsteak."

Clinton's voice chilled, fell away. "Take it, Merrick. Do yourself a favor and take it."

Merrick was watching Billy and Perch across the fire.

Billy's face was twisted with a secretive grin. Perch was watching him, contempt flaring his nostrils slightly.

"You, Billy. And Perch. You willing for me to share in that money?"

Billy laughed. "Sure. Take it."

Perch shrugged. "Why not?"

Valerie spoke for the first time. "Please."

Clinton said, "You take the money, Merrick. Now, we got to stay reasonable. You know what's in our minds. We mean to take them horses and head north."

"And me — I'm gettin' sick of jawing about it," Perch said. "You want the thousand, you take it, and we head north. Take it, mister, because you ain't got much choice."

"Turn back — and stay alive," Billy said. "It's real simple."

Merrick's voice was level. "Not quite. You see, there's an epidemic down there in San Carlos."

Perch laughed. "Maybe you don't realize it, mister. There's an epidemic right here — and you're about to die from it."

Clinton's curse stopped Perch. "Now listen to me, Merrick. We can still stay friendly about this thing. The boys and me — we come up from the south. Between here and San Carlos there ain't nothing but godforsaken country and hostiles. Now if we headed north, in less than a day we might meet a patrol from Fort Ambush if we lathered them horses. It don't make sense any way at all to go south. Nobody would hold it against you if you turned back — nobody expects you to get killed to get medicine down to that mission."

"Stop talking about it, Hardhead." Perch leaned forward. "Tell him. We're heading out of here before morning. Going north — with him, or without him."

"You race that wagon north," Merrick said. "Two things are sure to happen. You'll be sure to kill that man down there — he'd bleed to death. The other thing is that those same Apaches would trail you, and that would mean getting this woman killed . . . and it still don't mean you'd make it."

Perch snorted his derision. "Man, you really worry about things, don't you? Sick people got to have medicine. A man might bleed. Oh, boy, what you got is Southern honor."

"Kinda like a sickness," Billy said. "A man could die with it. You ever see a man die with that Southern honor sickness, Perch?"

"Hell, I seen them rebel nogoods die in packs. Man, I marched through that country once. The roads are terrible. Them rebels call it a highway — and up home we'd call it a pig track."

Billy shook his head. "Me? I heard so much about them big plantations. Most of them Southern trash I saw was living on grits and sidemeat."

"Listen," Perch said. "Whilst we was marching, we kept hearing about Southern hams. Southern hams, Hell, we stole a few. Now, I ain't lying to you, it was so full of fat you couldn't cook it."

"Sure," Billy said. "They ain't got nothing else, so they sit around telling each other they got Southern honor. So, why don't you get smart, Merrick? You been out here long enough to get some sense. Take a thousand dollars and let's get out of here."

Merrick poured the dregs from his coffee cup. He felt Valerie's eyes on him. He did not look at her. He kicked sand into the fire so it sputtered and died.

Darkness shrouded them. It flooded in, drowning out everything. While it was black dark, Merrick got to his feet and moved away from the overhang.

"Merrick?" Clinton's deep voice stabbed after him in the darkness.

Leaning against a boulder, Merrick answered him.

"I want no trouble with you, Merrick," Clinton said.

"That's fine."

"But I better tell you. I'll kill you and take them horses if that's the only way I can get to Fort Ambush. You think that over."

"I want you three to sleep well, too, Clinton," Blade said. "So think about me across that pool. I'll be there when you come to take that wagon."

He moved away in the darkness. He heard Valerie get up and hurry through the darkness to the gray blotch that was the wagon. He could hear the rustle of her skirts in the silence.

There was no movement from the over-hang. He flopped down on his blanket, mouth twisted. Nobody would get much rest tonight. If they slept at all up there, it would be the sleep of watchful men.

TEN

"Merrick . . . Blade."

He pulled up against the boulder. She was standing near him. She was only a dim outline in the darkness, but the soft feminine fragrance of her was midday clear. He felt tense. She brought danger with her. It was different from the danger of the men across the pool, but it was none the less potent.

Above the rim of the sump he saw the stars were beginning to show. The first darkness was clearing away and the sky seemed to melt as the stars appeared, making each separate planet seem to burn bright and singly, just out of reach.

The cry of the wind was faint. The men across the pool seemed far away. He wondered if for a moment he had fallen into a light sleeping state. He had to watch that. At the moment he was dazed, and only the woman's nearness had reality.

The men across the pool were wide awake. They had heard Valerie's whisper.

"The woman with you again, Merrick?" Clinton called. "How's her man going to take that?"

"Bleeding to death ain't the only way for a man to die," Perch said.

Young Billy laughed. "What is it you got, Merrick, that it don't have?"

Perch laughed. "Why, it ain't that a-tall, Billy-boy. What he's got is that old Southern honor. Man's nothing but honor and the woman trusts him. It's plumb a caution the way she has come to rely on Blade Merrick."

"That's a living fact," Billy said.

Their taunting voices rode across the pool.

Perch swore. "Why, it's like as though good-looking Mrs. Butler don't trust us at all — us that tried to keep her alive and away from the Injuns."

Clinton's voice had no laughter in it, but the taunt barbed it. "Let her fool around with him, and the Injuns *will* get her."

"She'll know who to trust," Perch said. "But it's going to be too late when the Injuns get their hands in that pretty mess of red hair."

Billy emitted a mock moan. "Oh, what a sin it would be to waste anything like that on Injuns."

The three men laughed. Merrick strained to hear their movement. It seemed to him they must be crouched at the very rim of the overhang, staring down at the boulder.

He heard the affection in old Clinton's voice. "Billy, you're growing into a right fine man. I'm proud of you. You got taste in women, boy," Clinton said into the silence.

Blade kept his voice low. "They'd like to get me to answer them," he said. "They'd take a shot at me if they were sure the first would get me."

"Jeff — is awake."

"Is he feeling better?"

"Yes. His fever is gone." She bent toward him, keeping her voice low. He could smell the woman-fragrance of her hair and her body. The fresh clean smell assailed him, and he wanted to tell her to get away from him, to stay away. She'd been out here long enough to know how scarce women were. God knew this was worse. He admitted it was different. He had been near women in the towns, at the army posts — few as they were, he could have been with some of them if he had wanted to. But it looked as though hell was playing a dirty trick on him. All his desire was congealed and focused on this woman. And she didn't have sense enough to stay away from him.

"You've saved his life," she whispered. "I never met a better man than you, Blade."

Sure, he thought. *What a fool you are.* He looked at her, yearning in the darkness.

"You're a gentleman. I haven't met many like you — out here."

He sighed, thinking, *And I haven't met any like you.* Then he warned himself that she could be here because she wanted just what the Clintons wanted — to turn that wagon north to Fort Ambush.

"I'm glad your husband's better."

"He sent me over," she said. "He's awake, and feeling better. He wants to talk to you."

"I want to thank you," Butler said when Merrick hunkered down beside his blanket.

He extended his slender hand. Blade took it. There were no calluses on Butler's palm. If he had worked for his woman since he came out here, he must have done it in saloons, over gambling tables. Hell, he told himself, forget it. It's none of your business, and you got worries enough. She chose this man. Let her live with him.

He frowned. Would he be so critical of her husband if he was not all ripped up about the woman?

"It's all right." His voice was brusque. "You'd do as much for me."

"That's it, old buddy. I don't know. You see, Val told me about that bullet. It was deep. She said you took it out like you were digging for precious metal."

"I don't know too much about a man's insides. I probe careful because I don't want to open something I can't close." Blade wished Jeff Butler would get to the point. He found himself disliking even the young fellow's voice. Funny how you could hate a man just because he had something you wanted, so that even his voice fretted and angered you. Jefferson Calhoun Butler had a Carolina drawl that was almost a whine.

And Valerie's skirts rustled as she knelt by Jeff, across from him. The wind filled his nostrils with that perfume that wasn't perfume at all, but *her*.

Jeff said, "Well, you saved my life. I'm glad you saw fit to be so careful."

"How do you feel now?"

"Like you left your right hand in my side."

"It'll be better. Bound to be sore for a while. If you don't bleed any more, you'll make it."

"That's what I want to talk to you about." Jeff's whine drew out each word so that Merrick flinched at the sound.

"Yeah?"

"I guess I don't have to tell you in a lot of words, Merrick. I was never meant for this country. Sure, I thought I was. Val and I —

we talked ourselves into it. Back home, I guess I'd be as good as the next man."

"Sure." Merrick glanced at Valerie, wondering what had first attracted her to this man. There wasn't much laughter in a man as weak as this one.

"I mean, I went all through the war. I was on the general's staff, sure. But we went into the fighting."

"I know."

"Sometimes the fighting came up to us. I never ran away from it. After the war, I went back home, and I felt I was as good as the next man. You know? I don't feel that way out here. There's too much you got to know, just to stay alive." He tried to laugh, but his voice quavered. "Hell, I thought I knew south from north — and east from west. But once Val and I got in that wagon — I even lost my sense of direction."

"It happens. All the time."

"I hate to depend on another man. But Val and I talked it over. We need help. Bad. She told me how Clinton and the other two threatened you."

He glanced up at Valerie. "She's filled you in with everything that's happened, eh?"

"I woke up a while ago." The drawling whine sawed at Merrick's taut-drawn nerves. "I heard you people talking up there.

When Val came back, I asked her about it. Now, I — I know you're going to do what's best — for all of us — eh, Merrick?"

Merrick stared at Butler a moment, lifted his gaze to Valerie. Even in the darkness she could not meet his gaze. He heard the low-toned conversation from the overhang, the distant cry of the wind. Somewhere in the wastes a coyote bayed.

"I don't know," he said at last. He stood up. He didn't want to hear the man whine and beg, not in front of the woman. At the moment all he wanted was to escape both of them. "I reckon I'll do what I have to."

"Sure. Sure."

"A man's got to live with himself."

He walked away down the incline, hearing the soft whisper of the water running out of the well, falling on a stone. He could hear the muted conversation of the Clintons, but he paid no attention to it.

He walked quietly, thinking it over, the man and his woman that were nothing to him, and the way he would remember her every night as long as he lived.

His grin was acrid. It happened that way sometimes. Hard, sudden and complete. And when it hit you, it was too bad. You could run away from it, but you couldn't stay in the same world with it . . . . not and

556

do nothing about it.

He shook his head, hating his thoughts. Jeff Butler had so little now; it was almost as if the woman were his last reservoir of strength — take her away, and what was left of him?

He heard the whisper of sound behind him. He slowed, feeling panic only because he knew it was Valerie. "Could I talk to you — just a minute?"

"If it's about heading north, I can't do it."

"No. It's about — Jeff." Her voice dropped.

He caught his breath. *Good God,* he thought, *don't apologize. Whatever you do, don't apologize for him.*

"He's sick," she said. "The bullet — the loss of blood. Really, he's very charming, and not afraid. Why, like he said, he went all through the war."

"He seems a good fellow."

"No. He was whining. I saw you — the way you withdrew."

"He's bad hurt."

"But there's more than that, and you know it. He's frightened — he's almost more afraid of living than — than of dying from that wound."

"A man gets down low, he can't help how he feels."

557

"It'll be worse. He heard what those men think of Southerners — he heard them trying to rile you into fighting. If they start on him —" She shuddered, standing close to him in the darkness. "You — you're from Virginia. You're one of us. Won't you try to help him?"

He spread his hands. "What could I do?"

"Don't let him be afraid — not in front of them."

"You might as well know — because a man is from Carolina or Virginia doesn't mean he's either brave or a coward. Like all places — there are both. A man is smart to know when to be scared."

"But —" her voice faltered — "fear is paralyzing him — and that's not smart."

"No." His voice was cold. "You're right. It ain't smart to be scared all the time."

ELEVEN

She went away from him, up the incline to the wagon. Merrick heard her moving around for some minutes and then could hear her lie down beside her husband.

He shivered with something more than the cold in the wind. He scooped out a place for his hipbone under the roll of the boulder and lay down on his blanket.

The horses were restless in the grass clump. He heard them blowing, pulling against their stakes. A small night animal slithered near him, and he heard the wind die, and the rustling of the trees as it rose again in the night.

The stars looked yellow and swollen, and the sky beyond them had paled, fading. He did not know how late it was but knew it did not matter. He could not sleep. He yawned, knowing he had never been more exhausted.

His eyelids were heavy. He felt drowsy, almost as if he had been drugged. The coffee had not helped much. He'd been afraid it would not. It had been served up with tension and hatreds that you could almost touch.

Lying on his side, he strained his eyes, staring at the depression beneath the over-hanging boulder across the pool. Soon, enough moonlight and starlight would fade the darkness to gray, but at the moment he could not see them over there.

He propped his head on his arm. Clinton had warned him clearly enough. They meant to take the wagon and the horses and move out tonight. They would not even hesitate to kill him if he opposed them. He wondered if they would bother to take

559

Valerie and Jeff Butler with them. It was certain that neither Billy nor Perch would want to leave her here. No. They'd take her if they ran before dawn, but the odds were they'd leave her husband and him dead — if they could get away with it.

He glanced at the sky, needing just a little more light under that overhang. He had to see them moving. They had plotted for hours. Whatever their plan was, it should now be well-discussed.

He sighed. Clinton had a neat purpose in warning him that he could expect them during the night. It had not been to prepare him. They knew he waited. Clinton wanted him to worry about *when* it would happen.

He heard Valerie and Jeff whispering in the darkness. He let his thoughts touch her because there was more pleasure, if no less danger, in thinking about her.

He had no idea how long he'd lain there when he heard the first whisper of movement.

The gray starlight had touched the depression beneath the overhang where the Clintons were. This light on the three shadowy forms over there, along with his own fatigue, had lulled him.

He waited, pressed against the boulder, tense. The sound was louder now, the noise a mouse might make, or a man moving across the crust of the sand.

He lifted his head, stared at the wagon. He could see the outlines of Valerie and Jeff over there. He moved his gaze around. The hell of it was there were still three forms under that overhang . . . or there appeared to be.

For a moment he thought it might be an Apache. If this were true, they'd lose the horses and he ought to call out to Clinton for help.

But he did not call out. He could not delay any longer. He got to his knees, letting the blanket fall away from him. He kicked his boot free.

There was the sound of a footstep in the darkness to his right around the boulder. The sound died and silence followed, as if someone held his breath.

Merrick worked his gun free of its holster. Thumbing back the hammer, he got to his knees, pressing close against the boulder, slithering cautiously. He took two steps, paused.

He glanced across the pool at the overhang. They could be waiting for him to step away from the shadow of the boulder, to show himself in the moonlight.

There was no movement under the overhang. Still, he had the nagging sense of wrong in this. He pressed himself back into the shadowed dark of the boulder.

A horse pawed the earth, so that part of it was all right: the horses hadn't been stolen yet. The wind chose this moment to die away. Merrick closed his mouth, forcing himself to breathe through his nose. The splash of water on the stone inside the pool seemed exaggeratedly loud. It was as if it were the regular heartbeat of this place.

Sweat broke out across his forehead. It was too quiet, an unnatural tension, drawing tighter and tighter like a wire that's going to snap. The Butlers asleep beside the wagon. The sound of the water dropping. The three dark forms that might be the Clintons, or else blankets piled on stones to look like them. The sky was lightening. He had no idea what time it was, only that it was hours until daybreak; the sky would darken over completely again before dawn. He waited, feeling the chill touch of the wind on his sweated face.

The sound of a footstep on the alkali crust was repeated; brush crackled. Some of the tension went out of Merrick and he almost laughed. The danger wasn't lessened, but there was no longer any doubt. They were begging him to investigate that noise. It was as if they whispered across the darkness, *Step out there, Merrick. Please. Come on out where we can see you.*

He moved cautiously to the left of the boulder, away from the sound of the brush and the footsteps. He pressed his body against the boulder, sliding around it.

In the darkness of the boulder, he crouched and stared through the gloom.

The set-up hit him with the impact of a fist. It rocked him on his heels to think they believed he'd fall for such a simple plot. A few yards away from him, across a clearing, Billy Clinton stood near a mesquite bush. In his right hand Billy had his gun, in the other he held a forked stick. He punched at the mesquite and it rattled faintly: the sound a man might make creeping up on his prey.

Perch was the joker in the trap — out there in the clearing; Billy was the bait. The plan was simple enough; catch Merrick in the space between them and cut him down in the crossfire.

He waited another moment, holding his breath. Perch was only a few feet from him, poised in the shadows, gun drawn, awaiting a signal from Billy. There was a chance the trap had another snapper — old Clinton could be the cincher, but there was not time to look for him. In a moment, Perch's instinct would warn him, or he'd hear Merrick breathing behind him.

Merrick twisted the gun, making a club of it. He braced himself and sprang toward the crouching Perch.

Clinton's warning yell came from across the water hole. It rattled against the rocks.

"Look out, Perch! Look out behind you!"

Perch straightened, spinning around on his heel. He was fast, but not fast enough. He brought his gun upward but did not get to fire it. Driven by his anxiety, Merrick chopped down with the gun butt. He could feel the shock of the blow all the way to his shoulder. There was the sound of wood and metal against Perch's skull.

Perch uttered an exhaling sound of agony and crumpled at the knees, pitching toward Merrick.

Blade moved to his left, away from Perch's toppling body.

Across the clearing in the mesquite, Billy Clinton hurled the stick from him and turned toward them, firing in the darkness.

The bullet chipped stone from the boulder beside Blade's face. Billy ran toward him, into the clearing, ready to fire again.

Blade did not hurry it. He crouched slightly in the shadows, leveled his gun at Billy's hand-carved belt. He pressed off his shot coldly. The impact of the bullet caught Billy squarely in the chest, knocking him his own length backwards into the dirt.

Merrick waited. There was a faint sobbing cry from within the clearing. In the faint light he saw that Billy's gun had been knocked from his hand as he fell. It lay some feet from him.

Billy had landed on his back, turned slightly on his side. He did not move.

Merrick felt the sickness well up in him. It had nothing to do with the killing; that was self-defense. Maybe it was the kid's age, the way he had laughed, had tilted his hat.

"Blade! Merrick? Are you all right?"

He heard Valerie calling from the wagon. He hoped she had sense enough to stay where she was. Clinton was going to be firing at anything that moved.

Clinton yelled. "Billy? Billy-boy. You all right?"

The wind rose, and the night chill deepened around the water hole.

"Billy! Perch! Billy! Goddamm it, boy, answer me." His gun ready, Merrick knelt and caught Perch by the collar. He dragged him around the boulder.

"Perch. That you, boy?"

Clinton's voice was frantic. He forgot himself enough to run out from beneath the overhang.

Merrick raised his gun.

"Hold it, Clinton. Right out there in the open where you are."

Clinton stopped as though he'd been poled. He held his gun at his side.

"You toss that gun away from you, Clinton," Merrick said.

"Billy?"

There was no answer. After a moment Clinton dropped the gun. He stood, swaying slightly, near the water hole. Merrick dragged Perch around the rim of the pool.

"Stand quiet, Clinton. You make a move, you're tagged."

Clinton seemed not to hear him. He was staring at the opening between the wagon and the boulder. They'd set the trap out there, set it with Billy as the bait, laughing as they planned it because nothing could go wrong. They'd live forever, all three of them, and share the loot from their latest haul in a Tucson saloon.

Merrick moved to within three feet of Hardhead Charley Clinton. He released his hold on Perch's shirt collar and stepped back.

Clinton did not see him, or Perch. His craggy face was rigid. His eyes were distended, fixed on that open place between wagon and boulder. In a moment Billy had to saunter through there, hat rakish, thumb in his belt.

The sound was ripped from Clinton's throat.

"Billy!"

The wind was his answer; the wind, the silence, and the whisper of the water in the pool.

"Boy. Billy, boy!"

Clinton shook his head, said, "Ah-h-h." The pain was intolerable, and yet he was numb, beyond pain.

"Goddam it, Billy-boy. You hear me, Billy? You hear me? You answer me."

Clinton stepped toward that opening, going down the incline. He almost stepped on Perch's face.

Merrick's voice was rasping. "Hold it. Right there, Clinton."

Clinton stopped, but did not turn around. He sobbed, standing there, his big shoulders shaking. The noises from his mouth were animal sounds, full of grieving and loss. Billy was dead, and he had to believe it. Billy was never going to die and Billy was dead.

He turned slowly. Tears were running from his eyes. His nose was running and when his mouth moved, he slobbered. He looked down at Perch Fisher as though he had never seen him.

"My boy. My boy." He lifted his head, a pirate out of time and place. His mouth twisted. "My boy. I had nothing else. You've killed my boy. I'm looking at you, Merrick. You killed my boy. God help you, Merrick. You'll never live — you'll never close your eyes again on this earth — not until I kill you. . . ."

Merrick stood there with the whine of the wind loud through the rocks. A faint film of dust sifted across the pool. He heard Valerie Butler's sharp intake of breath from the shadow beside the wagon. He did not take his gaze from Clinton.

He saw Clinton's hand falter toward his holster, find it empty. Clinton moaned again.

He stared at Merrick across Perch's prostrate body. Then he pulled his gaze away. Merrick saw him find the gun where he'd dropped it, saw him quiver toward it, almost lunging toward it though Merrick stood with his own gun, waiting.

At last, Clinton quieted, pulled his gaze away from his gun.

Merrick knelt slowly, watching Clinton. He removed Perch's gun from its holster. Clinton remained immobile.

Merrick backed up the incline, gathered the three rifles from beneath the overhang. He came back to where Clinton stood, gaze riveted on his gun on the ground.

Merrick said, "Take Perch up there to the overhang, Clinton. Do what you want to for him. He may die."

Clinton stared at him, bent down, caught Perch's collar, dragged him up the incline. Merrick gathered up the gun, went down to his boulder.

He heard Clinton pacing back and forth across the water hole. He walked to the clearing.

Merrick knelt beside Billy's body. The boy was dead. He found his gun, went slowly back to the sump.

Clinton was standing near the wagon. In another moment he would have made it to the boulder and the guns.

When he saw Merrick, Clinton swung around. His voice shook. "Butler, give me your gun. Give it to me. I'll kill him. I got to kill him or I can't go on living. Give me the gun."

Merrick moved near to Clinton. "Get back to your cage, Clinton. You tried a kill and it didn't work. You can thank God you're still walking around."

Clinton shrugged his shirt up on his

shoulders, eyes locked upon Merrick, burning his face into his mind.

Merrick said, voice cold and dead, "In the morning you better bury your boy, Clinton, unless you want the buzzards helping the Apaches find you quicker than they will anyhow."

He heard Clinton moan, helpless and torn with inner rage. He turned his back on Clinton, walked down to his blanket. He was more tired than he had ever been in all his life before.

TWELVE

In the darkest hour before daybreak, Merrick left the boulder, going quietly around it. He walked past Billy Clinton's body, twisted like something broken in the sand.

He went up on the highest point above the sump. The rocks crowded him and the wind whispered around them, a cold whisper of trouble and sudden death.

He searched the land with sleepless eyes. The ache in them extended to the crown of his head now. He rubbed them with the heel of his hands, turning slowly to search every point of the compass.

Nothing stirred out there. He didn't know what he expected to find at this hour. If the

Indians had found the horses they would be gorging themselves on roasted meat. If that were true, they had found the tracks leading south to Patchee Wells. But it might be also true that the Apache might lie around on his full belly, spend a few more hours making medicine. But if they were feasting on roasted meat there should be a fire reflected in the darkness from the valley.

There was nothing out there. The silence pressed in upon him. Whatever the Apache was about, he was not going to learn it up here.

He went down the incline, untied the horses and led them down to the pool, let them drink. He saw Perch was sprawled on the ground at the lip of the overhang. Clinton had sworn he would not sleep, but his grief and anguish had overcome him. He was toppled back against the wall of the depression. He snored in his sleep.

Merrick led the horses to the wagon, backed them between the shafts, hitched them to the wagon.

"Are you leaving?"

He turned, finding Valerie standing at the corner of the wagon, watching him.

"Maybe. If your husband hasn't bled too much during the night. If he feels well enough."

"Are you still going south?"

"I have all the guns."

"Not all of them."

"Would you shoot me?"

"I don't know. You should have taken Jeff's gun when you took the others."

He straightened the lines, checking them. His voice was level. "Thanks for warning me."

"Too late now, Mr. Merrick. Jeff and I talked it over last night. He won't give you his gun. You'll have to shoot him — like you did that boy."

"That *boy* missed me by inches. Was I supposed to stand there? You are just as dead, killed by a boy."

"I know you did what you had to do. You miss my point. I was trying to tell you, we were on your side. You were good to us; you saved Jeff's life. But this is different. This is our chance to get back home. . . ."

"So you've thrown in with Clinton and Perch."

"We don't know yet. That's up to you. We know he has a lot of money. He is very anxious to go north. He wants to go south to San Carlos even less than Jeff and I do. If you force him to travel south, you'll have to fight him every step of the way."

He was bent over checking a horseshoe.

He released the horse, straightened.

"That's where you're wrong. I'm not forcing anyone to go south with me. I told you people. *I'm* going south. If you want to go with me, fine. But it's up to you."

He heard her sharp intake of breath. "You'd leave them — or us, in this Indian country?"

"I'd hate it," he told her. "But as I said, it's your choice."

"I'm glad I see you for what you are. You're less than human."

He shrugged. "Maybe, Mrs. Butler. But it's a long ways to San Carlos, and there are Apaches — I'll have enough to do without battling the people riding with me."

She moved her hand upward from the folds of her dress. He saw the gleam of the long gun barrel.

"Put that thing down," he said.

"Stay where you are, Merrick. I've given this a lot of thought. If you think I won't shoot you, you just don't know how badly I want to get back east."

"Pull the trigger," he said.

"W-what?"

"You heard me. You're not going to shoot me unless you pull that trigger. And you're not getting these horses unless you kill me."

She breathed in deeply. He saw her brush

at a lock of hair on her forehead,

"Don't try any tricks," she said.

"The tricks are up to you. Coming over here with a sweet, friendly tone and pulling a gun. Go on, shoot me. Then let's see you people get north past those Mescaleros."

"We — can try it."

"Sure you can. You tried it once before. Only there was one more of you than there is now — and Perch Fisher has a cracked skull this morning. Don't count much on him. And you've got a long run ahead of you in that wagon, and the rattling around is sure to start your husband to bleeding — so you can count him as dead —"

"Shut up!"

Her cry rang against the inner wall of the sump. Old Clinton came to his feet in the first thin rays of daylight. He stared down at Valerie holding the gun on Merrick and roared.

"You just hold that, Miz Butler," he yelled. "I'm a-coming to take over."

Valerie turned to look at him. From the blanket Jeff yelled her name in warning. But it was too late.

Merrick sprang forward, grabbing her arm, twisting it and pulling her around between him and the running Clinton.

He wrested the gun from her hand, held it

toward Clinton.

"All right, old man. Stop right there."

Clinton took three more long running steps before he was able to halt.

"Godamighty, woman, why didn't you watch him?"

Blade was more aware of the pressures of her body against him than of Clinton's swearing, or of Jeff Butler propped on his elbows watching them from the blanket. He would have sworn he could feel the frantic thudding of her heart, or perhaps it was just the echo of his own. He thrust her away from him.

She stumbled and fell on the blanket beside Jeff. He did not look at her. His mouth was pulled down in petulant anger.

In the shelter of the boulder where he'd spent most of the night, Merrick made a small fire, banked with stones. He heated coffee, fried biscuits and warmed meat.

By the time the smell of coffee had filled the sump, Clinton was watching him from the lip of the overhang.

Valerie had walked to the edge of the wagon.

He poured a cup of coffee. "Will you join me?"

She came around the pool slowly. She would not look at him.

"Don't feel badly," he said. "You did as well as any of them. Better. You got nearer to me than I would have let them get."

He handed her a cup of coffee, a tin plate of warm meat, beans and fried biscuits.

She drank the hot coffee and ate hungrily. Merrick watched her a moment, glanced up at Clinton. "Come down here and get a plate, Clinton."

Clinton came down around the pool.

"All right," Merrick said when he was ten feet from the fire, "you can hold that."

He placed a cup of coffee on a stone in front of Clinton, then put a plate of food beside it.

Clinton squatted beside the stone and began to eat. He did not say anything. Merrick saw that Clinton's eyes were red-rimmed, his face stark, pallid.

Perch stood up slowly, walked dazedly down to the pool. He sank down beside it, bathing his face and moaning.

Merrick set a plate of food and coffee near him. Perch turned, looking at the food. The sudden turn made his head pain, and he touched at his skull.

"Must have walked into something in your sleep last night," Merrick said.

Perch touched his holster, found it empty. His face went blank and he paled beneath his sunburn. His gaze moved slowly around the camp.

Clinton was staring up at him. "Billy is dead," Clinton told him.

A muscle worked in Fisher's heavy-jowled face. His eye twitched. He glanced at the water, at the rising sun, back at Merrick. After a moment he sat down in front of his food.

Merrick carried a plate and a cup of coffee up the slight incline to the wagon. Butler was propped against the wheel.

Butler gave him a level smile, nodded his thanks. He drank the coffee and began to eat greedily.

Merrick glanced at Butler's bandages, found them only faintly blood-tinged.

He went to the rear of the wagon, took out two small army shovels. He tossed them down the incline so they fell near Clinton.

"You'll find my brother's grave down that incline, Clinton," he said, voice cold and meaningful. "You might dig your son's grave beside it."

THIRTEEN

Clinton did not move for a long time. Finally, he cleaned the scraps from his plate, tossed it along with the fork beside the smoldering fire. He picked up the two shovels.

For a second he held one as if it were a club. His red-rimmed eyes were fixed on Merrick up the incline beside the wagon. Merrick stood there, watching him.

"Come on, Perch," Clinton said.

The big gunman got up, tossing his plate and cup beside Clinton's. He was still groggy and massaged at his tousled head where Merrick had hit him. He took one of the shovels and the two men walked between the wagon and the boulder to the clearing where Billy Clinton's body was twisted on the ground.

Valerie remained sitting on a stone near the pool. She did not glance toward Merrick or her husband. She turned slightly so that she could watch Clinton and Perch Fisher digging out in the clearing. She stayed like that, her hands locked, immobile.

Merrick walked down the incline. He kicked sand into the fire and fanned away the last flare of smoke. He looked at Valerie a moment, but she did not turn. Clinton and Perch were working slowly, but turning deep spadefuls of earth each time. They spoke infrequently, and stopped to glance down the incline toward the sump where Merrick and their guns were.

It seemed to Merrick that the very look of the world this morning reflected his own inner disturbed feelings. The sun had given a coppery cast to the sky, to the few clouds that fringed the lower ceiling, and to the alkali ground. There was no breeze. It was already hot, though the sun was barely visible. It would be a hot and breathless day. He sighed, thinking it was going to be a deadly one.

He glanced toward Clinton and Perch. The earth was hard to dig in, and the work was slow. His mouth twisted. He knew that, for he had dug in that same ground. He tried to calculate how long it would take them to bury the boy.

He glanced toward the dull, coppery ball of sun. "We ought to be pulling out of here."

Valerie did not answer.

Jeff pulled higher against the wheel. "Mr. Merrick?"

For an instant, Valerie's head pulled around and she stared at her husband, face pallid. Then she exhaled, turned again to watch the men digging in the clearing.

Merrick went up the incline.

Butler said, "I'm feeling a lot better this morning."

"You feel up to traveling?"

"You mean would I rather take a chance

on bleeding to death in a moving wagon than lying here waiting for those Apaches to come back. Help me up there and let's go."

"Then you have nothing against going south?"

A shadow flickered in Butler's eyes. "I've everything against it — but after all, you have my gun, mine host."

"Yes. I reckon that changes things all right."

"I've lain here, Merrick, heard old Clinton offer you a thousand dollars, heard Valerie plead with you, and Fisher threaten to kill you. Looks like nothing we can say will turn you back from San Carlos."

"I'm afraid not — I've been in towns where kids died of epidemic fever."

"It's a long, lonely way to San Carlos."

"Yes."

"Through Indian territory."

"So I've been told."

"We're much nearer a Fort Ambush patrol to the north . . ."

"Yes."

"You were a soldier, Merrick. Common sense ought to tell you when to retreat."

"I was a sergeant — never on the general's staff."

Jeff Butler's pale face flushed. Then he grinned, and for him it was easy. He seldom let his anger show through his charm, which was something he wore on the surface.

"Then why not take the advice of a man who was?" he said, smiling.

Merrick glanced toward the men digging. "I've a lot to do if we're going to clear out of here as soon as they bury the boy. If that's all you wanted —"

"But it isn't." Butler's face grew warm again, and Merrick saw something happening to his eyes.

Butler lowered his voice, the whine disappearing, a kind of difficulty with his breathing showing in each word. "I've one more offer to make you, Merrick — if you'll turn north."

"Why don't you save your breath?"

"Won't you even listen? I think I can change your mind."

Merrick had turned away. Now he heeled around, his voice sharp. "All right. Let's have it."

"Let's talk it over a moment, Merrick." A look of bitterness showed in Butler's handsome face. "I've seen the way you've looked at Valerie."

"What are you talking about?"

"Oh, let's not get upset. You see — I've seen the way she looks at you, too." His laugh had a rancid sound. "I've been sick,

Merrick. Not blind."

"You're still sick."

Butler laughed at him. "You deny you want her?"

"I don't see the sense of talking about it at all."

"There's this sense . . . . I know a real man when I meet up with one, Merrick. You're the first completely whole man I've met since the general I served with in Virginia. I admired that man, ungrudgingly. . . . I can't say my admiration of you isn't a grudging kind. Because I can see without asking Valerie that she sees in you maybe the kind of man she thought I was when she married me. Though God knows, she should have known better even then."

"Is that all?"

Butler seemed not to have heard him. His mind was deeply entangled in his own bitter memories. "She knows well enough now. I failed her back in the East, Merrick, brought her out here with all kinds of glowing promises and I failed her worse than ever."

"That touches me. But there's nothing I can do about it."

Butler's mouth pulled into a hurting smile. "Yes. There is, Merrick. You can take advantage of it."

"I don't follow you."

"Yes, you do, Merrick. You're way ahead of me. You know and I know that after this Valerie is going to have an even lower estimation of me than before. If we get out of this alive, it'll be no thanks to me. Hell, I got us lost on a clear-marked trail and that got us into this hell in the first place."

"That happens."

"Yes. And it happens that when a woman finds herself married to a failure she can live with him — until she finds the kind of man she wants and — deserves. You think I don't know the truth, Merrick? When we get out of this, if Valerie goes back East with me — if she stays with me at all — it will only be out of a sense of loyalty. It will be you she'll be thinking about."

"Maybe you can sleep this off."

"Take us to Tucson, Merrick. When we get there . . . . I really got nothing to bargain any more. She despises me, she knows me for what I am — and worse, for what I'm not. . . . Take us to Tucson — and I swear I'll step out of this, Merrick — Valerie will be free."

Merrick stared at Butler. The handsome man leaned against the wagon wheel, watching him, his dry eyes narrowed and tortured, near to tears that he would never shed. The breath was ragged across Butler's parted lips. He had sunk as low as a man could sink. He despised himself more than anyone else could. He had failed Valerie in every possible way and now that she was all he had left he was bartering her for his life — even as he was asking himself why he believed anything as low as he was deserved to go on living.

The words struck Merrick hard, like the side of a hand across his Adam's apple. He swallowed hard, feeling blood surge against his temples. He was sure Butler could see the pulse bounce at the base of his throat.

His tongue touched his lips. They were parched. He moved his head to stare at the cool pool of water, suddenly thirsty. He let his gaze touch Valerie on the stone, the sun adding a coppery gloss to her red hair, the lines of her profile, the fullness of her breasts. He thought about her wild laughter and her stormy temper.

He inhaled deeply; his jaw tightened and he pulled his gaze away from her. He did not answer Butler.

Butler's bitter voice struck at him. "Deny you want her, Merrick? Last night, you thought I was asleep. I saw the way you looked at her. This morning when she might have killed you with my gun. She couldn't do it —"

"You make many deals like this for her?" Merrick was giving Butler a chance to flare into anger, to forget the suggestion he had made.

Jeff kept his voice low. "Look at her, Merrick. You know better than that. I've had — her loyalty. You could have —" Butler swallowed hard and did not finish that.

Merrick scowled. He wanted to walk away. He wanted to kick Butler's face. He did not move.

Butler's voice quavered. He was an ill man, a frightened one. "Listen to me, Merrick. You don't know what she's meant to me. But I know what she sees now when she looks at me — and it kills me. All I can save out of this hell is — maybe my life. I'm trying to buy my life. This is all I know. All I have."

Merrick stared at him.

"I know how scarce any woman is out here, Merrick . . . and you've never seen anything like Valerie — not anywhere."

"Then get her out of here."

"Can I do it? I'm doing what I can for her. You better think about what you can do for yourself, Merrick. There are a lot of Apaches between here and San Carlos — between here and anywhere."

585

Merrick did not answer.

"You think you'll ever see a woman like Valerie again?"

"Does she know you're — offering to leave her like this?"

"What do you care? Stop being holy. What difference does it make?"

"None, I reckon." Merrick turned, drawing his tongue across his parched lips again.

Butler's voice grabbed after him. "Make up your mind, Merrick. Turn north — to Tucson."

Merrick strode away from the wagon going down the incline. It seemed to him the sun had climbed crazily, burning the earth, drying him out, dehydrating his body. His eyes throbbed with the blood pumped fast behind them. A lizard skittered between the rocks and he felt himself go taut. They'd pulled his nerves tight, stringing them thin in the sun to stretch and dry and break.

"Merrick."

Valerie's voice touched at him as he passed the stone where she sat. Her voice was troubled.

He paused, stopped, legs apart, staring at her. His eyes felt hot and the pressure against them made them ache. She was a coppery blur before him. He felt the muscles in his stomach tighten. He closed his fists, turned to walk away from her.

"Merrick."

He stopped but did not look at her.

"They — they're almost ready. Let's go, Merrick. Please . . ."

He did not answer. He could hear Clinton's lowered voice from the clearing, hear the clods of earth as they struck the sides of the open grave, filling it. He could feel Butler's strangely dry gaze on him from the wagon. The sun scorched his shoulders and the back of his neck.

He walked to the edge of the water. He glanced across his shoulder and over Valerie's head to Clinton and Perch in the clearing.

He removed his gun belt, placed it on the ground close beside his boot. He pulled roughly at his shirt, jerking the buttons through the buttonholes, dragging his shirt-tails out of his belt.

He wore no undershirt. His back was baked brown, and muscles corded his shoulders, making lines to his lean hips. He dropped his shirt behind him, sank to his knees at the water's rim.

He cupped his hands and brought them brimming to his fevered face. This was not enough, and he bent forward, immersing his head in the cold water. He thought grimly, *This cold water can save a man more ways than one.*

He brought water up in his cupped hands, drinking thirstily, feeling the water falling against his chest, running along his flat stomach.

He bathed his eyes and then straightened up on his heels.

He could smell her. There was a warm, fresh excitement about her that was going to haunt him all the rest of his life. In that moment, crouching there, he could see his life, stretching hot and lonely ahead of him.

He had not heard her walk down close behind him, yet he knew he could turn and she would be there at his back.

"Blade."

There was something new in his name when she spoke it. She gave it a softness, she made a caress out of it. An old family name they'd given him in a burst of parental pride in bloodline. Funny what her voice could do to that name.

Merrick stood up slowly. The water ran down his face from his hair, off the squared planes of his jaw to his shoulders.

"Look at me, Blade."

And he thought, *The hell with everything else. The living, empty hell with loneliness, and what a man ought to do. What was a man to live with when he was alone? What he might have done, or what he had done? What else did a man regret except the good things he had left undone?*

There were a lot of Apaches between here — and anywhere.

Water coursed into the corners of his mouth. He felt his heart slugging against his ribs, knew that whatever had happened to Butler's eyes, happened now to his.

He turned around, suddenly, hands coming up from his sides.

He heard her catch her breath in a gasp that had horror in it. Her mouth sagged open, her green eyes distended, staring at the scar across his bare chest.

The life flowed downward out of him. He wanted to move, to speak, to curse; the anger and the agony was in him, but not the force.

His mouth twisted, and his eyes stung. Sure, a man lived with a scar, even one like this, for six years, it became part of him, and he lived with it, like any other infirmity. Sometimes, even, in moments like this one, a man forgot it entirely. God help him, after the look in her face, it would be a long time before he forgot it again.

His own gaze pulled down to the livid, jagged mark made by a knife, running from under his right collar bone like a streak of fantastic lightning across his rib cage, almost to his belt line. It had been laid bare by a knife, had healed this much, and would never heal any more.

His throat tightened. He stared down at her, hating the look of horror he saw in her pallid face. He wanted to rail at her. Not every man lived through hell and came out of it looking beautiful like Jeff Butler — if she wanted beautiful men, let her stay with her husband. But he didn't say any of that.

His voice grated, and he muttered between clenched teeth, "Next time you'll let a man know before you walk up on him like this."

The shock seeped out of her face, and something else replaced it. He did not see it. He didn't want to look at her any more.

He bent down, snatched up his shirt, thrust his arms into it.

She shook her head slowly, touched at her lips with her tongue. She tried to speak, but there was nothing to say, no words.

He picked up his gunbelt then, not even stopping to buckle it on. He strode away from her.

FOURTEEN

Merrick walked back to his rumpled blanket beside the boulder. Around him were the pans, the tin plates and cups, the ashes of the fire. Behind the small rock and under the boulder were the guns he'd stashed away. But he was not thinking about any of this.

He stood rigid for a moment, admitting the truth.

He was thinking about a saloon in Tucson. There was sawdust on the floor, and it was cool inside, out of the sun. The bartender knew him by name, but not by his capacity. Sometimes he went into the saloon and ordered a whiskey straight, and only one, never more. It would be something to see the bartender's face when he ordered a bottle and held his hand on its neck while he drank. The bartender would stare, thinking there was some mistake, thinking he didn't know Blade Merrick after all. Hell, who ever really knew any other person?

He buttoned his shirt, stuffing it into his trousers. Hell, a man had more than he could do on this earth even getting to know himself. Well, he had walked away from her. Not away from the soft flesh of her, the excitement of her hair, and the soft fra-

591

grance of her body. He had walked away from the look of horror in her face. He told himself he was glad he had done it, and the hell with the reason why. Only, all the time he knew what he wanted, and what he would always want.

He had to get things together, get that wagon out of here. The roast horsemeat would delay the Apaches for a while. It pleased him that they would gorge themselves first, but it was past time to hit the trail.

He buckled on his belt, his mind warning him it was time to leave, but his body longed to turn north, throw that goddam medicine out in the dirt. Maybe the Apaches would drink it, get drunk, even die from overdosage. He could turn north to Tucson, and that saloon. But the hell of it was, he was too honest. The saloon was only an excuse for thinking about Tucson. He wanted to get drunk; she was a poison in his bloodstream and he had to drink her out. But he knew if he went to Tucson he would have her. There weren't men enough; they didn't build walls high enough to keep him away from her.

He gathered up the cooking utensils, the plates and cups, dropping them into a sack. When he turned to go to the wagon he saw that Clinton and Perch were already there. They had thrown their shovels into the wagon bed. They were hunkered beside Butler and Valerie.

He stood there, watching them, knowing what they were saying without hearing the words. Clinton had some last-ditch plan. Clinton glanced toward Merrick, whispering urgently. Merrick saw Butler nod his head, and nod again. Butler's smile was charming, ingratiating.

He knelt down, gathered up the guns thonged together with a strip of leather. Carrying them under his right arm, dragging the sack, he went up the incline.

"Sorry to break up the meeting," he said. He moved his gaze from Perch to Clinton. Funny what depriving these men of their guns did to them. Where was Perch Fisher's contemptuous smile? "Perch, you and Clinton go over to the overhang. You got anything over there, get it ready to pull out of here."

He dropped the thonged guns under the front seat of the wagon.

"In case that looks inviting to you people," he said, "I better tell you, I'll shoot the first one of you that goes near that wagon until I give the word." He moved his gaze slowly across their faces, staring coldly at Valerie, including her. "You get the message?"

Clinton and Perch were on their feet. They did not answer, but walked slowly across the clearing to the overhang.

Merrick looked at Butler and Valerie for a moment. He turned on his heel, strode away.

He was almost to the clearing when Valerie's voice stopped him.

He paused and when she put out her hand asking him to stop, he leaned against a boulder where he could watch Clinton and Butler. A mouse skittered from a shattered rock across a sunny patch of ground to another shadow.

"I — want you to forgive me, Blade," she said.

"Nothing to forgive."

"Yes. I was startled when I saw that scar —"

"You're wasting time."

"No. I'm trying not to. There's something I must say. Jeff and I had talked all night — planning, not knowing what to do. Thinking —"

"About Tucson?" His voice was cold.

Her face colored faintly. Then her chin tilted. "Everything just piled up, one shocking thing after another —"

"It doesn't matter. I told you it doesn't

matter."

"First, last night when you killed Billy. I — know. You had to. It was your life or his. But he was so young. Just a boy. The thought of his dying shocked and upset me. Please understand."

His voice was chilled. "I know only one thing. Boy or not, if I hadn't killed Billy Clinton, someone else would have."

She nodded, her head lowered.

He persisted, voice rough. "He'd followed his old man too far. Once he might have been worth saving. I don't know."

"It's that it all added up to upset me —"

"And there's one more thing." He was speaking more to himself now than to her. "Somebody killed my brother. Right here at this water hole — somebody like the Clintons."

"The Clintons?"

"Three men. Men who'd robbed a Tucson bank and were on the run. All I know is they have saddlebags full of money — and now they're running north."

"But you have no proof."

"No. No proof."

She drew in a deep breath. She stared at his face, glanced over her shoulder at Butler sprawled beside the wagon, Clinton and Perch across the pool.

"I have something to tell you. I've got to tell you. No matter which way you plan to go."

He waited, watching her pallid face.

"They're going to jump you — they mean to take the wagon."

"I know that. You should be glad. The Clintons are going your way."

She bit her lip. "Maybe you knew they would jump you. But there's more. They talked it all over with Jeff and me."

"I didn't think you were exchanging recipes."

"Jeff told them he's willing to stand the trip — running all the way."

"Yes."

Her voice fell away. "They want me to — to let you — to get this gun from you — and remove the bullets."

His mouth was bitter. "I must be wearing what I want on my face. Everybody seems to know I've developed one weakness — and it's you."

"They hope so. They're gambling on it. They sent me after you now. They're watching — waiting."

He lifted his gaze from her face, feeling the working of the pulse in his throat. He wanted to laugh. Butler was staring at the sky, too casual. Clinton and Perch Fisher were talking together, watching something in another direction.

His mouth twisted. "Why the change of heart? Why are you telling me this?"

She shook her head. Her eyes filled with helpless tears. She looked away, staring at the clear pool with the boulders and the sky reflected in it.

She spread her hands. "I'm betraying my own husband."

"I asked you why."

Her voice went sharp. "I don't know why. Yes — I do. I know what he wanted me to do — to get him safely to Tucson. I — would do it, but maybe I'd never feel the same again toward him. I don't know."

"Are you hitting back at him already?"

"No. I know what you have done for me. And for Jeff. I know what Clinton is, and Perch. No matter what they say, I'm afraid to trust them. And — even though you won't turn north, it's you I trust. Suddenly, it's only you. I seem to know that my very life depends on you."

She looked up at him, her eyes tear-brimmed. "And then — when I saw the look in your face — there by the pool, I knew something I'd not known before. I knew you were a good man. Maybe the last good man I'll ever know. I could betray Jeff . . . but I couldn't betray you — not any more."

She pressed her knotted fist against her mouth. Tears struck her knuckles.

"All right." He kept his voice low. "Go back to them. Stall. Tell them you will come back to me — and that I want you to. That ought to please them."

She nodded, turned and walked slowly away from him. He stepped away from the boulder, looking at her. He felt an emptiness he'd never known.

He raised his voice. "Clinton. Perch. Move over to the wagon. I'll get up on the knoll and take a last look around. But stay away from those guns. I can see you just as easy from up there as I can from here."

He climbed the knoll, feeling the sun on his back. He glanced back at the four people beside the wagon. Valerie was talking dully to them. They watched him, but did not move toward the guns under the seat. Those guns were tied together. It would take time to loose one of them, and it might not be loaded. Merrick could kill any of them from the knoll. Common sense told them to trust Valerie's body and its magnetism for him, and to wait. . . .

He scanned the land before him, an inescapable feeling of wrong building in him. It was the sense of being trapped that he'd first felt when Billy Clinton shot the Apache scout yesterday afternoon, mixed now with all that had happened within the confines of the water wells, and all the unknown things that were happening with the Apaches out there somewhere in the wilderness.

He fixed his gaze on the far reaches of the heatswept land. Beyond, the crumpled badlands mountains lay against the sky, looking purple and cool. He pulled his gaze back to the flat, empty land between. The sun sucked the last moisture remaining from the night out of every plant, every grain of sand. A dust-devil rolled lazily, a hawk poised high in the stark, faded blue of the sky.

There was no movement out there, no trace of the Apaches. It didn't make sense that they had abandoned the hunt for the people they'd attacked in the valley, or that they would forgive the murder of the scout.

There was no sign of them in the vast tableland. The sun was coppery on the earth. A thought struck him. The Apaches may have moved up here last night. It would have been easy following the wheel tracks he'd left for them yesterday.

He leaned against the boulder, thinking about this. They had feasted on roast horse, followed a clear trail. He was almost afraid to turn and look behind him.

The first time he heard the sound beyond the forest of piñon and mesquite he tried to tell himself it was thunder, the pound of hooves, the beat of his own heart. But he knew better. It was the slow measured beat of a drum.

He stood there only a moment after that sound was repeated. He knew it was a good way to lose his scalp, but the desire to know outweighed his fear. He drew his gun, ran across the rocky ground and went as silently through the mesquite as he could move to the place where they had buried the Apache.

He stood there staring at the mesquite bush thrown aside, the grave open, and the Apache's body gone. He decided this was the moment when a man's whole life flashed through his mind. No matter what he had hoped for before, it was all over now. All wiped out by the mournful throb of the Apache drum out there below him.

Sweat coursed down his face. For a moment he could not pull himself away from that grave.

Hell, he thought, now I can't even go south.

He turned and walked blindly back to the clearing. He carried his gun at his side, but hardly knew he was carrying it.

He reached the rim of the descent to the water hole. He glanced over his shoulder. Nothing had changed; yet nothing was ever going to be the same again. The sun beat against the rocks, sucked life from the earth, glittered in the dust, but worse than the sun was the drum. It was everywhere, throbbing slowly like the last measured beats of a man's heart.

He walked slowly down the incline. Trying to think, but unable to do anything with the drum throbbing in the pit of his stomach, he moved toward the wagon.

He saw they were watching him. They had heard the drum, and knew what it meant, and suddenly he was their last hope. He wanted to laugh, looking at them. Butler had become the shade of ashes after a rain, and was chewing at his lips. Valerie stood immobile against the wagon. In her eyes were some of the swirling terrors he had seen there after the attack in the valley yesterday. All of it brought back to her by the pound of the drums. Perch, standing beside the blanket, reached instinctively for the gun that was no longer at his hip.

Charley Clinton stood staring up the incline toward the piñon forest and the sound of the drums. His legs were apart; sweat streaked his dust-patted face.

"Drums," Clinton said to Merrick. "The Indians out there?"

Merrick nodded. His mouth pulled into a bitter grin and his gaze struck hard against Clinton's. "You can quit worrying about the wagon — and which way you're going, Charley."

"We got any chance to get out of here?"

"None that I know. Not and get away from them. They found the Apache we buried and they dug him up. They're giving him an Apache burial. I figure we got until they get him cleansed of white burial and safely consigned to their gods."

"Hell," Perch Fisher said. "How much time we need? Let's get out of here."

FIFTEEN

"I got no hope they'll let us out of here," Merrick said, "but there's just one way to find out."

He nodded toward Butler, and Clinton moved with him to the wounded man on the blanket. They knelt on each side of him.

"How do you feel, Butler?" Merrick said.

"I'm too scared to feel anything," Butler said. "Let's go."

Merrick smiled at him, liking him for the first time since he'd known him. You had to admire anyone man enough to admit out loud to fear.

"Careful," Merrick said to Clinton. "Move him slow. We don't want to start him bleeding."

"Just move," Butler said, shaking his head. "My blood isn't going to run as numb as I am."

They lifted the wounded man. Valerie shook out the blanket and placed it in the body of the wagon. They set Butler inside the wagon.

Perch gathered up the three saddle bags and dropped them into the wagon.

Merrick laughed at him, but Perch said, "There's a lot of money there, Merrick, and as long as there's a chance I'll live to spend it, I'm hanging on to it."

Merrick shrugged. He told Valerie to get into the wagon. He helped her under the canvas with her husband.

"All right, Perch," he said. "You ride back there with the girl and the money."

Clinton spoke levelly. "There's one little matter, Merrick."

Merrick heeled around. "Yes?"

"We best throw in together until we get out of this here little difficulty, Merrick," Clinton said. "I hope you see fit to give us back our guns — or do you intend to let us bite our way past them Apaches?"

Merrick grinned and swung up on the front of the wagon. He loosed the thongs, tossed down rifles and pistols to Perch and Clinton.

"I admire you, Clinton," he said. "Admire the way you can make deals."

Clinton's mouth pulled into a wolfish grin. He stood a moment listening to the pound of the drums out there and the sudden wail of frenzied Indians.

"I'll make any deal, Merrick, that will get me what I want." He jerked his head toward the rear of the wagon. "Perch and me got that money — and we ain't dead yet."

Clinton climbed up on the seat. Merrick told him to pull the wagon around and head out of the sump, moving slowly.

Merrick ran across to the boulder where he'd built a fire. He kicked out all traces of the fire, pushed the discolored and fire-blackened stones into the pool.

He cut a scraggly mesquite brush and followed the wagon up the incline, brushing away all the wagon tracks and hoof marks. He had an empty feeling of futility about all this, but, like Clinton, he'd do what he had to, and he wasn't dead yet.

"Let's go," Perch whispered from the rear of the wagon. Clinton had stopped at the rim of the knoll.

Merrick glanced over his shoulder. That water hole looked peaceful, quiet, belonging to eternity.

He swung up on the seat beside Clinton. "Keep those horses light. One horseshoe against one rock and we'll interrupt that burial."

Clinton slapped the reins softly, the horses strained, and the wagon rolled out on the rocks.

From beyond the wooded area came the chanting cries of the reburial ceremony, and the sudden, rasping screams of hatred.

Clinton shuddered. "Sounds like that, makes a man think on his sins, all right."

Merrick sat tensely, rifle across his knees, a finger against its trigger. He watched all the land ahead of them, but it was tricky, a dangerous place of boulders, of brush, seeming open and flat, but now full of concealment for watching Apaches.

Clinton's voice was low. "Merrick, I been thinking. Back there in the valley when we were attacked. It was a small raiding party. Not more than seven."

"Yeah?"

"So now Billy took care of one of them. That leaves six. They're over there in a ceremony. If we rushed in there right now,

605

we could kill off them six before they got through wailing."

"You couldn't sell me that with a free gift on the side."

"Hell, man. They're in a frenzy of weeping — six of them."

"Six is plenty. There never were too many Apaches out here, but, mister, they'll remember the Apache as a warrior when all the other tribes are forgotten. You be glad the Army has 'em outnumbered in this territory, Clinton, or you'd be robbing banks east of the Mississippi right now."

Butler's voice came through the canvas. "What's there to see out there?"

"Nothing," Clinton told him. "You got a lot better view in there, mister. Enjoy it."

The wailing, keening cries of the Indians rose like dust into the sun, clouding and filtering out across the wasteland.

The wagon had rolled a few yards downslope with Clinton holding back on the reins. He glanced at Merrick. "You think it's about time to let 'em out, Mr. Merrick?"

"Ain't going to get any better," Merrick said. "Let's hit the road."

Clinton raised the reins high ready to slap them across the horses' rumps.

A rifle cracked almost at the animals' heads. The bullet whistled past like a hornet.

In that brief instant Merrick and Clinton considered the angles, the chances of running and getting out alive, the odds in favor of fighting back. Perch was concealed in the back, one more gun. But the army horses were too slow, they were hopelessly outnumbered, too far from any chance of aid.

"Hold it, Clinton," Merrick said. "Hold it hard. That shot meant stop. Next one is sure to mean one of us dead. If we got a chance at all of getting out alive — it'll be if we can talk our way out."

Clinton pulled hard on the reins.

The horses' heads came up high. Before they were quieted, three Indians stepped from behind boulders not nearly large enough to conceal them, yet they'd been concealed.

The three men held their rifles ready in the bend of their arms. Their faces were painted, and their bare chests were streaked with symbols. Their black hair was tied tightly against their heads.

Perch spoke from inside the wagon. "What's wrong, Hardhead? What you stopping for?"

Hardhead Charley spoke from the side of his mouth. "Hold what you got, Perch. Don't none of you make some fool move that might get us killed."

Perch's voice was awed. "Apaches?"

"Shore don't resemble a delegation of Quakers." There was silence from the body of the wagon.

"They know about the woman," Hardhead said from the corner of his mouth.

Merrick was staring at the Apaches. He had never seen any of the three before. They were young braves, would not have been on the trail six years ago, and had not been in any spots where they'd have met him since then.

"They know all about us," he said, wanting to silence Hardhead. "Keep your face straight no matter what they do."

One of the braves stepped forward beside the head of the right horse. He made a motion toward the rifle, the guns in their holsters. He jerked his head toward the ground.

"Throw 'em out," Merrick said, keeping his gaze level upon the braves. "Don't die a hero."

Clinton pulled his gun from its holster with his fingertips, tossed it to the ground. He watched the Apaches but they did not smile at his comedy. He did not feel particularly like smiling, either.

Merrick lifted the rifle with both hands and tossed it outward at the feet of the

Apaches. The Apaches barely looked at it, stood waiting for the handgun.

Merrick drew it from his holster, spun it and caught it by the barrel so they would not misread his intentions. He listened, heard the continued wailing from the burial. This was a time of evil for them — white men had desecrated one of their party, buried him flat in white-man fashion, a white man's burial for an Apache brave. It would take much wailing, much frenzy to cleanse this one's soul for eternity; it would take much blood to wash away the indignity and the insult.

He tossed out the gun to the Apache. The coppery-fleshed man caught the gun, inspected it, pushed it into the top of his breechcloth.

They did not even glance toward the rear of the wagon, though Merrick was certain they knew the two men and the woman were there. They were not concerned with what they could not see at the moment. They were very cold.

The brave now made a motion that told them to turn the wagon back toward the Wells.

Clinton nodded and pulled the heads of the horses around. Horseshoes clopped against outcroppings of stone. Merrick knew this was no longer important.

He heard the stifled crying of the woman inside the wagon. Something twisted inside him, but it did not displace the sense of helplessness that coursed through his body in his very bloodstream.

The measured pound of the drum struck against him, attacking his nerves at last.

The three braves walked silently beside the slow-moving wagon.

Clinton exhaled. "Dammit to goodbilly hell, Merrick. I told you yesterday afternoon. We ought to run. Yesterday. Before that scout showed."

"Run?" Merrick's voice was sharp and low. "Run where, Clinton? North? Right to them?"

"Hell, we had a chance yesterday, Merrick. What kind of chance we got now?"

"The same one we had yesterday."

"No. Yesterday them Apaches would have had full bellies and a roast-horse hangover. They wouldn't have had this here killing they had to avenge. Way they felt yesterday they might have wanted to get back to their squaws."

"You believe that?"

"Maybe not. But we were better off yesterday than we are today."

The wagon rolled slowly, with the gait of

a hearse, Merrick thought, up the incline and then started down toward the water hole.

It was the same water hole, but that was all. Everything about it was changed.

The drum had stopped from above the sump. Now there was silence. The three Apaches had moved through the mesquite and walked down the incline, leading the ponies.

The brave beside the wagon held up his hand. Clinton closed his fists on the reins. The horses stood poised. The three Apaches at the well did not turn around. They led the ponies to the water, allowed them to drink.

While the ponies drank, the brave who had ordered the guns thrown down went to the rear of the wagon. He threw back the flaps.

Merrick sat motionless on the boot. He heard Perch and Valerie get out of the wagon. The brave spoke then, his voice sharp.

Merrick knew he was telling Butler to get out of the wagon.

Perch said, "He's wounded. We'll have to help him out."

The Apache understood Perch Fisher. He said, voice cold, "Out."

Merrick did not move. He heard Butler crawl to the tail gate, try to pull himself over. He heard his frantic grasping and then heard the thud as his body struck the earth. The two braves nearest the wagon stared at him with interest but the three at the water seemed to hear none of this.

Valerie cried out.

"Up," the brave ordered.

Merrick stared straight ahead. He felt the wagon vibrate as Butler reached up and pulled himself to his feet against it.

The brave marched them forward around the wagon. Merrick saw then that he had the rest of their rifles. This seemed a very unimportant matter.

Butler staggered. Valerie caught his arm trying to support him, but he shook her hands down. He swayed slightly, but stood there tall, biting down on his mouth, sweat coursing down his forehead from his rumpled, curly hair. The side of his handsome face was dirt-smeared where he'd fallen onto the ground from the wagon. *By God,* Merrick thought with pride, *the devil was on the general's staff.*

The brave jerked his head at Clinton and Merrick. Merrick glanced at Hardhead. He nodded toward the ground. "After you."

Clinton swung down, stood with legs

apart, returning the cold stares of the Indians.

Merrick sprang from the wagon, stood beside Charley. The three braves walked behind them, prodded them forward on the incline.

One of the warriors at the pool led the last of the ponies away. Only then did the other two turn and inspect their prisoners, eyes chilled and contemptuous.

The taller stepped forward. No one had to introduce him as the leader. He may have been a minor chief of one of the roving tribes. Merrick did not know. He had never seen him before. But you didn't have to be acquainted to see the royal lineage he was heir to.

He was bare to the waist, as were the others. His face was marked along each cheek with a single yellow line. He held his corded shoulders straight, and his head was erect. His cheeks were hollowed, high-planed; he was a man who lived often with hunger, but when his belly was empty he had his pride. All of this was in his face, in the way he stood, and in the very way he studied the white people before him.

He let his gaze move over them, pulled his eyes back around, faced Merrick. "You are the leader of these people?" His voice was hesitant; the white man's language was a hateful thing as well as difficult.

Merrick lifted his shoulders, let them drop. "I will speak for them."

The leader's cold smile said there would not be a great deal to say. He jerked his head toward the wagon. "Crosses?"

"The army," Merrick said. "They thought they might mean something. I didn't. I was carrying medicines."

"Only medicines?" The Apache looked at the woman and the other three men.

"I picked up what you left, yesterday," Merrick said.

"And killed a brother of mine."

"About this I am sorry."

The Indian's face went rigid. He said, "If you do a thing, keep your pride in it when you die for it. It will not keep you alive to whine and beg."

"I neither whine nor beg. Still, I regret that death."

"And I spit out your apologies. I would admire more a man who could die proud of what he has done. And for that death you will die. You already died when you pulled the trigger that killed my brother."

Valerie caught her breath in a sob. Merrick spoke quickly, trying to pull the Apache's attention from her cry.

"You will see me die without asking mercy of you," Merrick said.

"The coyote brays loud before the trap springs on his throat. We shall see how you die. Believe that." He stepped back, dragging his cold gaze across them. "Vittorio has spoken."

SIXTEEN

There was a moment of intense, bitter silence. The Apache chieftain stood with his arms at his sides. One might have thought him relaxed except that his fists were tightly clenched, the muscles twisted in hard cords up his arm. The sun burned down upon the back of Merrick's neck. He watched the dust settle across the Wells, heard the patient slobbering of the ponies, the switch of their tails; but there was no end to the silence.

He heard Clinton's intake of breath when the Apache named himself for them. Merrick did not look but knew that Perch Fisher had sagged slightly, the hope dying in him. Neither man now felt so certain there was some way out, a time left for them to spend the loot in those swollen saddlebags. They had roamed the wastelands without meeting Vittorio face to face until today. They had heard of him.

The brave who had ordered them from the wagon was standing close behind Valerie. Merrick saw Vittorio's gaze pull from them to Valerie and he turned his head slightly enough to see what had attracted Vittorio's attention.

The brave was holding Valerie's red hair in his hands, letting it flow through his fingers. Then he drew the back of his hand softly across her cheek and down along her throat. He saw that Valerie shivered, that her eyes had the wild look of terror in them, but she stood perfectly still. In the sagged pull of her mouth he saw that she had abandoned hope, too. She did not know Vittorio's name or his reputation, but she was a woman and she could read his hatred and contempt in his face. There was not an atom of mercy in his black eyes.

The brave could not keep his hands off her.

In the Mescalero tongue, Vittorio snapped at the brave to cease.

The other braves stared at the young warrior and at Valerie. They laughed, but it was a brief sound, quickly dead and lost in the heat and stillness.

The brave reluctantly pulled his hands away from her, then caressed her cheek one more time with the backs of his fingers. He let his gaze move over her and then he walked forward to Vittorio.

The young brave, as tall as Vittorio, heavier, still lacked the arrogant look of strength the leader had. He had never known the hunger and the suffering Vittorio had known, and this deprived him of inner strengths rather than increasing them.

He spoke haltingly, in supplication and with much humility. At the same time there was urgency in the request he made. Merrick heard the brave ask for the woman. He was making promises of exchanges and sacrifices.

Clinton said, "The brave is asking for Butler's wife."

Merrick said, "Yes."

He heard Valerie's sobbing intake of breath.

Clinton said, "He wants the woman left alive — when the rest of us are killed."

Again Valerie caught her breath. Merrick glanced at her, afraid she would fall. His anger rose sharply at Clinton, then subsided.

"All right," he said. "Drop it."

"What the goodbilly hell," Clinton said. "She might as well know what's going to happen to her."

"We all know what's going to happen to us," Merrick said, speaking between clenched teeth. "You worry about how you'll take it when your turn comes."

Clinton laughed at him. The very existence of this final moment of danger gave the old pirate a sense of courage that would see him into eternity. Merrick could not help admiring the old man who had lived out his evil existence, taking what he wanted and asking nothing of anyone.

He touched his gaze upon the beefy Fisher and found him gone to lard. He was sweating, the streaks showing along his face and thick neck and upon his shirt. Merrick did not condemn Fisher for his fear. Fisher, like every other man who ever sat around a campfire out here at night, had heard tales of Indian tortures — and the Apache knew all the vulnerable areas of a man's body. They could keep you alive long after you wished you were dead.

Clinton watched the brave begging Vittorio for the right to keep the woman as his prize of this raid.

He turned slightly, glancing at Butler. His scraggly beard pulled beside his mouth. "Well, Butler, here's another chance for you. Maybe you can stay alive by trading off your woman to them Injuns."

Tears welled in Butler's eyes. He tried to stand straighter, but was too weak. He swayed slightly. A muscle worked in his jaw, but he did not answer Clinton. He did not look at him, but stared straight ahead of him.

Merrick looked at Valerie, saw that in a moment she was going to faint. Vittorio lifted his hand and the brave stepped back. Obviously, though Vittorio had promised nothing, the brave was hopeful. There was a touch of excitement about his face and he was staring at Valerie.

Merrick met Vittorio's gaze. He kept his face rigid, and did not lower his eyes under the chieftain's stare. The Apache chief was not impressed. He would yet see how arrogant the white man remained.

Merrick said, "So you are Vittorio?"

"You have heard of me?"

"I have heard of you. But I have never heard that you killed a wounded man." He nodded toward Butler whose stark white face showed the agony he endured standing there. But Butler remained erect, eyes forward. The old Confederate general would have been proud of his staff officer, Merrick thought.

He said, "Vittorio the brave kills wounded men and gives the man's wife as a prize.

619

Too bad I will not live after today. I would have a new story to tell about Vittorio the brave."

A slow flush crawled upward under Vittorio's flesh. He stepped toward Merrick.

Merrick did not flinch, kept his voice level and low, and deadly. "We are travelers, crossing your land in peace. We are not soldiers. The army wagon you see there is loaded with medicine. Is the Apache no longer a man that he must rob women and prey on the helpless?"

For an agonizing moment stretched long in time, Vittorio stared at Merrick. It looked as though Merrick had taunted the Apache beyond endurance and the man would kill him with his bare hands. That was what Vittorio wanted to do. There was no one at the water hole who could doubt that. Vittorio's fingers opened, closed, made an involuntary gesture toward Merrick's throat. He had moved the remaining distance between them, hardly seemed aware he had strode forward. He breathed through his mouth and in those dark eyes the hatred smoldered, while Vittorio remembered he was a prince and this was a white man, not worthy of forcing him to lose control for even a second. Vittorio took one step back. The anger had subsided and he was master again. He swept his gaze across his captives, looking at Valerie as though she, being a woman, did not exist.

He spoke to the brave who wanted her as his prize. The brave nodded, ran to the rear of the wagon. He inspected the boxes there, brought one and placed it at Vittorio's feet. They watched as Vittorio jerked his head and the brave ripped open the box. Vittorio stared at the bottles of medicine.

"Medicine," Clinton said. "All medicine. A town dies of fever and we head there." He nodded toward the south.

Vittorio did not look at Clinton. The Apache despised a liar and Vittorio did not bother to remind the big man that he had left them yesterday with a burning wagon that was headed north.

Vittorio spoke to the braves around them. The Apaches sprang to obey him. Working in pairs, the Apaches caught the white men, two at the arms, two at the feet, and slung them to the ground almost as if they were sheep to be sheared. They tied their wrists, staked them out, arms and legs spread wide.

It was accomplished speedily. Perch was the only one who fought. The butt of a rifle driven into his face took the fight out of him. Staked out on the ground, Perch rolled his head back and forth.

Merrick stared up at Valerie. The buck who desired her was standing at her back. He held her wrist, her arm twisted between her shoulder blades. This brave had lost some of the excitement of the torture in anticipation of carrying the woman to his lodge.

Merrick rolled his head, saw that Butler had been staked out beside him. Butler was in agony — they had broken open his wound. His bandage was stained the brownish-red of blood. Butler could not bite back the whimpering sounds of pain burned out of him by the bleeding wound in his side.

Merrick kept his voice low, hoping that Vittorio standing above them would not hear his words. "Try to swallow it, boy. There's no quicker way to get fed to the dogs — Apaches hate tears."

Vittorio strode tall and erect along the row of staked-out captives. His smile was full of contempt.

He looked over each of them slowly, particularly caught by the sight of Butler's blood darkening the bandage about his belly.

Vittorio said, "There is a question I will ask of you white men. It will buy you nothing to answer it, and yet for the one who answers it, I might order the torture ceased. This I do not promise. First I must hear your answer."

Perch rolled his head back and forth. His nose was bleeding. The other men remained still. The sun blazed into their faces, stinging the tears into their eyeballs.

"My question," Vittorio said. "I want one of you to name the man who shot my blood relative."

He waited. The silence pressed down upon them, and the sun blazed in their eyes. They did not move.

"You are very brave for now," Vittorio said. "I think maybe all of you will be begging to answer — soon." His mouth pulled and his gaze struck hard against Merrick's.

Vittorio paced before them. "I have so little regard for you — for all of you — that my blood is not appeased at the thought of watching you die crying and screaming in return for the death of my blood relative. That is not enough." His eyes distended and his mouth pulled back from his teeth. "I will give you something to live for. In a moment you will begin to die, one of you at the time. Each will have the pleasure of seeing the other die. If there is among you one who can endure Apache torture without tears —" he stared at Merrick who had insulted him — "prove yourself as much a man as any Apache is, I will allow all of you to live and go in peace from this place."

The buck holding Valerie cried out in protest. Vittorio raised his head slowly, and regarded the brave with a cold expression. For a moment protests bubbled across the buck's lips, but under the unrelenting stare of Vittorio they fell away.

Vittorio looked over the four men one more time. He walked back to the rim of the pool, stood with his back to them.

Merrick watched an Apache building a fire near them. There was a cry from another brave and Vittorio spun around on his heel.

The brave ran down the incline carrying the saddle bags. One was burst open and money spilled from it.

He dropped the saddlebags at Vittorio's feet. Vittorio said something to him, and he slashed open the other two bags, gold and Federal paper money spilling out.

Vittorio's eyes were sardonic, "Medicine?" He stared at the white men.

"We are very rich men," Clinton said. "Why don't you take the money, buy yourself many rifles and let us go?"

"The money I will take," Vittorio said. He knelt, caught some of it in his fist. "Vittorio will spend it as he believes best. Let you go?

624

You will buy your freedom, white man, in one way."

"Well, you tried," Merrick said to Clinton.

"As long as I'm alive, I will try, mister."

"Is that money from the bank at San Carlos?" Merrick said.

"I am pleased to tell you that it is," Clinton said. "We were headed north to spend it."

Merrick's mouth pulled taut. They were running north from San Carlos, just as a month ago the three of them had fled south from a bank robbery in Tucson. There was no longer any doubt why these men would have killed him rather than return with the army wagon south to San Carlos. His instinct and his hatred had pointed straight and true at these men. They had ridden into the water hole, found Ab there, shot him in the back and left him to the ants. Killed him simply to leave no witnesses to their trail.

He closed his eyes against the burn of the sun but could not escape seeing in his mind the way his brother had died, imagining the pleasure his death had brought to these men. Suddenly he regretted dying at the hand of the Apaches. He had covered many days and many miles looking for these men and proof against them. Now when he had found them, it was too late.

He heard Butler scream, crying out. He jerked his eyes open. One of the braves was ripping away Butler's bandage. The blood spurted from the tear in his side, coursing along his bare stomach and staining his trousers. The Indians had cut away Butler's shirt. The wounded man was biting at his mouth until his lips bled, but it was no good. He could not longer swallow his agony.

SEVENTEEN

Vittorio jabbed his thumb toward the sobbing Butler. "This one," he said, speaking at Merrick and spitting out the words, "weak as a woman. Weaker."

"Let Vittorio speak sometime with a bullet in his belly and his blood lost for two days," Merrick said.

Vittorio laughed at him, a bitter sound. With his lance he pressed at the tear in Butler's side, toying with him almost without interest.

"We settle this one first," Vittorio said, "lest he escape us by dying before we can kill him."

"In the name of God," Butler pleaded. "I can't stand any more. I'm dying. Mercy. In the name of God. Mercy."

Vittorio stared at him without changing expression, applying slight pressure to the lance.

"I'll tell you who killed your brother," Butler wailed.

Vittorio shrugged. His face said that he had been sure Butler would speak.

"It was none of us," Butler wept. "I swear it. It was one who lies dead now. It was Billy Clinton." He jerked his head toward Hardhead Charley. "Ask him. It was his son — and his son is dead."

Hardhead's voice had ironic laughter in it, and not a trace of fear. "It was my son, Vittorio. My son Billy. He shot your brother. Yesterday."

Vittorio stared at Butler, then at Clinton. He waved his hand downward at Butler, drew the blood-tipped lance away. He stepped back.

Vittorio looked down at Butler. "My thanks to you. I leave your eyes to the buzzards."

He turned his back on Butler.

From where he was staked out, Merrick could see they were heating the barrel end of his rifle in the fire that blazed, paled against the coppery brilliance of the sun. The brave was not hurried; he turned the barrel slowly in the hottest part of the fire.

Vittorio walked along the line of staked-out men. His warriors walked with him, converging on Perch Fisher.

Vittorio spoke to one of them. The brave hunkered on his haunches beside Perch's head.

From the surface crust of the earth, the brave carefully scooped fine thin sand. At a signal from Vittorio, he caught Perch by the hair and jerked his head back.

Perch did not make a sound. The blood had coagulated along his cheeks so he looked almost as painted as the Apaches. The Indian twisted his fist in Perch's hair so he was forced to twist his head back as far as his neck would allow.

With his head held back in the iron grip of the Apache, Fisher's flesh was stretched taut.

The Apache held his head above Perch's face and funneled a slow, steady stream of sand into his nostrils. With interest the Apaches stood watching to see how long Perch could endure the torment. Perch opened his mouth, gasping air through it, but the sand filled his nose, spilled in his throat and suddenly he could no longer breathe at all.

Perch screamed, rolling his head back and

forth, gasping, unable to speak.

Vittorio slashed his hand downward. The brave released Perch's head, stepped back from him. Vittorio stared at Perch for a moment, then spat on him.

Vittorio walked to Merrick, stared at him and then signaled toward Clinton. He strode forward, stood at Hardhead Charley's feet.

Clinton rolled his head on the side, staring at Merrick. "If you're impatient, Merrick, you can have my place in line."

Merrick lay there, staring at the sky as long as he could. From the thicket the braves brought greasewood, carefully shaved off the thorns.

Merrick saw them place thorns under each of Clinton's nails. The big man kept his face straight, his gaze fixed on the apex of the sky. With the flat of a knife they tapped the thorns into the quick under Clinton's nails.

His head rolled back and forth. He would lunge upward against his thongs but his face did not change, he did not speak.

When his nails were torn loose and his fingers were bloodied, Vittorio jerked his head at the braves. They jerked the thorns from Clinton's bleeding hands.

Vittorio gave another signal. Two braves

629

loosed the thongs on Clinton's left side, and crossed over, yanking him over.

A brave came down the incline with a thick limb. Vittorio tested it against his palm, handed it back to the brave and nodded.

When they brought the limb down across Clinton's kidneys the breath was forced in a rush across his mouth. He did not cry out. He writhed each time the limb was brought down. They could not make him beg for mercy even after he began to spit blood.

Vittorio spoke. The braves yanked the rawhide, pulling Clinton over on his back again. The stakes were driven into the ground. Two braves ripped away Clinton's shirt.

The old man's face was pale. Blood bubbled from the corner of his mouth, trickled into his beard. His eyes were open but were glazed slightly, very dry.

Vittorio bent at the waist, staring at Clinton. "Why don't you weep, white man? Cry out and beg. This Vittorio would like to see."

Clinton did not move.

Vittorio gave a dry laugh, jerked his head at the brave heating the rifle mouth in the fire.

The barrel was white hot. The brave

crossed to Clinton. Vittorio showed the gun to Clinton, nodded again.

Slowly the burning barrel was lowered toward Clinton's exposed navel. It touched his flesh. There was the acrid odor of burning flesh. Clinton moaned first, rolling his head back and forth, then he screamed, and kept screaming, the tears and the agony boiling from his mouth.

Vittorio sent the brave back to the fire. He stood at Merrick's feet until he decided the gun barrel was reheated properly. He spoke and the brave came running with the gun.

This time Vittorio himself handled the gun. He stepped forward standing across Merrick's chest. His mouth pulled into a taunting smile, the Apache stared down into Merrick's face.

Holding the gun by its butt, Vittorio lowered it straight down toward Merrick's eyes, moving slowly with deadly steadiness.

When the gun was still more than a foot away, Merrick felt the heat like lances ripping into his eyeballs. The white-hot gun barrel came closer. This was like having your eyes broiled in hell, like staring into the white hot ball of the midday sun, like having your soul burned from your body by fire.

The gun was so near now that he could

not see it. He writhed against the thongs. He had been sure Vittorio would press the gun against his face, burning out his eyes, but, for the moment anyhow, the Indian stayed the rifle inches from his brow.

Merrick felt his eyes go dry, felt them burn, seeming to constrict and lose all their fluid in the heat. It was as if the heat were a magnet painfully drawing the color from the pupils. The pain lanced through his head, striking at the raw nerve ends at the base of his skull. He could hear himself yelling, screaming, begging for mercy, and yet there could not have been a sound from him because the gun was not drawn away.

He tried to roll away from the killing heat but slowly, patiently and relentlessly the gun followed his head as it rolled back and forth against the ground.

His teeth chattered. Please God, let them put out my eyes. Let it end. It can only end when I'm blind, God, let it end.

He felt the reason swirling and disappearing from his brain, drawn out of him by the white-hot magnet. Sudden crazy memories raced disjointed through his mind. The first pony he'd ever owned, given to him by his father on a farm in Virginia. The way Ab's body had looked pumped full of bullets and left beside the pool. The look in Valerie

Butler's face when he had turned to her, scarred chest bared, from that pool. He could hear Mary Beth's screams, and she was no longer screaming for him to help her when he was helpless to aid her, she was begging them to kill her. They had not left her anything to live for, and by the time he had insanely chewed the thongs from his wrist and rushed at the men crouched over her, she was begging to die. He would not scream aloud. He would not ask any mercy of these people who had shown no mercy to his wife, making her live, making her suffer after she pleaded with them to let her die. He no longer knew if he were screaming, only that his head rolled on the earth and his eyes burned and there was no end to the burning.

He did not know how long Vittorio stood there, tracing his agonized rolls with the gun barrel. His wrists fought the thongs and half a dozen times they caught his arms and drove the stakes into the earth again.

The world had become a blazing inferno, a blanket of flowing blood even when he distended his eyes.

"Have mercy!" He heard a woman scream that. For an instant his brain told him it was Mary Beth, but Mary Beth was six years dead. It was Valerie who had cried out.

Suddenly the gun was gone from his face. He did not know how long it was gone. Even after the heated metal had been withdrawn, the agony burned into his eyes.

He stopped rolling his head. He stared into the sun, but saw nothing. There was a blur before his eyes.

Vittorio spoke, a sharp guttural order. Vittorio had moved away, was standing at his feet.

Through the pain that blazed inside his head, he felt them tearing away his shirt. He stretched his head upward. Now they would press the reheated gun against his navel. Clinton had screamed and begged for mercy. In a moment the gun would touch his vital and tender area and he would scream too. He looked forward to it. The hell would end for a moment. There would be nothing left except for the Apaches to kill them then.

The shirt was ripped away. Blade lay there, waiting. There was a moment of terrible, stunned silence.

The blur did not lessen. It was as though he could see blood flowing across his eyeballs, and that was all he could see.

"Get back." He heard Vittorio yell that. It was spoken in the Apache dialect and the warriors fell away from the men staked on the ground.

Through the agony in Merrick's brain came the realization that when they had ripped away his shirt Vittorio had been staring down at the knife scar across his chest.

Suddenly Vittorio lunged forward. Crouched over Merrick, he caught his throat in his right hand.

"Speak." The words spat through Vittorio's lips. "Your name, man."

"Merrick." Blade tried to hold his breath, to keep any quaver from his voice.

"Blade Merrick." It was a sound of agony across Vittorio's mouth. Still clutching Merrick's throat, Vittorio lifted his head, ordered the men released from the thongs.

Vittorio turned, staring down at Merrick. "Why didn't you speak?" His voice cut at Merrick.

Merrick felt his hands freed, felt the blood return to his wrists and fingers.

He caught Vittorio's hand and tore it loose from his throat.

Vittorio hunkered there. Merrick sat up, still seeing nothing but the fire and blood inside his own head.

For a long time Merrick slouched there, head bent.

"You had only to speak," Vittorio said.

Merrick breathed in deeply. His voice was

cold. "I beg no one. I beg no Apache for mercy."

"You did not have to beg — only to show this scar, speak your name."

"Did I? Would it have done any good? Did the Apache show my wife any mercy? Would you have shown mercy after your blood brother was killed yesterday?"

"Would you die then, rather than ask for your life?"

Merrick said, "I ask no more than an Apache. Six years ago I was as good as the Apache . . . better. I do not kill women as the Apache kills them."

"Vittorio kills no women."

"Vittorio's people killed my wife. Six years ago. Vittorio's people would have killed me." He raked his hand across the livid scar on his chest. "But the knife of Vittorio's people was not sharp enough to kill me — and the hand of Vittorio's people not strong enough to kill me — only strong enough to rape and kill my wife."

Vittorio stood up. His voice was very low. "Our gods looked down that day six years ago upon injustice. The injustice of the evil among our people attacking the house of the man trying to aid us. Our gods saw rape and murder even as you accuse. This evil still is spoken in the lodges and the wickiups of my people. Apaches among us wronged you by killing your wife and using the knife on you when you had come among us to aid us. That day the chief of all my people asked you to forgive, to remain free to live and hunt and travel our lands among us, never betraying my people, never betrayed by us."

Merrick sagged on the ground. He could not touch his face, the pain was too intense. He could not shut out the memories that raced even more fiery through his mind. He had gone among the Apaches during an epidemic that almost wiped them out, working with the Indian agent and army doctors, only to return home to find his house burning and his wife dying after brutal rape. They had tied him up and he had chewed, clawed his way free to fight them to death with his bare hands, to rip out tongues, to claw out eyes, to stop their breathing until they killed him, because he wanted to die, because Mary Beth was dead, but he would not stop fighting them until their knives ripped him open. The savage leader was raking at his guts, Merrick's hand twisting his knife wrist when the tribal leaders overtook the renegades.

Vittorio said, "Vittorio was not at that kill, nor were any of his people. The evil among us had struck at you. Yesterday the bad of your people killed my brother in blood."

Merrick heard the words, but he did not raise his head. The fire in his eyes was making him ill. He wanted to sprawl forward raving on the earth. He wanted to dig out his own eyes.

He remained motionless.

Vittorio said, "Vittorio respects the honorable agreement made between my people and you at the time of your tragedy. You are free now to go among my people — free as you have always been — free forever."

EIGHTEEN

Merrick pulled himself to his feet. Pain raged through him, burning downward from his eyes.

He stood for a moment swaying slightly, legs apart. He saw nothing; the blur before his eyes had not lessened. He shivered, thinking he was blind, to wander helpless the rest of his life in this country, alone and blind.

He moved his head, not attempting to see, but listening. He staggered toward the sound of the water.

He knelt beside the pool, holding his arms across his middle. He was ill.

After a long time he dipped his hands cupped into the water. It was icy against his fevered flesh. He brought the water up to his eyes and forehead as though he could never be cool enough again.

Behind him he heard Vittorio ordering the Apaches to mount. The young buck who had wanted Valerie lifted his voice in raging protest. Vittorio let him rage a moment, then silenced him with one sharp word. Merrick remained beside the pool on his knees. He did not hear the young brave speak again. As his head cooled he felt again the noon blaze of sun on his back. He heard the slow soft sound of the unshod ponies moving up the incline.

He heard someone beside him. He did not stop bathing his eyes. Dimly, as though through red-darkened glasses he saw the ripples of the water surface.

"Blade."

He tensed at the sound of her voice. He remained with his head bowed over the water.

"Is Jeff all right?" he said.

"I — fixed his bandages. The bleeding has stopped. He is lying beside the wagon."

"All right."

"They've gone. The Indians have gone."

"Yes."

She was silent a moment. He brought the water up against his face.

"They took Clinton's money — that's all they took with them."

"Clinton is lucky."

"Nobody's lucky," she answered. "If it had not been for you, we'd all be dead."

He did not answer. He held the water against his eyes until it spilled through his fingers, or grew warm against his flesh.

"Your wife," Valerie said. "I'm so sorry."

"It was a long time ago."

"Not to you."

"No. Not to me."

"I understand so much now. How you could travel alone through this country with medicine for the missions."

"The army thought I could."

"And you could have — except for us."

"It does not matter."

"It matters. You've been hurt enough . . . too much. I wish there were something I could do."

"There isn't anything."

"They've made you hate," she said. "When they killed your wife, you had nothing left but hate."

"No. It was just that Mary Beth was the only one. I never wanted anyone else."

"Only because you hated everybody."

He opened his mouth to deny this, then closed it. She was speaking the truth. He had lived six years with cold hatred. It was like living forever with ashes in your soul and in your mouth. He had walked through everything, never allowing himself to become part of anything, never seeing anything but the gray shades of the old hate. And then a month ago, the ashes smoldered and the hatred burned again. He saw his brother's stripped body. He hated again, the way he had hated that day when his wife was killed. For this long month, this new hatred had been livid in him. He had lived for one thing, to find the men who had killed his brother and see that they died.

He shuddered, his whole body quivering.

"Blade. Are you all right?"

He did not answer her. He straightened, sitting on his heels. He stared across the cool sump, feeling its coolness, but not seeing anything. He thought about Hardhead Charley Clinton and Perch Fisher and about the way Billy Clinton had died. In his smoky vision he saw the way the Apaches had funneled sand into Perch's nostrils. Perch had tried to save them by not yelling for mercy, even knowing the promise was made in jest. There was a chance that if he did not yell, the tortures might cease; at least the others might die in less than agony. Perch had tried until the sand clogged and scratched his nostril air passages, his throat. Old Clinton had tried, and because he was tougher, he had lasted longer. He had been through hell with them.

He stared at the falling water, sure that he could discern its shape, splashing against the stone at the far wall of the pool. The hatred that had driven him was cooled, only now there was not the taste of ashes, the sense of being dead. He did not want to kill Charley Clinton or Perch Fisher, not even to avenge his brother's death. The horror he'd gone through at Vittorio's hands had purged him of hatred, burned it out of him.

He stood up slowly, vaguely making out the shape of the pool. He would see again, he was sure of it; perhaps existence in the desert had toughened him. He felt only one thing, a need for the woman beside him, something he would never have.

He drew in a deep breath. There was one answer. He had to get out of here, get south to San Carlos. He would be busy there, and she would go her way with her husband, and he would never see her again. At least he had begun to live again, had rejoined the human race. She deserved the credit for this, even though he never could have her.

"We better clear out," he said.

She touched his arm. Her fingers dug into his flesh. He turned to face her. He could see her hair only as a bright halo. She was blurred before him.

Her voice sounded odd, full of tears. "Blade — it won't be the same — for us — after we leave here. We won't see each other again."

His voice was hard. "You'll be all right."

"Yes . . . I'll be all right."

"You take your husband and get back east. You'll be right."

"I — said I'd be all right." Her voice caught. She said again, whispering it, protesting. "I'll never see you again."

"We better clear out."

"I never knew anyone like you, Blade. Never even hoped any more I'd find anyone — like you."

His voice was low, desperately savage. "All right. And I want you. Is that what you want to hear? Is that what you need? You think that'll make it any easier?"

"I don't want it to be easier, Blade. I wanted you to know . . . that's all."

Suddenly she was pressed against him. He felt her quivering, crying against his chest. For one last moment he kept his arms at his sides. They came upward almost involuntarily, touching her, his hands hungry, pressing her closer. Her tear-streaked face tilted upward, and he cupped her head in his hand, pressed her mouth against his.

Clinton's voice sounded faraway, then suddenly came close, strong and loud. There was laughter in it, a crazy exultant sound that struck against the walls of the sump.

"That's fine, missy," Clinton shouted from behind Blade. "You just hold what you got. No way we planned it, you couldn't have trapped him better for me."

NINETEEN

Merrick stepped away from her and turned around. Instinctively he reached for his gun, found his holster empty. He stared toward the place from which Clinton's voice came. He could not see him, but he could hear his wild laughter, coming closer.

"You done fine, missy," Clinton said. He was only a few feet from Merrick now. He was like a dark blur in the bloody world.

"Real good," Perch said, and Merrick could dimly make out his form at Clinton's side.

"How does it feel to be the one without the guns?" Clinton's laughter taunted Merrick. "That Injun left us all our guns. You should have told your ever-loving Injun friend you didn't trust us with firearms."

"He should have known it looking at you."

Valerie stepped around him, pressed close against his side. "You got to believe me, Blade." Her voice was agonized. "I didn't know about this . . . I'd even forgotten what they told me to do."

His voice was cold. "It doesn't matter."

"It's all that matters." She pressed against him, between him and the gunmen. "You've got to believe me."

Clinton laughed. "Tell him you didn't know the Injuns gave us back our guns whilst he was bending over that pool. Tell him you didn't know it. You got him pretty well hooked. He'll believe anything."

Valerie straightened, turning to face them. "I knew. But I thought after all we'd been through . . . he'd saved your lives."

"You thought I'd forget my Billy's death just like that?"

"Yes. You owe him your own life now. We all do."

"Say thank you to the nice man, Perch," Clinton ordered.

"Thanks," Perch said, voice bitter.

"Now we thanked him, ma'am, you best get out the way. You're right where you could get hurt bad. Now, Perch and me are willing you should ride north with us to Tucson, but we ain't begging you . . . it's just up to you."

Merrick said, "You still think you'll get to Tucson?"

"A lot nearer than you'll ever get again." Clinton stopped laughing, his voice lowered. "You're a brave man, Merrick, I can't deny that, by God — maybe you're even a good man. When all the accounts are in, it's hard to hold everything against you. Looks like you done what you thought you had to — even can see now how you were trying to help us in your way. But I got to have them horses and that wagon."

Valerie said, "You're not going to make it. Those Apaches would like nothing better than to catch you out in that waste country — without Merrick. He's the only one who can get you safely through the Indian country."

"That might have been true. But I'm gambling they'll let his wagon through — if they find out later they been tricked, I can't cry about that. We'll get through. Now if you'll get back yonder to your husband where you belong, we'll clear up this business and get out of here."

Valerie's voice caught in a sob. She turned,

pressing against Merrick. "Blade. They'll kill you. There's no way to talk to them. Nothing means anything to them. Tell them you'll turn back — tell them you'll take them to Tucson if they'll let you live."

Merrick exhaled. He closed his arm about her, held her for a moment against him, spoke across her bright hair.

"Why don't you tell her, Clinton? Why don't you tell her the truth, that you couldn't let me live even if I agreed to turn back."

"That's all he wants," Valerie said. She spun around, faced Clinton. "That is all you want. Isn't it?"

Clinton looked at her, his pirate's face twisted. He gave a faint shrug.

"No," Merrick said, voice level. "It wouldn't matter to him even if I agreed to drive them north. It doesn't even matter that he knows he sent Billy out there to kill me and it didn't work out. What he isn't telling you, Valerie, is that if I don't die, he and Perch are lost."

Valerie shivered.

"A month ago," Merrick said, talking to Valerie but staring at the blurred images of Fisher and Clinton, "they robbed a bank in Tucson. I was there. They left town just ahead of me. I had no interest in the bank robbery. I had my brother on my mind. Well, they ran past here on their way to San Carlos. They killed my brother a month ago. Here at Patchee Wells. Now, they've robbed another bank, and even though the Apaches took their loot, they're still guilty of robbery — and murder. There's just one thing they could do — they could let me live to get them past the Injuns and almost to Fort Ambush. But then if they killed me there, they might have to face a murder charge. If they didn't kill me, they'd be sure I'd turn them in at Tucson. So they've got to gamble on the Indians not checking my wagon again. They've got to kill me here and take their chances on the law."

Clinton shrugged.

"And there's more," Merrick said. His voice hardened. "I knew you three had been here before we ever got here."

"Man, you're clever. How'd you figger that?"

"I took a drink from a canteen you had back there in the valley. Billy's canteen. I knew then. His canteen was filled with water from this pool. You killed Ab, but the three of you lied, said you'd never been to this water hole. Because by then the word had caught up with you. You knew the man you killed here was my brother — and you knew

I was looking for his killer."

Clinton shrugged. He spoke to Perch. "How about that, Perch? You ever see such a smart fellow?"

"Sin to see him die," Perch said.

Clinton said, "Get out of the way, Mrs. Butler. My temper is short, and it's gettin' late. I'd as soon leave you with him here as not — only you wouldn't enjoy it, because you'd both be dead."

TWENTY

"Clinton." Jeff's voice rattled down the incline from the wagon. Merrick raised his head, but could not see Jeff or the wagon. He heard Valerie's sharp intake of breath. She was staring past Clinton and Fisher.

"Don't bother me now, man," Clinton said over his shoulder.

"Clinton. Drop that gun. You, too, Perch."

Clinton turned enough to see Jeff. He had pulled himself to his feet and, propped against the wagon, had staggered around it. He was not able to lift the rifle to his shoulder, but held it at his side, his right hand grasping the trigger.

"Don't make me shoot you, Clinton," Jeff said. "Because I don't want to have to."

Clinton roared. It was the sound of a

wounded animal, an outraged pirate, a frustrated Viking yelling against the pound of the North Sea.

"What's the matter with you, Butler?" His voice shook. "You crossing me? I'm the one that'll get you to Tucson. Why you crossing me?"

"Drop your gun, Clinton, and we'll talk about it. I ain't got a lot of patience."

"Look at him." Clinton jerked his head toward Merrick, voice shaking. "He was down here loving up your woman — and you're crossing me for him? The man that's trying to take your wife?"

Butler's voice remained level. "That's my concern, Clinton. I know what I am. I know what he is. The choice between us is up to her."

"Don't be a fool, Butler."

"I'm not a fool. Not any more. I was. But I'm not. I know now what a real man is, what it is to be a man. I never have been one."

"All right, so he's a good man. He's still against everything we want."

"Everything *you* want, Clinton. Merrick has saved my life twice, and as it happens, I hate to be in any man's debt that far."

Perch moved to turn around. Butler said, "Take it easy, Perch. Drop that gun before you turn."

"Jeff. Look out!" Valerie screamed.

Clinton stepped wide and swung around, firing as he turned.

The sound of his gun struck against the crack of Jeff's rifle.

Clinton was struck in the chest. He yelled, and toppled backward down the incline.

Jeff stayed beside the wagon for a moment, long enough to pull Perch half around to shoot him in case Clinton had missed. But Clinton had not missed. The rifle slipped from Jeff's lifeless fingers. He sagged against the wagon wheel, slid down it and lay still in the sand.

In that moment, Merrick moved. He knew that Jeff had saved his life by shooting Clinton, had given him a chance to stay alive by pulling Perch Fisher around.

Perch was hardly more than a blurred image before him. Merrick lunged toward him, striking him in the side. He grasped at Perch's right wrist as they hit the ground.

Perch was striking at him. Merrick did not even attempt to protect himself. He battered Perch's gunhand against the rocks, kept hitting until the gun flew from Perch's hand.

Perch got his legs under Merrick and sent him reeling backward.

Perch turned, crouching to dive for his gun. Valerie had run to it, and scooped it up. She turned and ran up the incline. Perch came up off his knees.

Merrick landed on his shoulders, locking his arm under his throat and dragging him off balance. They toppled outward and fell into the pool.

They went under, kicking and thrashing.

Merrick fought his way upward. Fisher was beating at his head as he surfaced. He caught Fisher about the middle and dragged him under. His lungs felt as if they would burst. He put his foot in Perch's stomach and thrust downward. His head cleared the surface and he gasped for air. Perch caught him and pulled him under.

By now Perch was fighting for the surface, Merrick caught him by the throat and pulled him back. Perch fought frantically, his mouth opening, and he swallowed water.

Merrick managed to get his own head above the water without loosening his grasp on Fisher's throat. His fingers tightened and he pressed down. Fisher caught at his hands, pulling, but his fingers were already weakening, and then he was not fighting any more.

Merrick lunged away from him, pulled himself up on the rocks. He sat there for a long time, staring at the body in the pool.

A shiver wracked through him.

He caught Perch Fisher by the shirt collar and pulled him from the water.

Valerie came slowly down the incline. Her eyes were brimming with tears, but her head was tilted.

"Jeff," she said. "Jeff is dead."

But she said it with a sense of pride and a sense of loss. Merrick thought that no matter how low Jeff had sunk in her estimation, he had redeemed himself with her and he hadn't died in vain.

Merrick worked in the sun with the spade. The sun blazed, sinking slowly. The coppery sky was reflected in the pool. It was late afternoon before the three men were buried.

Valerie sat beside the Wells and waited for him. The darkness was settling when he tossed the spade into the wagon.

She got up and came to him.

"We better head out," he said. "We can be in San Carlos in the morning."

"Yes, Blade," she said, "I'm ready to go."

He touched her hand. Her fingers enclosed his. They walked up the incline. He helped her into the wagon, climbed to the seat beside her. He glanced at the graves down the incline from the Wells, gazed once more at the cool sump. He spoke to the horses, slapped the reins across them.

The wagon moved slowly up the incline, crested the rim and headed south.

Valerie did not look back again.

It was a long time before the wagon was out of sight of the water hole. Darkness came slowly, fading in from the mountains where the haze was purple, rolling in across the flat wastes. The wind came up, and it covered the heel prints in the sand, and blew the earth across the wagon tracks so there was no trace of them. The stillness settled with the night. White men had come here to Patchee Wells — and Indians. For a little while, the silence had been broken. But the white men passed, and the Indians; the silence settled again, breathless and un-broken.

The water hole was as it was before, as it was in the beginning, and forever.

The employees of Thorndike Press hope you have enjoyed this Large Print book. All our Thorndike, Wheeler, and Kennebec Large Print titles are designed for easy reading, and all our books are made to last. Other Thorndike Press Large Print books are available at your library, through selected bookstores, or directly from us.

For information about titles, please call:
(800) 223-1244

or visit our website at:
gale.com/thorndike

To share your comments, please write:
Publisher
Thorndike Press
10 Water St., Suite 310
Waterville, ME 04901